John Henry Newman

The Works Of Cardinal Newman

Vol. 5

John Henry Newman

The Works Of Cardinal Newman
Vol. 5

ISBN/EAN: 9783337319939

Printed in Europe, USA, Canada, Australia, Japan

Cover: Foto ©Raphael Reischuk / pixelio.de

More available books at **www.hansebooks.com**

PAROCHIAL AND PLAIN SERMONS

By JOHN HENRY NEWMAN, B.D.

FORMERLY VICAR OF ST. MARY'S, OXFORD

IN EIGHT VOLUMES

VOL. V.

NEW EDITION

RIVINGTONS

London, Oxford, and Cambridge

1870.

TO

JOSHUA WATSON, ESQ. D.C.L.

THE BENEFACTOR OF ALL HIS BRETHREN,

BY HIS LONG AND DUTIFUL MINISTRY,

AND PATIENT SERVICE,

TO HIS AND THEIR COMMON MOTHER,

THIS VOLUME IS INSCRIBED,

IN THE HOPE THAT HE WILL NOT BE DISPLEASED

BY AN UNSANCTIONED OFFERING

OF RESPECT AND GRATITUDE.

Oct. 21st, 1840.

CONTENTS.

SERMON VIIL

— THE STATE OF INNOCENCE.

(Christmas.)

𝔈𝔠𝔠𝔩𝔢𝔰𝔦𝔞𝔰𝔱𝔢𝔰 vii. 29.

SERMON IX.

CHRISTIAN SYMPATHY.

(Christmas.)

𝔥𝔢𝔟𝔯𝔢𝔴𝔰 ii. 16.

SERMON X.

RIGHTEOUSNESS NOT OF US, BUT IN US.

(Epiphany.)

1 ℭorint𝔥ians i. 30, 31.

SERMON XI.

THE LAW OF THE SPIRIT.

(Epiphany.)

𝔯omans x. 4.

SERMON XII.

THE NEW WORKS OF THE GOSPEL.

(*Epiphany.*)

2 Corinthians v. 17.

SERMON XIII.

THE STATE OF SALVATION.

(*Epiphany.*)

Ephesians iv. 24.

SERMON XIV.

TRANSGRESSIONS AND INFIRMITIES.

(*Epiphany.*)

Hebrews x. 38.

SERMON XV.

SINS OF INFIRMITY.

(*Epiphany.*)

Galatians v. 17.

SERMON XVI.

SINCERITY AND HYPOCRISY.

(*Epiphany.*)

2 Corinthians viii. 12.

SERMON XVII.

THE TESTIMONY OF CONSCIENCE.

(Epiphany.)

2 Corinthians i. 12.

SERMON XVIII.

MANY CALLED, FEW CHOSEN.

Septuagesima.)

1 Corinthians ix. 24.

SERMON XIX.

PRESENT BLESSINGS.

(Septuagesima.)

Philippians iv. 18.

SERMON XX.

ENDURANCE, THE CHRISTIAN'S PORTION.

(Sexagesima.)

Genesis xlii. 36.

SERMON XXI.

AFFLICTION, A SCHOOL OF COMFORT.

(Sexagesima.)

2 Corinthians i. 4.

SERMON I.

WORSHIP, A PREPARATION FOR CHRIST'S COMING.

(ADVENT.)

*" Thine eyes shall see the King in His beauty : they shall behold
the land that is very far off."*

YEAR after year, as it passes, brings us the same
warnings again and again, and none perhaps more
impressive than those with which it comes to us at this
season. The very frost and cold, rain and gloom,
which now befall us, forebode the last dreary days of the
world, and in religious hearts raise the thought of them.
The year is worn out; spring, summer, autumn, each in
turn, have brought their gifts and done their utmost;
but they are over, and the end is come. All is past
and gone, all has failed, all has sated; we are tired of
the past; we would not have the seasons longer; and
the austere weather which succeeds, though ungrateful
to the body, is in tone with our feelings, and acceptable.
Such is the frame of mind which befits the end of the
year; and such the frame of mind which comes alike
on good and bad at the end of life. The days have

come in which they have no pleasure; yet they would hardly be young again, could they be so by wishing it. Life is well enough in its way; but it does not satisfy. Thus the soul is cast forward upon the future, and in proportion as its conscience is clear and its perception keen and true, does it rejoice solemnly that "the night is far spent, the day is at hand," that there are "new heavens and a new earth" to come, though the former are failing; nay, rather that, because they are failing, it will "soon see the King in His beauty," and "behold the land which is very far off." These are feelings for holy men in winter and in age, waiting, in some dejection perhaps, but with comfort on the whole, and calmly though earnestly, for the Advent of Christ.

And such, too, are the feelings with which we now come before Him in prayer day by day. The season is chill and dark, and the breath of the morning is damp, and worshippers are few, but all this befits those who are by profession penitents and mourners, watchers and pilgrims. More dear to them that loneliness, more cheerful that severity, and more bright that gloom, than all those aids and appliances of luxury by which men nowadays attempt to make prayer less disagreeable to them. True faith does not covet comforts. It only complains when it is forbidden to kneel, when it reclines upon cushions, is protected by curtains, and encompassed by warmth. Its only hardship is to be hindered, or to be ridiculed, when it would place itself as a sinner before its Judge. They who realize that awful Day when they shall see Him face to face, whose eyes are as a flame of fire, will as little bargain to pray pleasantly now, as they will think of doing so then.

One year goes and then another, but the same warnings recur. The frost or the rain comes again; the earth is stripped of its brightness; there is nothing to rejoice in. And then, amid this unprofitableness of earth and sky, the well-known words return; the Prophet Isaiah is read; the same Epistle and Gospel, bidding us "awake out of sleep," and welcome Him "that cometh in the Name of the Lord;" the same Collects, beseeching Him to prepare us for judgment. O blessed they who obey these warning voices, and look out for Him whom they have not seen, because they "love His appearing!"

We cannot have fitter reflections at this Season than those which I have entered upon. What may be the destiny of other orders of beings we know not;—but this we know to be our own fearful lot, that before us lies a time when we must have the sight of our Maker and Lord face to face. We know not what is reserved for other beings; there may be some, which, knowing nothing of their Maker, are never to be brought before Him. For what we can tell, this may be the case with the brute creation. It may be the law of their nature that they should live and die, or live on an indefinite period, upon the very outskirts of His government, sustained by Him, but never permitted to know or approach Him. But this is not our case. We are destined to come before Him; nay, and to come before Him in judgment; and that on our first meeting; and that suddenly. We are not merely to be rewarded or punished, we are to be judged. Recompense is to come upon our actions, not by a mere general provision or course of nature, as it does at present, but from the Lawgiver Himself in person. We have to stand before His righteous Presence, and that one by one. One by one we shall have to endure His holy and searching eye. At present we are in a world of shadows. What we see is not substantial. Suddenly it will be rent in twain and vanish away, and our Maker will appear. And then, I say, that first appearance will be nothing less than a personal intercourse between the Creator and every creature. He will look on us, while we look on Him.

I need hardly quote any of the numerous passages of Scripture which tell us this, by way of proof; but it may impress the truth of it upon our hearts to do so. We are told then expressly, that good and bad shall see God. On the one hand holy Job says, "Though after my skin worms destroy this body, yet in my flesh shall I see God: whom I shall see for myself, and mine eyes shall behold, and not another." On the other hand unrighteous Balaam says, " I shall see Him, but not now; I shall behold Him, but not nigh ; there shall come a Star out of Jacob, and a Sceptre shall rise out of Israel." Christ says to His disciples, " Look up, and lift up your heads, for your redemption draweth nigh ;" and to His enemies, " Hereafter ye shall see the Son of man sitting on the right hand of power, and coming in the clouds of heaven." And it is said generally of all men, on the one hand, " Behold He cometh with clouds ; and every eye shall see Him, and they also which pierced Him; and all kindreds of the earth shall wail because of Him." And on the other, " When He shall appear, we shall be like Him; for we shall see Him as He is." Again, " Now we see through a glass, darkly; but then face to face:" and again, " They shall see His face; and His Name shall be in their foreheads."[1]

And, as they see Him, so will He see them, for His coming will be to judge them. " We must all appear before the judgment-seat of Christ," says St. Paul. Again, " We shall all stand before the judgment-seat of Christ. For it is written, As I live, saith the Lord, every knee shall bow to Me, and every tongue shall confess to God. So then every one of us shall give account of himself to God." And again, " When the Son of man shall come in His glory, and all the holy Angels with Him, then shall He sit upon the throne of His glory. And before Him shall be gathered all nations; and He shall separate them one from another, as a shepherd divideth his sheep from the goats."[2]

Such is our first meeting with our God; and, I say, it will be as sudden as it is intimate. " Yourselves know perfectly," says St. Paul, " that the day of the Lord so cometh as a thief in the night. For when they shall say, Peace and safety, then sudden destruction cometh upon them." This is said of the wicked,— elsewhere He is said to surprise good as well as bad. " While the Bridegroom tarried," the wise and foolish

[1] Job xix. 26, 27. Numb. xxiv. 17. Luke xxi. 28. Matt. xxvi. 64. Rev. i. 7. 1 John iii. 2. 1 Cor. xiii. 12. Rev. xxii. 4.
[2] 2 Cor. v. 10. Rom. xiv. 10—12. Matt. xxv. 31, 32.

virgins "all slumbered and slept.   And at midnight there was a cry made, Behold, the Bridegroom cometh ; go ye out to meet Him."[1]

Now, when this state of the case, the prospect which lies before us, is brought home to our thoughts, surely it is one which will lead us anxiously to ask, Is this all that we are told, all that is allowed to us, or done for us? Do we know only this, that all is dark now, and all will be light then; that now God is hidden, and one day will be revealed? that we are in a world of sense, and are to be in a world of spirits? For surely it is our plain wisdom, our bounden duty, to prepare for this great change;—and if so, are any directions, hints, or rules given us *how* we are to prepare? "Prepare to meet thy God," "Go ye out to meet Him," is the dictate of natural reason, as well as of inspiration. But *how* is this to be?

Now observe, that it is scarcely a sufficient answer to this question to say that we must strive to obey Him, and so to approve ourselves to Him. This indeed might be enough, were reward and punishment to follow in the mere way of nature, as they do in this world. But, when we come steadily to consider the matter, appearing before God, and dwelling in His presence, is a very different thing from being merely subjected to a system of moral laws, and would seem to require another preparation, a special preparation of thought and affection, such as will enable us to endure His countenance, and to hold communion with Him as we ought. Nay, and, it may be, a preparation of

<hr>

[1] 1 Thess. v. 2, 3. Matt. xxv. 5, 6.

the soul itself for His presence, just as the bodily eye must be exercised in order to bear the full light of day, or the bodily frame in order to bear exposure to the air.

But, whether or not this be safe reasoning, Scripture precludes the necessity of it, by telling us that the Gospel Covenant is intended, among its other purposes, to prepare us for this future glorious and wonderful destiny, the sight of God,—a destiny which, if not most glorious, will be most terrible. And in the worship and service of Almighty God, which Christ and His Apostles have left to us, we are vouchsafed means, both moral and mystical, of approaching God, and gradually learning to bear the sight of Him.

This indeed is the most momentous reason for religious worship, as far as we have grounds for considering it a true one. Men sometimes ask, Why need they *profess* religion? Why need they go to church? Why need they observe certain rites and ceremonies? Why need they watch, pray, fast, and meditate? Why is it not enough to be just, honest, sober, benevolent, and otherwise virtuous? Is not this the true and real worship of God? Is not activity in mind and conduct the most acceptable way of approaching Him? How can they please Him by submitting to certain religious forms, and taking part in certain religious acts? Or if they must do so, why may they not choose their own? Why must they come to church for them? Why must they be partakers in what the Church calls Sacraments? I answer, they must do so, first of all and especially, because God tells them so to do. But besides this, I observe that we see this plain reason why, that they are one day to change their state of being. They are not to be here for ever. Direct intercourse with God on their part now, prayer and the like, may be necessary to their meeting Him suitably hereafter: and direct intercourse on His part with them, or what we call sacramental communion, may be necessary in some incomprehensible way, even for preparing their very nature to bear the sight of Him.

Let us then take this view of religious service; it is "going out to meet the Bridegroom," who, if not seen " in His beauty," will appear in consuming fire. Besides its other momentous reasons, it is a preparation for an awful event, which shall one day be. What it would be to meet Christ at once without preparation, we may learn from what happened even to the Apostles when His glory was suddenly manifested to them. St. Peter said, " Depart from me, for I am a sinful man, O Lord." And St. John, " when he saw Him, fell at His feet as dead." [1]

This being the case, it is certainly most merciful in God to vouchsafe to us the means of preparation, and such means as He has actually appointed. When Moses came down from the Mount, and the people were dazzled at his countenance, he put a veil over it. That veil is so far removed in the Gospel, that we are in a state of preparation for its being altogether removed. We are with Moses in the Mount so far, that we have a sight of God ; we are with the people beneath it so far, that Christ does not visibly show Himself. He has put a veil on, and He sits among us silently and secretly.

[1] Luke v. 8. Rev. i. 17.

When we approach Him, we know it only by faith; and when He manifests Himself to us, it is without our being able to realize to ourselves that manifestation.

Such then is the spirit in which we should come to all His ordinances, considering them as anticipations and first-fruits of that sight of Him which one day must be. When we kneel down in prayer in private, let us think to ourselves, Thus shall I one day kneel down before His very footstool, in this flesh and this blood of mine; and He will be seated over against me, in flesh and blood also, though divine. I come, with the thought of that awful hour before me, I come to confess my sin to Him now, that He may pardon it then, and I say, "O Lord, Holy God, Holy and Strong, Holy and Immortal, in the hour of death and in the day of judgment, deliver us, O Lord!"

Again, when we come to church, then let us say :— The day will be when I shall see Christ surrounded by His Holy Angels. I shall be brought into that blessed company, in which all will be pure, all bright. I come then to learn to endure the sight of the Holy One and His Servants; to nerve myself for a vision which is fearful before it is ecstatic, and which they only enjoy whom it does not consume. When men in this world have to undergo any great thing, they prepare themselves beforehand, by thinking often of it, and they call this making up their mind. Any unusual trial they thus make familiar to them. Courage is a necessary step in gaining certain goods, and courage is gained by steady thought. Children are scared, and close their eyes, at the vision of some mighty warrior or glorious king. And when Daniel saw the Angel, like St. John, " his comeliness was turned in him into corruption, and he retained no strength." [1] I come then to church, because I am an heir of heaven. It is my desire and hope one day to take possession of my inheritance: and I come to make myself ready for it, and I would not see heaven yet, for I could not bear to see it. I am allowed to be in it without seeing it, that I may learn to see it And by psalm and sacred song, by confession and by praise, I learn my part.

And what is true of the ordinary services of religion, public and private, holds in a still higher or rather in a special way, as regards the sacramental ordinances of the Church. In these is manifested in greater or less degree, according to the measure of each, that Incarnate Saviour, who is one day to be our Judge, and who is enabling us to bear His presence then, by imparting it to us in measure now. A thick black veil is spread between this world and the next. We mortal men range up and down it, to and fro, and see nothing. There is no access through it into the next world. In the Gospel this veil is not removed; it remains, but every now and then marvellous disclosures are made to us of what is behind it. At times we seem to catch a glimpse of a Form which we shall hereafter see face to face. We approach, and in spite of the darkness, our hands, or our head, or our brow, or our lips become, as it were, sensible of the contact of something more than earthly. We know not where we are, but we have been bathing in water, and a voice tells us that it is blood.

[1] Dan. x. 8.

Or we have a mark signed upon our foreheads, and it spake of Calvary. Or we recollect a hand laid upon our heads, and surely it had the print of nails in it, and resembled His who with a touch gave sight to the blind and raised the dead. Or we have been eating and drinking ; and it was not a dream surely, that One fed us from His wounded side, and renewed our nature by the heavenly meat He gave. Thus in many ways He, who is Judge to us, prepares us to be judged,—He, who is to glorify us, prepares us to be glorified, that He may not take us unawares ; but that when the voice of the Archangel sounds, and we are called to meet the Bridegroom, we may be ready.

Now consider what light these reflections throw upon some remarkable texts in the Epistle to the Hebrews. If we have in the Gospel this supernatural approach to God and to the next world, no wonder that St. Paul calls it an "enlightening," "a tasting of the heavenly gift," a being "made partaker of the Holy Ghost," a "tasting of the good word of God, and the powers of the world to come." No wonder, too, that utter apostasy after receiving it should be so utterly hopeless; and that in consequence, any profanation of it, any sinning against it, should be so perilous in proportion to its degree. If He, who is to be our Judge, condescend here to manifest Himself to us, surely if that privilege does not fit us for His future glory, it does but prepare us for His wrath.

And what I have said concerning Ordinances, applies still more fully to Holy Seasons, which include in them the celebration of many Ordinances. They are times

when we may humbly expect a larger grace, because
they invite us especially to the means of grace. This
in particular is a time for purification of every kind.
When Almighty God was to descend upon Mount
Sinai, Moses was told to "sanctify the people," and bid
them "wash their clothes," and to " set bounds to them
round about :" much more is this a season for "cleansing
ourselves from all defilement of the flesh and spirit,
perfecting holiness in the fear of God ;"[1] a season for
chastened hearts and religious eyes ; for severe thoughts,
and austere resolves, and charitable deeds ; a season for
remembering what we are and what we shall be. Let
us go out to meet Him with contrite and expectant
hearts ; and though He delays His coming, let us watch
for Him in the cold and dreariness which must one day
have an end. Attend His summons we must, at any
rate, when He strips us of the body ; let us anticipate,
by a voluntary act, what will one day come on us of
necessity. Let us wait for Him solemnly, fearfully,
hopefully, patiently, obediently ; let us be resigned to
His will, while active in good works. Let us pray Him
ever, to "remember us when He cometh in His kingdom ;" to remember all our friends ; to remember our
enemies ; and to visit us according to His mercy here,
that He may reward us according to His righteousness
hereafter.

[1] Exod. xix. 10—12. 2 Cor. vii. 1.

SERMON II.

REVERENCE, A BELIEF IN GOD'S PRESENCE.

(ADVENT.)

*" Thine eyes shall see the King in His beauty: they shall behold
the land that is very far off."*

THOUGH Moses was not permitted to enter the land
of promise, he was vouchsafed a sight of it from a
distance. We too, though as yet we are not admitted
to heavenly glory, yet are given to see much, in preparation for seeing more. Christ dwells among us in His
Church really though invisibly, and through its Ordinances fulfils towards us, in a true and sufficient sense,
the promise of the text. We are even now permitted to
" see the King in His beauty," to " behold the land that
is very far off." The words of the Prophet relate to our
present state as well as to the state of saints hereafter.
Of the future glory it is said by St. John, " They shall
see His face, and His name shall be in their foreheads."[1]
And of the present, Isaiah himself speaks in passages
which may be taken in explanation of the text: " The
glory of the Lord shall be revealed, and all flesh shall

[1] Rev. xxii. 4.

see it together;" and again, "They shall see the glory of the Lord, and the excellency of our God."[1] We do not see God face to face under the Gospel, but still, for all that, it is true that "we know in part;" we see, though it be "through a glass darkly;" which is far more than any but Christians are enabled to do. Baptism, by which we become Christians, is an illumination; and Christ, who is the Object of our worship, is withal a Light to worship by.

Such a view is strange to most men; they do not realize the presence of Christ, nor admit the duty of realizing it. Even those who are not without habits of seriousness, have almost or quite forgotten the duty. This is plain at once: for, unless they had, they would not be so very deficient in reverence as they are. It is scarcely too much to say that awe and fear are at the present day all but discarded from religion. Whole societies called Christian make it almost a first principle to disown the duty of reverence; and we ourselves, to whom as children of the Church reverence is as a special inheritance, have very little of it, and do not feel the want of it. Those who, in spite of themselves, are influenced by God's holy fear, too often are ashamed of it, consider it even as a mark of weakness of mind, hide their feeling as much as they can, and, when ridiculed or censured for it, cannot defend it to themselves on intelligible grounds. They wish indeed to maintain reverence in their mode of speaking and acting, in relation to sacred things, but they are at a loss how to answer objections, or how to resist received customs

---

[1] Isa. xl. 5; xxxv. 2.

and fashions; and at length they begin to be suspicious and afraid of their own instinctive feelings. Let us then take occasion from the promise in the text both to describe the religious defect to which I have alluded, and to state the remedy for it.

There are two classes of men who are deficient in awe and fear, and, lamentable to say, taken together, they go far to make up the religious portion of the community. This is lamentable indeed, if so it is: it is not wonderful that sinners should live without the fear of God; but what shall we say of an age or country, in which even the more serious classes, those who live on principle, and claim to have a judgment in religious matters, who look forward to the future, and think that their account stands fair, and that they are in God's favour, when even such persons maintain, or at least act as if they maintained, that "the spirit of God's holy fear" is no part of religion? "If the light that is in us be darkness, how great is that darkness!"

These are the two classes of men who are deficient in this respect: first, those who think that they never were greatly under God's displeasure; next, those who think that, though they once were, they are not at all now for all sin has been forgiven them;—those on the one hand who consider that sin is no great evil in itself, those on the other who consider that it is no great evil in them, because their persons are accepted in Christ for their faith's sake.

Now it must be observed that the existence of fear in religion does not depend on the circumstance of our being sinners; it is short of that. Were we pure as the Angels, yet in His sight, one should think, we could not but fear, before whom the heavens are not clean, nor the Angels free from folly. The Seraphim themselves veiled their faces while they cried, Glory! Even then were it true that sin was not a great evil, or was no great evil in us, nevertheless the mere circumstance that God is infinite and all-perfect is an overwhelming thought to creatures and mortal men, and ought to lead all persons who profess religion to profess also religious fear, however natural it is for irreligious men to disclaim the feeling.

And next let it be observed, it is no dispute about terms. For at first sight we may be tempted to think that the only question is whether the word "fear" is a good or bad word;—that one man makes it all one with slavish dread, and another with godly awe and reverence;—and that therefore the two seem to oppose each other, when they do not,—as if both parties agreed that reverence is right and selfish terror wrong, and the only point between them were, whether by the word fear was meant terror or reverence. This is not the case: it is a question not of words but of things; for these persons whom I am describing plainly consider that state of mind wrong, which the Church Catholic has ever prescribed and her Saints have ever exemplified.

To show that this is so, I will in a few words state what the two sets of opinion are to which I allude; and what that fault is, which, widely as they differ in opinion from each other, they have in common.

The one class of persons consists of those who think

the Catholic Creed too strict,—who hold that no certain doctrines need be believed in order to salvation, or at least question the necessity; who say that it matters not what a man believes, so that his conduct is respectable and orderly,—who think that all rites and ceremonies are mere niceties (as they speak) and trifles, and that a man pleases God equally by observing them or not,—who perhaps go on to doubt whether Christ's death is strictly speaking an atonement for the sin of man,—who, when pressed, do not allow that He is strictly speaking and literally God,—and who deny that the punishment of the wicked is eternal. Such are the tenets, more or less clearly apprehended and confessed, which mark the former of the two classes of which I speak.

The other class of men are in their formal doctrines widely different from the former. They consider that, though they were by nature children of wrath, they are now by God's grace so fully in His favour, that, were they to die at once, they would be certain of heaven,— they consider that God so absolutely forgives them day by day their trespasses, that they have nothing to answer for, nothing to be tried upon at the Last Day,—that they have been visited by God's grace in a manner quite distinct from all around them, and are His children in a sense in which others are not, and have an assurance of their saving state peculiar to themselves, and an interest in the promises such as Baptism does not impart;—they profess to be thus beyond the reach of doubt and anxiety, and they say that they should be miserable without such a privilege.

I have alluded to these schools of religion, to show how widely a feeling must be spread which such contrary classes of men have in common. Now, what they agree in is this: in considering God as simply a God of love, not of awe and reverence also,—the one meaning by love *benevolence*, and the other *mercy;* and in consequence neither the one nor the other regard Almighty God with *fear;* and the signs of want of fear in both the one and the other, which I proposed to point out, are such as the following.

For instance:—they have no scruple or misgiving in speaking freely of Almighty God. They will use His Name as familiarly and lightly, as if they were open sinners. The one class adopts a set of words to denote Almighty God, which remove the idea of His personality, speaking of Him as the "Deity," or the "Divine Being;" which, as they use them, are of all others most calculated to remove from the mind the thought of a living and intelligent Governor, their Saviour and their Judge. The other class of men, going into the other extreme, but with the same result, use freely that incommunicable Name by which He has vouchsafed to denote to us His perfections. When He appeared to Moses, He disclosed His Name; and that Name has appeared so sacred to our translators of Scripture, that they have scrupled to use it, though it occurs continually in the Old Testament, substituting the word "Lord' out of reverence. Now, the persons in question delight in a familiar use, in prayers and hymns and conversation, of that Name by which they designate Him before whom Angels tremble. Not even our fellow-men do we freely call by their own names, unless we are at our ease with them; yet sinners can bear to be familiar with the Name by which they know the Most High has distinguished Himself from all creatures.

Another instance of want of fear, is the bold and unscrupulous way in which men speak of the Holy Trinity and the Mystery of the Divine Nature. They use sacred terms and phrases, should occasion occur, in a rude and abrupt way, and discuss points of doctrine concerning the All-holy and Eternal, even (if I may without irreverence state it) over their cups, perhaps arguing against them, as if He were such a one as themselves.

Another instance of this want of fear is found in the peremptory manner in which men lay down what Almighty God must do, what He cannot but do, as if they were masters of the whole scheme of salvation, and might anticipate His high providence and will.

And another is the confidence with which they often speak of their having been converted, pardoned, and sanctified, as if they knew their own state as well as God knows it.

Another is the unwillingness so commonly felt, to bow at the Name of Jesus, nay the impatience exhibited towards those who do; as if there were nothing awful in the idea of the Eternal God being made man, and as if we did not suitably express our wonder and awe at it by practising what St. Paul has in very word prescribed.

Another instance is the careless mode in which men

speak of our Lord's earthly doings and sayings, just as if He were a mere man. He was man indeed, but He was more than man : and He did what man does, but then those deeds of His were the deeds of God,—and we can as little separate the deed from the Doer as our arm from our body. But, in spite of this, numbers are apt to use rude, familiar, profane language, concerning their God's childhood, and youth, and ministry, though He is their God.

And another is the familiarity with which many persons address our Lord in prayer, applying epithets to Him and adopting a strain of language which does not beseem creatures, not to say sinners.

And another is their general mode of prayer; I mean, in diffuse and free language, with emphatic and striking words, in a sort of coloured or rich style, with pomp of manner, and an oratorical tone, as if praying were preaching, and as if its object were not to address Almighty God, but to impress and affect those who heard them.

And another instance of this want of reverence is the introduction, in speaking or writing, of serious and solemn words, for the sake of effect, to round, or to give dignity to, a sentence.

And another instance is irreverence in church, sitting instead of kneeling in prayer, or pretending to kneel but really sitting, or lounging or indulging in other unseemly attitudes ; and, much more, looking about when prayers are going on, and observing what others are doing.

These are some out of a number of peculiarities

which mark the religion of the day, and are instanced, some in one class of men, some in another; but all by one or other;—and they are specimens of what I mean when I say that the religion of this day is destitute of *fear.*

Many other instances might be mentioned of very various kinds. For instance, the freedom with which men propose to alter God's ordinances, to suit their own convenience, or to meet the age; their reliance on their private and antecedent notions about sacred subjects; their want of interest and caution in inquiring what God's probable will is; their contempt for any view of the Sacraments which exceeds the evidence of their senses; and their confidence in settling the order of importance in which the distinct articles of Christian faith stand;—all which shows that it is no question of words whether men have fear or not, but that there *is* a something they really have not, whatever name we give it.

So far I consider to be plain:—the only point which can be debated is this, whether the feelings which I have been describing are necessary; for each of the two classes which I have named contends that they are unnecessary; the one decides them inconsistent with reason, the other with the Gospel; the one calls them superstitious, and the other legal or Jewish. Let us then consider, are these feelings of fear and awe Christian feelings or not? A very few words will surely be sufficient to decide the question.

I say this, then, which I think no one can reasonably dispute. They are the class of feelings we *should* have,—yes, have in an intense degree—if we literally had the sight of Almighty God; therefore they are the class of feelings which we shall have, *if* we realize His presence. In proportion as we believe that He is present, we shall have them; and not to have them, is not to realize, not to believe that He is present. If then it is a duty to feel as though we saw Him, or to have faith, it is a duty to have these feelings; and if it is a sin to be destitute of faith, it is a sin to be without them. Let us consider this awhile.

Who then is there to deny, that if we saw God, we should fear? Take the most cold and secular of all those who explain away the Gospel; or take the most heated and fanatic of those who consider it peculiarly their own; take those who think that Christ has brought us nothing great, or those who think He has brought it all to themselves,—I say, would either party keep from fearing greatly if they saw God? Surely it is quite a truism to say that any creature would fear. But why would he fear? would it be merely because he saw God, or because he knew that God was present? If he shut his eyes, he would still fear, for his eyes had conveyed to him this solemn truth; to *have* seen would be enough. But if so, does it not follow at once, that, if men do not fear, it is because they do not act as they would act if they saw Him, that is,—they do not feel that He is present? Is it not quite certain that men would not use Almighty God's Name so freely, if they thought He was really in hearing,—nay, close beside them when they spoke? And so of those other instances of want of godly fear, which I mentioned, they one and all come from deadness to the presence of God. If a man believes Him present, he will shrink from addressing Him familiarly, or using before Him unreal words, or peremptorily and on his own judgment deciding what God's will is, or claiming His confidence, or addressing Him in a familiar posture of body. I say, take the man who is most confident that he has nothing to fear from the presence of God, and that Almighty God is at peace with him, and place him actually before the throne of God; and would he have no misgivings? and will he dare to say that those misgivings are a weakness, a mere irrational perturbation, which he ought not to feel?

This will be seen more clearly, by considering how differently we feel towards and speak of our friends as present or absent. Their presence is a check upon us; it acts as an external law, compelling us to do or not do what we should not do or do otherwise, or should do but for it. This is just what most men lack in their religion at present,—such an external restraint arising from the consciousness of God's presence. Consider, I say, how differently we speak of a friend, however intimate, when present or absent; consider how we feel, should it so happen that we have begun to speak of him as if he were not present, on finding suddenly that he is; and that, though we are conscious of nothing but what is loving and open towards him. There is a tone of voice and a manner of speaking about persons absent, which we should consider disrespectful, or at least inconsiderate, if they were present. When that is the case, we are ever thinking more or less, even though unconsciously to ourselves, how they will take what we say, how it will affect them, what they will say to us or think of us in turn. When a person is absent, we are tempted perhaps confidently to say what his opinion is on certain points;—but should he be present, we qualify our words; we hardly like to speak at all, from the vivid consciousness that we may be wrong, and that he is present to tell us so. We are very cautious of pronouncing what his feelings are on the matter in hand, or how he is disposed towards ourselves; and in all things we observe a deference and delicacy in our conduct towards him. Now, if we feel this towards our fellows, what shall we feel in the presence of an Angel? and if so, what in the presence of the All-knowing, All-searching Judge of men? What is respect and consideration in the case of our fellows, becomes godly fear as regards Almighty God; and they who do not fear Him, in one word, do not believe that He sees and hears them. If they did, they would cease to boast so confidently of His favourable thoughts of them, to foretell His dealings, to pronounce upon His revelations, to make free with His Name, and to address Him familiarly.

Now, in what has been said, no account has been taken, as I have already observed, of our being sinners, a corrupt, polluted race at the best, while He is the All-holy God,—which must surely increase our fear and awe greatly, and not at all the less because we have been so wonderfully redeemed. Nor, again, has account been taken of another point, on which I will add two or three words.

There is a peculiar feeling with which we regard the dead. What does this arise from?—that he is absent? No; for we do not feel the same towards one who is merely distant, though he be at the other end of the earth. Is it because in this life we shall never see him again? No, surely not; because we may be perfectly certain we shall never see him when he goes abroad, we may know he is to die abroad, and perhaps he does die abroad; but will any one say that, when the news of his death comes, our feeling when we think of him is not quite changed? Surely it is the passing into another state which impresses itself upon us, and makes us speak of him as we do,—I mean, with a sort of awe. We cannot tell what he is now,—what his relations to us,—what he knows of us. We do not understand him, —we do not see him. He is passed into the land "that is very far off;" but it is not at all certain that he has not some mysterious hold over us. Thus his not being seen with our bodily eyes, while perchance he is present, makes the thought of him more awful. Apply this to the subject before us, and you will perceive that there is a sense, and a true sense, in which the *invisible* presence of God is more awful and overpowering than if we saw it. And so again, the presence of Christ, now that it is invisible, brings with it a host of high and mysterious feelings, such as nothing else can inspire. The thought of our Saviour, absent yet present, is like that of a friend taken from us, but, as it were, in dream returned to us, though in this case not in dream, but in reality and truth. When He was going away, He said to His disciples, "I will see you again, and your heart shall rejoice." Yet He had at another time said, "The days will come when the Bridegroom shall be taken from them, and then shall they fast in those days." See what an apparent contradiction, such as attends the putting any high feeling into human language! they were to joy because Christ was come, and yet weep because He was away; that is, to have a feeling so refined, so strange and new, that nothing could be said of it, but that it combined in one all that was sweet and soothing in contrary human feelings, as commonly experienced. As some precious fruits of the earth are said to taste like all others at once, not as not being really distinct from all others, but as being thus best described, when we would come as near the truth as we can, so the state of mind which they are in who believe that the Son of God is here, yet away,—is at the right hand of God, yet in His very flesh and blood among us,—is present, though invisible,—is one of both joy and pain, or rather one far above either; a feeling of awe, wonder, and praise, which cannot be more suitably expressed than by the Scripture word *fear;* or by holy Job's words, though he spoke in grief, and not as being possessed of a blessing. "Behold, I go forward, but He is not there; and backward, but I cannot perceive Him: on the left hand, where He doth work, but I cannot behold Him: He hideth Himself on the right hand, that I cannot see Him. Therefore am I troubled at His presence; when I consider, I am afraid of Him."[1]

To conclude. Enough has been said now to show that godly fear must be a duty, if to live as in God's sight

[1] Job xxiii. 8, 9, 15.

is a duty,—must be a privilege of the Gospel, if the spiritual sight of "the King in His beauty" be one of its privileges. Fear follows from faith necessarily, as would be plain, even though there were not a text in the Bible saying so. But in fact, as it is scarcely needful to say, Scripture abounds in precepts to fear God Such are the words of the Wise Man: "The fear of the Lord is the beginning of knowledge." Such again is the third commandment, in which we are solemnly bidden not to take God's Name in vain. Such the declaration of the prophet Habakkuk, who beginning by declaring "The just shall live by his faith," ends by saying, "The Lord is in His Holy Temple; let the whole earth keep silence before Him." Such is St. Paul's, who, in like manner, after having discoursed at length upon faith as "the realizing of things hoped for, the evidence of things not seen," adds: "Let us have grace, whereby we may serve God acceptably with reverence and godly fear." Such St. Luke's account of the Church militant on earth, that "walking in the fear of the Lord and in the comfort of the Holy Ghost," it was "multiplied." Such St. John's account of the Church triumphant in heaven, "Who shall not fear Thee," they say, "O Lord, and glorify Thy Name; for Thou only art Holy?" Such the feeling recorded of the three Apostles on the Mount of Transfiguration, who, when they heard God's voice, "fell on their face, and were sore afraid."[1] And now, if this be so, can anything be clearer than that the *want* of fear is nothing else but *want* of faith, and that in

[1] Prov. i. 7. Hab. ii. 4, 20. Heb. xii. 28. Acts ix. 31. Rev. xv. 4. Matt. xvii. 6.

consequence we in this age are approaching in religious temper that evil day of which it is said, " When the Son of Man cometh, shall He find faith on the earth ?"[1]   Is it wonderful that we have no fear in our words and mutual intercourse, when we exercise no *acts* of faith? What, you will ask, are acts of faith?   Such as these, —to come often to prayer, is an act of faith; to kneel down instead of sitting, is an act of faith; to strive to attend to your prayers, is an act of faith; to behave in God's House otherwise than you would in a common room, is an act of faith; to come to it on week-days as well as Sundays, is an act of faith; to come often to the most Holy Sacrament, is an act of faith; and to be still and reverent during that sacred service, is an act of faith.   These are all acts of faith, because they all are acts such as we should perform, if we saw and heard Him who *is* present, though with our bodily eyes we see and hear Him *not*.   But, " blessed are they who have not seen, and yet have believed;" for, be sure, if we thus act, we shall, through God's grace, be gradually endued with the spirit of His holy fear.   We shall in time, in our mode of talking and acting, in our religious services and our daily conduct, manifest, not with constraint and effort, but spontaneously and naturally, that we fear Him while we love Him.

<hr>

[1] Luke xviii. 8.

SERMON III

UNREAL WORDS.

ISAIAH xxxiii. 17.

*" Thine eyes shall see the King in His beauty: they shall behold
the land that is very far off."*

THE Prophet tells us, that under the Gospel covenant
God's servants will have the privilege of seeing those
heavenly sights which were but shadowed out in the
Law. Before Christ came was the time of shadows;
but when He came, He brought truth as well as grace;
and as He who is the Truth has come to us, so does He
in return require that we should be true and sincere in
our dealings with Him. To be true and sincere is really
to see with our minds those great wonders which He
has wrought in order that we might see them. When
God opened the eyes of the ass on which Balaam rode,
she saw the Angel and acted upon the sight. When
He opened the eyes of the young man, Elisha's servant,
he too saw the chariots and horses of fire, and took
comfort. And in like manner, Christians are now under
the protection of a Divine Presence, and that more
wonderful than any which was vouchsafed of old time.

God revealed Himself visibly to Jacob, to Job, to Moses, to Joshua, and to Isaiah; to us He reveals Himself not visibly, but more wonderfully and truly; not without the co-operation of our own will, but upon our faith, and for that very reason more truly; for faith is the special means of gaining spiritual blessings. Hence St. Paul prays for the Ephesians "that Christ may dwell in their hearts by faith," and that "the eyes of their understanding may be enlightened." And St. John declares that "the Son of God hath given us an understanding that we may know Him that is true: and we are in Him that is true, even in His Son Jesus Christ."[1]

We are no longer then in the region of shadows: we have the true Saviour set before us, the true reward, and the true means of spiritual renewal. We know the true state of the soul by nature and by grace, the evil of sin, the consequences of sinning, the way of pleasing God, and the motives to act upon. God has revealed Himself clearly to us; He has "destroyed the face of the covering cast over all people, and the veil that is spread over all nations." "The darkness is past, and the True Light now shineth."[2] And therefore, I say, He calls upon us in turn to "walk in the light as He is in the light." The Pharisees might have this excuse in their hypocrisy, that the plain truth had not been revealed to them; we have not even this poor reason for insincerity. We have no opportunity of mistaking one thing for another: the promise is expressly made to us that "our teachers shall not be removed into a corner any

---

1 Ephes. iii. 17; i. 18.　1 John v. 20.
2 Isa. xxv. 7.　1 John ii. 8.

more, but our eyes shall see our teachers;" that "the eyes of them that see shall not be dim;" that every thing shall be called by its right name; that "the vile person shall be no more called liberal, nor the churl said to be bountiful;"[1] in a word, as the text speaks, that "our eyes shall see the King in His beauty; we shall behold the land that is very far off." Our professions, our creeds, our prayers, our dealings, our conversation, our arguments, our teaching must henceforth be sincere, or, to use an expressive word, must be *real*. What St. Paul says of himself and his fellow-labourers, that they were true because Christ is true, applies to all Christians: " Our rejoicing is this, the testimony of our conscience, that in simplicity and godly sincerity, not with fleshly wisdom, but by the grace of God, we have had our conversation in the world, and more abundantly to you-ward. . . . The things that I purpose, do I purpose according to the flesh, that with me there should be yea yea, and nay nay? But as God is true, our word toward you was not yea and nay. For the Son of God, Jesus Christ, . . . was not yea and nay, but in Him was yea. For all the promises of God in Him are yea, and in Him Amen, unto the glory of God by us."[2]

And yet it need scarcely be said, nothing is so rare as honesty and singleness of mind; so much so, that a person who is really honest, is already perfect. Insincerity was an evil which sprang up within the Church from the first; Ananias and Simon were not open opposers of the Apostles, but false brethren. And, as foreseeing what was to be, our Saviour is remarkable

---

[1] Isa. xxx. 20; xxxii. 3, 5.   [2] 2 Cor. i. 12—20.

in His ministry for nothing more than the earnestness
of the dissuasives which He addressed to those who came
to Him, against taking up religion lightly, or making
promises which they were likely to break.

Thus He, " the True Light, which lighteth every man
that cometh into the world," " the Amen, the faithful
and true Witness, the Beginning of the creation of
God,"[1] said to the young Ruler, who lightly called Him
" Good Master," " Why callest thou Me good ?" as
bidding him weigh his words; and then abruptly told
him, " One thing thou lackest." When a certain man
professed that he would follow Him whithersoever He
went, He did not respond to him, but said, " The foxes
have holes, and the birds of the air have nests, but the
Son of Man hath not where to lay His head." When St.
Peter said with all his heart in the name of himself and
brethren, " To whom shall we go ? Thou hast the words
of eternal life," He answered pointedly, " Have not I
chosen you twelve, and one of you is a devil ?" as if He
said, " Answer for thyself." When the two Apostles
professed their desire to cast their lot with Him, He
asked whether they could " drink of His cup, and be
baptized with His baptism." And when " there went
great multitudes with Him," He turned and said, that
unless a man hated relations, friends, and self, he could
not be His disciple. And then he proceeded to warn all
men to " count the cost" ere they followed Him. Such
is the merciful severity with which He repels us that
He may gain us more truly. And what He thinks
of those who, after coming to Him, relapse into a

<hr>

[1] John i. 9. Rev. iii. 14.

hollow and hypocritical profession, we learn from His language towards the Laodiceans : " I know thy works, that thou art neither cold nor hot : I would thou wert cold or hot. So then, because thou art lukewarm, and neither cold nor hot, I will cast thee out of My mouth."[1]

We have a striking instance of the same conduct on the part of that ancient Saint who prefigured our Lord in name and office, Joshua, the captain of the chosen people in entering Canaan. When they had at length taken possession of that land which Moses and their fathers had seen " very far off," they said to him, " God forbid that we should forsake the Lord, and serve other gods. We will ... serve the Lord, for He is our God." He made answer, " Ye cannot serve the Lord ; for He is a holy God ; He is a jealous God ; He will not forgive your transgressions nor your sins."[2] Not as if he would hinder them from obeying, but to sober them in professing. How does his answer remind us of St. Paul's still more awful words, about the impossibility of renewal after utterly falling away !

And what is said of profession of *discipleship* applies undoubtedly in its degree to *all* profession. To make professions is to play with edged tools, unless we attend to what we are saying. Words have a meaning, whether we mean that meaning or not; and they are imputed to us in their real meaning, when our not meaning it is our own fault. He who takes God's Name in vain, is not counted guiltless because he means

---

[1] Mark x. 17—21. Matt. viii. 20. John vi. 68—70. Matt. xx. 22. Luke xiv. 25—28. Rev. iii. 15, 16.

[2] Josh. xxiv. 16—19.

nothing by it,—he cannot frame a language for him-self; and they who make professions, of whatever kind, are heard in the sense of those professions, and are not excused because they themselves attach no sense to them. " By thy words thou shalt be justified, and by thy words thou shalt be condemned."[1]

Now this consideration needs especially to be pressed upon Christians at this day ; for this is especially a day of professions. You will answer in my own words, that all ages have been ages of profession. So they have been, in one way or other, but this day in its own especial sense;—because this is especially a day of individual profession. This is a day in which there is (rightly or wrongly) so much of private judgment, so much of separation and difference, so much of preaching and teaching, so much of authorship, that it involves individual profession, responsibility, and recompense in a way peculiarly its own. It will not then be out of place if, in connexion with the text, we consider some of the many ways in which persons, whether in this age or in another, make unreal professions, or seeing see not, and hearing hear not, and speak without mastering, or trying to master, their words. This I will attempt to do at some length, and in matters of detail, which are not the less important because they are minute.

Of course it is very common in all matters, not only in religion, to speak in an unreal way ; viz., when we speak on a subject with which our minds are not familiar. If you were to hear a person who knew nothing about military matters, giving directions how soldiers on

[1] Matt. xii. 37.

service should conduct themselves, or how their food and lodging, or their marching, was to be duly arranged, you would be sure that his mistakes would be such as to excite the ridicule and contempt of men experienced in warfare. If a foreigner were to come to one of our cities, and without hesitation offer plans for the supply of our markets, or the management of our police, it is so certain that he would expose himself, that the very attempt would argue a great want of good sense and modesty. We should feel that he did not understand us, and that when he spoke about us, he would be using words without meaning. If a dim-sighted man were to attempt to decide questions of proportion and colour, or a man without ear to judge of musical compositions, we should feel that he spoke on and from general principles, on fancy, or by deduction and argument, not from a real apprehension of the matters which he discussed. His remarks would be theoretical and unreal.

This unsubstantial way of speaking is instanced in the case of persons who fall into any new company, among strange faces and amid novel occurrences. They sometimes form amiable judgments of men and things, sometimes the reverse,—but whatever their judgments be, they are to those who know the men and the things strangely unreal and distorted. They feel reverence where they should not; they discern slights where none were intended; they discover meaning in events which have none; they fancy motives; they misinterpret manner; they mistake character; and they form generalizations and combinations which exist only in their own minds.

Again, persons who have not attended to the subject of morals, or to politics, or to matters ecclesiastical, or to theology, do not know the relative value of questions which they meet with in these departments of knowledge. They do not understand the difference between one point and another. The one and the other are the same to them. They look at them as infants gaze at the objects which meet their eyes, in a vague unapprehensive way, as if not knowing whether a thing is a hundred miles off or close at hand, whether great or small, hard or soft. They have no means of judging, no standard to measure by,—and they give judgment at random, saying yea or nay on very deep questions, according as their fancy is struck at the moment, or as some clever or specious argument happens to come across them. Consequently they are inconsistent; say one thing one day, another the next;—and if they must act, act in the dark; or if they can help acting, do not act; or if they act freely, act from some other reason not avowed. All this is to be unreal.

Again, there cannot be a more apposite specimen of unreality than the way in which judgments are commonly formed upon important questions by the mass of the community. Opinions are continually given in the world on matters, about which those who offer them are as little qualified to judge as blind men about colours, and that because they have never exercised their minds upon the points in question. This is a day in which all men are obliged to have an opinion on all questions, political, social, and religious, because they have in some way or other an influence upon the decision; yet the multitude are for the most part absolutely without capacity to take their part in it. In saying this, I am far from meaning that this need be so,—I am far from denying that there is such a thing as plain good sense, or (what is better) religious sense, which will see its way through very intricate matters, or that this is in fact sometimes exerted in the community at large on certain great questions; but at the same time this practical sense is so far from existing as regards the vast mass of questions which in this day come before the public, that (as all persons who attempt to gain the influence of the people on their side know well) their opinions must be purchased by interesting their prejudices or fears in their favour;—not by presenting a question in its real and true substance, but by adroitly colouring it, or selecting out of it some particular point which may be exaggerated, and dressed up, and be made the means of working on popular feelings. And thus government and the art of government becomes, as much as popular religion, hollow and unsound.

And hence it is that the popular voice is so changeable. One man or measure is the idol of the people to-day, another to-morrow. They have never got beyond accepting shadows for things.

What is instanced in the mass is instanced also in various ways in individuals, and in points of detail. For instance, some men are set perhaps on being eloquent speakers. They use great words and imitate the sentences of others; and they fancy that those whom they imitate had as little meaning as themselves, or they perhaps contrive to think that they themselves have a meaning adequate to their words.

Another sort of unreality, or voluntary profession of what is above us, is instanced in the conduct of those who suddenly come into power or place. They affect a manner such as they think the office requires, but which is beyond them, and therefore unbecoming. They wish to act with dignity, and they cease to be themselves.

And so again, to take a different case, many men, when they come near persons in distress and wish to show sympathy, often condole in a very unreal way. I am not altogether laying this to their fault; for it is very difficult to know what to do, when on the one hand we cannot realize to ourselves the sorrow, yet withal wish to be kind to those who feel it. A tone of grief seems necessary, yet (if so be) cannot under our circumstances be genuine. Yet even here surely there is a true way, if we could find it, by which pretence may be avoided, and yet respect and consideration shown.

And in like manner as regards religious emotions. Persons are aware from the mere force of the doctrines of which the Gospel consists, that they ought to be variously affected, and deeply and intensely too, in consequence of them. The doctrines of original and actual sin, of Christ's Divinity and Atonement, and of Holy Baptism, are so vast, that no one can realize them without very complicated and profound feelings. Natural reason tells a man this, and that if he simply and genuinely believes the doctrines, he must have these feelings; and he professes to believe the doctrines absolutely, and therefore he professes the correspondent feelings. But in truth he perhaps does *not* really believe them absolutely, because such absolute belief is the work of long time, and therefore his profession of feeling outruns the real inward existence of feeling, or he becomes unreal. Let us never lose sight of two truths,—that we ought to have our hearts penetrated with the love of Christ and full of self-renunciation; but that if they be not, professing that they are does not make them so.

Again, to take a more serious instance of the same fault, some persons pray, not as sinners addressing their God, not as the Publican smiting on his breast, and saying, "God be merciful to me a sinner," but in such a way as they conceive to be becoming *under* circumstances of guilt, in a way becoming such a strait. They are self-conscious, and reflect on what they are about, and instead of actually approaching (as it were) the mercy-seat, they are filled with the thought that God is great, and man His creature, God on high and man on earth, and that they are engaged in a high and solemn service, and that they ought to rise up to its sublime and momentous character.

Another still more common form of the same fault, yet without any definite pretence or effort, is the mode in which people speak of the shortness and vanity of life, the certainty of death, and the joys of heaven. They have commonplaces in their mouths, which they bring forth upon occasions for the good of others, or to console them, or as a proper and becoming mark of attention towards them. Thus they speak to clergymen in a professedly serious way, making remarks true and sound, and in themselves deep, yet unmeaning in their mouths; or they give advice to children or young men; or perhaps in low spirits or sickness they are led to speak in a religious strain as if it was spontaneous. Or when they fall into sin, they speak of man being frail, of the deceitfulness of the human heart, of God's mercy, and so on:—all these great words, heaven, hell, judgment, mercy, repentance, works, the world that now is, the world to come, being little more than "lifeless sounds, whether of pipe or harp," in their mouths and ears, as the "very lovely song of one that hath a pleasant voice and can play well on an instrument,"—as the proprieties of conversation, or the civilities of good breeding.

I am speaking of the conduct of the world at large, called Christian; but what has been said applies, and necessarily, to the case of a number of well-disposed or even religious men. I mean, that before men come to know the realities of human life, it is not wonderful that their view of religion should be unreal. Young people who have never known sorrow or anxiety, or the sacrifices which conscientiousness involves, want commonly that depth and seriousness of character, which sorrow only and anxiety and self-sacrifice can give. I do not notice this as a fault, but as a plain fact, which may often be seen, and which it is well to bear in mind. This is the legitimate use of this world, to make us seek for another. It does its part when it repels us and disgusts us and drives us elsewhere. Experience of it gives experience of that which is its antidote, in the case of religious minds; and we become real in our view of what is spiritual by the contact of things temporal and earthly. And much more are men unreal when they have some secret motive urging them a different way from religion, and when their professions therefore are forced into an unnatural course in order to subserve their secret motive. When men do not like the conclusions to which their principles lead, or the precepts which Scripture contains, they are not wanting in ingenuity to blunt their force. They can frame some theory, or dress up certain objections, to defend themselves withal; a theory, that is, or objections, which it is difficult to refute perhaps, but which any rightly-ordered mind, nay, any common bystander, perceives to be unnatural and insincere.

What has been here noticed of individuals, takes place even in the case of whole Churches, at times when love has waxed cold and faith failed. The whole system of the Church, its discipline and ritual, are all in their origin the spontaneous and exuberant fruit of the real principle of spiritual religion in the hearts of its members. The invisible Church has developed itself into the Church visible, and its outward rites and forms are nourished and animated by the living power which dwells within it. Thus every part of it is real, down to the minutest details. But when the seductions of the world and the lusts of the flesh have eaten out this divine inward life, what is the outward Church but a hollowness and a mockery, like the whited sepulchres of which our Lord speaks, a memorial of what was and is not? and though we trust that the Church is nowhere thus utterly deserted by the Spirit of truth, at least according to God's ordinary providence, yet may we not say that in proportion as it approaches to this state of deadness, the grace of its ordinances, though not forfeited, at least flows in but a scanty or uncertain stream?

And lastly, if this unreality may steal over the Church itself, which is in its very essence a practical institution, much more is it found in the philosophies and literature of men. Literature is almost in its essence unreal; for it is the exhibition of thought disjoined from practice. Its very home is supposed to be ease and retirement; and when it does more than speak or write, it is accused of transgressing its bounds. This indeed constitutes what is considered its true dignity and honour, viz. its abstraction from the actual affairs of life; its security from the world's currents and vicissitudes; its saying without doing. A man of literature is considered to preserve his dignity by doing nothing; and when he proceeds forward into action, he is thought to lose his position, as if he were degrading his calling by enthusiasm, and becoming a politician or a partisan. Hence mere literary men are able to say strong things against the opinions of their age, whether religious or political, without offence; because no one thinks they mean anything by them. They are not expected to go forward to act upon them, and mere words hurt no one.

Such are some of the more common or more extended specimens of profession without action, or of speaking without really seeing and feeling. In instancing which, let it be observed, I do not mean to say that such profession, as has been described, is always culpable and wrong; indeed I have implied the contrary throughout. It is often a misfortune. It takes a long time really to feel and understand things as they are; we learn to do so only gradually. Profession beyond our feelings is only a fault when we might help it;—when either we speak when we need not speak, or do not feel when we might have felt. Hard insensible hearts, ready and thoughtless talkers, these are they whose unreality, as I have termed it, is a sin; it is the sin of every one of us, in proportion as our hearts are cold, or our tongues excessive.

But the mere fact of our saying more than we feel is not necessarily sinful. St. Peter did not rise up to the full meaning of his confession, " Thou art the Christ," yet he was pronounced blessed. St. James and St. John said, " We are able," without clear apprehension, yet without offence. We ever promise things greater than we master, and we wait on God to enable us to perform them. Our promising involves a prayer for light and strength. And so again we all say the Creed, but who comprehends it fully? All we can hope is, that we are in the way to understand it; that we partly understand it ; that we desire, pray, and strive to understand it more and more. Our Creed becomes a sort of prayer. Persons are culpably unreal in their way of speaking, not when they say more than they feel, but when they say things different from what they feel. A miser praising almsgiving, or a coward giving rules for courage, is unreal; but it is not unreal for the less to discourse about the greater, for the liberal to descant upon munificence, or the generous to praise the noble-minded, or the self-denying to use the language of the austere, or the confessor to exhort to martyrdom.

What I have been saying comes to this :—be in earnest, and you will speak of religion where, and when, and how you should; aim at things, and your words will be right without aiming. There are ten thousand ways of looking at this world, but only one right way. The man of pleasure has his way, the man of gain his, and the man of intellect his. Poor men and rich men, governors and governed, prosperous and discontented, learned and unlearned, each has his own way of looking at the things which come before him, and each has a wrong way. There is but one right way; it is the way in which God looks at the world. Aim at looking at it in God's way. Aim at seeing things as God sees them. Aim at forming judgments about persons, events, ranks, fortunes, changes, objects, such as God forms. Aim at looking at this life as God looks at it. Aim at looking at the life to come, and the world unseen, as God does. Aim at "seeing the King in His beauty." All things that we see are but shadows to us and delusions, unless we enter into what they really mean.

It is not an easy thing to learn that new language which Christ has brought us. He has interpreted all things for us in a new way; He has brought us a religion which sheds a new light on all that happens. Try to learn this language. Do not get it by rote, or speak it as a thing of course. Try to understand what you say. Time is short, eternity is long; God is great, man is weak; he stands between heaven and hell; Christ is his Saviour; Christ has suffered for him. The Holy Ghost sanctifies him; repentance purifies him, faith justifies, works save. These are solemn truths, which need not be actually spoken, except in the way of creed or of teaching; but which must be laid up in the heart. That a thing is true, is no reason that it should be said, but that it should be done; that it should be acted upon; that it should be made our own inwardly.

Let us avoid talking, of whatever kind; whether mere empty talking, or censorious talking, or idle profession, or descanting upon Gospel doctrines, or the affectation of philosophy, or the pretence of eloquence. Let us guard against frivolity, love of display, love of being talked about, love of singularity, love of seeming original. Let us aim at meaning what we say, and saying what we mean; let us aim at knowing when we understand a truth, and when we do not. When we do not, let us take it on faith, and let us profess to do so. Let us receive the truth in reverence, and pray God to give us a good will, and divine light, and spiritual strength, that it may bear fruit within us.

SERMON IV.

SHRINKING FROM CHRIST'S COMING.

(ADVENT.)

ISAIAH xxxiii. 17.

*"Thine eyes shall see the King in His beauty: they shall behold
the land that is very far off."*

BEFORE Christ came, the faithful remnant of Israel
were consoled with the promise that "their eyes
should see" Him, who was to be their "salvation."
"Unto you that fear My Name shall the Sun of righteousness arise with healing in His wings." Yet it is
observable that the prophecy, though cheering and
encouraging, had with it something of an awful
character too. First, it was said, "The Lord whom ye
seek shall suddenly come to His Temple, even the
messenger of the Covenant whom ye delight in." Yet
it is soon added, "But who may abide the day of His
coming? and who shall stand when He appeareth? for
He is like a refiner's fire, and like fullers' soap."[1]

The same mixture of fear with comfort is found in
the Disciples after His Resurrection. The women
departed from the sepulchre "with fear and great joy."

[1] Mal. iv. 2; iii. 1, 2.

They "trembled and were amazed: neither said they any thing to any man, for they were afraid." The Apostles "were terrified and affrighted, and supposed that they had seen a spirit." "They believed not for joy, and wondered." And our Lord said to them, "Why are ye troubled? and why do thoughts arise in your hearts?" On another occasion, "None of the disciples durst ask him, Who art thou? knowing that it was the Lord."[1] It might be from slowness to believe, or from misconception, or from the mere perplexity of amazement, but so it was; they exulted and they were awed.

Still more remarkable is the account of our Lord's appearance to St. John in the Book of Revelation; more remarkable because St. John had no doubt or perplexity. Christ had ascended; the Apostle had received the gift of the Holy Ghost; yet he "fell at His feet as dead."

This reflection leads us on to a parallel thought concerning the state and prospects of all Christians in every age. We too are looking out for Christ's coming, —we are bid look out,—we are bid pray for it; and yet it is to be a time of judgment. It is to be the deliverance of all Saints from sin and sorrow for ever; yet they, every one of them, must undergo an awful trial. How then can any look forward to it with joy, not knowing (for no one knows) the certainty of his own salvation? And the difficulty is increased when we come to pray for it,—to pray for its coming soon: how can we pray that Christ would come, that the day of

[1] Matt. xxviii. 8. Mark xvi. 8. Luke xxiv. 37, 38. John xxi. 12.

judgment would hasten, that His kingdom would come, that His kingdom may be at once,—may come on us this day or to-morrow,—when by so coming He would be shortening the time of our present life, and cut off those precious years given us for conversion, amendment, repentance and sanctification? Is there not an inconsistency in professing to wish our Judge already come, when we do not feel ourselves ready for Him? In what sense can we really and heartily pray that He would cut short the time, when our conscience tells us that, even were our life longest, we should have much to do in a few years?

I do not deny that there is some difficulty in the question, but surely not more so than there is on every side of us in religious matters. Religion has (as it were) its very life in what are paradoxes and contradictions in the eye of reason. It is a seeming inconsistency how we can pray for Christ's coming, yet wish time to "work out our salvation," and " make our calling and election sure." It was a seeming contradiction, how good men were to desire His first coming, yet be unable to abide it; how the Apostles feared, yet rejoiced after His resurrection. And so it is a paradox how the Christian should in all things be sorrowful yet always rejoicing, and dying yet living, and having nothing yet possessing all things. Such seeming contradictions arise from the want of depth in our minds to master the whole truth. We have not eyes keen enough to follow out the lines of God's providence and will, which meet at length, though at first sight they seem parallel.

I will now try to explain how these opposite duties

of fearing yet praying to have the sight of Christ are not necessarily inconsistent with each other. Why we should fear it, is not strange. Surely when a man gets himself steadily to contemplate a state of things beyond this life, he is in the way to be overpowered by the thoughts which throng upon him. How dreadful to the imagination is every scene of that unknown hereafter! This life indeed is full of dangers and pains, but we know what they are like ; we do not know what shall be in the world to come. "Lord, whither goest Thou?" said the Apostles ; " we know not whither Thou goest." Supposing a man told that he should suddenly be carried off to some unknown globe in the heavens,—this is the kind of trouble in its least fearful shape, which the future presents, when dwelt upon. And still more trying is the peculiar prospect which presents itself of Christ's coming in judgment. What a prospect. to be judged for all our doings by an unerring Judge Try to trace back the history of your life in memory, and fancy every part of it confessed by you in words, put into words before some intimate friend, how great would be your shame ! but how gladly would you in that day resign yourself to a disclosure to a fellow-sinner, how gladly to a disclosure to a world of sinners, compared with the presence of an All-holy, All-seeing Creator with His eyes upon you, "beholding you," as the gospel speaks of Him in the days of His flesh,—and one deed of evil after another told forth, while all your best actions and best qualities fade away and become as discoloured and unsightly as if there were nothing good in them; and you the while uncertain how the decision shall be. I do not presume to say that all this will happen in detail; but this is what is meant by a judgment in the earthly sense of the word, and that awful trial is surely not called a judgment for nothing, but that we may gain some ideas from it. Think of all this, and you will not deny that the thought of standing before Christ is enough to make us tremble. And yet His presence is held out to us by Himself as the greatest of goods; all Christians are bound to pray for it, to pray for its hastening; to pray that we may speedily look on Him whom none can see "without holiness," none but "the pure in heart;"—and now the question is, How can we pray for it with sincerity?

1. Now first, though we could not at all reconcile our feelings about ourselves with the command given us, still it is our duty to obey the latter on faith. If Abraham could lift up his knife to slay his son, we may well so far subdue our fears as to pray for what nevertheless is terrible. Job said, "Though he slay me, yet I will trust in him." Under all circumstances surely, we may calmly resign ourselves into His hands. Can we suppose that He would deceive us? deal unkindly or hardly with us? Can He make use of us, if I may say so, against ourselves? Let us not so think of the most merciful Lord. Let us do what He bids, and leave the rest to Him. Thus, I say, we might reason with ourselves, if nothing else could be said.

2. But next, I observe, that when we pray for the coming of Christ, we do but pray in the Church's words,

that He would "*accomplish the number* of His elect and would hasten His kingdom." That is, we do not pray that He would simply cut short the world, but, so to express myself, that He would make time go quicker, and the wheels of His chariot speed on. Before He comes, a certain space must be gone over; all the Saints must be gathered in; and each Saint must be matured. Not a grain must fall to the ground; not an ear of corn must lose its due rain and sunshine. All we pray is, that He would please to crowd all this into a short space of time; that He would "finish the work and cut it short *in righteousness*," and "make a short work upon the earth;" that He would accomplish,—not curtail, but fulfil,—the circle of His Saints, and hasten the age to come without disordering this. Indeed it cannot be otherwise. All God's works are in place and season; they are all complete. As in nature, the structure of its minutest portions is wrought out to perfection, and an insect is as wonderful as Leviathan; so, when in His providence He seems to hurry, He still keeps time, and moves upon the deep harmonies of truth and love. When then we pray that He would come, we pray also that we may be ready; that all things may converge and meet in Him; that He may draw us while He draws near us, and makes us the holier the closer He comes. We pray that we may not fear that which at present we justly do fear; "that when He shall appear, we may have confidence, and not be ashamed before Him at His coming."[1] He can condense into an hour a life of trial. He who frames

---

[1] 1 John ii. 28.

the worlds in a moment, and creates generations by the breath of His mouth, and melts, and hardens, and deluges, and dries up the solid rocks in a day, and makes bones to live, grow, and die, and buries them in the earth, and changes them into stone, apart from time and at His mere will, more wondrously can He deal with the world of spirits, who are never subject to the accidents of matter. He can by one keen pang of agony punish the earthly soul, or by one temptation justify it, or by one vision glorify it. Adam fell in a moment; Abraham was justified upon his seizing the knife; Moses lost Canaan for a word; David said, "I have sinned," and was forgiven; Solomon gained wisdom in a dream; Peter made one confession and received the keys; our Lord baffled Satan in three sentences; He redeemed us in the course of a day; He regenerates us by a form of words. We know not how "fearfully and wonderfully" our souls "are made." To men in sleep, in drowning, or in excitement, moments are as years. They suddenly become other men, nature or grace dispensing with time.

3. But again, you say, How can I pray to see Christ, who am so unclean? You say well that you are un-clean. But in what time do you propose to become otherwise? Do you expect in this life ever to be clean? Yes, in one sense, by the presence of the Holy Ghost within you; but that presence we trust you have now. But if by "clean," you mean free from that infection of nature, the least drop of which is sufficient to dis-honour all your services, clean you never will be till you have paid the debt of sin, and lose that body which

Adam has begotten. Be sure that the longer you live, and the holier you become, you will only perceive that misery more clearly. The less of it you have, the more it will oppress you; its full draught does but confuse and stupify you; as you come to yourself, your misery begins. The more your soul becomes one with Him who deigns to dwell within it, the more it sees with His eyes. You dare not pray for His presence now;— would you pray for it had you lived Methuselah's years? I trow not. You will never be good enough to desire it; no one in the whole Church prays for it except on conditions implied. To the end of the longest life you are still a beginner. What Christ asks of you is not sinlessness, but diligence. Had you lived ten times your present age, ten times more service would be required of you. Every day you live longer, more will be required. If He were to come to-day, you would be judged up to to-day. Did He come to-morrow, you would be judged up to to-morrow. Were the time put off a year, you would have a year more to answer for. You cannot elude your destiny, you cannot get rid of your talent; you are to answer for your opportunities, whatever they may be, not more nor less. You cannot be profitable to Him even with the longest life; you can show faith and love in an hour. True it is, if you have turned from Him, and served sin, and in proportion as you have done this, you have a great work before you,—to undo what you have done. If you have given years to Satan, you have a double duty, to repent as well as to work; but even then you may pray without dread; for in praying for His presence you still are praying, as I have said, to be ready for it.

4. But once more.   You ask, how you can make up your mind to stand before your Lord and God; I ask in turn, how do you bring yourself to come before Him now day by day?—for what is this but meeting Him? Consider what it is you mean by praying, and you will see that, at that very time that you are asking for the coming of His kingdom you are anticipating that coming, and accomplishing the thing you fear. When you pray, you come into His presence. Now reflect on yourself, what your feelings are in coming. They are these: you seem to say,—I am in myself nothing but a sinner, a man of unclean lips and earthly heart.   I am not worthy to enter into His presence.   I am not worthy of the least of all His mercies.   I know He is All-holy, yet I come before Him; I place myself under His pure and piercing eyes, which look me through and through, and discern every trace and every motion of evil within me.   Why do I do so?   First of all, for this reason.   To whom should I go?   What can I do better?   Who is there in the whole world that can help me?   Who that will care for me, or pity me, or have any kind thought of me, if I cannot obtain it of Him? I know He is of purer eyes than to behold iniquity; but I know again that He is All-merciful, and that He so sincerely desires my salvation that He has died for me.   Therefore, though I am in a great strait, I will rather fall into His hands, than into those of any creature.   True it is I could find creatures more like myself, imperfect or sinful: it might seem better to betake

myself to some of these who have power with God, and to beseech them to interest themselves for me. But no; somehow I cannot content myself with this;—no, terrible as it is, I had rather go to God alone. I have an instinct within me which leads me to rise and go to my Father, to name the Name of His well-beloved Son, and having named it, to place myself unreservedly in His hands, saying. " If Thou, Lord, wilt be extreme to mark what is done amiss, O Lord, who may abide it ? But there is forgiveness with Thee."—This is the feeling in which we come to confess our sins, and to pray to God for pardon and grace day by day; and observe, it is the very feeling in which we must prepare to meet Him when He comes visibly. Why, even children of this world can meet a judicial process and a violent death with firmness. I do not say that we must have aught of their pride or their self-trusting tranquillity. And yet there is a certain composure and dignity which become us who are born of immortal seed, when we come before our Father. If indeed we have habitually lived to the world, then truly it is natural we should attempt to fly from Him whom we have pierced. Then may we well call on the mountains to fall on us, and on the hills to cover us. But if we have lived, however imperfectly, yet habitually, in His fear, if we trust that His Spirit is in us, then we need not be ashamed before Him. We shall then come before Him, as now we come to pray—with profound abasement, with awe, with self-renunciation, still as relying upon the Spirit which He has given us, with our faculties about us, with a collected and determined mind, and with hope.

He who cannot pray for Christ's coming, ought not in consistency to pray at all.

I have spoken of coming to God in prayer generally; but if this is awful, much more is coming to Him in the Sacrament of Holy Communion; for this is in very form an anticipation of His coming, a near presence of Him in earnest of it. And a number of men feel it to be so; for, for one reason or another, they never come before Him in that most Holy Ordinance, and so deprive themselves of the highest of blessings here below. Thus their feeling is much the same as theirs would be, who from fear of His coming, did not dare look out for it. They indeed who are in the religious practice of communicating, understand well enough how it is possible to feel afraid and yet to come. Surely it is possible, and the case is the same as regards the future day of Christ. You must tremble, and yet pray for it. We have all of us experienced enough even of this life, to know that the same seasons are often most joyful and also most painful. Instances of this must suggest themselves to all men. Consider the loss of friends, and say whether joy and grief, triumph and humiliation, are not strangely mingled, yet both really preserved. The joy does not change the grief, nor the grief the joy, into some third feeling; they are incommunicable with each other, both remain, both affect us. Or consider the mingled feelings with which a son obtains forgiveness of a father,—the soothing thought that all displeasure is at an end, the veneration, the love, and all the undescribable emotions, most pleasurable, which cannot be put into words,—yet his bitterness against himself.

Such is the temper in which we desire to come to the Lord's table; such in which we must pray for His coming; such in which His elect will stand before Him when He comes.

5. Lastly, let me say more distinctly what I have already alluded to, that in that solemn hour we shall have, if we be His, the inward support of His Spirit too, carrying us on towards Him, and " witnessing with our spirits that we are the children of God." God is mysteriously threefold; and while He remains in the highest heaven, He comes to judge the world;—and while He judges the world, He is in us also, bearing us up and going forth in us to meet Himself. God the Son is without, but God the Spirit is within,—and when the Son asks, the Spirit will answer. That Spirit is vouchsafed to us here; and if we yield ourselves to His gracious influences, so that He draws up our thoughts and wills to heavenly things, and becomes one with us, He will assuredly be still in us and give us confidence at the Day of Judgment. He will be with us, and strengthen us; and how great His strength is, what mind of man can conceive? Gifted with that supernatural strength, we may be able to lift up our eyes to our Judge when He looks on us, and look on Him in turn, though with deep awe, yet without confusion of face, as if in the consciousness of innocence.

That hour must come at length upon every one of us. When it comes, may the countenance of the Most Holy quicken, not consume us; may the flame of judgment be to us only what it was to the Three Holy Children, over whom the fire had no power!

SERMON V.

EQUANIMITY.

(CHRISTMAS.)

PHIL. iv. 4.

" Rejoice in the Lord alway, and again I say, Rejoice."

IN other parts of Scripture the prospect of Christ's coming is made a reason for solemn fear and awe, and a call for watching and prayer, but in the verses connected with the text a distinct view of the Christian character is set before us, and distinct duties urged on us. "The Lord is at hand," and what then?—why, if so, we must "rejoice in the Lord;" we must be conspicuous for "moderation;" we must be "careful for nothing;" we must seek from God's bounty, and not from man, whatever we need; we must abound in "thanksgiving;" and we must cherish, or rather we must pray for, and we shall receive from above, "the peace of God which passeth all understanding," to "keep our hearts and minds through Christ Jesus."

Now this is a view of the Christian character definite and complete enough to admit of commenting on,—and it may be useful to show that the thought of Christ's coming not only leads to fear, but to a calm and cheerful frame of mind.

Nothing perhaps is more remarkable than that an Apostle,—a man of toil and blood, a man combating with powers unseen, and a spectacle for men and Angels, and much more that St. Paul, a man whose natural temper was so zealous, so severe, and so vehement,—I say, nothing is more striking and signi·ficant than that St. Paul should have given us this view of what a Christian should be. It would be nothing wonderful, it *is* nothing wonderful, that writers in a day like this should speak of peace, quiet, sobriety, and cheerfulness, as being the tone of mind that becomes a Christian ; but considering that St. Paul was by birth a Jew, and by education a Pharisee, that he wrote at a time when, if at any time, Christians were in lively and incessant agitation of mind ; when persecution and rumours of persecution abounded ; when all things seemed in commotion around them ; when there was nothing fixed ; when there were no churches to soothe them, no course of worship to sober them, no homes to refresh them ; and, again, considering that the Gospel is full of high and noble, and what may be called even romantic, principles and motives, and deep mysteries ;—and, further, considering the very topic which the Apostle combines with his admonitions is that awful subject, the coming of Christ ;—it is well worthy of notice, that, in such a time, under such a covenant, and with such a prospect, he should draw a picture of the Christian character as free from excitement and effort, as full of repose, as still and as equable, as if the great Apostle wrote in some monastery of the desert or some country parsonage. Here surely is the finger of God; here is the evidence of supernatural influences, making the mind of man independent of circumstances! This is the thought that first suggests itself; and the second is this, how deep and refined is the true Christian spirit!—how difficult to enter into, how vast to embrace, how impossible to exhaust! Who would expect such composure and equanimity from the fervent Apostle of the Gentiles? We know St. Paul could do great things; could suffer and achieve, could preach and confess, could be high and could be low: but we might have thought that all this was the limit and the perfection of the Christian temper, as he viewed it; and that no room was left him for the feelings which the text and following verses lead us to ascribe to him.

And yet he who "laboured more abundantly than all" his brethren, is also a pattern of simplicity, meekness, cheerfulness, thankfulness, and serenity of mind. These tempers were especially characteristic of St Paul, and are much insisted on in his Epistles. For instance.—" Mind not high things, but condescend to men of low estate. Be not wise in your own conceits. ... Provide things honest in the sight of all men. If it be possible, as much as lieth in you, live peaceably with all men." He enjoins, that "the aged men be sober, grave, temperate, sound in faith, in charity, in patience." "The aged woman likewise ... not false accusers, not given to much wine, teachers of good things, that they may teach the young women to be sober, to love their husbands, to love their children, to be discreet, chaste, keepers at home, good, obedient to their own husbands." And "young men" to be "sober-minded." And it is remarkable that he ends this exhortation with urging the same reason as is given in the verse after the text: "looking for that blessed hope, and the glorious appearing of our great God and Saviour Jesus Christ." In like manner, he says, that Christ's ministers must show "uncorruptness in doctrine, gravity, sincerity, sound speech that cannot be condemned;" that they must be "blameless, not self-willed, not soon angry .... lovers of good men, sober, just, holy, temperate."[1] All this is the description of what seems almost an ordinary character; I mean, it is so staid, so quiet, so unambitious, so homely. It displays so little of what is striking or extraordinary. It is so negligent of this world, so unexcited, so singleminded.

It is observable, too, that it was foretold as the peculiarity of Gospel times by the Prophet Isaiah: "The work of righteousness shall be peace; and the effect of righteousness, quietness and assurance for ever. And My people shall dwell in a peaceable habitation, and in sure dwellings, and in quiet resting-places."[2]

Now then let us consider more particularly what is this state of mind, and what the grounds of it. These seem to be as follows:—The Lord is at hand; this is not your rest; this is not your abiding-place. Act then

---

[1] Rom. xii. 16—18. Titus ii. 2—13; i. 7, 8.
[2] Isa. xxxii. 17, 18.

as persons who are in a dwelling not their own; who are not in their own home; who have not their own goods and furniture about them; who, accordingly, make shift and put up with anything that comes to hand, and do not make a point of things being the best of their kind. "But this I say, brethren, the time is short." What matters it what we eat, what we drink, how we are clothed, where we lodge, what is thought of us, what becomes of us, since we are not at home? It is felt every day, even as regards this world, that when we leave home for a while we are unsettled. This, then, is the kind of feeling which a belief in Christ's coming will create within us. It is not worth while establishing ourselves here; it is not worth while spending time and thought on such an object. We shall hardly have got settled when we shall have to move.

This being apparently the general drift of the passage, let us next enter into the particular portions of it.

1. "Be careful for nothing," he says, or, as St. Peter, "casting all your care upon Him," or, as He Himself, "Take no thought" or care "for the morrow, for the morrow will take thought for the things of itself."[1] This of course is the state of mind which is directly consequent on the belief, that "the Lord is at hand." Who would care for any loss or gain to-day, if he knew for certain that Christ would show Himself to-morrow? no one. Well, then, the true Christian feels as he would feel, did he know for certain that Christ would be here to-morrow. For he knows for certain, that at least Christ will come to him when he dies; and faith

---

[1] 1 Peter v. 7. Matt. vi. 34.

anticipates his death, and makes it just as if that distant day, if it *be* distant, were past and over. One time or another Christ will come, for certain : and when He once *has* come, it matters not what length of time there was before He came ;—however long that period may be, it has an end. Judgment is coming, whether it comes sooner or later, and the Christian realizes that it is coming ; that is, time does not enter into his calculation. or interfere with his view of things. When men expect to carry out their plans and projects, then they care for them ; when they know these will come to nought, they give them over, or become indifferent to them.

So, again, it is with all forebodings, anxieties, mortifications, griefs, resentments of this world. "The time is short." It has sometimes been well suggested, as a mode of calming the mind when set upon an object, or much vexed or angered at some occurrence, what will you feel about all this a year hence ? It is very plain that matters which agitate us most extremely now, will then interest us not at all ; that objects about which we have intense hope and fear now, will then be to us nothing more than things which happen at the other end of the earth. So will it be with all human hopes, fears, pleasures, pains, jealousies, disappointments, successes, when the last day is come. They will have no life in them ; they will be as the faded flowers of a banquet, which do but mock us. Or when we lie on the bed of death, what will it avail us to have been rich, or great, or fortunate, or honoured, or influential ? All things will then be vanity. Well, what this world will be understood by all to be then, such is it felt to be by the Christian now. He looks at things as he then will look at them, with an uninterested and dispassionate eye, and is neither pained much nor pleased much at the accidents of life, because they are accidents.

2. Another part of the character under review is, what our translation calls moderation; "Let your moderation be known unto all men," or, as it may be more exactly rendered, your consideration, fairness, or equitableness. St. Paul makes it a part of a Christian character to have a reputation for candour, dispassionateness, tenderness towards others. The truth is, as soon and in proportion as a person believes that Christ is coming, and recognises his own position as a stranger on earth, who has but hired a lodging in it for a season, he will feel indifferent to the course of human affairs. He will be able to look on, instead of taking a part in them. They will be nothing to him. He will be able to criticise them, and pass judgment on them, without partiality. This is what is meant by "our moderation" being acknowledged by all men. Those who have strong interests one way or the other, cannot be dispassionate observers and candid judges. They are partisans; they defend one set of people, and attack another. They are prejudiced against those who differ from them, or who thwart them. They cannot make allowances, or show sympathy for them. But the Christian has no keen expectations, no acute mortifications. He is fair, equitable, considerate towards all men, because he has no temptation to be otherwise.

He has no violence, no animosity, no bigotry, no party feeling. He knows that his Lord and Saviour must triumph; he knows that He will one day come from heaven, no one can say how soon. Knowing then the end to which all things tend, he cares less for the road which is to lead to it. When we read a book of fiction, we are much excited with the course of the narrative, till we know how things will turn out; but when we do, the interest ceases. So is it with the Christian. He knows Christ's battle will last till the end; that Christ's cause will triumph in the end; that His Church will last till He comes. He knows what is truth and what is error, where is safety and where is danger; and all this clear knowledge enables him to make concessions, to own difficulties, to do justice to the erring, to acknowledge their good points, to be content with such countenance, greater or less, as he himself receives from others. He does not fear; fear it is that makes men bigots, tyrants, and zealots; but for the Christian, it is his privilege, as he is beyond hopes and fears, suspense and jealousy, so also to be patient, cool, discriminating, and impartial;—so much so, that this very fairness marks his character in the eyes of the world, is "known unto all men."

3. Joy and gladness are also characteristics of him, according to the exhortation in the text, "Rejoice in the Lord alway," and this in spite of the fear and awe which the thought of the Last Day ought to produce in him. It is by means of these strong contrasts that Scripture brings out to us what is the real meaning of its separate portions. If we had been told merely

to fear, we should have mistaken a slavish dread, or the gloom of despair, for godly fear; and if we had been told merely to rejoice, we should perhaps have mistaken a rude freedom and familiarity for joy; but when we are told both to fear and to rejoice, we gain thus much at first sight, that our joy is not to be irreverent, nor our fear to be desponding; that though both feelings are to remain, neither is to be what it would be by itself. This is what we gain at once by such contrasts. I do not say that this makes it at all easier to combine the separate duties to which they relate; that is a further and higher work; but thus much we gain at once, a better knowledge of these separate duties themselves. And now I am speaking about the duty of rejoicing, and I say, that whatever be the duty of fearing greatly and trembling greatly at the thought of the Day of Judgment, and of course it is a great duty, yet the command so to do cannot reverse the command to rejoice; it can only so far interfere with it as to explain what is meant by rejoicing. It is as clear a duty to rejoice in the prospect of Christ's coming, as if we were not told to fear it. The duty of fearing does but perfect our joy; that joy alone is true Christian joy, which is informed and quickened by fear, and made thereby sober and reverent.

How joy and fear can be reconciled, words cannot show. Act and deed alone can show how. Let a man try both to fear and to rejoice, as Christ and His Apostles tell him, and in time he will learn how; but when he has learned, he will be as little able to explain how it is he does both, as he was before. He will seem inconsistent, and may easily be proved to be so, to the satisfaction of irreligious men, as Scripture is called inconsistent. He becomes the paradox which Scripture enjoins. This is variously fulfilled in the case of men of advanced holiness. They are accused of the most opposite faults; of being proud, and of being mean; of being over-simple, and being crafty; of having too strict, and, at the same time, too lax a conscience; of being unsocial, and yet being worldly; of being too literal in explaining Scripture, and yet of adding to Scripture, and superseding Scripture. Men of the world, or men of inferior religiousness, cannot understand them, and are fond of criticising those who, in seeming to be inconsistent, are but like Scripture teaching.

But to return to the case of joy and fear. It may be objected, that at least those who fall into sin, or who have in times past sinned grievously, cannot have this pleasant and cheerful temper which St. Paul enjoins. I grant it. But what is this but saying that St. Paul enjoins us *not* to fall into sin? When St. Paul warns us against sadness and heaviness, of course he warns us against those things which make men sad and heavy; and therefore especially against sin, which is an especial enemy of joyfulness. It is not that sorrowing for sin is wrong when we *have* sinned, but the *sinning* is wrong which causes the sorrowing. When a person has sinned, he cannot do anything better than sorrow. He ought to sorrow; and so far as he does sorrow, he is certainly *not* in the perfect Christian state; but it is his sin that has forfeited it. And yet even here sorrow is not inconsistent with rejoicing. For there are few men, who are really in earnest in their sorrow, but after a time may be conscious that they are so; and, when man knows himself to be in earnest, he knows that God looks mercifully upon him; and this gives him sufficient reason for rejoicing, even though fear remains. St. Peter could appeal to Christ, " Lord, Thou knowest all things; Thou knowest that I love Thee." We of course cannot appeal so unreservedly—still we can timidly appeal—we can say that we humbly trust that, whatever be the measure of our past sins, and whatever of our present self-denial, yet at bottom we do wish and strive to give up the world and to follow Christ; and in proportion as this sense of sincerity is strong upon our minds, in the same degree shall we rejoice in the Lord, even while we fear.

4. Once more, peace is part of this same temper also. " The peace of God," says the Apostle, " which passeth all understanding, shall keep your hearts and minds through Christ Jesus." There are many things in the Gospel to alarm us, many to agitate us, many to transport us, but the end and issue of all these is *peace.* " Glory to God in the highest, and on earth peace." It may be asked indeed whether warfare, perplexity, and uncertainty be not the condition of the Christian here below; whether St. Paul himself does not say that he has " the care," or the anxiety, " of all the Churches," and whether he does not plainly evince and avow in his Epistles to the Galatians and Corinthians much distress of mind? " Without were fightings, within fears."[1] I grant it; he certainly shows at times much

1 2 Cor. vii. 5.

agitation of mind; but consider this. Did you ever look at an expanse of water, and observe the ripples on the surface? Do you think that disturbance penetrates below it? Nay; you have seen or heard of fearful tempests on the sea; scenes of horror and distress, which are in no respect a fit type of an Apostle's tears or sighings about his flock. Yet even these violent commotions do not reach into the depths. The foundations of the ocean, the vast realms of water which girdle the earth, are as tranquil and as silent in the storm as in a calm. So is it with the souls of holy men. They have a well of peace springing up within them unfathomable; and though the accidents of the hour may make them seem agitated, yet in their hearts they are not so. Even Angels joy over sinners repentant, and, as we may therefore suppose, grieve over sinners impenitent,—yet who shall say that they have not perfect peace? Even Almighty God Himself deigns to speak of His being grieved, and angry, and rejoicing,—yet is He not the unchangeable? And in like manner, to compare human things with divine, St. Paul had perfect peace, as being stayed in soul on God, though the trials of life might vex him.

For, as I have said, the Christian has a deep, silent, hidden peace, which the world sees not,—like some well in a retired and shady place, difficult of access. He is the greater part of his time by himself, and when he is in solitude, that is his real state. What he is when left to himself and to his God, that is his true life. He can bear himself; he can (as it were) joy in himself, for it is the grace of God within him, it is the presence of the Eternal Comforter, in which he joys. He can bear, he finds it pleasant, to be with himself at all times,—"never less alone than when alone." He can lay his head on his pillow at night, and own in God's sight, with overflowing heart, that he wants nothing,—that he "is full and abounds,"—that God has been all things to him, and that nothing is not his which God could give him. More thankfulness, more holiness, more of heaven he needs indeed, but the thought that he can have more is not a thought of trouble, but of joy. It does not interfere with his peace to know that he may grow nearer God. Such is the Christian's peace, when, with a single heart and the Cross in his eye, he addresses and commends himself to Him with whom the night is as clear as the day. St. Paul says that "the peace of God shall *keep* our hearts and minds." By "keep" is meant "guard," or "garrison," our hearts; so as to keep out enemies. And he says, our "hearts and minds" in contrast to what the world sees of us. Many hard things may be said of the Christian, and done against him, but he has a secret preservative or charm, and minds them not.

These are some few suggestions on that character of mind which becomes the followers of Him who was once "born of a pure Virgin," and who bids them as "new-born babes desire the sincere milk of the Word, that they may grow thereby." The Christian is cheerful, easy, kind, gentle, courteous, candid, unassuming; has no pretence, no affectation, no ambition, no singularity; because he has neither hope nor fear about this world. He is serious, sober, discreet, grave, moderate, mild, with so little that is unusual or striking in his bearing, that he may easily be taken at first sight for an ordinary man. There are persons who think religion consists in ecstasies, or in set speeches;—he is not of those. And it must be confessed, on the other hand, that there is a common-place state of mind which does show itself calm, composed, and candid, yet is very far from the true Christian temper. In this day especially it is very easy for men to be benevolent, liberal, and dispassionate. It costs nothing to be dispassionate when you feel nothing, to be cheerful when you have nothing to fear, to be generous or liberal when what you give is not your own, and to be benevolent and considerate when you have no principles and no opinions. Men nowadays are moderate and equitable, not because the Lord is at hand, but because they do not feel that He is coming. Quietness is a grace, not in itself, only when it is grafted on the stem of faith, zeal, self-abasement, and diligence.

May it be our blessedness, as years go on, to add one grace to another, and advance upward, step by step, neither neglecting the lower after attaining the higher, nor aiming at the higher before attaining the lower. The first grace is faith, the last is love; first comes zeal, afterwards comes loving-kindness; first comes humiliation, then comes peace; first comes diligence, then comes resignation. May we learn to mature all graces in us;—fearing and trembling, watching and repenting, because Christ is coming; joyful, thankful, and careless of the future, because He is come.

SERMON VI.

REMEMBRANCE OF PAST MERCIES.

(CHRISTMAS.)

GEN. xxxii. 10.

*" I am not worthy of the least of all the mercies, and of all the truth,
which Thou hast showed unto Thy servant."*

THE spirit of humble thankfulness for past mercies
which these words imply, is a grace to which we
are especially called in the Gospel. Jacob, who spoke
them, knew not of those great and wonderful acts of
love with which God has since visited the race of man.
But though he might not know the depths of God's
counsels, he knew himself so far as to know that he
was worthy of no good thing at all, and he knew also
that Almighty God had shown him great mercies and
great truth: mercies, in that He had done for him
good things, whereas he had deserved evil; and truth,
in that He had made him promises, and had been
faithful to them. In consequence, he overflowed with
gratitude when he looked back upon the past; mar-
velling at the contrast between what he was in himself
and what God had been to him.

Such thankfulness, I say, is eminently a Christian

grace, and is enjoined on us in the New Testament. For instance, we are exhorted to be "thankful," and to let "the Word of Christ dwell in us richly in all wisdom; teaching and admonishing one another in psalms and hymns and spiritual songs, singing with grace in our hearts to the Lord."

Elsewhere, we are told to "speak to ourselves in psalms and hymns and spiritual songs, singing and making melody in our heart to the Lord: giving thanks always for all things unto God and the Father, in the Name of our Lord Jesus Christ."

Again: "Be careful for nothing: but in every thing by prayer and supplication, with thanksgiving, let your requests be made known unto God."

Again: "In every thing give thanks: for this is the will of God in Christ Jesus concerning you."[1]

The Apostle, who writes all this, was himself an especial pattern of a thankful spirit: "Rejoice in the Lord alway," he says: "and again I say, Rejoice." "I have learned, in whatsoever state I am, therewith to be content. I have all and abound; I am full." Again: "I thank Christ Jesus our Lord, who hath enabled me, for that He counted me faithful, putting me into the ministry; who was before a blasphemer and a persecutor, and injurious. But I obtained mercy, because I did it ignorantly in unbelief. And the grace of our Lord was exceeding abundant, with faith and love which is in Christ Jesus."[2] O great Apostle! how could it be otherwise, considering what he had

---

[1] Col. iii. 15, 16. Eph. v. 19, 20. Phil. iv. 6. 1 Thess. v. 18.
[2] Phil. iv. 4, 11, 18. 1 Tim. i. 12—14.

been and what he was,—transformed from an enemy to a friend, from a blind Pharisee to an inspired preacher? And yet there is another Saint, besides the patriarch Jacob, who is his fellow in this excellent grace,—like them, distinguished by great vicissitudes of life, and by the adoring love and the tenderness of heart with which he looked back upon the past:— I mean, "David, the son of Jesse, the man who was raised up on high, the anointed of the God of Jacob, and the sweet Psalmist of Israel."[1]

The Book of Psalms is full of instances of David's thankful spirit, which I need not cite here, as we are all so well acquainted with them. I will but refer to his thanksgiving, when he set apart the precious materials for the building of the Temple, as it occurs at the end of the First Book of Chronicles; when he rejoiced so greatly, because he and his people had the heart to offer freely to God, and thanked God for his very thankfulness. "David, the king . . rejoiced with great joy; wherefore David blessed the Lord before all the congregation; and David said, Blessed be Thou, Lord God of Israel, our Father, for ever and ever. . . Both riches and honour come of Thee, and Thou reignest over all; and in Thine hand is power and might, and in Thine hand it is to make great, and to give strength unto all. Now, therefore, our God, we thank Thee, and praise Thy glorious Name. But who am I, and what is my people, that we should be able to offer so willingly after this sort? for all things come of Thee, and of Thine own have we given Thee."[2]

<hr>

[1] 2 Sam. xxiii. 1.   [2] 1 Chron. xxix. 9--14.

Such was the thankful spirit of David, looking back upon the past, wondering and rejoicing at the way in which his Almighty Protector had led him on, and at the works He had enabled him to do; and praising and glorifying Him for His mercy and truth. David, then, Jacob, and St. Paul, may be considered the three great patterns of thankfulness, which are set before us in Scripture;—saints, all of whom were peculiarly the creation of God's grace, and whose very life and breath it was humbly and adoringly to meditate upon the contrast between what, in different ways, they had been, and what they were. A perishing wanderer had unexpectedly become a patriarch; a shepherd, a king; and a persecutor, an apostle: each had been chosen, at God's inscrutable pleasure, to fulfil a great purpose, and each, while he did his utmost to fulfil it, kept praising God that he was made His instrument. Of the first, it was said, "Jacob have I loved, but Esau have I hated;" of the second, that "He refused the tabernacle of Joseph, and chose not the tribe of Ephraim, but chose the tribe of Judah, even the hill of Sion, which He loved: He chose David also His servant, and took him away from the sheepfolds." And St. Paul says of himself, "Last of all, He was seen of me also, as of one born out of due time."[1]

These thoughts naturally come over the mind at this season, when we are engaged in celebrating God's grace in making us His children, by the incarnation of His Only-begotten Son, the greatest and most wonderful of all His mercies. And to the Patriarch Jacob our minds

[1] Rom. ix. 13. Ps. lxxviii. 68—71. 1 Cor. xv. 8.

are now particularly turned, by the First Lessons for this day,[1] taken from the Prophet Isaiah, in which the Church is addressed and comforted under the name of Jacob. Let us then, in this season of thankfulness, and at the beginning of a new year, take a brief view of the character of this Patriarch ; and though David and Isaiah be the prophets of grace, and St. Paul its special herald and chief pattern, yet, if we wish to see an actual specimen of a habit of thankfulness occupied in the remembrance of God's mercies, I think we shall not be wrong in betaking ourselves to Jacob.

Jacob's distinguishing grace then, as I think it may be called, was a habit of affectionate musing upon God's providences towards him in times past, and of over-flowing thankfulness for them. Not that he had not other graces also, but this seems to have been his distin-guishing grace. All good men have in their measure all graces ; for He, by whom they have any, does not give one apart from the whole : He gives the root, and the root puts forth branches. But since time, and circum-stances, and their own use of the gift, and their own disposition and character, have much influence on the mode of its manifestation, so it happens, that each good man has his own distinguishing grace, apart from the rest, his own particular hue and fragrance and fashion, as a flower may have. As, then, there are numberless flowers on the earth, all of them flowers, and so far like each other ; and all springing from the same earth, and nourished by the same air and dew, and none without beauty ; and yet some are more beautiful than others ;

[1] Second Sunday after Christmas.

and of those which are beautiful, some excel in colour, and others in sweetness, and others in form; and then, again, those which are sweet have such perfect sweetness, yet so distinct, that we do not know how to compare them together, or to say which is the sweeter: so is it with souls filled and nurtured by God's secret grace. Abraham, for instance, Jacob's forefather, was the pattern of faith. This is insisted on in Scripture, and it is not here necessary to show that he was so. It will be sufficient to say, that he left his country at God's word; and, at the same word, took up the knife to slay his own son. Abraham seems to have had something very noble and magnanimous about him. He could realize and make present to him things unseen. He followed God in the dark as promptly, as firmly, with as cheerful a heart, and bold a stepping, as if he were in broad daylight. There is something very great in this; and, therefore, St. Paul calls Abraham *our* father, the father of Christians as well as of Jews. For we are especially bound to walk by faith, not by sight; and are blessed in faith, and justified by faith, as was faithful Abraham. Now (if I may say it, with due reverence to the memory of that favoured servant of God, in whose praise I am now speaking) that faith in which Abraham excelled was not Jacob's characteristic excellence. Not that he had not faith, and great faith, else he would not have been so dear to God. His buying the birthright and gaining the blessing from Esau were proofs of faith. Esau saw nothing or little precious in them,—he was profane; easily parted with the one, and had no high ideas of the other. However, Jacob's faith, earnest and vigorous as it was, was not like Abraham's. Abraham kept his affections loose from everything earthly, and was ready, at God's word, to slay his only son. Jacob had many sons, and may we not even say that he indulged them overmuch? Even as regards Joseph, whom he so deservedly loved, beautiful and touching as his love of him is, yet there is a great contrast between his feelings towards the "son of his old age" and those of Abraham towards Isaac, the unexpected offspring of his hundredth year,—nor only such, but his long-promised only son, with whom were the promises. Again : Abraham left his country,—so did Jacob ; but Abraham, at God's word,—Jacob, from necessity on the threat of Esau. Abraham, from the first, felt that God was his portion and his inheritance, and, in a great and generous spirit, he freely gave up all he had, being sure that he should find what was more excellent in doing so. But Jacob, in spite of his really living by faith, wished (if we may so say), as one passage of his history shows, to see before he fully believed. When he was escaping from Esau and came to Bethel, and God appeared to him in a dream and gave him promises, but not yet the performance of them,—what did he do? Did he simply accept them? He says, "*If* God will be with me, and will keep me in this way that I go, and will give me bread to eat, and raiment to put on, so that I come again to my father's house in peace, *then* shall the Lord be my God."[1] He makes his obedience, in some sense, depend on a condition ; and although we must not, and need not, take the words as if he meant that he would not

[1] Gen. xxviii. 20, 21.

serve God *till* and *unless* He did for him what He had promised, yet they seem to show a fear and anxiety, gentle indeed, and subdued, and very human (and therefore the more interesting and winning in the eyes of us common men, who read his words), yet an anxiety which Abraham had not. We feel Jacob to be more like ourselves than Abraham was.

What, then, was Jacob's distinguishing grace, as faith was Abraham's? I have already said it: I suppose, thankfulness. Abraham appears ever to have been looking forward in *hope,*—Jacob looking back in *memory:* the one rejoicing in the future, the other in the past; the one setting his affections on the future, the other on the past; the one making his way towards the promises, the other musing over their fulfilment. Not that Abraham did not look back also, and Jacob, as he says on his death-bed, did not "wait for the salvation" of God; but this was the difference between them, Abraham was a hero, Jacob "a plain man, dwelling in tents."

Jacob seems to have had a gentle, tender, affectionate, timid mind—easily frightened, easily agitated, loving God so much that he feared to lose Him, and, like St. Thomas perhaps, anxious for sight and possession from earnest and longing desire of them. Were it not for faith, love would become impatient, and thus Jacob desired to possess, not from cold incredulity or hardness of heart, but from such a loving impatience. Such men are easily downcast, and must be treated kindly; they soon despond, they shrink from the world, for they feel its rudeness, which bolder natures do not. Neither Abraham nor Jacob loved the world. But Abraham did not fear, did not feel it. Jacob felt and winced, as being wounded by it. You recollect his touching complaints, " All these things are against me !"—" Then shall ye bring down my grey hairs with sorrow to the grave."—" If I am bereaved of my children, I am bereaved." Again, elsewhere we are told, " All his sons and all his daughters rose up to comfort him, but he refused to be comforted." At another time, " Jacob's heart fainted, for he believed them not." Again, " The spirit of Jacob their father revived."[1] You see what a child-like, sensitive, sweet mind he had. Accordingly, as I have said, his happiness lay, not in looking forward to the hope, but backwards upon the experience, of God's mercies towards him. He delighted lovingly to trace, and gratefully to acknowledge, what had been given, leaving the future to itself.

For instance, when coming to meet Esau, he brings before God in prayer, in words of which the text is part, what He had already done for him, recounting His past favours with great and humble joy in the midst of his present anxiety. " O God of my father Abraham," he says, " and God of my father Isaac, the Lord which saidst unto me, Return unto thy country, and to thy kindred, and I will deal well with thee : I am not worthy of the least of all the mercies, and of all the truth, *which Thou hast showed unto Thy servant ; for with my staff I passed over this Jordan, and now I am become two bands."* Again, after he had returned to his own land, he proceeded to fulfil the promise he had made to consecrate Bethel as a house of God, " Let us

[1] Gen. xlii. 36, 38 ; xliii. 14 ; xxxvii. 35 ; xlv. 26, 27.

arise, and go up to Bethel; and I will make there an altar unto God, *who answered me in the day of my distress, and was with me in the way which I went.*" Again, to Pharaoh, still dwelling on the past: " The days of the years of my pilgrimage are an hundred and thirty years; few and evil have the days of the years of my life been," he means, in themselves, and as separate from God's favour, " and have not attained unto the days of the years of the life of my fathers, in the days of their pilgrimage." Again, when he was approaching his end, he says to Joseph, " God Almighty *appeared unto me* at Luz," that is, Bethel, " in the land of Canaan, and blessed me." Again, still looking back, " As for me, when I came from Padan, Rachel died by me in the land of Canaan, in the way, when yet there was but a little way to come to Ephrath; and I buried her there in the way of Ephrath." Again, his blessing upon Ephraim and Manasseh : " God, before whom my fathers Abraham and Isaac did walk, *the God which fed me all my life long unto this day*, the Angel which redeemed me from all evil, bless the lads." Again he looks back on the land of promise, though in the plentifulness of Egypt: " Behold, I die, but God shall be with you, and bring you again unto the land of your fathers." And when he gives command about his burial, he says : " I am to be gathered unto my people; bury me with my fathers in the cave that is in the field of Ephron the Hittite." He gives orders to be buried with his fathers ; this was natural, but observe, he goes on to *enlarge* on the subject, after his special manner: " There they buried Abraham and Sarah his wife; there they buried Isaac

and Rebekah his wife; and *there I buried Leah.*"   And
further on, when he speaks of waiting for God's salvation, which is an act of hope, he so words it as at the
same time to dwell upon the past: " I *have* waited," he
says, that is, all my life long, " I have waited for Thy
salvation, O Lord." [1]   Such was Jacob, living in memory
rather than in hope, counting times, recording seasons,
keeping days; having his history by heart, and his past
life in his hand; and as if to carry on his mind into
that of his descendants, it was enjoined upon them,
that once a year every Israelite should appear before
God with a basket of fruit of the earth, and call to mind
what God had done for him and his father Jacob, and
express his thankfulness for it.   " A Syrian ready to
perish was my father," he had to say, meaning Jacob;
" and he went down into Egypt, and sojourned there,
and became a nation, great, mighty, and populous. . . . . .
And the Lord brought us forth out of Egypt with an
outstretched arm, and with great terribleness, and with
signs, and with wonders; and hath brought us into this
land . . . . that floweth with milk and honey.   And
now, behold, I have brought the first-fruits of the land,
which Thou, O Lord, hast given me." [2]

Well were it for us, if we had the character of mind
instanced in Jacob, and enjoined on his descendants;
the temper of dependence upon God's providence, and
thankfulness under it, and careful memory of all He has
done for us.   It would be well if we were in the habit

[1] Gen. xxxii. 9, 10; xxxv. 3; xlvii. 9; xlviii. 3, 7, 15, 16, 21;
xlix. 29—31, 18.   [2] Deut. xxvi. 5—10.

of looking at all we have as God's gift, undeservedly given, and day by day continued to us solely by His mercy. He gave; He may take away. He gave us all we have, life, health, strength, reason, enjoyment, the light of conscience; whatever we have good and holy within us; whatever faith we have; whatever of a renewed will; whatever love towards Him; whatever power over ourselves; whatever prospect of heaven. He gave us relatives, friends, education, training, knowledge, the Bible, the Church. All comes from Him. He gave; He may take away. Did He take away, we should be called on to follow Job's pattern, and be resigned: "The Lord gave, and the Lord hath taken away. Blessed be the Name of the Lord."[1] While He continues His blessings, we should follow David and Jacob, by living in constant praise and thanksgiving, and in offering up to Him of His own.

We are not our own, any more than what we possess is our own. We did not make ourselves; we cannot be supreme over ourselves. We cannot be our own masters. We are God's property by creation, by redemption, by regeneration. He has a triple claim upon us. Is it not our happiness thus to view the matter? Is it any happiness, or any comfort, to consider that we *are* our own? It may be thought so by the young and prosperous. These may think it a great thing to have everything, as they suppose, their own way,—to depend on no one,—to have to think of nothing out of sight,—to be without the irksomeness of continual acknowledgment, continual prayer, continual

[1] Job i. 21.

reference of what they do to the will of another. But as time goes on, they, as all men, will find that independence was not made for man—that it is an unnatural state—may do for a while, but will not carry us on safely to the end. No, we are creatures; and, as being such, we have two duties, to be resigned and to be thankful.

Let us then view God's providences towards us more religiously than we have hitherto done. Let us try to gain a truer view of what we are, and where we are, in His kingdom. Let us humbly and reverently attempt to trace His guiding hand in the years which we have hitherto lived. Let us thankfully commemorate the many mercies He has vouchsafed to us in time past, the many sins He has not remembered, the many dangers He has averted, the many prayers He has answered, the many mistakes He has corrected, the many warnings, the many lessons, the much light, the abounding comfort which He has from time to time given. Let us dwell upon times and seasons, times of trouble, times of joy, times of trial, times of refreshment. How did He cherish us as children! How did He guide us in that dangerous time when the mind began to think for itself, and the heart to open to the world! How did He with His sweet discipline restrain our passions, mortify our hopes, calm our fears, enliven our heavinesses, sweeten our desolateness, and strengthen our infirmities! How did He gently guide us towards the strait gate! how did He allure us along His everlasting way, in spite of its strictness, in spite of its loneliness, in spite of the dim twilight in which it lay! He has been all things to us. He has been, as He was to Abraham, Isaac, and

Jacob, our God, our shield, and great reward, promising and performing, day by day. "Hitherto hath He helped us." "He hath been mindful of us, and He will bless us." He has not made us for nought; He has brought us thus far, in order to bring us further, in order to bring us on to the end. He will never leave us nor forsake us; so that we may boldly say, "The Lord is my Helper; I will not fear what flesh can do unto me." We may "cast all our care upon Him, who careth for us." What is it to us how our future path lies, if it be but His path? What is it to us whither it leads us, so that in the end it leads to Him? What is it to us what He puts upon us, so that He enables us to undergo it with a pure conscience, a true heart, not desiring anything of this world in comparison of Him? What is it to us what terror befalls us, if He be but at hand to protect and strengthen us? "Thou, Israel," He says, "art My servant Jacob, whom I have chosen, the seed of Abraham My friend." "Fear not, thou worm Jacob, and ye men of Israel; I will help thee, saith the Lord, and thy Redeemer, the Holy One of Israel." "Thus saith the Lord that created thee, O Jacob, and He that formed thee, O Israel, Fear not; for I have redeemed thee, I have called thee by thy name; thou art Mine. When thou passest through the waters, I will be with thee; and through the rivers, they shall not overflow thee; when thou walkest through the fire, thou shalt not be burned; neither shall the flame kindle upon thee. For I am the Lord thy God, the Holy One of Israel, thy Saviour."[1]

<hr>

[1] Isa. xli. 8, 14; xliii. 1—3.

SERMON VII.

THE MYSTERY OF GODLINESS.

(CHRISTMAS.)

HEBREWS ii. 11.

*" Both He that sanctifieth and they who are sanctified are all of one:
for which cause He is not ashamed to call them brethren."*

OUR Saviour's birth in the flesh is an earnest, and,
as it were, beginning of our birth in the Spirit.
It is a figure, promise, or pledge of our new birth, and
it effects what it promises.   As He was born, so are we
born also ; and since He was born, therefore we too are
born.   As He is the Son of God by nature, so are we
sons of God by grace ; and it is He who has made us
such.   This is what the text says ; He is the "Sanctifier,"
we the "sanctified."   Moreover, He and we, says the
text, "are all of one."   God sanctifies the Angels, but
there the Creator and the creature are not of one.   But
the Son of God and we are of one ; He has become
"the firstborn of every creature ;" He has taken our
nature, and in and through it He sanctifies us.   He
is our brother by virtue of His incarnation, and, as the

text says, " He is not ashamed to call us brethren;" and, having sanctified our nature in Himself, He communicates it to us.

1. This is the wonderful economy of grace, or mystery of godliness, which should be before our minds at all times, but especially at this season, when the Most Holy took upon Him our flesh of "a pure Virgin," " by the operation of the Holy Ghost, without spot of sin, to make us clean from all sin." God "dwelleth in the Light which no man can approach unto ;" He "is Light, and in Him is no darkness at all." "His garment," as described in the Prophet's Vision, is "white as snow, and the hair of His head like the pure wool; His throne the fiery flame, and His wheels burning fire." And in like manner the Son of God, because He is the Son, is light also. He is "the True Light, which lighteth every man that cometh into the world." On His transfiguration "His face did shine as the sun," and "His raiment became shining, exceeding white as snow," "white and glistering." And when He appeared to St. John, "His head and His hairs were white like wool, as white as snow; and His eyes were as a flame of fire: and His feet like unto fine brass, as if they burnt in a furnace; and His countenance was as the sun shineth in his strength."[1] Such was our Lord's holiness because He was the Son of God from eternity. There was always the Father, always the Son : always the Father, *therefore* always the Son, for the Name of Father implies

[1] 1 Tim. vi. 16.   1 John i. 5.   Dan. vii. 9.   John i. 9.   Matt. xvii. 2.   Mark ix. 3.   Luke xi. 29.   Rev. i. 14—16.

the Son, and never was there a time when the Father Almighty was not, and in the Father the Son also. He it is who is spoken of in the beginning of St. John's Gospel, when it is said, "In the beginning was the Word, and the Word was with God, and the Word was God." Soon after, the same Apostle speaks of Him as "in the bosom of the Father." And He speaks Himself of "the glory which He had with the Father before the world was." And St. Paul calls Him "the Brightness of God's glory, and the express Image of His Person." And elsewhere, "the Image of the Invisible God." Thus what our Lord is, that none other can be; He is the Only-begotten Son; He has the Divine nature, and is of one substance with the Father, which cannot be said of any creature. He is one with God, and His nature is secret and incommunicable. Hence St. Paul contrasts His dignity with that of Angels, the highest of all creatures, with a view of showing the infinite superiority of the Son. "Unto which of the Angels said He at any time, Thou art My Son, this day have I begotten Thee?" Again, "When He bringeth in the first-begotten into the world, He saith, And let all the Angels of God worship Him." And again, "To which of the Angels saith He at any time, Sit on My right hand until I make Thine enemies Thy footstool?" Of the Angels we are told, "He putteth no trust in His saints; yea, the heavens are not clean in His sight;" but our Lord is His "beloved Son, in whom He is well pleased."[1]

[1] John i. 1; xvii. 5. Heb. i. 3, *et seq.* Col. i. 15. Job xv. 15. Matt. iii. 17.

He it was who created the worlds; He it was who interposed of old time in the affairs of the world, and showed Himself to be a living and observant God, whether men thought of Him or not. Yet this great God condescended to come down on earth from His heavenly throne, and to be born into His own world; showing Himself as the Son of God in a new and second sense, in a created nature, as well as in His eternal substance. Such is the first reflection which the birth of Christ suggests.

2. And next, observe, that since He was the All-holy Son of God, though He condescended to be born into the world, He necessarily came into it in a way suitable to the All-holy, and different from that of other men. He took our nature upon Him, but not our sin; taking our nature in a way above nature. Did He then come from heaven in the clouds? did He frame a body for Himself out of the dust of the earth? No; He was, as other men, "made of a woman," as St. Paul speaks, that He might take on Him, not another nature, but the nature of man. It had been prophesied from the beginning, that the Seed of the woman should bruise the serpent's head. "I will put enmity," said Almighty God to the serpent at the fall, "between thee and the woman, and between thy seed and her Seed; It shall bruise thy head."[1] In consequence of this promise, pious women, we are told, were in the old time ever looking out in hope that in their own instance peradventure the promise might find its accomplishment. One after another hoped in turn that she herself might

[1] Gen. iii. 15.

be mother of the promised King ; and therefore marriage was in repute, and virginity in disesteem, as if then only they had a prospect of being the Mother of Christ, if they waited for the blessing according to the course of nature, and amid the generations of men. Pious women they were, but little comprehending the real condition of mankind. It was ordained, indeed, that the Eternal Word should come into the world by the ministration of a woman ; but born in the way of the flesh He could not be. Mankind is a fallen race ; ever since the Fall there has been a "fault and corruption of the nature of every man that naturally is engendered of the offspring of Adam ; . . . so that the flesh lusteth always contrary to the Spirit, and therefore in every person born into this world it deserveth God's wrath and damnation." And "the Apostle doth confess that concupiscence and lust hath of itself the nature of sin." "That which is born of the flesh, is flesh." "Who can bring a clean thing out of an unclean ?" "How can he be clean that is born of a woman ?" Or as holy David cries out, "Behold, I was shapen in wickedness, and in sin hath my mother conceived me."[1] No one is born into the world without sin; or can rid himself of the sin of his birth except by a second birth through the Spirit. How then could the Son of God have come as a Holy Saviour, had He come as other men ? How could He have atoned for our sins, who Himself had guilt ? or cleansed our hearts, who was impure Himself? or raised up our heads, who was Himself the son of shame? Surely

______
[1] John iii. 6.   Job xiv. 4; xxv. 4.   Ps. li. 5.

any such messenger had needed a Saviour for his own
disease, and to such a one would apply the proverb,
"Physician, heal thyself." Priests among men are
they who have to offer "first for their own sins,
and then for the people's;"[1] but He, coming as the
immaculate Lamb of God, and the all-prevailing Priest,
could not come in the way which those fond persons
anticipated. He came by a new and living way, by which
He alone has come, and which alone became Him. The
Prophet Isaiah had been the first to announce it: "The
Lord Himself shall give you a sign," he says, "Behold,
a Virgin shall conceive and bear a Son, and shall call
His Name Immanuel." And accordingly St. Matthew,
after quoting this text, declares its fulfilment in the
instance of the Blessed Mary. "All this," he says,
"was done that it might be fulfilled which was spoken
by the prophet." And further, two separate Angels,
one to Mary, one to Joseph, declare who the adorable
Agent was, by whom this miracle was wrought.
"Joseph, thou son of David," an Angel said to him,
"fear not to take unto thee Mary thy wife, for that
which is conceived in her is of the Holy Ghost;" and
what followed from this? He proceeds, "And she shall
bring forth a Son, and thou shalt call His Name Jesus,
for He shall save His people from their sins." Because
He was "incarnate by the Holy Ghost of the Virgin
Mary," therefore He was "Jesus," a "Saviour from sin."
Again, the Angel Gabriel had already said to Mary,
"Hail, thou that art highly favoured, the Lord is with
thee: blessed art thou among women." And then he

[1] Heb. vii. 27.

proceeds to declare, that her Son should be called Jesus; that He " should be great, and should be called the Son of the Highest;" and that "of His Kingdom there shall be no end." And he concludes by announcing, "The Holy Ghost shall come upon thee, and the power of the Highest shall overshadow thee; therefore that Holy Thing which shall be born of thee shall be called the Son of God." [1]   Because God the Holy Ghost wrought miraculously, therefore was her Son a " Holy Thing," " the Son of God," and " Jesus," and the heir of an everlasting kingdom.

3. This is the great Mystery which we are now celebrating, of which mercy is the beginning, and sanctity the end: according to the Psalm, "Righteousness and peace have kissed each other." He who is all purity came to an impure race to raise them to His purity. He, the brightness of God's glory, came in a body of flesh, which was pure and holy as Himself, "without spot, or wrinkle, or any such thing, but holy and without blemish;" and this He did for our sake, "that we might be partakers of His holiness." He needed not a human nature for Himself,—He was all-perfect in His original Divine nature; but He took upon Himself what was ours for the sake of us.   He who "hath made of one blood all nations of men," so that in the sin of one all sinned, and in the death of one all died, He came in that very nature of Adam, in order to communicate to us that nature as it is in His Person, that "our sinful bodies might be made clean by His Body, and our souls washed through His most precious

[1] Matt. i. 20, 21. Luke i. 23—35.

Blood;" to make us partakers of the Divine nature; to sow the seed of eternal life in our hearts; and to raise us from "the corruption that is in the world through lust," to that immaculate purity and that fulness of grace which is in Him. He who is the first principle and pattern of all things, came to be the beginning and pattern of human kind, the firstborn of the whole creation. He, who is the everlasting Light, became the Light of men; He, who is the Life from eternity, became the Life of a race dead in sin; He, who is the Word of God, came to be a spiritual Word, " dwelling richly in our hearts," an " engrafted Word, which is able to save our souls ;" He, who is the co-equal Son of the Father, came to be the Son of God in our flesh, that He might raise us also to the adoption of sons, and might be first among many brethren. And this is the reason why the Collect for the season, after speaking of our Lord as the Only-begotten Son, and born in our nature of a pure Virgin, proceeds to speak of our new birth and adopted sonship, and renewal by the grace of the Holy Ghost.

4. And when He came into the world, He was a pattern of sanctity in the circumstances of His life, as well as in His birth. He did not implicate and contaminate Himself with sinners. He came down from heaven, and made a short work in righteousness, and then returned back again where He was before. He came into the world, and He speedily left the world; as if to teach us how little He Himself, how little we His followers, have to do with the world. He, the Eternal Ever-living Word of God, did not outlive Methuselah's years, nay, did not even exhaust the

common age of man; but He came and He went,
before men knew that He had come, like the lightning
shining from one side of heaven unto the other, as
being the beginning of a new and invisible creation,
and having no part in the old Adam. He was in the
world, but not of the world; and while He was here,
He, the Son of man, was still in heaven: and as well
might fire feed upon water, or the wind be subjected
to man's bidding, as the Only-begotten Son really be
portion and member of that perishable system in which
He condescended to move. He could not rest or tarry
upon earth; He did but do His work in it; He could
but come and go.

And while He was here, since He could not acquiesce
or pleasure Himself in the earth, so He would none of
its vaunted goods. When He humbled himself unto His
own sinful creation, He would not let that creation
minister to Him of its best, as if disdaining to receive
offering or tribute from a fallen world. It is only
nature regenerate which may venture to serve the Holy
One. He would not accept lodging or entertainment,
acknowledgment, or blandishment, from the kingdom of
darkness. He would not be made a king; He would
not be called, Good Master; He would not accept
where He might lay His head. His life lay not in
man's breath. or man's smile; it was hid in Him from
whom He came and to whom He returned.

"The Light shineth in darkness, and the darkness
comprehended it not." He seemed like other men to
the multitude. Though conceived of the Holy Ghost,
He was born of a poor woman, who, when guests were

numerous, was thrust aside, and gave birth to Him in a place for cattle. O wondrous mystery, early manifested, that even in birth He refused the world's welcome! He grew up as the carpenter's son, without education, so that when He began to teach, His neighbours wondered how one who had not learned letters, and was bred to a humble craft, should become a prophet. He was known as the kinsman and intimate of humble persons ; so that the world pointed to them when He declared Himself, as if their insufficiency was the refutation of His claims. He was brought up in a town of low repute, so that even the better sort doubted whether good could come out of it. No; He would not be indebted to this world for comfort, aid, or credit; for "the world was made by Him, and the world knew Him not." He came to it as a benefactor, not as a guest; not to borrow from it, but to impart to it.

And when He grew up, and began to preach the kingdom of heaven, the Holy Jesus took no more from the world then than before. He chose the portion of those Saints who preceded and prefigured Him, Abraham, Moses, David, Elijah, and His forerunner John the Baptist. He lived at large, without the ties of home or peaceful dwelling; He lived as a pilgrim in the land of promise; He lived in the wilderness. Abraham had lived in tents in the country which his descendants were to enjoy. David had wandered for seven years up and down the same during Saul's persecutions. Moses had been a prisoner in the howling wilderness, all the way from Mount Sinai to the borders of Canaan. Elijah wandered back again from Carmel to Sinai. And the Baptist had remained in the deserts from his youth. Such in like manner was our Lord's manner of life, during His ministry: He was now in Galilee, now in Judæa; He is found in the mountain, in the wilderness, and in the city; but He vouchsafed to take no home, not even His Almighty Father's Temple at Jerusalem.

Now all this is quite independent of the special objects of mercy which brought Him upon earth. Though He had still submitted Himself by an incomprehensible condescension to the death on the cross at length, yet why did He from the first so spurn this world, when He was not atoning for its sins? He might at least have had the blessedness of brethren who believed in Him; He might have been happy and revered at home; He might have had honour in His own country; He might have submitted but at last to what he chose from the first; He might have delayed His voluntary sufferings till that hour when His Father's and His own will made Him the sacrifice for sin.

But He did otherwise; and thus He becomes a lesson to us who are His disciples. He, who was so separate from the world, so present with the Father even in the days of His flesh, calls upon us, His brethren, as we are in Him and He in the Father, to show that we really are what we have been made, by renouncing the world while in the world, and living as in the presence of God.

Let them consider this, who think the perfection of our nature still consists, as before the Spirit was given, in the exercise of all its separate functions, animal and mental, not in the subjection and sacrifice of what is inferior in us to what is more excellent. Christ, who is the beginning and pattern of the new creature, lived out of the body while He was in it. His death indeed was required as an expiation; but why was His life so mortified, if such austerity be not man's glory?

Let us at this season approach Him with awe and love, in whom resides all perfection, and from whom we are allowed to gain it. Let us come to the Sanctifier to be sanctified. Let us come to Him to learn our duty, and to receive grace to do it. At other seasons of the year we are reminded of watching, toiling, struggling, and suffering; but at this season we are reminded simply of God's gifts towards us sinners. " Not by works of righteousness which we have done, but according to His mercy He saved us." We are reminded that we can do nothing, and that God does everything. This is especially the season of grace. We come to see and to experience God's mercies. We come before Him as the helpless beings, during His ministry, who were brought on beds and couches for a cure. We come to be made whole. We come as little children to be fed and taught, " as new-born babes, desiring the sincere milk of the word, that we may grow thereby." [1] This is a time for innocence, and purity, and gentleness, and mildness, and contentment, and peace. It is a time in which the whole Church seems decked in white, in her baptismal robe, in the bright and glistering raiment which she wears upon the Holy Mount. Christ comes at other times with garments dyed in blood; but now

[1] 1 Pet. ii. 2.

He comes to us in all serenity and peace, and He bids us rejoice in Him, and to love one another. This is not a time for gloom, or jealousy, or care, or indulgence, or excess, or licence:—not for " rioting and drunkenness," not for " chambering and wantonness," not for " strife and envying,"[1] as says the Apostle; but for putting on the Lord Jesus Christ, " who knew no sin, neither was guile found in His mouth."

May each Christmas, as it comes, find us more and more like Him, who as at this time became a little child for our sake, more simple-minded, more humble, more holy, more affectionate, more resigned, more happy, more full of God.

[1] Rom. xiii. 12.

SERMON VIII.

THE STATE OF INNOCENCE.

(CHRISTMAS.)

" God hath made man upright, but they have sought out many inventions."

THE state of our parents as God made them " upright," and " very good," in the day that they were
created, presents much to excite our interest and sympathy, though we, their descendants, have passed away
into a far different state. Since that time our nature
has gone through many fortunes,—through much evil
to greater good. That primeval state is no longer ours.
It is no longer ours, though it is no longer forfeited.
The penalties are removed; the flaming sword no
longer bars the entrance of Eden; yet have we not
returned to it. For so is it with all that happens to
us,—the past *never* returns, not in what it contained,
any more than in itself. Each time has its own peculiar attributes; it is impressed with its own characters.
We recognise them in memory. When from time to
time this or that passage of our lives rises in our minds,

H 2

it comes to us with its own savour. We know it as if
by taste and scent, and we know that that peculiar and
indescribable token, be it good or bad, never can attach
to anything else. And what is true of indifferent
things, is true also when right and wrong come into
question, and in the great destinies of man. If we sin
and forfeit what God has given, not God Himself (such
seems to be His will), not God Himself, in the fulness
of His mercies, ever brings back what we were. He
may wash out our sin,—He may give us blessings,
greater blessings than we had,—He does not give us the
same. When man was driven out of Paradise, it was
for good and all,—he never has returned,—he never
will return,—he has been born again, but not into possession of the garden of innocence : he has a rest in
store, and a happier one,—a more glorious paradise, but
still another.

This being so, it would seem as if there was little to
interest us now in the first condition of Adam. As lost,
it would only raise remorse and distress; as found
again, it is something new. And yet, though Almighty
God does not bring back the past, His dispensations
move forward in an equable uniform way, like circles
expanding about one centre;—the greater good to
come being, not indeed the same as the past good, but
nevertheless resembling it, as a substance resembles its
type. In the past we see the future as if in miniature
and outline. Indeed how can it be otherwise ? seeing
that all goods are but types and shadows of God Himself the Giver, and are like each other because they are
like Him. Hence the garden of Eden, though long

past away, is brought again and again to our notice in the progress of God's dealings with us, not only in order to instruct us by the past, but unavoidably, if I may so speak, from the resemblance which one condition of God's favour bears to another;—of Adam's first state to the Law, and of the Law to the Gospel, and of the Gospel to the state of rest after death, and of that to heaven. For instance, the land that flowed with milk and honey, was a sort of visible return of the lost garden ; and in a manner reversed the sentence of banishment which God has laid upon our first parents. Again, the reign of Christ too is imaged as a state in which the beasts return to the dominion of man, and are harmless;— when the serpent is no longer venomous, and when "the desert shall rejoice, and blossom as the rose," and "instead of the thorn shall come up the fir-tree, and instead of the brier shall come up the myrtle-tree;" when "the mountains and the hills shall break forth into singing, and all the trees of the field shall clap their hands."[1] And so of the intermediate state ; for our Lord says to the penitent thief, "To-day shalt thou be with Me in *paradise.*" And lastly, to describe heaven too, in the last words which God has vouch-safed to us, ending His revelations as he began them, He sets before us the vision of a happy garden. "He showed me a pure river of water of life, clear as crystal, proceeding out of the throne of God and of the Lamb. In the midst of the street of it, and on either side of the river, was there the Tree of Life, which had twelve manner of fruits, and yielded her fruit every month;

[1] Isa. xxxv. 1 ; lv. 18, 12.

and the leaves of the Tree were for the healing of the nations."[1] Thus God takes away the less to give the greater,—not reversing the past, but remedying and heightening it; preserving the pattern of it, and so keeping us from forgetting it.

Therefore we may well look back on the garden of Eden, as we would on our own childhood. That childhood is a type of the perfect Christian state; our Saviour so made it when He said that we must become as little children to enter His kingdom. Yet it too is a thing past and over. We are not, we cannot be children; grown men have faculties, passions, aims, principles, views, duties, which children have not; still, however, we must become *as* little children; in them we are bound to see Christian perfection, and to labour for it with them in our eye. Indeed there is a very much closer connexion between the state of Adam in Paradise and our state in childhood, than may at first be thought; so that in surveying Eden, we are in a way looking back on our own childhood; and in aiming to be children again, we are aiming to be as Adam on his creation. Let us then now compare together these two parallel states, and in doing so let us have an eye to that third state, higher than either; I mean our regenerate state in Christ, of which these two are both types.

There is, for what we know, a very mysterious real connexion between the garden of Eden and our childhood, on which, however, I am not going to enlarge. I mean, the doctrine of original sin does connect together, in some unknown and awful way, Adam and each of us.

[1] Rev. xxii. 1, 2.

If, as we believe, Adam's sin is imputed to each of us, if we enter into the world with it upon us, in all its consequences, just as if it were ours, certainly we cannot be in Adam's state when he was in Eden (rather what he was when leaving it), but still so much may be said, that our childhood is in some sense a continuation of Adam's state when in Eden, a carrying it on through and after his fall, and not a beginning; though in thus speaking we use words beyond our own meaning.

But dismissing this subject, I would have you observe, that as far as we are given to know it, Adam's state in Eden seems to have been like the state of children now—in being simple, inartificial, inexperienced in evil, unreasoning, uncalculating, ignorant of the future, or (as men now speak) unintellectual. The tree of the knowledge of good and evil was kept from him. Also, I would observe, that whereas we who do know good and evil, are bid to become as simple children; so again we are promised a paradise in which shall be no Tree of Knowledge. St. John describes to us the future paradise, and tells us of the Tree of Life there, but it has no Tree of Knowledge; instead of which " the glory of God doth lighten it, and the Lamb is the light thereof." It would seem then, taking human nature according to what it was on its creation, according to what it is in childhood (which is the type of its perfection), and according to what is implied about its future state, that in all these states the "knowledge of good and evil" is away, whatever be the meaning of that phrase, and that instead of it the Lord is our Light, "and in His light shall we see light." This remarkably corresponds with the words of the text: "God hath made man upright, but they have sought out many *inventions*." But to return to our first parents.

The state in Eden seems, I say, to be very much what is called the life of innocents, of such as are derided and contemned by men, as they now are,—their degenerate descendants.

1. First Adam and Eve were placed in a garden to cultivate it; how much is implied even in this! "The Lord God took the man and put him into the garden of Eden, to dress it and to keep it." If there was a mode of life free from tumult, anxiety, excitement, and fever of mind, it was the care of a garden. You will say it could not be otherwise, while he was but one man in the whole world;—the accumulation of human beings, the mutual action of mind on mind, this it is which creates all the hurry and variety of life. Adam was a hermit, whether he would or no. True; but does not this very circumstance that God made him such, point out to us what is our true happiness, if we were given it, which we are not? At least we see in type what our perfection is, in these first specimens of our nature, which need not, unless God had so willed, have been created in this solitary state, but might have been myriads at once, as the Angels were created. And let it be noted, that, when the Second Adam came, He returned, nay, more than returned to that life which the First had originally been allotted. He too was alone, and lived alone, the immaculate Son of a Virgin Mother; and He chose the mountain summit or the garden as His home. Save always, that in His case sorrow and pain went with His

loneliness ; not, like Adam, eating freely of all trees but one, but fasting in the wilderness for forty days—not tempted to eat of that one through wantonness, but urged in utter destitution of food to provide Himself with some necessary bread,—not as a king giving names to fawning brutes, but one among the wild beasts,—not granted a help meet for His support, but praying alone in the dark morning,—not dressing the herbs and flowers, but dropping blood upon the ground in agony, —not falling into a deep sleep in His garden, but buried there after His passion ;—yet still like the first Adam, solitary,—like the first Adam, living with His God and Holy Angels. And this is the more remarkable, both because He came to do a great work in a short ministry, and because the same characteristic will be found in His servants also ; nay, in His most laboriously employed and most successfully active servants, before and after Him. Abraham, Isaac, and Jacob, were as " plain men dwelling in tents;" Moses lived for forty years a shepherd's life; and when at length he was set over the chosen people, still in one of the most critical moments of his government, he had long retirements in the Mount with God. Samuel was brought up within the Temple : Elijah lived in the deserts ; so did the Baptist, his antitype. Even the Apostles had their seasons of solitude. We hear of St. Peter at Joppa ; and St. Paul had his labours again and again suspended by imprisonment; as if such occasional respite from exertion were as necessary for the spirit as sleep is necessary for the body. If then the life of Christ and His servants be any guide to us, certainly it would appear as if the simplicity and the repose of life, with which human nature began, is an indication of its perfection. And again, does not our infancy teach us the same lesson? which is especially a season when the soul is left to itself, withdrawn from its fellows as effectually as if it were the only human being on earth, like Adam in his inclosed garden, fenced off from the world, and visited by Angels.

2. Fenced off from the world, nay, fenced off even from himself; for so it is, and most strange too, that our infant and childish state is hidden from ourselves. We cannot recollect it. We know not what it was, what our thoughts in it were, and what our probation, more than we know Adam's. This is a remarkable analogy for such persons as question and object to the account of our first parents in Eden. To what does their difficulty amount at the utmost, but to this, that they do not know what their state was? that there is a depth and a secret about the Word of God, which they cannot penetrate? And is it greater than that which hangs over themselves personally, in their own most mysterious infancy? the history of which, doubtless, if it could be put into words, and set before us, would be as strange and foreign to us, would be as little recognised by us as our own, as the second and third chapters of Genesis. And here again occurs a parallel in our state of perfection; "we know not what we *shall* be." We know not what we are tending to, any more than what we have started from. St. Paul was once caught up to Paradise, and he witnesses to the incomprehensible nature of that life, which was begun and broken off

in Eden. "I knew such a man . . . how he was caught up into Paradise, and heard *unspeakable* words, which it is not lawful for a man to utter."[1] And all this is further paralleled by the state of regeneration in the present world, as far as this, that those who advance far in the divine life, both are themselves hidden, and see things hidden from common men. "The light shineth in darkness, and the darkness comprehended it not." "The world was made by Him, and the world knew Him not." "The world knoweth us not because it knew Him not. And on the other hand, "The secret of the Lord is with them that fear Him." " He that believeth in the Son of God, hath the witness in himself." " To him that overcometh will I give a white stone, and in the stone a new name written, which no man knoweth saving he that receiveth it."[2]

3. Another resemblance between the state of Adam in paradise, and that of children is this, that children are saved, not by their purpose and habits of obedience, not by faith and works, but by the influence of baptismal grace; and into Adam God " breathed the breath of life, and man became a living soul." Far different is our state since the fall:—at present our moral rectitude, such as it is, is acquired by trial, by discipline: but what does this really mean? by sinning, by suffering, by correcting ourselves, by improving. We advance to the truth by experience of error; we succeed through failures. We know not how

---

[1] 2 Cor. xii. 3, 4.
[2] John i. 5, 10. 1 John iii. 1. Ps. xxv. 14. 1 John v. 10. Rev. i. 17.

to do right except by having done wrong. We call virtue a mean,—that is, as considering it to lie between things that are wrong. We know what is right, not positively, but negatively;—we do not see the truth at once and make towards it, but we fall upon and try error, and find it is *not* the truth. We grope about by touch, not by sight, and so by a miserable experience exhaust the possible modes of acting till nought is left, but truth, remaining. Such is the process by which we succeed; we walk to heaven backward; we drive our arrows at a mark, and think him most skilful whose shortcomings are the least.

So it is not with children baptized and taken away. So was it not while Adam was still upright, as God created him. Adam might probably have matured in holiness, had he remained in his first state, without experience of evil, whether pain or error; for he had that within him which was to him more than all the habits which trial and discipline painfully form in us. Unless it be presumptuous to say it, grace was to him instead of a habit; grace was his clothing within and without. Grace dispensed with efforts towards holiness, for holiness lived in him. We do not know what we mean by a habit, except as a state or quality of mind *under* which we act in this or that particular way; it is a permanent power in the mind; and what is grace but this? What then man fallen gains by dint of exercise, working up towards it by religious acts, that Adam already acted *from*. He had that light within him, which he might make brighter by obedience, but which he had not to create. Not till he fell, did he lose that supernatural endowment, which raised him into a state above himself, and made him in a certain sense more than man, and what the Angels are, or Saints hereafter. This robe of innocence and sanctity he lost when he fell; he knew and confessed that he had lost it; but while he possessed it, he was sinless and perfect, and acceptable to God, though he had gone through nothing painful to obtain it. He tired of it; he tired of being upright from the heart only, and not in the way of reason. He desired to obey, not in the way of children, but of those who choose for themselves. He ate of the forbidden fruit, that he might choose with his eyes open between good and evil, and his eyes *were* opened, and he "knew that he was naked;" for the strength of God's inward glory went from him, and he was left henceforth to struggle on towards obedience as he best might in his fallen state by experience of sin and misery. And here again let it be observed, as in former points of the parallel, that this gift which sanctified Adam and saves children, does become the ruling principle of Christians generally when they advance to perfection. According as habits of holiness are matured, principle, reason, and self-discipline are unnecessary; a moral instinct takes their place in the breast, or rather, to speak more reverently, the Spirit is sovereign there. There is no calculation, no struggle, no self-regard, no investigation of motives. We act from love. Hence the Apostles say, "Ye have an unction from the Holy One, and ye know all things;" "Ye are the temple of the living God; as God hath said, I will dwell in them, and walk in them." [1]

[1] 1 John ii. 20. 2 Cor. vi. 16.

Now if the doctrine on which this parallel is founded be true, which one cannot doubt, how miserable that state, which is so often praised and magnified as the perfection of our nature, whereas it is the very curse that has come upon us,—the knowledge of evil. Yet can anything be more certain than that men do glory in it; glory in their shame, and consider they are advancing in moral excellence, when they are but gaining a knowledge of moral evil?

For instance, I suppose great numbers of men think that it is slavish and despicable to go on in that narrow way in which they are brought up as children, without experience of the world. It *is* the narrow way, and they call it narrow in contumely. They fret at the restraints of their father's roof, and wish to judge and act for themselves. They think it manly to taste the pleasures of sin; they think it manly to know what sin is before condemning it. They think they are then better judges, when they are not blindly led by others, but have taken upon them, by their own act, the yoke of evil. They think it a fine thing to curse and swear, and to revel, and to ridicule God's sacred truth, and to profess themselves the devil's scholars. They look down upon the innocent, upon women and children, and solitaries, and holy and humble men of heart, who, like the Cherubim, see God and worship, as unfit for the great business of life, and worthless in the real estimate of things. They think it no great harm to leave off a correct life for a time, so that they return to it at length. They consider that it is even more pleasing to God, a more " reasonable service" to subdue evil than to follow good. They consider that to bring "the motions of sin" under, and show their power over it, is a higher thing than not to have them to fight against.[1] They think it more noble to have an enemy to overcome and rebels to control than to be in peace. Alas! they commonly do not acknowledge so much as that there is a rebel power within them; they call sin but a venial evil, and no wonder that, so thinking, they can bear to talk of trying it, and cannot understand that it is better to be ever pure than to have been at one time stained.

This is one kind of knowledge, and most miserable doubtless, which we have gained by the fall, to know sin by experience;—not to gaze at it with awe as the Angels do, or as children when they wonder how there can be wicked men in the world, but to admit it into our hearts. Alas! ever since the fall this has been more or less the state of the natural man, to live in sin; and though here and there, under the secret stirrings of God's grace, he has sought after God and obeyed Him, it has been in a grovelling sort, like worms working their way upwards through the dust of the earth, turning evil against itself, and unlearning it from having known it. And such too seems to be one chief way in which Providence carries on His truth even under the Gospel; not by a direct flood of light upon the Church, but by setting one mischief upon another, bidding one serpent destroy another, the less the greater; thus gradually thinning the brood of sin, and wasting them by their own contrariety. And in this

___
[1] *Vide* Froude's Sermons, XIII.

way doubtless we are to regard sects and heresies, as witnesses and confessors of particular truths, as God's means of destroying evil,—mortal themselves, yet greedy of each other.

4. The mention of heresy and error opens upon us a large subject to which I will but allude. What then is intellect itself, as exercised in the world, but a fruit of the fall, not found in paradise or in heaven, more than in little children, and at the utmost but tolerated in the Church, and only not incompatible with the regenerate mind? Children do not go by reason: Adam in his state of innocence had no opportunity for aught but what we should call a calm and simple life. To God Most High we ascribe moral excellences, truth, faithfulness, love, justice, holiness: again we speak of His power, knowledge, and wisdom: but it would be profane even to utter His great Name in connexion with those powers of mind which we call ability, and prize so highly. Christ again displays no eloquence or power of words, no subtle or excursive reasoning, no brilliancy, ingenuity, or fertility of thought, such as the world admires. Nay, the same truth holds as regards our own regenerate state; for though doubtless every power of the intellect has its use in the Church, yet surely, after all, faith is made supreme, and reason then only is considered in place when it is subordinate. "Blessed are they," says our Lord, "that have not seen and yet have believed;" and Paul again, "The Jews require a sign, and the Greeks seek after wisdom; but we preach Christ crucified, unto the Jews a stumbling-block, and to the Greeks foolishness; but unto them

which are called, both Jews and Greeks, Christ the power of God and the wisdom of God." [1] What a contrast to such passages is presented by a mere catalogue of the powers of mind by which men succeed in life, and by which the structure of society is kept together! Take the world as it is, with its intelligence, its bustle, its feverish efforts, its works, its results, the ceaseless ebb and flow of the great tide of mind: view society, I mean, not in its adventitious evil, but in its essential characters, and what is all its intellectual energy but a fruit of the tree of the knowledge of good and evil, and though not sinful, yet, in fact, the consequence of sin? Consider its professions, trades, pursuits, or, in the words of the text, "inventions;" trace them down to their simplest forms and first causes, and what is their parent, but the loss of original uprightness? What place have its splendours, triumphs, speculations, or theories in that pure and happy region which was our cradle, or in that heaven which is to be our rest? Dexterity, promptness, presence of mind, sagacity, shrewdness, powers of persuasion, talent for business, what are these but developments of intellect which our fallen state has occasioned, and probably far from the highest which our mind is capable of? And are not these and others at best only of use in remedying the effects of the fall, and, so far, indeed, demanding of us deep thankfulness towards the Giver, but not having a legitimate employment except in a world of sickness and infirmity?

Now, in thus speaking, let it be observed, I am not

[1] John xx. 29.   1 Cor. i. 22—24.

using light words of what is a great gift of God, and one distinguishing mark of man over the brutes, our reason; I have but spoken of the *particular exercises and developments*, in which it has its life in the world, as we see them; and these, though in themselves excellent, and often admirable, yet would not have been but for sin, and now that they are, subserve the purposes of sin. Reason, I say, is God's gift; but so are the passions; Adam had the gift of reason, and so had he passions; but he did not *walk* by reason, nor was he led by his passions; he, or at least Eve, was tempted to follow passion and reason, instead of her Maker, and she fell. Since that time passion and reason have abandoned their due place in man's nature, which is one of subordination, and conspired together against the Divine light within him, which is his proper guide. Reason has been as guilty as passion here. God made man upright, and grace was his strength; but he has found out many inventions, and his strength is reason.

To conclude: Let us learn from what has been said, whatever gifts of mind we have, henceforth to keep them under, and to subject them to innocence, simplicity, and truth. Let our characters be formed upon faith, love, contemplativeness, modesty, meekness, humility. I know well that men differ so much here one from another, that it were folly to expect their outward character to appear one and the same. One man carries his gentleness on the surface, or his humbleness, or his simplicity; and his intellectual gifts are hid within him. We look at him, and cannot understand how he should possess those endowments of mind, which we know he has. Another's graces are buried, or nearly so ; he overflows with thought, or is powerful in speech, or takes a keen view of the world, and is ever present and ready wherever he is ; while he keeps his self-abasement and seriousness to himself. These are accidents; "the Lord seeth not as man seeth ; for man looketh on the outward appearance, but the Lord looketh on the heart."[1] Let us labour to approve ourselves to Christ. If we be in a crowd, still be we as hermits in the wilderness; if we be rich as if poor, if married as single, if gifted in mind, still as little children. Let the tumult of error teach us the simplicity of truth ; the miseries of guilt the peace of innocence ; and "the many inventions" of the reason the stability of faith. Let us, with St. Paul, be "all things to all men," while we "live unto God ;" "wise as serpents and harmless as doves," "in malice children, in understanding men."

[1] 1 Sam. xvi. 7.

SERMON IX.

CHRISTIAN SYMPATHY.

(CHRISTMAS.)

HEB. ii. 16.

" For verily He took not on Him the nature of Angels, but He took on Him the seed of Abraham."

WE are all of one nature, because we are sons of Adam ; we are all of one nature, because we are brethren of Christ. Our old nature is common to us all, and so is our new nature. And because our old nature is one and the same, therefore is it that our new nature is one and the same. Christ could not have taken the nature of every one of us, unless every one of us had the same nature already. He could not have become our brother, unless we were all brethren already ; He could not have made us His brethren, unless by becoming our Brother; so that our brotherhood in the first man is the means towards our brotherhood in the second.

I do not mean to limit the benefits of Christ's atoning death, or to dare to say that it may not effect ends infinite in number and extent beyond those expressly recorded. But still so far is plain, that it is by taking our nature that He has done for us what He has done for none else; that, by taking the nature of Angels, He would not have done for us what He has done; that it is not only the humiliation of the Son of God, but His humiliation in our nature, which is our life. He might have humbled Himself in other natures besides human nature; but it was decreed that "the Word" should be "made flesh." "Forasmuch as the children are partakers of flesh and blood, He also Himself likewise took part of the same." And, as the text says, "He took not hold of Angels, but He took hold of the seed of Abraham.

And since His taking on Him our nature is a necessary condition of His imparting to us those great benefits which have accrued to us from His death, therefore, as I have said, it was necessary that we should, one and all, have the same original nature, in order to be redeemed by Him; for, in order to be redeemed, we must all have that nature which He the Redeemer took. Had our natures been different, He would have redeemed one and not another. Such a common nature we have, as being one and all children of one man, Adam; and thus the history of our fall is connected with the history of our recovery.

Christ then took our nature, when He would redeem it; He redeemed it by making it suffer in His own Person; He purified it, by making it pure in His own Person He first sanctified it in Himself, made it righteous, made it acceptable to God, submitted it to an expiatory passion, and then He imparted it to us.

He took it, consecrated it, broke it, and said, "Take, and divide it among yourselves."

And moreover, He raised the condition of human nature, by submitting it to trial and temptation; that what it failed to do in Adam, it might be able to do in Him. Or, in other words, which it becomes us rather to use, He condescended, by an ineffable mercy, to be tried and tempted in it; so that, whereas He was God from everlasting, as the Only-begotten of the Father, He took on Him the thoughts, affections, and infirmities of man, thereby, through the fulness of His Divine Nature, to raise those thoughts and affections, and destroy those infirmities, that so, by God's becoming man, men, through brotherhood with Him, might in the end become as gods.

There is not a feeling, not a passion, not a wish, not an infirmity, which we have, which did not belong to that manhood which He assumed, except such as is of the nature of sin. There was not a trial or temptation which befalls us, but was, in kind at least, presented before Him, except that He had nothing within Him, sympathizing with that which came to Him from without. He said upon His last and greatest trial, "The Prince of this world cometh and hath nothing in Me;" yet at the same time we are mercifully assured that "we have not a High Priest which cannot be touched with the feeling of our infirmities, but" one, who "was in all points tempted like as we are, yet without sin." And again, "In that He Himself hath suffered being tempted, He is able to succour them that are tempted."[1]

<hr>

[1] Heb. iv. 15; ii. 18

But what I would to-day draw attention to, is the thought with which I began, viz. the comfort vouchsafed to us in being able to contemplate Him whom the Apostle calls "the man Christ Jesus," the Son of God in our flesh. I mean, the thought of Him, "the beginning of the creation of God," "the firstborn of every creature," binds us together by a sympathy with one another, as much greater than that of mere nature, as Christ is greater than Adam. We were brethren, as being of one nature with him, who was "of the earth, earthy;" we are now brethren, as being of one nature with "the Lord from heaven." All those common feelings, which we have by birth, are far more intimately common to us, now that we have obtained the second birth. Our hopes and fears, likes and dislikes, pleasures and pains, have been moulded upon one model, have been wrought into one image, blended and combined unto "the measure of the stature of the fulness of Christ." What they become, who have partaken of "the Living Bread, which came down from heaven," the first converts showed, of whom it is said that they "had all things common;" that "the multitude of them that believed were of one heart and of one soul;" as having "one body, and one Spirit, one hope, one Lord, one Faith, one Baptism, one God and Father of all."[1] Yes, and one thing needful; one narrow way; one business on earth; one and the same enemy; the same dangers; the same temptations; the same afflictions; the same course of life; the same death; the same resurrection; the same judgment. All these things

----

[1] Acts ii. 44; iv. 32. Eph. iv. 4—6.

being the same, and the new nature being the same, and from the Same, no wonder that Christians can sympathise with each other, even as by the power of Christ sympathising in and with each of them.

Nay, and further, they sympathise together in those respects too, in which Christ has not, could not have, gone before them; I mean in their common sins. This is the difference between Christ's temptation and ours: His temptations were without sin, but ours with sin. Temptation with us almost certainly involves sin. We sin, almost spontaneously, in spite of His grace. I do not mean, God forbid, that His grace is not sufficient to subdue all sin in us; or that, as we come more and more under its influence, we are not less and less exposed to the involuntary impression of temptation, and much less exposed to voluntary sin; but that so it is, our evil nature remains in us in spite of that new nature which the touch of Christ communicates to us; we have still earthly principles in our souls, though we have heavenly ones, and these so sympathise with temptation, that, as a mirror reflects promptly and of necessity what is presented to it, so the body of death which infects us, when the temptations of this world assail it, —when honour, pomp, glory, the world's praise, power, ease, indulgence, sensual pleasure, revenge are offered to it,—involuntarily responds to them, and sins—sins because it *is* sin; sins before the better mind can control it, because it exists, because its life is sin; sins *till* it is utterly subdued and expelled from the soul by the gradual growth of holiness and the power of the Spirit. Of all this, Christ had nothing. He was " born of a pure Virgin," the immaculate Lamb of God; and though He was tempted, yet it was by what was good in the world's offers, though unseasonable and unsuitable, and not by what was evil in them. He overcame what it had been unbecoming to yield to, while he felt the temptation. He overcame also what was sinful, but He felt no temptation to it.

And yet it stands to reason, that though His temptations differed from ours in this main respect, yet His presence in us makes us sympathise one with another, even in our sins and faults, in a way which is impossible without it; because, whereas the grace in us is common to us all, the sins against that grace are common to us all also. We have the same gifts to sin against, and therefore the same powers, the same responsibilities, the same fears, the same struggles, the same guilt, the same repentance, and such as none can have but we. The Christian is one and the same, wherever found; as in Christ, who is perfect, so in himself, who is training towards perfection; as in that righteousness which is imputed to him in fulness, so in that righteousness which is imparted to him only in its measure, and not yet in fulness.

This is a consideration full of comfort, but of which commonly we do not avail ourselves as we might. It is one comfortable thought, and the highest of all, that Christ, who is on the right hand of God exalted, has felt all that we feel, sin excepted; but it is very comfortable also, that the new and spiritual man, which He creates in us, or creates us into,—that is, the Christian, as he is naturally found everywhere,—has everywhere the same temptations, and the same feelings under them, whether innocent or sinful; so that, as we are all bound together in our Head, so are we bound together, as members of one body, in that body, and believe, obey, sin, and repent, all in common.

I do not wish to state this too strongly. Doubtless there are very many differences between Christian and Christian. Though their nature is the same, and their general duties, hindrances, helps, privileges, and rewards the same, yet certainly there are great differences of character, and peculiarities belonging either to individuals or to classes. High and low, rich and poor, Jew and Gentile, man and woman, bond and free, learned and unlearned, though equal in the Gospel, do in many respects differ, so that descriptions of what passes in the mind of one will often appear strange and new to the other. Their temptations differ, and their diseases of mind. And the difference becomes far greater, by the difficulty persons have of expressing exactly what they mean, so that they convey wrong ideas to one another, and offend and repel those who really do feel what they feel, though they would express themselves otherwise.

Again, of course there is this great difference between Christians, that some are penitents, and some have never fallen away since they were brought near to God; some have fallen for a time, and grievously; others for long years, yet perhaps only in lesser matters. These circumstances will make real differences between Christian and Christian, so as sometimes even to remove the possibility of sympathy almost altogether. Sin certainly does contrive this victory in some cases, to hinder us being even fellows in misery; it separates us while it seduces, and, being the broad way, has different lesser tracks marked out upon it.

But still, after all such exceptions, I consider that Christians, certainly those who are in the same outward circumstances, are very much more like each other in their temptations, inward diseases, and methods of cure, than they at all imagine. Persons think themselves isolated in the world ; they think no one ever felt as they feel. They do not dare to expose their feelings, lest they should find that no one understands them. And thus they suffer to wither and decay what was destined in God's purpose to adorn the Church's paradise with beauty and sweetness. Their "mouth is not opened," as the Apostle speaks, nor their "heart enlarged;" they are "straitened" in themselves, and deny themselves the means they possess of at once imparting instruction and gaining comfort.

Nay, instead of speaking out their own thoughts, they suffer the world's opinion to hang upon them as a load, or the influence of some system of religion which is in vogue. It very frequently happens that ten thousand people all say what not any one of them feels, but each says it because every one else says it, and each fears not to say it lest he should incur the censure of all the rest. · Such are very commonly what are called the opinions of the age. They are bad principles or doctrines, or false notions or views, which live in the mouths of men, and have their strength in their public recognition. Of course by proud men, or blind, or carnal, or worldly, these opinions which I speak of are really felt and entered into; for they are the natural growth of their own evil hearts. But very frequently the same are set forth, and heralded, and circulated, and become current opinions, among vast multitudes of men who do not feel them. These multitudes, however, are obliged to receive them by what is called the force of public opinion; the careless of course, carelessly, but the better sort superstitiously. Thus ways of speech come in, and modes of thought quite alien to the minds of those who give in to them, who feel them to be unreal, unnatural, and uncongenial to themselves, but consider themselves obliged, often from the most religious principles, not to confess their feelings about them. They dare not say, they dare not even realize to themselves their own judgments. Thus it is that the world cuts off the intercourse between soul and soul, and substitutes idols of its own for the one true Image of Christ, in and through which only souls can sympathise. Their best thoughts are stifled, and when by chance they hear them put forth elsewhere, as may sometimes be the case, they feel as it were conscious and guilty, as if some one were revealing something against them, and they shrink from the sound as from a temptation, as something pleasing indeed but forbidden. Such is the power of false creeds to fetter the mind and bring it into captivity; false views of things, of facts, of doctrines, are imposed on it tyrannically, and men live and die in bondage, who were destined to rise to the stature of the fulness of Christ. Such, for example, I consider to be, among many instances, the interpretation which is popularly received among us at present,

of the doctrinal portion of St. Paul's Epistles, an interpretation which has troubled large portions of the
Church for a long three hundred years.

But, I repeat, we are much more like each other,
even in our sins, than we fancy. I do not of course
mean to say, that we are one and all at the same point
in our Christian course, or have one and all had the
same religious history in times past; but that, even
taking a man who has never fallen from grace, and one
who has fallen most grievously and repented, even they
will be found to be very much more like each other in
their view of themselves, in their temptations, and feelings upon those temptations, than they might fancy
beforehand. This we see most strikingly instanced
when holy men set about to describe their real state.
Even bad men at once cry out, "This is just our case,"
and argue from it that there is no difference between
bad and good. They impute all their own sins to the
holiest of men, as making their own lives a sort of
comment upon the text which his words furnish, and
appealing to the appositeness of their own interpretation in proof of its correctness. And I suppose it cannot be denied, concerning all of us, that we are generally
surprised to hear the strong language which good men
use of themselves, as if such confessions showed them
to be more like ourselves, and much less holy than we
had fancied them to be. And on the other hand, I
suppose, any man of tolerably correct life, whatever his
positive advancement in grace, will seldom read accounts
of notoriously bad men, in which their ways and feelings are described, without being shocked to find that

these more or less cast a meaning upon his own heart, and bring out into light and colour lines and shapes of thought within him, which, till then, were almost invisible. Now this does not show that bad and good men are on a level, but it shows this, that they are of the same nature. It shows that the one has within him in tendency, what the other has brought out into actual existence; so that the good has nothing to boast of over the bad, and while what is good in him is from God's grace, there is an abundance left, which marks him as being beyond all doubt of one blood with those sons of Adam who are still far from Christ their Redeemer. And if this is true of bad and good, much more is it true in the case of which I am speaking, that is of good men one with another; of penitents and the upright. They understand each other far more than might at first have been supposed. And whereas their sense of the heinousness of sin rises with their own purity, those who are holiest will speak of themselves in the same terms as impure persons use about themselves; so that Christians, though they really differ much, yet as regards the power of sympathising with each other will be found to be on a level. The one is not too high or the other too low. They have common ground; and as they have one faith and hope, and one Spirit, so also they have one and the same circle of temptations, and one and the same confession.

It were well if we understood all this. Perhaps the reason why the standard of holiness among us is so low, why our attainments are so poor, our view of the truth so dim, our belief so unreal, our general notions so artificial and external is this, that we dare not trust each other with the secret of our hearts. We have each the same secret, and we keep it to ourselves, and we fear that, as a cause of estrangement, which really would be a bond of union. We do not probe the wounds of our nature thoroughly ; we do not lay the foundation of our religious profession in the ground of our inner man ; we make clean the outside of things ; we are amiable and friendly to each other in words and deeds, but our love is not enlarged, our bowels of affection are straitened, and we fear to let the intercourse begin at the root ; and, in consequence, our religion, viewed as a social system, is hollow. The presence of Christ is not in it.

To conclude. If it be awful to tell to another in our own way what we are, what will be the awfulness of that Day when the secrets of all hearts shall be disclosed! Let us ever bear this in mind when we fear that others should <u>know</u> what we are really :—whether we are right or wrong in hiding our sins now, it is a vain notion if we suppose they will always be hidden. The Day shall declare it ; the Lord will come in Judgment ; He " will bring to light the hidden things of darkness, and will make manifest the counsels of the hearts." [1] With this thought before us, surely it is a little thing whether or not man knows us here. *Then* will be knowledge without sympathy : then will be shame with everlasting contempt. Now, though there be shame, there is comfort and a soothing relief ; though there be awe, it is greater on the side of him who hears than of him who makes avowal.

[1] 1 Cor. iv. 5.

SERMON X.

RIGHTEOUSNESS NOT OF US, BUT IN US.

(EPIPHANY.)

1 Cor. i. 30, 31.

"Of Him are ye in Christ Jesus, who of God is made unto us wisdom, and righteousness, and sanctification, and redemption; that, according as it is written, He that glorieth, let him glory in the Lord."

ST. PAUL is engaged, in the chapter from which these words are taken, in humbling the self-conceit of the Corinthians. They had had gifts given them; they did not forget they had them; they used, they abused them; they forgot, not that they were theirs, but that they were given them. They seem to have thought that those gifts were theirs by a sort of right, because they were persons of more cultivation of mind than others, of more knowledge, more refinement. Corinth was a wealthy place; it was a place where all nations met, and where men saw much of the world; and it was a place of science and philosophy. It had indeed some good thing in it which Athens had not. The wise men of Athens heard the Apostle and despised him, but of Corinth it was said to him by

Christ Himself, " I have much people in this city."[1]
Yet, though there were elect of God at Corinth, yet in
a place of so much luxury and worldly wisdom, difficulties so great stood in the way of a simple, humble
faith, as to seduce, if it were possible, even the elect,—
as to bring it to pass that those who were saved were
saved "as by fire." In spite of the clear views which
the Apostle had doubtless given them on their conversion of their utter nothingness in themselves ; in spite
too of their confessing it (for we can hardly suppose
that they said in so many words that their gifts were
their own), yet they did not feel that they came from
God. They seemed, as it were, to claim them, or at
least to view their possession of them as a thing of
course ; they acted as if they were their own, not with
humbleness and gratitude towards their Giver, not with
a sense of responsibility, not with fear and trembling,
but as if they were lords over them, as if they had
sovereign power to do what they would with them,
as if they might use them from themselves and for
themselves.

Our bodily powers and limbs also come from God,
but they are in such sense part of our original formation,
or (if I may say so) of our essence, that though we ought
ever to lift up our hearts in gratitude to God while we
use them, yet we use them as *our* instruments, organs,
and ministers. They spring from us, and (as I may
say) hold of us, and we use them for our own purposes.
Well, this seems to have been the way in which the
Corinthians used their supernatural gifts, viz. as if they

<hr>

[1] Acts xviii. 10.

were parts of themselves,—as natural faculties, instead
of influences *in* them, but not *of* them, *from* the Giver
of all good,—not with awe, not with reverence, not with
worship.   They considered themselves, not members of
the Kingdom of saints, and dependent on an unseen Lord,
but mere members of an earthly community, still rich
men, still scribes, still philosophers, still disputants, who
had the *addition* of certain gifts, who had aggrandized
their existing position by the reception of Christianity.
They became proud, when they should have been thankful.
They had forgotten that to be members of the Church
they must become as little children; that they must
give up all, that they might win Christ; that they must
become poor in spirit to gain the true riches; that they
must put off philosophy, if they would speak wisdom
among the perfect.   And, therefore, St. Paul reminds
them that "not many wise men after the flesh, not
many mighty, not many noble are called;" and that
all true power, all true wisdom flows from Christ, who
is "the power of God, and the wisdom of God;" and
that all who are Christians indeed, renounce their own
power and their own wisdom, and come to Him that He
may be the Source and Principle of their power, and of
their wisdom; that they may depend on Him, and hold of
Him, not of themselves; that they may exist in Him, or
have Him in them; that they may be (as it were) His
members; that they may glory simply in Him, not in
themselves. For, whereas the wisdom of the world is but
foolishness in God's sight, and the power of the world
but weakness, God had set forth His Only-begotten Son
to be the First-born of creation, and the standard and

original of true life; to be a wisdom of God and a power of God, and a "righteousness, sanctification, and redemption" of God, to all those who are found in Him. "Of Him," says he, "are ye in Christ Jesus, who is made unto us a wisdom from God, namely, righteousness, and sanctification, and redemption; that according as it is written, He that glorieth, let him glory in the Lord."

In every age of the Church, not in the primitive age only, Christians have been tempted to pride themselves on their gifts, or at least to forget that they were gifts, and to take them for granted. Ever have they been tempted to forget their own responsibilities, their having received what they are bound to improve, and the duty of fear and trembling, while improving it. On the other hand, how they ought to behave under a sense of their own privileges, St. Paul points out when he says to the Philippians, "Work out your own salvation with fear and trembling, *for* it is God which worketh in you both to will and to do of His good pleasure."[1] God is in you for righteousness, for sanctification, for redemption, through the Spirit of His Son, and you must use His influences, His operations, not as your own (God forbid !), not as you would use your own mind or your own limbs, irreverently, but as His presence in you. All your knowledge is from Him; all good thoughts are from Him; all power to pray is from Him; your Baptism is from Him; the consecrated elements are from Him; your growth in holiness is from Him. You are not your own, you have been bought with a price, and a mysterious power is working

---

[1] Phil. ii. 13.

in you. Oh that we felt all this as well as were convinced of it!

This then is one of the first elements of Christian
knowledge and a Christian spirit, to refer all that is
good in us, all that we have of spiritual life and righteousness, to Christ our Saviour; to believe that He works
in us, or, to put the same thing more pointedly, to
believe that saving truth, life, light, and holiness are not
of us, though they must be *in* us. I shall now enlarge
on each of these two points.

1. Whatever we have, is not of us, but of God. This
surely it will not take many words to prove. Our unassisted nature is represented in Scripture as the source
of much that is evil, but not of anything that is good.
We read much in Scripture of *evil* coming out of the
natural heart, but nothing of good coming out of it.
When did not the multitude of men turn away from
Him who is their life? when was it that the holy were
not the few, and the unholy the many? and what does
this show but that the law of man's nature tends
towards evil, not towards good? As is the tree, so is its
fruit; if the fruit be evil, therefore the tree must be
evil. When was the face of human society, which is
the fruit of human nature, other than evil? When was
the power of the world an upholder of God's truth?
When was its wisdom an interpreter of it? or its rank
an image of it? Shall we look at the early age of the
world? What fruit do we find there? "The earth
was corrupt before God, and the earth was filled with
violence." "God saw that the wickedness of man was
great upon the earth, and that every imagination of he

thoughts of his heart was only evil continually. And it repented the Lord that He had made man on the earth, and it grieved Him at His heart." Shall we find good in man's nature after the flood more easily than before? "And the Lord said, Behold, the people is one, and they have all one language; and this they begin to do, and now nothing will be restrained from them which they have imagined to do . . . . So the Lord scattered them abroad from thence upon the face of all the earth." Shall we pass on to the days of David? "The Lord looked down from heaven upon the children of men, to see if there were any that did understand and seek God. They are all gone aside, they are all together become filthy; there is none that doeth good, no not one." Thus three times did God look down from heaven, and three times was man the same, God's enemy, a rebel against his Maker. Let us see if Solomon will lighten this fearful testimony. He says, "The heart of the sons of men is full of evil, and madness is in their heart while they live, and after that they go to the dead." Shall we ask of the prophet Isaiah? He answers, "We are all as an unclean thing, and all our righteousnesses are as filthy rags; and we all do fade as a leaf; and our iniquities as the wind have taken us away." Or Jeremiah? "The heart is deceitful above all things, and desperately wicked." Or what did our Lord Himself, when He came in the flesh, witness of the fruits of the heart? He said, "Out of the heart proceed evil thoughts, murders, adulteries, fornications, thefts, false witnesses, blasphemies." And will His coming have improved the world? How will it be, when He comes again? " When the Son of Man cometh, shall He find faith on the earth?"[1] What then human nature *tends* to, is very plain, and according to the end, so I say must be the beginning. If the end is evil, so is the beginning; if the termination is astray, the first direction is wrong. " Out of the abundance of the heart the mouth speaketh," and the hand worketh; and such as is the work and the word, such is the heart. Nothing then can be more certain, if we go by Scripture, not to speak of experience, than that the present nature of man is evil, and not good; that evil things come from it, and not good things. If good things come from it, they are the exception, and therefore not of it, but in it merely; first given to it, and then coming from it; not of it by nature, but in it by grace. Our Lord says expressly, " That which is born of the flesh, is flesh; and that which is born of the Spirit, is spirit. Marvel not that I say unto thee, Ye must be born again."[2] And again, " Without Me ye can do nothing;"[3] and St. Paul, " I can do all things through Christ, that strengtheneth me." And again, in the Epistle before us, " Who maketh thee to differ from another? and what hast thou that thou didst not receive? now if thou didst receive it, why dost thou glory, as if thou hadst not received it?"[4]

This is that great truth which is at the foundation of all true doctrine as to the way of salvation. All teaching about duty and obedience, about attaining heaven, and

---

[1] Gen. vi. 11, 5, 6; xi. 6—8. Ps. xiv. 2, 3. Eccl. ix. 3. Isa. lxiv. 6. Jer. xvii. 9. Matt. xv. 19. Luke xviii. 8.
[2] John iii. 7.   [3] John xv. 5.   [4] 1 Cor. iv. 7.

about the office of Christ towards us, is hollow and unsubstantial, which is not built *here*, in the doctrine of our original corruption and helplessness; and, in consequence, of original guilt and sin. Christ Himself indeed is the foundation, but a broken, self-abased, self-renouncing heart is (as it were) the ground and soil in which the foundation must be laid; and it is but building on the sand to profess to believe in Christ, yet not to acknowledge that without Him we can do nothing. It is what is called the Pelagian heresy, of which many of us perhaps have heard the name. I am not, indeed, formally stating what that heresy consists in, but I mean, that, speaking popularly, I may call it the belief, that "holy desires, good counsels, and just works," can come of *us*, can be *from* us, as well as *in* us: whereas they are from God only; from whom, and not from ourselves, is that righteousness, sanctification, and redemption, which is in us,—from whom is the washing away of our inward guilt, and the implanting in us of a new nature. But when men take it for granted that they are natural objects of God's favour,—when they view their privileges and powers as natural things,—when they look upon their Baptism as an ordinary work, bringing about its results as a matter of course,—when they come to Church without feeling that they are highly favoured in being allowed to come,—when they do not understand the necessity of prayer for God's grace,—when they refer everything to system, and subject the provisions of God's free bounty to the laws of cause and effect,—when they think that education will do everything, and that education is in their

own power,—when, in short, they think little of the
Church of God, which is the great channel of God's
mercies, and look upon the Gospel as a sort of literature or philosophy, contained in certain documents,
which they may use as they use the instruction of other
books; then, not to mention other instances of the same
error, are they practically Pelagians, for they make
themselves their own centre, instead of depending on
Almighty God and His ordinances.

2. And, secondly, while truth and righteousness are
not of us, it is quite as certain that they are also in us
if we be Christ's; not merely nominally given to us and
imputed to us, but really implanted in us by the
operation of the Blessed Spirit. Our Lord and Saviour
Jesus Christ, when He came on earth in our flesh,
made a perfect atonement, "sacrifice, oblation, and
satisfaction for the sins of the whole world." He was
born of a woman, He wrought miracles, He fasted and
was tempted in the desert, He suffered and was crucified, He was dead and buried; He rose again from the
dead, He ascended on high, and "liveth ever" with the
Father,—all for our sakes. And as His incarnation and
death were in order to our salvation, so also He really
accomplished the end which that humiliation had in
view. All was done that needed to be done, except what
could not be done at a time, when they were not yet in
existence on whom it was to be done. All was done
for us except the actual grant of mercy made to us one
by one. He saved us by anticipation, but we were not
yet saved in fact, for as yet we were not. But everything short of this was then finished. Satan was

vanquished; sin was atoned for; the penalty was paid; God was propitiated; righteousness, sanctification, redemption, life, all were provided for the sons of Adam, and all that remained to do was to dispense, to impart, these divine gifts to them one by one. This was not done, because it could not be done all at once; it could not be done forthwith to individuals, and salvation was designed in God's counsels to be an individual gift. He did not once for all restore the whole race, and change the condition of the world in His sight immediately on Christ's death. The sun on Easter-day did not rise, nor did He rise from the grave, on a new world, but on the old world, the sinful rebellious outcast world as before. Men were just what they had been, both in themselves and in His sight. They were guilty and corrupt before His crucifixion, and so they were after it; so they remain to this day, except so far as He by His free bounty and at His absolute will, vouchsafes to impart the gift of His passion to this man or that. He provided, not gave salvation, when He suffered; and there must be a giving or applying in the case of all those who are to be saved. The gift of life is in us, as truly as it is not of us; it is not only *from* Him but it is *unto* us. This must carefully be borne in mind, for as there are those who consider that life, righteousness, and salvation are of us, so there are others who hold that they are not in us; and as there are many who more or less forget that justification is of God, so there are quite as many who more or less forget that justification must be in man if it is to profit him. And it is hard to say which of the two errors is the greater.

But there is another ground for saying that Christ did not finish His gracious economy by His death; viz. because the Holy Spirit came in order to finish it. When He ascended, He did not leave us to ourselves; so far the work was not done. He sent His Spirit. Were all finished as regards individuals, why should the Holy Ghost have condescended to come? But the Spirit came to finish in us, what Christ had finished in Himself, but left unfinished as regards us. To Him it is committed to apply to us severally all that Christ had done for us. As then His mission proves on the one hand that salvation is not from ourselves, so does it on the other that it must be wrought in us. For if all gifts of grace are with the Spirit, and the presence of the Spirit is within us, it follows that these gifts are to be manifested and wrought in us. If Christ is our sole hope, and Christ is given to us by the Spirit, and the Spirit be an inward presence, our sole hope is in an inward change. As a light placed in a room pours out its rays on all sides, so the presence of the Holy Ghost imbues us with life, strength, holiness, love, acceptableness, righteousness. God looks on us in mercy, because He sees in us "the mind of the Spirit," for whoso has this mind has holiness and righteousness within him. Henceforth all his thoughts, words, and works, as done in the Spirit, are acceptable, pleasing, just before God; and whatever remaining infirmity there be in him, that the presence of the Spirit hides. That divine influence, which has the fulness of Christ's grace to purify us, has also the power of Christ's blood to justify.

Let us never lose sight of this great and simple view,

which the whole of Scripture sets before us. What was actually done by Christ in the flesh eighteen hundred years ago, is in type and resemblance really wrought in us one by one even to the end of time. He was born of the Spirit, and we too are born of the Spirit. He was justified by the Spirit, and so are we. He was pronounced the well-beloved Son, when the Holy Ghost descended on Him; and we too cry Abba, Father, through the Spirit sent into our hearts. He was led into the wilderness by the Spirit; He did great works by the Spirit; He offered Himself to death by the Eternal Spirit; He was raised from the dead by the Spirit; He was declared to be the Son of God by the Spirit of holiness on His resurrection: we too are led by the same Spirit into and through this world's temptations; we, too, do our works of obedience by the Spirit; we die from sin, we rise again unto righteousness through the Spirit; and we are declared to be God's sons,—declared, pronounced, dealt with as righteous,—through our resurrection unto holiness in the Spirit. Or, to express the same great truth in other words; Christ Himself vouchsafes to repeat in each of us in figure and mystery all that He did and suffered in the flesh. He is formed in us, born in us, suffers in us, rises again in us, lives in us; and this not by a succession of events, but all at once : for He comes to us as a Spirit, all dying, all rising again, all living. We are ever receiving our birth, our justification, our renewal, ever dying to sin, ever rising to righteousness. His whole economy in all its parts is ever in us all at once; and this divine presence constitutes the title of each of us to heaven; this is what He will acknowledge and accept at the last day. He will acknowledge Himself,—His image in us,—as though we reflected Him, and He, on looking round about, discerned at once who were His; those, namely, who gave back to Him His image. He impresses us with the seal of the Spirit, in order to avouch that we are His. As the king's image appropriates the coin to him, so the likeness of Christ in us separates us from the world and assigns us over to the kingdom of heaven.

Scripture is full of texts to show that salvation is such an inward gift. For instance : What is it that rescues us from being reprobates ? "Know ye not," says St. Paul, " that Jesus Christ is in you, except ye be reprobates ?" What is our hope ? "Christ in us, the hope of glory." What is it that hallows and justifies ? "The Name of the Lord Jesus, and the Spirit of our God." What makes our offerings acceptable ? "Being sanctified by the Holy Ghost." What is our life ? "The Spirit is life because of righteousness." How are we enabled to fulfil the law ? "The righteousness of the law is fulfilled in us who walk not after the flesh, but after the Spirit." Who is it makes us righteous ? "The fruit of the *Spirit* is in all goodness, and righteousness, and truth." [1]

To conclude.—I have said that there are two opposite errors : one, the holding that salvation is not of God; the other, that it is not in ourselves. Now it is remarkable that the maintainers of both the one and the other

---

[1] 2 Cor. xiii. 5.　Col. i. 27.　1 Cor. vi. 11.　Rom. xv. 16.　Rom. viii. 10.　Eph. v. 9.

error, whatever their differences in other respects, agree in this,—in depriving a Christian life of its mysteriousness. He who believes that he can please God of himself, or that obedience can be performed by his own powers, of course has nothing more of awe, reverence, and wonder in his personal religion, than when he moves his limbs and uses his reason, though he might well feel awe then also. And in like manner he also who considers that Christ's passion once undergone on the Cross absolutely secured his own personal salvation, may see mystery indeed in that Cross (as he ought), but he will see no mystery, and feel little solemnity, in prayer, in ordinances, or in his attempts at obedience. He will be free, familiar, and presuming, in God's presence. Neither will " work out their salvation with fear and trembling ; " for neither will realize, though they use the words, that God is in them " to will and to do." Both the one and the other will be content with a low standard of duty : the one, because he does not believe that God requires much ; the other, because he thinks that Christ in His own person has done all. Neither will honour and make much of God's Law : the one, because he brings down the Law to his own power of obeying it ; the other, because he thinks that Christ has taken away the Law by obeying it in his stead. They only feel awe and true seriousness who think that the Law remains ; that it claims to be fulfilled by them ; and that it can be fulfilled in them through the power of God's grace. Not that any man alive arises up to that perfect fulfilment, but that such fulfilment is not impossible ; that it is begun in all true Christians;

that they all are tending to it; are growing into it; and are pleasing to God because they are becoming, and in proportion as they are becoming like Him who, when He came on earth in our flesh, fulfilled the Law perfectly.

SERMON XI.

THE LAW OF THE SPIRIT.

(EPIPHANY.)

ROM. x. 4.

" Christ is the end of the Law for righteousness to every one that believeth."

IN the Epistle to the Romans, St. Paul argues against Jews who rejected the Gospel ; in his Epistles to the Corinthians, he rebukes Christians who had abused it. The sin of the fickle and vain-glorious Corinthians was very different from that of the hard-hearted Jews ; and yet in either case it rose from one and the same root, pride. Both Jews and Greeks prided themselves on what they were, on what Moses had left them, or what Christ's Apostles had brought them; both forgot that whatever they had was God's gift, and that it was their duty to be dependent and watchful.   But in appearance they differed : the Jews insisted on God's former mercies unseasonably ; and the Greeks of Corinth thought even of His last and best, lightly and unthankfully.

Sinful feelings and passions generally take upon themselves the semblance of reason, and affect to argue.

It was in this way that the Jews, whom St. Paul is opposing in the text, disguised from themselves their own unbelief; and this has turned out a benefit to the Church ever since, as having led St. Paul, in consequence, to set forth views of the Gospel which otherwise might not have come to us with the authority of inspiration. The text contains such a view, expressed very concisely, which I now propose to explain; and after doing so, I will add a few words on the feelings of the Jews, in contrast with the doctrine it contains.

St. Paul tells us, that "Christ is the end of the Law for righteousness to every one that believeth." Here are three subjects which call for remark: the Law, Righteousness, and Faith. I will speak of them in succession.

1. In the first place, of "the Law." By the Law is meant the eternal, unchangeable Law of God, which is the revelation of His will, the standard of perfection, and the mould and fashion to which all creatures must conform, as they would be happy. God is holy, and His Law is holy. His Law is the image of Himself; it is the word of Life and Truth commanding that, of which He is the perfect pattern. "Be ye holy," He says, "for I am holy." "Be ye perfect, even as your Father which is in heaven is perfect."[1] His Law is the declaration of His infinite and glorious attributes, and thereby becomes the rule by which all beings imitate, approach, and resemble Him. And when He created them, He provided that it should be to them what it ought to be. God loves holiness, and therefore, as became a good and

<hr>

1 Pet. i. 16.   Matt. v. 48.

kind Father, He created all His children holy. He created them to be His children, not His enemies; beings in whom He might take pleasure; who might be near Him, not far off from Him; whom He might love and reward. He formed them upon the pattern of the Law; He moulded them into symmetry by means of it. He created man "in His own image, and after His likeness;" that is, upon the type of the Law. He put His Spirit within him, and set up the Law in his heart; so that, what He is in His infinite nature, such was man, such was Adam in a finite nature,—perfect after his kind.

And in this sense, the Law given to the Israelites from Mount Sinai is called in Scripture, and may be considered, the holy and eternal Law of God. Not that any number of commandments, uttered in man's language and written upon tables, could be commensurate with what is of an infinite and of a spiritual nature; not that a code of precepts, addressed to one portion of a fallen race, in one country, and in one particular state of moral and social existence, could rise to the majesty and beauty of what is perfect;—but that the Law of Moses represented the Law of God in its place and age; was the fullest revelation of it, and the nearest approximation to it, then vouchsafed; and was that Law, as far as it went. As Adam, a child of the dust, was also an "image of God," so the Jewish Law, though earthly and temporary, had at the same time a divine character. It was the light of God shining in a gross medium, in order that it might be "comprehended;" and if it did not teach the chosen people all, it taught them much, and in the only way in which they could be taught it.

And hence, as in the text, St. Paul, when on the subject of the Jews, speaks of their Law as if it were the eternal Law of God; and so it was, but only as brought down to its hearers, and condescending to their infirmity.

2. Such is "the Law," as spoken of in the text; and by "Righteousness" is meant conformity to the Law,— that one state of soul which is pleasing to God. It is a relative word, having reference to a standard set up, and expressing the fulfilment of its requirements. To be righteous is to act up to the Law, whatever the Law be, and thereby to be acceptable to Him who gave it. Such Adam was in Paradise; the Law was his inward life, and Almighty God dealt with him accordingly,— He called, accounted, dealt with him as righteous, because he was righteous.

It was far otherwise with him when he had fallen. He then forfeited the presence of the Holy Spirit; he no longer fulfilled the Law; he lost his righteousness, and he knew he had lost it. He knew it before God told him; he condemned himself, he pronounced himself unrighteous, before God formally rejected him from his state of justification. And in this unrighteous state he has remained, viewed in himself, ever since; knowing the Law, but not doing it; admiring, not loving; assenting, not following; not utterly without the Law, yet not with it; with the Law not within him, but before him, —not any longer in his heart, as the pillar of a cloud, which was a gracious token and a guide to the Israelites, but departing from him, and moving away, and taking up its place, as it were over against him, and confronting him as an enemy, accuser, and avenger. It was a cloud of thick darkness, instead of a pillar of light ; and from it the Lord looked out upon him, and troubled him. Or in St. Paul's words, "the commandment, which was ordained to life, he found to be unto death."[1] What had been a law of innocence, became a law of conscience ; what was freedom, became bondage ; what was peace, became dread and misery.

Let us thank God that dread and misery are left us. Better is it that the Law remain to us externally, and in the way of an upbraiding conscience, than that it should be utterly removed. While, and so far as it so remains, our own judgment upon ourselves is a warning to us, what the judgment of God will be hereafter, what His view of us is at present. For is not the pain of a bad conscience different from any other pain that we know ? I do not ask whether it is greater or less than other pain, but whether it is not unlike any other, peculiar and individual. Can that pain be compensated and overcome by the wages of sin, whatever they be,—or rather, does it not, while it lasts, remain distinctly perceptible and entire in the midst of them ? In conscience, then, we have the figure of the wrath of God upon transgressors of the Law ; the pain which it inflicts on us at times, or in certain cases, is a sort of indication how God regards, and will one day visit, all sins, according to the sure word of Scripture. Take an instance, which, though extreme, will serve to explain what I would say. What accounts do we read of the frightful sleepless remorse which murderers have before now shown ! so much so that, though no one knew their crime, yet they could

[1] Rom. vii. 10.

not help confessing it,—as if death were a lighter suffering than a bad conscience. Here you see the misery of being unjustified. Or, again, consider the peculiar piercing distress which follows upon the commission of sins of impurity;—here you have a corroboration in a particular instance of what Scripture affirms generally, concerning the misery of sinning. Or, think of those indescribable feelings in our nature, to which our first parent alludes, when he says, " I heard Thy voice in the garden, and I was afraid, because I was naked; and I hid myself." [1] Are not these feelings a type of the horror with which Angels now look, with which we shall look hereafter, upon all transgression of the Law, or unrighteousness?

Unrighteousness then is a state of misery, frightful as the murderer's, acute as theirs who follow Belial, and overpowering as Adam's when he fled from God. And from this state Christ came to save us, by bringing us back again to righteousness. Man was righteous at the first, because the Law of God ruled him; he became unrighteous when this Law ceased to rule him; and he becomes righteous again by the Law of God once more ruling him. He was righteous at the first by the presence of the Holy Spirit, which enabled him to obey the Law; and such too is his second righteousness. And thus the words of the text are fulfilled; " Christ is the end of the Law for" or unto "righteousness." He effects what the Law contemplates and enjoins, but cannot accomplish, our righteousness. And how? St. Paul does not mention it in the text, but in many other

<hr>

[1] Gen. iii. 10.

places in his Epistles; viz. by that great gift of His passion, the abiding influence of the Holy Ghost, which enables us to offer to God an acceptable obedience, such as by nature we cannot offer.

Now let me show from Scripture some of these points on which I have been insisting.

First, not much need be said to make it plain that by nature we cannot please God, or, in other words, have no principle of righteousness in us. St. Paul says in so many words, "They that are in the flesh cannot please God;" and just before, "The carnal mind is enmity against God; for it is not subject to the Law of God, neither indeed can be." In the foregoing chapter he says, "We know that the Law is spiritual; but I am carnal, sold under sin. For that which I do, I allow not; for what I would, that do I not: but what I hate, that do I. I know that in me (that is, in my flesh) dwelleth no good thing." Again, "By the deeds of the Law there shall no flesh be justified in His sight · for by the Law is the knowledge of sin." In like manner the prophet Isaiah says, "We are all as an unclean thing; and all our righteousnesses are as filthy rags."[1] Such is our state by nature: the best things we do are displeasing to God in themselves, as savouring of the Old Adam, and being works of the flesh and not spiritual.

And as this is our natural state, so the desire of religious men, and the one promise of a merciful God has ever been, that we should be made obedient to the Law, or righteous. Thus David says, "Thou

---

[1] Rom. viii. 7. 8 ; vii. 14. 15, 18 ; iii. 20. Isa. lxiv. 6.

requirest truth *in the inward parts*; and shalt make me to understand wisdom secretly. Thou shalt purge me with hyssop, and I shall be clean; Thou shalt wash me, and I shall be *whiter than snow*. Make me a *clean heart*, O God, and renew a right spirit within me. O give me the comfort of Thy help again; and stablish me with Thy free Spirit." Again, "I will wash my hands in *innocency*, O Lord, and so will I go to Thine altar." Again, "Give me understanding, and I shall keep Thy Law, yea, *I shall keep it* with my *whole heart.* ... Behold, my delight is in Thy commandments. O quicken me in Thy righteousness." "Teach me to do the thing that pleaseth Thee; for Thou art my God: let Thy loving Spirit lead me forth into the land of *righteousness.*"[1]

And what Psalmists ask, Prophets promise. They make it the one great distinction of Gospel times, that that original righteousness which is so necessary for us, and from which we are so far gone, should be vouchsafed again to us, and that through the Spirit. Daniel states the object of Christ's coming to be the "making reconciliation for iniquity, *and* bringing in everlasting *righteousness.*" Malachi says that Christ should "purify the sons of Levi," that they may "offer unto the Lord an offering in *righteousness.*" In Isaiah, Almighty God speaks to them "that know *righteousness,*" viz. "the people in whose heart is My *law;*" and he also speaks of "the *Spirit* being poured upon us from on high," and in consequence of "*righteousness* remaining in the fruitful field, and the work of righteousness being *peace,*

---

[1] Ps li. 6, 7, 10, 12; xxvi. 6; cxix. 30, 40; cxliii. 10.

and the effect of righteousness, *quietness and assurance
for ever."* Still more clear is the prophet Jeremiah
in declaring what the Gospel gift consists in ; " Behold,
the days come, saith the Lord, that I will make a new
covenant with the house of Israel and with the house
of Judah : I will *put My law in their inward parts,*
and write it in their hearts." In similar terms does
the prophet Ezekiel describe the great gift of the
Gospel, "*A new heart* also will I give you, and a *new
spirit* will I put within you ; and I will put *My Spirit*
within you, and *cause you* to walk in My statutes, and
ye shall keep My judgments and do them." Again
elsewhere the prophet Isaiah calls this new nature,
or righteousness, or gift of the Spirit, which the Gospel
furnishes, a sort of garment or robe of the soul, being
that glory which Adam had before sin stripped him
of it ; "He hath clothed me with the garment of salvation, He hath covered me with *the robe of righteousness,* as a bridegroom decketh himself with ornaments,
and as a bride adorneth herself with her jewels." With
this passage must be compared St. John's words in the
Revelations, "The marriage of the Lamb is come, and
His wife hath made herself ready. And to her was
granted that she should be arrayed in fine linen, clean
and white ; *for the fine linen is the righteousness of
saints.*" Our Lord also speaks of the great gift of the
Gospel under the same figure, when he tells us of the
man who came to the marriage feast without a wedding-
garment, that is, without righteousness or holiness.[1]

____

[1] Dan. ix. 24. Mal. iii. 3. Isa. li. 7 ; xxxii. 15, 16, 17. Jer.
xxxi. 31. Ez. xxxvi. 26, 27. Isa. lxi. 10. Rev. xix. 7, &.

Thus, if we listen to the voices of the Prophets, we must believe that the righteousness of the Law really *is* fulfilled in us under the Gospel through the Spirit;—but as this is a truth in this day denied by some persons, it may be well to insist upon it.

Now that it is a plain truth of Scripture, is proved, in addition to what has been said, by those numerous passages which speak of holy men as "righteous *before God.*" This is an expression to which we shall do well to attend, as being an additional explanation of the word "righteousness;" for if holy men are righteous *before God,* they come up to God's *standard* of perfection. The phrase "in the sight of " or "before" often occurs in Scripture, and it means "in the *judgment,*" "with the *witness*" of him or them to whom it is applied. Thus in the last chapter of St. Luke, where it is said, "Their words seemed to them as idle tales," this stands in the original Greek, "Their words seemed *in their sight*" or "*before them,*" that is, "*in their judgment.*" And hence when St. Paul speaks with an oath, he uses these words, "Now the things which I write unto you, behold, *before God,* I lie not," that is, "with the *witness* of God." And so Peter and John answer the council, "Whether it be right *in the sight of God* to hearken unto you more than unto God, judge ye," *i.e.* "in the *presence*" and "with the *witness* of God." And hence the Angels are said "to stand in the *presence* of God," or to be "before His throne," for they can bear it. And on the other hand, the prodigal son says, "Father, I have sinned *before Thee,*" that is, I know that Thou art conscious of my sin. When then it is said, as it so often is said in Scripture, that the righteous are righteous "before God," this means that their righteousness is not merely the name or semblance of righteousness, nor righteousness up to an earthly standard, but a real and true righteousness which approves itself to God. They are able to stand before God and yet not be condemned. They are not sinners before God, but they are righteous before God, and bear His scrutiny. By nature no one can stand in His presence. "All the world becomes guilty *before God.*" "By the deeds of the Law no flesh shall be justified in *His sight.*" *How* then are we able to come before Him? How shall we stand in His sight? The answer is given us in the Old Testament, in the words of Balaam to Balak. Balak asked, "Wherewith shall I *come before the Lord*, and bow myself before the High God?" and the answer was, "He hath showed thee, O man, what is good; and what doth the Lord require of thee, but to do justly, and to love mercy, and to walk humbly with thy God?" Or again, the answer may be given in the words of Zacharias, who blesses the Lord God of Israel for fulfilling His promise, and enabling us to come into His presence to "serve Him, *without fear*, in holiness and righteousness *before Him.*" And accordingly, to come to the case of individuals, Noah, even before the Gospel times, is said to have "found grace in the eyes of the Lord." Why? Because, in the words of Almighty God to him, "*Thee* have I seen righteous *before Me*," or, in My sight, "in this generation;" and Daniel escaped the lions,

"forasmuch as *before God* innocency was found in him."
In like manner Zacharias and Elizabeth "were both
righteous *before* God," or in the judgment of God. It
was told to Cornelius that "his prayers and alms had
come up for a memorial *in the sight*," or judgment,
of God. And St. Paul speaks of intercession for
governors being "good and acceptable *in the sight* of
God our Saviour." And he prays for his brethren
that God would "work *in* them that which is well
pleasing in *His sight*," or judgment. St. Peter too
speaks of a "meek and quiet spirit," being, "in the
sight of God, of great price." And St. John, that
"we receive what we ask of Him, because we do
those things that are pleasing *in His sight*." And
Christ warns the Church of Sardis to "be watchful,
and strengthen the things which remain, which are
ready to die;" for He says, "I have not found thy
works perfect *before God*," or in the witness of God.
And accordingly the word "witness" is itself used
elsewhere to express the same thing, as in the instance
of Abel, who, St. Paul says, by his "more excellent
sacrifice," "*obtained witness* that he was righteous;
God testifying of his gifts."[1] If then it is plain from
Scripture, as it is, that by nature we are unrighteous
in God's sight, and cannot stand before God, the same
Scripture also proves that by the gift of grace we *are*
righteous, and can can stand before Him; and it is

---

[1] Luke xxiv. 11. Gal. i. 20. Acts iv. 19. Luke i. 19. Rev. viii. 2;
i. 5. Rom. iii. 19. Mic. vi. 8. Luke i. 74, 75. Gen. vii. 1.
Dan. vi. 22. Luke i. 6. Acts x. 4. 1 Tim. ii. 3. Heb. xiii. 21.
1 Pet. iii. 4. 1 John iii. 22. Rev. iii. 2. Heb. xi. 4.

us easy, by some evasion, to explain away the Scripture proofs for the doctrine of original sin, as to get rid of those which Scripture furnishes us for the doctrine of implanted righteousness, and that through the Spirit.

St. Paul has a number of other passages concerning the office of the Holy Spirit, which are equally apposite to show that He it is who vouchsafes to give us inward righteousness under the Gospel, or to justify, or make us acceptable to God. For instance, he says, "Ye are washed, ye are sanctified, ye are *justified* in the Name of the Lord Jesus, and by the *Spirit* of our God. Elsewhere he first calls the Gospel "the ministration of the *Spirit*," and in the next verse, "the ministration of righteousness." Elsewhere he speaks of the Holy Ghost as "the Spirit of *adoption*." And he intimates that "the *righteousness* of the law" is "*fulfilled*" in those "who walk after the *Spirit*." Again he says that the presence of the Spirit in us pleads, as it were, for us with the Father, "making intercession for us with plaints unutterable;" and that God, "who searcheth the hearts," "*knoweth* what is the mind of the Spirit, because He maketh intercession for the saints, according," or, in a way acceptable, "to God." And elsewhere he contrasts the state of nature and the state of grace in this plain way, clearly implying that that inward gift of righteousness which we lost in Adam we have recovered in Christ; "As by the offence of one, judgment came upon all men to condemnation, even so by the righteousness of One the free gift came upon all men unto justification *of life.* For *as* by one man's disobedience many were made sinners, *so* by the obedience of One shall many be *made righteous* ... that, as sin hath reigned unto death, even so might grace reign through righteousness unto eternal life by Jesus Christ our Lord."[1] Sin, which we derive through Adam, is not a name merely, but a dreadful reality; and so our new righteousness also is a real and not a merely imputed righteousness. It is real righteousness, because it comes from the Holy and Divine Spirit, who vouchsafes, in our Church's language, to pour His gift into our hearts, and who thus makes us acceptable to God, whereas by nature, on account of original sin, we are displeasing to Him. We are "not in the flesh, but in the Spirit," and therefore in a state of *grace*. Again, St. Paul speaks of the "offering of the Gentiles being *acceptable*." How acceptable? He proceeds, "being sanctified by the Holy Ghost." He speaks of presenting our "bodies as a living sacrifice, holy, *acceptable* unto God." He says that Christ has "saved us, according to His mercy, by the washing of regeneration, and the renewing of the Holy Ghost," and that we are able thereby to "walk worthy of the Lord unto all *pleasing*."[2]

Such then is the meaning of the words of the text, "Christ is the end of the Law for righteousness." As if the Apostle said, Would you fulfil the righteousness of the Law? You cannot in your own strength. You cannot without that divine gift which His passion has purchased, the gift of the Spirit; with it "the

---

[1] 1 Cor. vi. 11. 2 Cor. iii. 8, 9. Gal. iv. 5, 6. Rom. viii. 26, 27; v. 18—21.

[2] Rom. xv. 16; xii. 1. Tit. iii. 5. Col. 1. 10.

righteousness of the Law *may* be fulfilled in you." Christ then is the end of the Law for righteousness, because He effects the purpose of the Law. He brings that about which "the Law cannot do, because it is weak through the flesh," through our unregenerate, unrenewed, carnal nature.

3. But here this question may be asked,—"How can we be said to *fulfil* the Law, and to offer an *acceptable* obedience, since we do not obey *perfectly?* At best we only obey in part; the best obedience of ours is sullied with imperfection. Even with the gift of the Spirit, we do nothing which will bear the strict inspection of a holy and just Judge. Adam, on the other hand, had no sinful nature at all, before his fall; there was nothing in him to counteract or to defile the influences of grace. He then might be justified by his inward righteousness, but we cannot."

I answer as follows:—We can only be justified, certainly, by what is perfect; no work of ours, as far as it is ours, is perfect : and therefore by no work of ours, viewed in its human imperfections, are we justified. But when I speak of our righteousness I speak of the work of the Spirit, and this work, though imperfect, considered as ours, is perfect as far as it comes from Him. Our works, done in the Spirit of Christ, have a justifying *principle* in them, and that is the presence of the All-holy Spirit. His influences are infinitely pleasing to God, and able to overcome in His sight all our own infirmities and demerits. This we are expressly told by St. Paul, in reference to one work of the Holy Ghost, the exercise of prayer, as I just now quoted his words. "He that searcheth the hearts, knoweth what is the mind of the Spirit, because He maketh intercession for the saints," that is, in their hearts, "according to God."[1] Not then for anything of our own are we acceptable to God, but for the work of grace in us; and as having this work of grace in us we *are* acceptable. And this Divine Presence in us, makes us altogether pleasing to God. It makes those works pleasing to God, which it produces, though human infirmity be mixed with them: it hallows those acts, that life, that obedience of which it is the original cause, and which it orders and fashions; so that our new obedience or righteousness is justifying, though imperfect, not for its own sake, but for this new and heavenly principle of grace infused into it.

But again, there is another reason why, for Christ's sake, we are dealt with as perfectly righteous, though we be not so. Not only for the Spirit's presence in us, but for what is ours;—not indeed what is now ours, but for what we shall be. We are not unreprovable, and unblemished in holiness yet, but we shall be at length through God's mercy. They who persevere to the end, will be perfect in soul and body, when they stand before God in heaven; and now that perfection is beginning in them, now they have a gift in them which will in due time, through God's mercy, leaven the whole mass within them. They will one day be presented blameless before the Throne, and they are now to labour towards, and begin that

[1] Rom. viii. 27.

perfect state. And in consideration that it is begun in them, God of His great mercy imputes it to them as if it were already completed. He anticipates what will be, and treats them as that which they are labouring to become. This is what is meant by faith being imputed for righteousness, which St. Paul often insists on, and which is implied in the last words of the text, which I have not yet explained. "Christ is the end of the Law for righteousness *to every one that believeth.*" Faith is the element of all perfection ; he who begins with faith, will end in unspotted and entire holiness. It is the earnest of a great deal more than itself, and therefore is allowed, in God's consideration, to stand for, to be a pledge of, to be taken in advance for that, which it for certain will end in. He who believes has not yet perfect righteousness and unblameableness, but he has the first fruits of it. And all through a man's life, whether his righteous deeds be more or less, or his righteousness of heart more or less, his faith is something quite distinct from anything he had in a state of nature, and though it does not satisfy the requirements of God's law, yet since it tends to perfection, it is mercifully taken as perfection. "Abraham believed God, and it was counted to him for righteousness," because God, who sees the end from the beginning, knew it would end in perfect and unblemished righteousness. And in like manner to us "it shall be imputed, if we believe on Him that raised up Jesus our Lord from the dead, who was delivered for our offences, and raised again for our justification."[1]

[1] Rom. iv. 24, 25.

4. Lastly, such being the Law, such our rightecus-
ness, such the work of Christ in us through the
Spirit, and such the office of faith, we see what the
mistake of the Jews was, of which so much is said
in St. Paul's Epistle to the Romans, and which seems
to be the reason why the text itself was written.
They were in a path which never would lead to
holiness and heaven. They were in a state which
was destitute of grace and help. They were under
the threatening and condemning Law. Many good
men doubtless there had been and were under the
Law, but their spiritual excellence was not from the
Law, but from the Gospel, the blessings of which were
anticipated under it, and which the Apostle was at
that time preaching throughout the world. But the
Pharisees and others, not understanding the real nature
and office of their Law, and the reason why God had
given it through Moses, thought to be saved by it,
—thought it led to heaven. Whereupon St. Paul
attempted to show them that they were, as I may say,
in the wrong road. They aimed at eternal life ; that
was the object towards which they professed to · be
travelling. Now St. Paul told them that the Jewish
Law did not lead to it. He said that if they desired
to reach the eternal rest of heaven, they must betake
themselves to another road. And that they could not
as it were, cross over into it, but that they must go
back and enter in at the gate, and that this gate was
faith. He said that the further they went on in their
present course, the less they would really advance,
towards their object ; and, though it seemed lost time

to go back, it was not so. They might do as many works and services as they would in their present state, but these would not advance them at all, and why?—not that works were not necessary, God forbid! but that such works were not good works; that no works were good works but those done in the Spirit, and that nothing could gain them the gift of the Spirit but faith in Christ. They desired to be righteous; it was well; but Christ alone was " the end of the Law for righteousness to every one that believed." They desired to fulfil the Law; well then, let them seek " the Law of the Spirit of life," whereby " the righteousness of the Law might be fulfilled in them." They desired the reward of righteousness: be it so; let them then " wait through the Spirit for the hope of righteousness by faith."[1] But they were too proud to confess that they had anything to learn, that they had to begin again, to submit to be taught, to believe in Him they had crucified, to come suppliantly for the gift of the Spirit. They refused the true righteousness which God had provided, thinking they were righteous as they were, and that they could be saved in the flesh. Hence St. Paul says, " They, being ignorant of God's righteousness, and going about to establish their own righteousness, have not submitted themselves unto the righteousness of God."[2] They thought that faith was something mean and weak,—so it was; and, therefore, that it was unable to do great things,—so it was not; for Christ's strength is made perfect in weakness, and He has chosen the despicable things of this world to put to shame such as are highly

---

[1] Gal. v. 5.   [2] Rom. x. 3.

esteemed. They considered that they were God's people by a sort of right, that they did not need grace, and that their outward ceremonies and their dead works would profit them. Therefore the Apostle warned them, that Abraham himself was justified, not by circumcision, but by faith; that circumcision was not taken for righteousness in his case, for it never would arrive at righteousness, but that faith would arrive, and therefore it was taken; that "to him that worketh not, but believeth on him that justifieth the ungodly, his faith is counted for righteousness;"[1] that "by grace are we saved through faith, not of works, for we are *God's* workmanship, *created in* Christ Jesus *unto* good works;"[2] that "if by grace, then is it no more of works, otherwise grace is no more grace; but if it be of works, then is it no more grace, otherwise work is no more work."[3] However, the Jews still preferred their old works to good works; they refused to go the way by which alone their persons, thoughts, words, actions, services could be made acceptable to God; they would not exercise that loving faith which alone could gain for them the gift of the Spirit, and was fruitful in true righteousness; they refused to be justified in God's way, and determined to use the Law of Moses for a purpose for which it was never given, for their justification in His sight, and for attaining eternal life.

And in consequence God turned from them, and gave to others what was first offered to them. He manifested Himself to the Gentiles. Those who had hitherto been without any tokens of God's favour, outstripped in the

[1] Rom. iv. 5.   [2] Eph. ii. 8–10.   [3] Rom. xi. 6.

race those who had long enjoyed it. The first became last, and the last first. "The Gentiles, which followed not after righteousness, have attained to righteousness, even the righteousness which is of faith; but Israel, which followed after the law of righteousness, hath not attained to the law of righteousness. Wherefore? Because they sought it, not by faith, but, as it were, by the works of the Law; for they stumbled at that stumbling-stone." [1]

Let us see to it, lest in any way we too stumble at God's commands or promises; let us beg of Him to lead us on in His perfect and narrow way, and to be "a lantern to our feet, and a light to our path," while we walk in it.

[1] Rom. xi. 30–32.

SERMON XII.

THE NEW WORKS OF THE GOSPEL.

2 Cor. v. 17

*If any man be in Christ, he is a new creature: old things are passed
away; behold, all things are become new."*

NOTHING, is more clearly stated, or more strongly
insisted on, by St. Paul, than the new creation, or
second beginning, or regeneration, of the world, which
has been vouchsafed in Christ. It had been announced
in prophecy. "Behold, I create *new* heavens and a *new*
earth; and the former shall not be remembered, nor,
come into mind." Again: " Behold, the days come,
saith the Lord, that I will make a *new* covenant with
the house of Israel and with the house of Judah. . . . I
will put My law in their inward parts, and write it in
their hearts; and will be their God, and they shall be
My people." And again : " A *new* heart will I give
you, and a *new* spirit will I put within you; and I will
take away the stony heart out of your flesh, and I will
give you an heart of flesh. And I will put My Spirit
within you, and cause you to walk in My statutes, and

ye shall keep My judgments and do them."[1]   In the
text, St. Paul declares the fulfilment of these promises
in the Gospel.   "If any man be in Christ, he is a *new*
creature ; *old things are passed away,*" as the heavens
and earth shall pass away, at the end of the world ;
"behold, all things are become *new.*"   And hence he
calls Christ, not only "the Image of the Invisible God,"
but also "the *first-born* of every creature ;" or, as He
calls Himself in the book of Revelation, "the *beginning*
of the creation of God."[2]   St. Paul also speaks of
"the *new* and living way which He hath consecrated
for us through His flesh ;" of Christians having "put
off the old man with his deeds," and having "put on
the *new* man, which is renewed in knowledge, after
the Image of Him that created him ;" of "*newness* of
life," and "*newness* of spirit ;" of "ministers of the
New Testament, not of the letter, but of the Spirit ;"
and of our being God's "workmanship, *created* in
Christ Jesus unto good works."[3]   Elsewhere he says,
that true and availing "circumcision is that of the
heart, in the Spirit and not in the letter, whose praise
is not of men, but of God ;" and that "circumcision is
nothing, and uncircumcision is nothing, but the keeping
the commandments of God."[4]

Now it may be asked, Is there not some contrariety
in these statements ?   The Gospel is said to be a *new*
covenant, and yet, after all, it is to consist in "walking

<hr>

[1] Isa. lxv. 17.   Jer. xxxi. 31, 33.   Ez. xxxvi. 26, 27.

[2] Col. i. 15.   Rev. iii. 14.

[3] Heb. x. 20.   Col. iii. 9, 10.   Rom. vi. 4 ; vii. 6.   2 Cor. iii. 6
Eph. 2. 10.

[4] Rom. ii. 29.   1 Cor. vii. 19.

in God's statutes" and "doing His judgments," and "keeping His commandments," and being "created unto good works." Now these were but the terms of the old covenant: "Fear God and keep His commandments;" "If thou wilt enter into life, keep the commandments;" "The man that doeth those things shall live by them."[1] If the new Covenant be of works too, how is the Gospel other than the Law? how can it justly be called new? If the way of salvation be now what it ever has been, how are we gainers? What privilege is there in being brought under the Gospel? What has Christ done for us? Hence some persons have concluded that salvation under the Gospel is *not* of works; and in confirmation of this they urge, that St. Paul elsewhere speaks expressly of salvation as being not of works but of faith; and they allege that faith *is* a new way of salvation, though works of obedience are not and cannot be.

Now there can be no doubt at all that salvation is by faith, and that its being by faith is one of those special circumstances which make the Gospel a new covenant; but still it may be by works also; for, to use a familiar illustration, obedience is the *road* to heaven, and faith the *gate*. Those who attempt to be saved simply without works, are like persons who should attempt to travel to a place, not along the road, but across the fields. If we wish to get to our journey's end, we shall keep to the road; but even then we may go the *wrong* road. This was the case with the Jews. They professed to go along the road of works,—they

---

[1] Eccles. xii. 13. Rom. x. 5.

did not wander into the fields,—so far well: but they took the wrong road. That particular road of which faith is the gate, that particular obedience, those particular works, which commence in faith, these are the only right and sure road to heaven. It is wrong to leave the road for the open country ; again, it is wrong to go along the wrong road ;—but it is not wrong to go along the right road. And in like manner it is sinful to attempt no obedience whatever ; it is blind perversity to attempt obedieuce by the Jewish law or the law of nature ; but it is not sinful, it is not perverse, it is nothing else than wisdom, nothing else than true godliness, to follow after that obedience which is of faith.

The illustration may be pursued further. A road may want repairing,—it may get worse and worse as we go on, till it ceases to be a road : it may fall off from a road into a lane, from a lane to a path, or a wild heath, or a marsh ; or it may be cut off by high impassable mountains ; so that a person who attempts that way will never arrive at his journey's end. This was the case with the works of the Law by which the Jews thought to gain heaven,—this is the case with all works done in our natural strength : they are like a road over fens or precipices, which is sure to fail us. At first we might seem to go on well, but we should find at length that we made no progress. We should never get to our journey's end. Our best obedience in our own strength is worth nothing ; it is altogether unsound, it is ever failing, it never grows firmer, it never can be reckoned on, it does nothing well, it has nothing in it pleasing or acceptable to God :—and not only so, it is the obedience of souls born and living under God's wrath, for a state of nature is a state of wrath. On the other hand, obedience which is done in faith is done with the aid of the Holy Spirit; it is holy and acceptable in God's sight; it grows habitual and consistent; it tends to possess the soul wholly; and it leads straight onward to heaven. This was the very promise of the Gospel as the prophet Isaiah announces it. " An highway shall be there and a way, and it shall be called the *way of holiness :* the unclean shall not pass over it . . . the way-faring men, though fools, shall not err therein." [1] This being understood, we shall have no difficulty in under-standing St. Paul's language. The way of salvation is by works, as under the Law, but it is by " works which spring out of faith," and which come of " the inspira-tion of the Spirit." It is because works are living and spiritual, from the heart, and by faith, that the Gospel is a new covenant. Hence in the passages above quoted we are told again and again of "the law *in our inward parts;* " a new *heart;* " "a new *spirit ;* " the Holy "*Spirit within us ;* " " newness of *life*," and " circum-cision of the *heart* in the Spirit." And hence St. Paul says, that though we have not been " saved by works," yet we are " *created* unto *good* works ; " and that " the blood of Christ purges the conscience from *dead* works to *serve* the *living* God." Salvation then is not by dead works, but by living works. The Jews could but do dead works ; but Christians can do good and spiri-tual works. The Gospel Covenant, then, is both a new

[1] Isa. xxxv. 8   [2] Heb. ix. 14.

way and not a new way. It is not a new way, seeing it is *in* works : it is a new way, in that it is *by* faith. It is, as St. Paul words it, the " obedience of faith ; "— new because of faith, old because of obedience.

And thus there is no opposition between St. Paul and St. James. St. James says, that justification is by works, and St. Paul that it is by· faith : but, observe, St. James does not say that it is by dead or Jewish works ; he mentions expressly *both* faith *and* works ; he only says, "not faith *only* but works also : "— and St. Paul is far from denying it is by works, he only says that it is by faith and denies that it is by *dead* works. And what proves this, among other circumstances, is, that he never calls those works, which he condemns and puts aside, *good* works, but simply works : whenever he speaks of good works in his Epistles, he speaks of Christian works ; not of Jewish. On the whole, then, salvation is both by faith and by works. St. James says, not *dead* faith, and St. Paul, not *dead* works. St. James, " not by faith *only*," for that *would* be dead faith : St. Paul, " not by works only," for such *would* be dead works. Faith alone can make works living ; works alone can make faith living. Take away either, and you take away both ;—he alone has faith who has works,—he alone has works who has faith.

It is not at all wonderful, then, that though the way of salvation under the Gospel is new, still in certain respects it is still what the Jews, nay, and what the heathen thought it to be. The way of justification has in all religions been by means of works ; so it is under the Gospel ; but in the Gospel alone it is by the means of good works.

However, this statement, simple and obvious as it is, is a hard saying to many persons, who think that the way of salvation should be altogether new under the Gospel, altogether different from what is prescribed under other religions; whereas they think little has been gained for us by Christ, if after all He has left us, as before, to be saved by obedience. This is a difficulty with them. They think Christianity is made Jewish, or almost heathen, if salvation is attained by what is the old way; and this being the case, I shall make some remarks, with the hope of reconciling the mind to it.

I observe, then, that whether it came from Noah after the flood or not, so it is, that all religions, the various heathen religions as well as the Mosaic religion, have many things in them which are very much the same. They seem to come from one common origin, and so far have the traces of truth upon them. They are all branches, though they are corruptions and perversions, of that patriarchal religion which came from God. And of course the Jewish religion came entirely and immediately from God. Now God's works are like each other, not different; if, then, the Gospel is from God, and the Jewish religion was from God, and the various heathen religions in their first origin were from God, it is not wonderful, rather it is natural, that they should have in many ways a resemblance one with another. And, accordingly, that the Gospel is in certain points like the religions which preceded it, is but an argument that "God is One, and that there is none other but He;"—the difference between them being that the heathen religions are a true religion corrupted; the Jewish, a true religion dead; and Christianity, the true religion living and perfect. The heathen thought to be saved by works, so did the Jews, so do Christians; but the heathen took the works of darkness for good works, the Jews thought cold, formal and scanty works to be good works, and Christians believe that works done in the Spirit of grace, the fruit of faith, and offered up under the meritorious intercession of Christ, that these only are good works, but that these really *are* good:—so that while the heathen thinks to be saved by sin, and the Jew by self, the Christian relies on the Spirit of Him who died on the Cross for him. Thus they differ; but they all agree in thinking that works are the means of salvation; they differ in respect to the quality of these works.

Let us take some parallel instances in religious doctrine and worship, for they abound.

1. For example : Religion, considered in itself, cannot but have much which is the same in all systems, true and false. It is the worship of God. This involves saying prayers, postures of devotion, and the like, whatever the particular worship be; nor is the Gospel less a new covenant, because it retains these old usages, unless it ceases to be new, because it retains religion. While man is man, it could not be otherwise. These observances are right when performed well, evil when performed ill; evil as performed by the heathen, right as performed by Christians. The heathen worship devils, as St. Paul tells us. As is their god, such is their service. The Gospel came to

destroy the worship of devils, not to destroy worship; we do not cease to have a new worship, because we worship, not devils, but Almighty God.

2. Again, meetings for worship have been in all religions from the first. But it does not follow from this that "old things" have not been made to pass away, till coming to church is denounced as a sin. On the contrary, St. Paul expressly tells us *not* to forsake the assembling of ourselves together, though " all things have become new." What had been done of old time for bad purposes or in a bad way, is to be done for a holy purpose and in a heavenly way under the Gospel. A new life is infused into what once was evil, or at least profitless; so that, whereas of old time men came together to worship as " dry bones," in consequence of the creative power of Christ, " the dead bones live."

3. Again, religion has ever existed in a large organized body, with orders and officers, with ministers and people. It has always exercised an influence over the State, and it has ever been what is called established, or had rank and property. Now there is abundant evidence that this was intended to be the condition of religion under the Gospel, in spite of its being a new religion. Ranks existed from the first,—Apostles, Evangelists, Prophets, Bishops, and Deacons, as we read in Scripture. And property was held by the Church, for the rich gave up their wealth, and laid it at the Apostles' feet. And St. Paul used his privilege as a citizen of Rome. Here again, then, though salvation be of faith, and religion be spiritual, and old things be passed away, and all

things have become new, yet the old framework remains as far as this, that there are men set apart to preach the Gospel, and that they " live by the Gospel."

4. Again, all religions, before the Gospel came, had their mysteries; I mean alleged disclosures of Truth, which could not be fully understood all at once, if at all, and which were open to some more than to others. The Gospel, though it be light and liberty, has not materially altered things here. It has mysteries as we all know; such as the doctrines of the Holy Trinity, and the Incarnation. And these mysteries cannot be equally entered into by all, but in proportion as men are humble and holy, and intellectually gifted, and blessed with leisure. St. Paul speaks of " the hidden wisdom;" and declares that " the natural man receiveth not the things of the Spirit of God, for they are foolishness unto him; neither can he know them, because they are spiritually discerned." And elsewhere he declines to speak to the Hebrews about Melchizedec, " of whom " he had " many things to say, and hard to be uttered, seeing " they were " dull of hearing." [1]

5. Again, religions before Christ came ever had holy days and festivals, both among heathen and Jews. The Gospel has not done away with holy days, only it has changed them, and made them more truly holy. For instance, it has not destroyed the Feast of one day in seven, or the Lord's day; not to mention other instances. This is the more remarkable, because St. Paul's words are at first sight very strong against the observance, under the Gospel, of any days above others,

[1] 1 Cor. ii. 14. Heb. v. 11.

as a matter of religion. He finds fault with the Galatians, because they observe " days, and months, and times, and years." And he bids the Colossians not to let any man " judge them in meat or in drink, or in respect of an holy day, or of the new moon, or of the Sabbath days, which are a shadow of things to come, but the body is of Christ." [1] Who would not, at first sight, suppose from these words, that all holy days, all holy seasons, were to be done away, under the Gospel, as mere shadows,—Sunday, Christmas-day, Easter-tide, Lent, and all the rest ? Yet it is not so. The Apostles in the Acts, and St. John in the Revelation, observe and recognise the Lord's day as a Gospel festival. Jewish days *are* shadows, but Christian are not ; just as Jewish works, or works of the Law, avail not, but Christian works avail. The weekly festival is not one of the " old things " which have " passed away " in Christ, neither have righteous works. The Sabbath has " become new " by becoming the Lord's day ; works become new, by becoming spiritual.

6. Again, washing with water was a heathen rite of purification, and also a Jewish rite. Yet it remains under the Gospel ; and with the same change. The " divers washings " of the Jews were " carnal ordinances ;" [2] but Baptism, our washing, is a washing of the Spirit ; and because the former are annulled, it does not follow that the latter should be. On the contrary, our Lord distinctly commanded His Apostles, " Go ye and teach all nations, baptizing them." [3]

[1] Gal. iv. 10. Col. ii. 16, 17.
[2] Heb. ix. 10.   [3] Matt. xxviii. 19.

7. Once more. The heathen had temples; the Jews had a temple; and our Lord said to the Samaritan woman, that the hour was coming when the true worshippers should worship, not in the temple at Jerusalem, but "in spirit and in truth." But this did not mean that there were to be no Christian temples, or churches, as we call them; at least it has never been taken so to mean. All it would seem to mean is, that the Jewish temple is not like a Christian temple, but differs in some essential points.

I have said enough to explain St. Paul's statement in the text, that "old things are passed away," and "all things new" under the Gospel. By all things being "*new*" is meant that they are *renewed;* by "old things *passing away*" is meant that they are *changed.* The substance remains; the form, mode, quality, and circumstances are different and more excellent. Religion has still forms, ordinances, precepts, mysteries, duties, assemblies, festivals, and temples as of old time; but, whereas all these were dead and carnal before, now, since Christ came, they have a life in them. He has brought life to the world; He has given life to religion; He has made everything spiritual and true by His touch, full of virtue, full of grace, full of power: so that ordinances, works, forms, which before were unprofitable, now, by the inward meritorious influence of His blood imparted to them, avail for our salvation.

This one point, in addition, is clear from what has been said; that if all Christian worship is "in spirit and in truth," nothing has a place under the Gospel which is *not* spiritual. It is very inconsistent then, to say, as some people do say, that Baptism should be observed, and yet that it does not convey Divine grace, and is a mere outward ordinance ; for if so, it is nothing better than a Jewish rite, and instead of being observed, it ought to be abolished altogether.   And again, unless the Church itself, and the ministerial order attached to it, be a means of grace and the instrument of the Holy Ghost, they are no better than the Jewish temple and the Jewish priests, which have come to nought, and have no part in the spiritual system of the Gospel. And so, in like manner, works of obedience also, if they are no better than "the works of the Law," which cannot justify ; if they are not pleasing to God, if they be filthy rags, as some persons say, and as the works of nature *are* ; if so, then I do not see that they need be attempted at all ; for all works of the Law are done away.   Everything is done away in the Gospel but what is spirit and truth ; and our works, our ordinances, our discipline, are spirit and truth, or they are done away.

And, lastly, hereby we see why justification must be of faith : because, as Christ, by means of His Spirit, makes a new beginning in us, so faith, on our part, receives that new beginning, and co-operates with Him. And it is the only principle which can do this : for as things spiritual are unseen, so faith is in its very nature that which apprehends and uses things unseen.   We renounce our old unprofitable righteousness, which is from Adam, and accept, through faith, that new righteousness which is imparted by the Spirit ; or, in St. Paul's words, "we, through the Spirit, wait for the hope of righteousness by faith."

To conclude. Let us think much, and make much, of the grace of God; let us beware of receiving it in vain; let us pray God to prosper it in our hearts, that we may bring forth much fruit. We see how grace wrought in St. Paul: it made him labour, suffer, and work righteousness almost above man's nature. This was not his own doing; it was not through his own power. He says himself, "Yet not I, but the grace of God which was in me." God's grace was "sufficient for him." It was its triumph in him, that it made him quite another man from what he was before. May God's grace be efficacious in us also. Let us aim at doing nothing in a dead way; let us beware of dead works, dead forms, dead professions. Let us pray to be filled with the spirit of love. Let us come to Church joyfully; let us partake the Holy Communion adoringly; let us pray sincerely; let us work cheerfully; let us suffer thankfully; let us throw our heart into all we think, say, and do; and may it be a spiritual heart! This is to be a new creature in Christ; this is to walk by faith.

SERMON XIII.

THE STATE OF SALVATION.

" That ye put on the new man, which after God is created in righteous-
ness and true holiness."

THESE words express very strongly a doctrine which
is to be found in every part of the New Testament,
that the Gospel covenant is the means of introducing us
into a state of life so different from that in which we
were born, and should otherwise continue, that it may
not unfitly be called a new creation. As that which
is created differs from what is not yet created, so the
Christian differs from the natural man. He is brought
into a new world, and, as being in that new world, is
invested with powers and privileges which he absolutely
had not in the way of nature. By nature his will is
enslaved to sin, his soul is full of darkness, his conscience is under the wroth of God; peace, hope, love,
faith, purity, he has not; nothing of heaven is in him;
nothing spiritual nothing of light and life. But in
Christ all these blessings are given: the will and the

power; the heart and the knowledge; the light of faith, and the obedience of faith. As far as a being can be changed without losing his identity, as far as it is sense to say that an existing being can be new created, so far has man this gift when the grace of the Gospel has its perfect work and its maturity of fruit in him. A brute differs less from a man, than does man, left to himself with his natural corruption allowed to run its course, differ from man fully formed and perfected by the habitual indwelling of the Holy Spirit.

Hence, in the text, the Apostle speaks of the spiritual state which Christ has bought for us, as being a "new creature in righteousness and true holiness." Elsewhere he says, "If any man be in Christ he is a new creature; old things are passed away; behold all things are become new." Elsewhere, "Be ye transformed by the renewing of your mind." Elsewhere, "Ye are dead, and your life is hid with Christ in God." Elsewhere, "We are buried with Him by baptism into death; that, like as Christ was raised up from the dead by the glory of the Father, even so we also should walk in newness of life."[1]

What then is this new state in which a Christian finds himself, compared with the state of nature? It is worth the inquiry.

Now, first, there ought to be no difficulty in our views about it so far as this: that there *is* a certain new state, and that a state of salvation; and that Christ came to bring into it all whom He had chosen out of the world. Christ "gave Himself for our sins (says St. Paul), that

2 Cor. v. 17. Rom. xii. 2. Col. iii. 3. Rom. vi. 4.

He might deliver us from the present evil world." He "hath delivered us from the power of darkness, and hath translated us into the kingdom of His dear Son." He came "to gather together in one the children of God, which are scattered abroad." "As many as received Him, to them gave He power to become the sons of God."[1] This is most clear. There can be no doubt, at all that there is a certain state of grace now vouchsafed to us, who are born in sin and the children of wrath, such that those who are to be saved hereafter are (to speak generally) those, and those only, who are placed in that saving state here. I am not going on to the question, whether or not there is a visible Church; but I insist only on this, that it has not seemed fit to Almighty God to transplant His elect at once from this world and from a state of nature to the eternal happiness of heaven. He does not suffer them to die as they were born, and then, on death, change them outwardly and inwardly; but He brings them into a saving state here, preparatory to heaven;—a state which the Catechism calls a "state of salvation;" and which St. Luke denotes, when he says, "The Lord added daily to the Church such as should be saved;"[2] that is, persons called to salvation, placed in a saving state.

No one ought to deny this; though in this day, when all kinds of error abound, some persons seem to have taken up a notion that the world was fully reconciled all at once by Christ's death at the very time of it, and wholly transferred into a state of acceptance; so that there is no new state necessary now for those who shall

<hr>

[1] Gal. i. 4. Col. i. 13. John xi. 52; i. 12.   [2] Acts ii. 47.

ultimately be benefited by it; that they have but to do their duty, and they will be rewarded accordingly; whereas it does certainly appear, from such texts of Scripture as have been quoted, that there is a certain state, or kingdom of Christ, into which all must enter here who shall be saved hereafter. We cannot attain to heaven hereafter, without being in this new kingdom here; we cannot escape from the miseries and horrors of the Old Adam, except by being brought into this Kingdom, as into an asylum, and there remaining.

And further, this new state is one of "righteousness and true holiness," as the text speaks. Christ brings us into it by coming to us through His Spirit; and, as His Spirit is holy, we are holy, if we are in the state of grace. Christ is present in that heart which He visits with His grace. So that to be in His kingdom is to be in righteousness, to live in obedience, to breathe, as it were, an atmosphere of truth and love.

Now it is necessary to insist upon this also: for here again some men go wrong; and while they go so far as to acknowledge that there is a new state, or kingdom, into which souls must be brought, in order to salvation, yet they consider it as a state, not of holiness and righteousness, but merely or mainly of acceptance with God. It has been maintained by some persons, that human nature, even when regenerate, is not, and cannot be, really holy; nay, that it is idle to suppose that, even with the aid of the Holy Spirit, it can do any thing really good in any degree; that our best actions are sins; and that we are always sinning, not only in slighter matters, but so as to need pardon in all we do, in the same sense in which we needed it when we were as yet unregenerate; and, consequently, that it is vain to try to be holy and righteous, or, rather, that it is presumptuous.

Now, of course it is plain, that even the best of men are full of imperfections and failings; so far is undeniable. But, consider, by nature we are in a state of death. Now, is this the state of our hearts under the Gospel? Surely not; for, while "to be carnally minded is death," "to be spiritually minded is life and peace." I mean, that the state of salvation in which we stand is not one in which "our righteousnesses are" what the prophet calls "filthy rags," but one in which we can help sinning unto death,—can help sinning in the way men do sin when left in a state of nature. If we do so sin, we *cease* to be in that state of salvation; we fall back into a state resembling our original state of wrath, and must pass back again from wrath to grace (if it be so), as we best may, in such ways as God has appointed: whereas it is not an uncommon notion at this time, that a man may be an habitual sinner, and yet be in a state of salvation, and in the kingdom of grace. And this doctrine many more persons hold than think they do; not in words, but in heart. They think that faith is all in all; that faith, if they have it, blots out their sins as fast as they commit them. They sin in distinct acts in the morning,—their faith wipes all out; at noon,—their faith still avails; and in the evening,—still the same. Or they remain contentedly in sinful habits or practices, under the dominion of sin, not warring against it, in ignorance what is sin and what is not; and they think that the only business of a Christian is, not to be holy, but to have faith, and to think and speak of Christ; and thus, perhaps, they are really living, whether by habit or by act, in extortion, avarice, envy, rebellious pride, self-indulgence, or worldliness, and neither know nor care to know it. If they sin in habits, they are not aware of these at all; if by acts, instead of viewing them one and all together, they take them one by one, and set their faith against each separate act. So far has this been carried, that some men of name in the world have, before now, laid it down as a great and high principle, that there is no mortal sin but one, and that is want of faith; and have hereby meant, not that he who commits mortal sin cannot be said to have faith, but that he who has faith cannot be said to commit mortal sin; or, to speak more clearly, they have, in fact, defined a state of salvation to be nothing more or less than a state *in which* our sins are forgiven; a state of mere acceptance, not of substantial holiness. Persons who hold these opinions, consider that the great difference between a state of nature and a state of salvation is, that, in a state of nature when we sin, we are not forgiven (which is true); but that, in a state of salvation, when we sin, our sins are forgiven us, because we *are* in that state. On the other hand, I would maintain from Scripture, that a state of salvation is so far from being a state in which sins of every kind are forgiven, that it is a state in which there are not sins of every kind to forgive; and that, if a man commit them, so far from being forgiven *by* his state, he falls at once *from* his state by committing them; so far from being justified by faith, he, for that very reason, has not faith whereby to justify him. I say, our state of grace is a state of holiness; not one in which we may be *pardoned*, but in which we are *obedient*. He who acts unworthily of it, is not sheltered by it, but forfeits it. It is a state in which power is given us to act rightly, and therefore punishment falls on us if we act wrongly.

This is plain, from Scripture, on many reasons; of which I will here confine myself to one or two.

1. Let us first consider such Parables of our Lord as speak of the Christian state, to see what its characteristics are. These will be found not to recognise at all the case of instable, variable minds, falling repeatedly into gross sins, and saved by that state of grace in which they have been placed. The Christian state does not shelter a man who sins, but it lets him drop. Just as we cannot hold in our hands a thing in flames, but however dear it be to us, though it be a child, we are forced at length to let it go; so wilful sin burns like fire, and the Church drops us, however unwillingly, when we sin wilfully. Not our faith, not our past services, not God's past mercies, avail to keep us in a state of grace, if "we sin wilfully after receiving the knowledge of the truth."[1] Now I say, agreeably with this, we shall find our Saviour's parables divide Christians into two states, those who continue in God's favour, and those who lose it; and those who continue in it are said

<hr>

[1] Heb. x. 26.

to be, not those who merely have repentance and faith, who sin, but ever wash out their sins by coming for pardon, but those who do not sin ;—not those whose one great aim is to obtain *forgiveness*, but those who (though they abound in infirmities, and so far have much to be forgiven) yet are best *described* by saying that they aim at *increasing* their talents, aim at " laying up for themselves a good foundation for the time to come, that they may lay hold of eternal life."[1]

For example, in our Saviour's first parable, who is he who builds his house upon a rock? not he who has faith merely, but he, who having doubtless faith to begin the work, has faith also strong enough to perfect it; who " heareth *and doeth.*"

Again, in the parable of the Sower, the simple question considered is, who they are who profit by what they have received; what a Christian has to do is represented as a *work*, a process which has a beginning, middle, and end; a consistent course of obedience, not a state in which we have done nothing more at the end of our lives than at the beginning, except sin the oftener, according to its length. In that parable one man is said not to admit the good seed; a second admits it, but its root withers; a third goes further, the seed strikes root, and shoots upwards, but its leaves and blossoms get entangled and overlaid with thorns. The fourth takes root, shoots upwards, and does more, bears fruit to perfection. This then is the Christian's great aim, viz. not to come short after grace given him. This forms his peculiar danger, and his special

---

[1] 1 Tim. vi. 19.

dread. Of course he is not secure from peril of gross sin; of course he is continually defiled with sins of infirmity; but whereas, how to be forgiven is the main inquiry for the natural man, so, how to fulfil his calling, how to answer to grace given, how to increase his Lord's money, how to attain, this is the great problem of man regenerate. Faith gained him pardon; but works gain him a reward.

Again, the Net had two kinds of fish, good and bad, just and wicked; they differ in character and conduct; whereas men allow themselves to speak as if, in point of moral condition, the saved and the reprobate were pretty much on a level; the real difference being, that the one have faith appropriating Christ's merits, and a spiritual conviction of their own perishing state, and the other have not. And so I might go on to the parables of the Ten Virgins, the Talents, and others, and show in like manner that the state of a Christian, as our Lord contemplates it, is one in which he is, not lamenting the victories of sin, but working out salvation; beginning, continuing, and at last perfecting, a course of obedience.

2. This being the doctrine of the Gospels, we shall understand why it is that so little is said in the Epistles of the sins of Christians. Indeed, no one can be sufficiently aware, till he inquires into the subject, how very few texts can be produced from the Apostles' writings containing a promise of forgiveness when Christians sin.[1] And yet this apparent omission is not difficult to explain. They had sins before they

---

[1] *Vide* of these Sermons, Vol. iv. Serm. vii.

were Christians; they were forgiven that they might not sin again. St. Paul and his brethren never pray that Christians' sins may be pardoned, but that they may fulfil their calling. Their description of the state of the Church is almost like an account of Angels and the spirits of the just. "Our conversation is in heaven," says St. Paul, thus summing up in few words what almost all his Epistles testify to us. We hear of their "glorying in tribulations," their being "alive from the dead," their "joy and peace in believing," their being "fruitful in every good work," their "increasing in the knowledge of God," their "work of faith, and labour of love, and patience of hope." This is a picture of those whom the Apostle acknowledges as true Christians; as if in the case of true Christians gross transgression were impossible. They were far beyond that; what they had to avoid was shortcoming in the end. They were day by day to lessen the distance between themselves and their goal. They were to produce something positive, and they were gifted with the grace of the Holy Spirit for this purpose. There was nothing generous, nothing grateful, nothing of the high temper of faith, in sitting at home and merely praying for pardon. This might be well enough, it was all that they could do, while they were in a state of unassisted nature, in the house of bondage, with fetters upon them, and the iron entering into them. But their chains had been struck off; they could work, they could run; and they had a work to do, a road to journey. If they wilfully transgressed, they *left* the road, they *abandoned* the work. Then they were like Demas, who went back, and they had to be restored; to be pardoned, not *in* the state of grace, but, if I may so say, *into* it.

3. Let us now turn our thoughts to St. John's description of the Christian state. For instance, in his first Epistle he expressly tells us, " Whosoever is born of God *sinneth not*, but he that is begotten of God keepeth himself, and that wicked one toucheth him not."[1] Such is the state of the true Christian; he is not only born again, but is born of God. All who are baptized, indeed, are born of God, as well as born again; but those who fall into sin, though they cannot undo what once has been, and are still born again, yet they are born again to their greater condemnation, and, therefore, not born again of God any longer, but, till they repent, born again unto judgment. But he in whom the divine birth is realized, "sinneth not, but keepeth himself," and what is the consequence? "that wicked one toucheth him not:" why? because he is in the kingdom of God. Satan cannot touch any one who keeps within that kingdom. God has "translated us from the power of darkness into the kingdom of His dear Son." It is by seducing us out of that kingdom that Satan destroys us; but while we continue within the sheepfold, the wolf cannot harm us. And hence the prophecy, which belongs to all Christ's followers in their degree as well as to our Lord Himself, "He shall give His Angels charge over thee to keep thee *in all thy ways*." "He shall deliver thee from the snare of the hunter, and from the noisome pestilence. He shall defend thee under His wings, and thou shalt be

[1] 1 John v. 18.

safe under His feathers. There shall no evil happen unto thee, neither shall any plague come nigh thy dwelling. Thou shalt go upon the lion and adder: the young lion and the dragon shalt thou tread under thy feet."[1] The serpent can but tempt, he cannot harm us, while we are in the paradise of God. This, I repeat, is the state of salvation, of which the Catechism speaks, and St. John assures us that they only are thus kept from the touch of that wicked one, who are so born of God as not to sin.

Again, "Whosoever is born of God, doth not commit sin, for His *seed remaineth* in him; and he cannot sin, because he is born of God." Again He says, "He that saith he abideth in Him, ought himself also so to walk even as He walked." Again, "If that which ye have heard from the beginning shall abide in you, ye also shall abide in the Son and in the Father." What is this but to say, that if it did not, they were no longer in grace? "Whosoever abideth in Him, sinneth not." Again, "We know that we have passed from death unto life, because we love the brethren."[2]

And on the other hand the same Apostle plainly declares, that they who do sin are *not* in a state of grace. For instance, "If we say that we have fellowship with Him, and walk in darkness, we lie, and do not the truth." "He that saith he is in the light, and hateth his brother, is in darkness even until now." Again, "Whosoever committeth sin, transgresseth also the law, for sin is the transgression of the law. . . . Whosoever sinneth, hath not seen Him, neither known

[1] Ps. xci. 11, 3, 10, 13.   [2] 1 John iii. 9; ii. 6, 24; iii. 6, 14.

Him." "He that committeth sin is of the devil." "Whosoever transgresseth, and abideth not in the doctrine of Christ, hath not God."[1]

You see here are two states distinctly mentioned, and two states only; a state of grace, and a state of wrath; and he who sins in the state of grace, falls at once into the state of wrath. There is no such person under the Gospel as a "justified sinner," to use a phrase which is sometimes to be heard. If he is justified and accepted, he has ceased to be a sinner. The Gospel only knows of justified saints; if a saint sins, he ceases to be justified, and becomes a *condemned* sinner. Some persons, I repeat, speak as if men might go on sinning, and sinning ever so grossly, yet without falling from grace, without the necessity of taking direct and formal means to get back again. They *can* get back, praised be God, but still they *have* to get back, and the error I am speaking of is forgetfulness that they *have* fallen, and *have* to return.

4. That they who sin fall into a hopeless state,—that is hopeless *while* they continue in it, so that they can only gain hope *by leaving* it,—is shown more forcibly still in St. Paul's Epistle to the Hebrews. For instance, the inspired writer says, "If we sin wilfully, after that we have received the knowledge of the truth, there remaineth no more sacrifice for sins, but a certain fearful looking for of judgment and fiery indignation, which shall devour" or eat "the adversaries."[2] Here it is expressly said that wilful sin against knowledge does not leave us as it found us. We cannot receive pardon

1 John i. 6; ii. 9; iii. 4, 6, 8. 2 John 9.   2 Heb. x 27.

as we received it at the first, freely and instantly, merely on faith, we are thrown out of grace; and though our prospects are not at once hopeless, yet our *state* is hopeless, tends to perdition, nay, in itself, is perdition, one in which, *while* we are in it, we are lost. Hence all through this Epistle St. Paul, equally with St. John, speaks of but two states, a state of grace and glory in the heavenly Jerusalem, a communion with God, Christ, Angels, saints departed, saints on earth; and, on the other hand, a state of wrath; and he warns his brethren that they cannot sin without falling into the state of wrath. "We are not of them that draw back unto perdition, but of them that believe to the saving of the soul."[1]   He does not speak of sin and sinners tenderly; he does not merely say, "If you sin, you are an evidence of human frailty; you are *inconsistent;* you ought to keep from sin from *gratitude;* you should be deeply *humbled* at your sins; you should betake yourselves to the atonement of Christ if you sin." All this is true, but it would be short of the real state of the case; and St. Paul, therefore, says much more: "If you sin wilfully, you throw yourselves out of God's kingdom; you by the very act disinherit yourselves, you bring yourselves into a dreadful region;" and he leaves it to them to draw the inference what they ought to do to get back again. He urges against them "the terrors of the Lord." He bids them not deceive themselves, for sinners have no inheritance in the kingdom. Accordingly he warns them "to look diligently, lest any man come short of the grace of God;" and to "fear, lest a promise

---

[1] Heb. x. 39.

being left us of entering into His rest, any of them should seem to *come short* of it."[1]

Such is the new state of "righteousness and true holiness," in which Christians are created, and such is the state of those who draw back from it; and if any one asks whether St. Paul does not say that "by *faith* we stand?" I answer, as I have already answered, that doubtless faith does keep us in a state of grace, and is the means of blotting out for us those sins which we commit in it. But *what* are those sins which we do commit? Sins of infirmity;—all other sins faith itself excludes. If we do commit greater sins, we have not faith. Faith we cannot use to blot out the greater sins, for faith we have not at all, if we commit such. That faith which has not power over our hearts to keep us from transgressing, has not power with God to keep Him from punishing.

To conclude. This is our state :—Christ has healed each of us, and has said to us, "See thou sin no more, lest a worse thing come unto thee."[2] If we commit sin, we fall,—not at once back again into the unredeemed and lost world; no, but at least we fall out of the kingdom, though for a while we may linger on the skirts of the kingdom. We fall into what will in the event lead us back *into* the lost world, or rather into what is worse, unless we turn heavenward, and extricate ourselves from our fearful state as speedily as we can. We come into what may be called the passage or vestibule of hell; a place full of those unclean spirits who "seek rest and find none," and rejoice in getting posses-

Heb. xii. 15 ; iv. 1.   [2] John v. 14.

sion of souls, from which they were once cast out. We are no longer in the light of God's countenance, and though (blessed be His Name) doubtless we can through His help get back into it, yet we have to get back into it;—and then the whole subject becomes an anxious and serious one. Yes, it is indeed very serious, considering how the common run of Christians go on. If wilful sin throws us out of a state of grace, and if men do sin wilfully, and then forget that they have done so, and years pass away, and they merely smooth over what has happened by forgetting it, and assume that they are still in a state of grace, making no efforts by true repentance to be put into it again, only assuming that they are in it; and then go about their duties as Christians, just as if they were still God's children in the sense in which Baptism made them, and were not presumptuously intruding without leave, and not by the door, into a house whence they have been sent out; and if they so live and so die, what are we to say about them? Alas! what a dreadful thought it is, that there may be numbers outwardly in the Christian Church, nay, who at present are in a certain sense religious men, who, nevertheless, have no principle of *growth* in them, because they have sinned, and never duly repented. They may be under a disability for past sins, which they have never been at the pains to remove, or to attempt to remove. Alas! to think that they do not know their state at all and esteem themselves in the unreserved enjoyment of God's favour, when, after all, their religion is for the most part but the reflection from without upon their surface, not a light within them, or at least but the remains of grace once given.   O dreadful thought, if we are in the number!   O most dreadful thought, if an account lies against us in God's books, which we have never manfully encountered, never inquired into, never even prayed against, only and simply *forgotten;* which we leave to itself to be settled as it may; and if at any time some sudden memory of it comes across us, we think of it without fear, as if what has gone out of our minds had been forgotten of God also !—or even, as the way of some is, if, when we recollect any former sins of whatever kind, we palliate them, give them soft names, make excuses, saying they were done in youth or under great temptation, or cannot be helped now, or have been forsaken.   May God give us all grace ever to think of these things; to reflect on the brightness of that state in which God once placed us, its purity, its sweetness, its radiance, its beauty, its majesty, its glory: and to think, in contrast of the wretchedness and filthiness of that load of sin, with which our own wilfulness has burdened us: and to pray Him to show us how to unburden ourselves,—how to secure to ourselves again those gifts which, for what we know, we have forfeited.

SERMON XIV.

TRANSGRESSIONS AND INFIRMITIES.

HEB. x. 38.

" Now the just shall live by faith; but if any man draw back, My soul shall have no pleasure in him."

WARNINGS such as this would not be contained in Scripture, were there no danger of our drawing back, and thereby losing that "life" in God's presence which faith secures to us. The blessedness of a creature is to "live before God,"[1] to have an "access"[2] into the court of the King of kings, that state of grace and glory which Christ has purchased for us. Faith is the tenure upon which this divine life is continued to us: by faith the Christian lives, but if he draws back he dies; his faith profits him nothing; or rather, his drawing back to sin is a reversing of his faith; after which, God has no pleasure in him. And yet, clearly as this is stated in Scripture, men in all ages have fancied that they might sin grievously, yet maintain their Christian hope. They have comforted themselves with thoughts

[1] Gen. xvii. 18. [2] Rom. v. 2.

o 2

of the infinite mercy of God, as if He could not punish the sinner; or they have laid the blame of their sins on their circumstances; or they have hoped that zeal for the truth, or that almsgiving, would make up for a bad life; or they have relied upon repenting in time to come. And not the least subtle of such excuses is that which results from a doctrine popularly received at this day, that faith in Christ is compatible with a very imperfect state of holiness, or with unrighteousness, and avails for the pardon of an unrighteous life. So that a man may, if so be, go on pretty much like other men, with this only difference, that he has what he considers faith,—a certain spiritual insight into the Gospel scheme, a renunciation of his own merit, and a power of effectually pleading and applying to his soul Christ's atoning sacrifice, such as others have not;—that he sins indeed much as others, but then is deeply grieved that he sins; that he *would* be under the wrath of God as others are, had he not faith to remove it withal. And thus the necessity of a holy life is in fact put out of sight quite as fully as if he said in so many words, that it was not required; and a man may, if it so happen, be low-minded, sordid, worldly, arrogant, imperious, self-confident, impure, self-indulgent, ambitious or covetous, nay, may allow himself from time to time in wilful acts of sin which he himself condemns, and yet, by a great abuse of words, may be called spiritual.

Now I quite grant that there are sins which faith is the means of blotting out continually, so that the "just" still "lives" in God's sight in spite of them. There is no one but sins continually so far as this, that all that he does might be more perfect, entire, blameless than it is. We are all encompassed by infirmities, weaknesses, ignorances ; and all these besetting sins are certainly, as Scripture assures us, pardoned on our faith; but it is another thing to assert this of greater and more grievous sins, or what may be called transgressions. For faith keeps us from transgressions, and they who transgress, for that very reason, have not true and lively faith ; and, therefore, it avails them nothing that faith, as Scripture says, is imputed to Christians for righteousness, for they have not faith. Instead of faith blotting out transgressions, transgressions blot out faith. Faith, if it be true and lively, both precludes transgressions and gradually triumphs over infirmities; and while infirmities continue, it regards them with so perfect an hatred, as avails for their forgiveness, and is taken for that righteousness which it is gradually becoming. And such *is* a holy doctrine ; for it provides for our pardon without dispensing with our obedience.

This distinction in the character of sins, viz. that some argue absence of faith and involve the loss of God's favour, and that others do not, is a very important one to insist upon, even though we cannot in all cases draw the line and say what sins imply the want of faith, and what do not ; because, if we know that there *are* sins which do throw us out of grace, though we do not know *which* they are, this knowledge, limited as it is, will, through God's mercy, put us on our guard against acts of sin of any kind ; both from the dread we shall feel lest these in particular, whatever they are, may be of that fearful nature, and next, from knowing that at least they tend that way. The common mode of reasoning adopted by the religion of the day is this : some sins are compatible with true faith, viz. sins of infirmity ; therefore, wilful transgression, or what the text calls " departing " from God, is compatible with it also. Men do not, and say they cannot, draw the line ; and thus, from putting up with small sins, they go on to a sufferance of greater sins. Well, I would take the reverse way, and begin at the other end. I would force upon men's notice that there are sins which do forfeit grace ; and then if, as is objected, that we cannot draw the line between one kind of sin and another, this very circumstance will make us shrink not only from transgressions, but also from infirmities. From hatred and abhorrence of large sins, we shall, please God, go on to hate and abhor the small.

Now then let us betake ourselves to Scripture, in proof of this distinction between sin and sin. I say then this : first, that there are sins which forfeit a state of grace ; next, that there are sins which do not forfeit it ; and, lastly, that sins which do not forfeit it, nevertheless tend to forfeit it.

1. No one surely can doubt that there are sins which exclude a man, while he is under their power, from salvation. This is brought home to us by all that meets us on the very surface of the inspired text. " He that committeth sin, is of the devil," says St. John ; " whosoever doeth not righteousness, is not of God." And, again, St. Paul, " Many walk, of whom I have told you often, and now tell you even weeping, that they are the enemies of the Cross of Christ ; whose end is destruction."

Again, "Christ is of no effect unto you, whosoever of you are justified by the Law; ye are fallen from grace."[1] Again, in the text, "The just shall live by faith, but if he draw back, My soul shall have no pleasure in him." Here are instances, at first sight, of sins which forfeit our hope of salvation; but let me be more particular.

(1.) All habits of vice are such. For instance, St. Paul says, "Know ye not that the unrighteous shall not inherit the Kingdom of God? Be not deceived: neither fornicators, nor idolaters, nor adulterers, nor effeminate, nor drunkards," and so he proceeds, "shall inherit the kingdom of God."[2] As, then, Baptism made us "inheritors of the kingdom of heaven," so sins such as these forfeit that kingdom. Accordingly, the Apostle goes on, by way of contrast, to speak of what they had become in Christ,—"And such were some of you; but ye are washed, but ye are sanctified, but ye are justified."

(2.) Next, it is fearful to think (fearful, because, among ourselves at this day, men are almost blind to the sin), that covetousness is mentioned in connexion with sins of the flesh, as incurring forfeiture of grace equally with them. St. Paul says, "neither adulterers, nor effeminate, nor *covetous*." Again, to the Ephesians, "This ye know, that no whoremonger, nor unclean person, nor *covetous man*, who is an idolater, hath any inheritance in the kingdom of Christ and of God." This accords with our Lord's warning, "ye cannot serve God and mammon;"[3] as much as to say, If you serve

---

[1] John iii. 8, 10.   Phil. iii. 18, 19.   Gal. v. 4.
[2] 1 Cor. vi. 9, 10.   [3] Eph. v. 5.   Matt. vi. 24.

mammon, you forthwith quit God's service; you cannot serve two masters at once; you have passed into the kingdom of mammon, that is, of Satan.

(3.) All violent breaches of the law of charity are inconsistent with a state of grace; for the Apostle, in the places just cited, speaks of "thieves, revilers, and extortioners." In like manner St. John says in the Book of Revelations, "Without are dogs, and sorcerers, and *murderers.*"[1]

(4.) And in like manner all profaneness, heresy, and false worship; thus St. John speaks of "idolaters," with murderers; and St. Paul says that Esau, as being "a profane person," lost the blessing; and declares of all who "preach any other Gospel" than the true one, "Let him be accursed."[2]

(5.) And further, "hardness of heart," or going against light; according to the text, "Let us labour to enter into that rest, lest any man fall after the same example of unbelief;" and "To-day, if ye will hear his voice, harden not your hearts."[3]

Such are greater sins or transgressions. They are here specified, not as forming a complete list of such sins, which indeed cannot be given, but in proof of what ought not to be doubted, that there are sins which are not found in persons in a state of grace.

2. In the next place, that there are sins of infirmity, or such as do not throw the soul out of a state of salvation, is evident directly it is granted that there are sins which do; for no one will pretend to say that all sins exclude from grace, else no one can be saved, for

---

[1] Rev. xxii. 15.   [2] Heb. xii. 16. Gal. i. 8.   [3] Heb. iv. 7, 11.

there is no one who is sinless. However, Scripture expressly recognises sins of infirmity as distinct from transgressions, as shall now be shown.

For instance: St. Paul says to the Galatians, "The flesh lusteth against the Spirit, and the Spirit against the flesh; and these are contrary the one to the other, so that ye cannot do the things that ye would."[1] In these words he allows that it is possible for the power of the flesh and the grace of the Spirit to co-exist in the soul; neither the flesh quenching the Spirit, nor the Spirit all at once subduing the flesh. Here then is a sinfulness which is compatible with a state of salvation.

Again, the same Apostle says, that we have a High Priest who is "touched with the feeling of our *infirmities*," in that He had them Himself, *all but* their sin :— this implies that we have sinful infirmities, yet of that light nature that they can be said to be in substance partaken by One who was pure from all sin. Accordingly, in the next verse St. Paul bids us "come boldly to the throne of grace, that we may obtain mercy." Such words do not imply a return *into* a state of salvation, but pardon *in* that state, and they correspond to what he afterwards says, "Let us draw near with a true heart in full assurance of faith, having boldness to enter into the holiest by the blood of Jesus," that is, by a continual approach; or as he says to the Romans, By Christ "we have access," or admission, "by faith into this grace wherein we *stand*."[2]

---

[1] Gal. v. 17.
[2] Heb. iv. 15, 16; x. 19—22. Rom. v. 2.

In like manner he says, that "the Spirit helpeth our infirmities,"[1] whereas transgression on the contrary quenches the Spirit.

And somewhat parallel to this is his language about himself, when, after speaking of a trial to which he was subjected, he says that Christ said to him, " My grace is sufficient for thee, for My strength is made perfect in weakness ; " and he adds, " Most gladly therefore will I rather glory in my infirmities, that the power of Christ may rest upon me."[2]

And so in an earlier part of the same Epistle he says, apparently with the same meaning, " We have this treasure," the knowledge of the Gospel, " in earthen vessels, that the excellency of the power may be of God, and not of us."[3]

Sins of infirmity seem also intended in his exhortation to the Corinthians in another part of the same Epistle. After showing that righteousness has no fellowship with unrighteousness, and bidding them "be separate, and touch not the unclean thing," he adds, " Having therefore these promises, let us cleanse ourselves from all defilement of the flesh and spirit, *perfecting holiness* in the fear of God."[4]

In like manner St. John says, " If we walk in the light, as He is in the light, we have fellowship one with another ; and the blood of Jesus Christ His Son cleanseth us from all sin."   It seems then that there is sin which is consistent with " walking in the light," and that from this sin " the blood of Christ cleanseth us."[5]

---

[1] Rom. viii. 26.   [2] 2 Cor. xii. 9.   [3] 2 Cor. iv. 7.
[4] 2 Cor. vii. 1.   [5] 1 John i. 7.

Again, the same Apostle says soon after, "My little children, these things write I unto you, that ye sin not; and if any man sin, we have an Advocate with the Father, Jesus Christ the Righteous, and He is the Propitiation for our sins." Here sins are contemplated as attaching to a Christian, and as passed over in the view of Christ's righteousness; yet presently St. John says, "Whosoever is born of God, doth not commit sin,"[1] that is, infirmities he may admit, transgressions he cannot.

And St. James says, "In many things we all offend," that is, we all stumble. We are ever stumbling along our course, while we walk; but if we actually fall in it, we fall from it.

And St. Jude: "Of some have compassion, making a difference; and others save with fear, pulling them out of the fire."[2] Distinct kinds of sins are evidently implied here.

And lastly, our Lord Himself had already implied that there are sins which are not inconsistent with a state of grace, when He said of His Apostles, "The spirit is willing, but the flesh is weak."[3]

3. It remains to show that these sins of infirmity tend to those which are greater, and forfeit grace; which is not the least important point which comes under consideration.

An illustration will explain what I mean, and may throw light on the whole subject. You know it continually happens that some indisposition overtakes a man, such that persons skilled in medicine, when asked

---

[1] 1 John ii. 1 ; iii. 9.   [2] Jude 22, 23.
[3] Matt. xxvi. 41.

if it is dangerous, answer, "Not at present, but they do not know what will come of it; it may turn out something very serious; but there is nothing much amiss yet; at the same time, if it be not checked, and, much more, if it be neglected, it will be serious." This, I conceive, is the state of Christians day by day, as regards their souls; they are always ailing, always on the point of sickness; they are sickly, easily disarranged, obliged to take great care of themselves against air, sun, and weather; they are full of tendencies to all sorts of grievous diseases, and are continually showing these tendencies, in slight symptoms; but they are not yet in a dangerous way. On the other hand, if a Christian falls into any serious sin, then he is at once cast out of grace, as a man who falls into a pestilential fever is quite in a distinct state from one who is merely in delicate health.

Now with respect to this progress of sin from infirmity to transgression, here, as before, we have no need to go to Scripture in proof of a truth which every day teaches us, that men begin with little sins and go on to great sins, that the course of sin is a continuous declivity, with nothing to startle those who walk along it, and that the worst transgressions seem trifles to the sinner, and that the lightest infirmities are grievous to the holy. "He that despiseth small things," says the wise man, "shall fall by little and little;" this surely is the doctrine of inspired Scripture throughout; and here I will do no more than cite two passages from two Apostles in behalf of it. St. James says expressly, "When lust hath conceived, it bringeth forth sin; and sin, *when it is finished*, bringeth forth *death."* [1] You see that from the first it tends to death ; for it ends in death, but not *till* it ends, till it is *finished.* Again, St. Paul says, " Make straight paths for your feet, *lest* that which is *lame* be *turned out of the way;* but let it rather be healed." [2] We are ever in a degree lame in this world, even in our best estate. All Christians are such ; but when in consequence of their lameness they proceed to turn aside, or, as the text says, to " draw back," then they differ from those who are merely lame, as widely as those who halt along a road differ from those who fall out of it. Those who have turned aside, have to return ; they have fallen into a different state : those who are lame must be " healed " *in* the state of grace in which they are, and while they are in it ; and that, *lest* they " turn out " of it. Thus lameness is at once distinct from backsliding, yet leads to it.

And here an observation may be made concerning that sin against the Holy Ghost, which shall never be forgiven. I am very far from denying that there is a certain special sin to which that awful title belongs, though I will not undertake to say what it is ; but I observe thus much :—that, whereas it is the unpardonable sin, there is not a sin which we do but may be considered to tend towards it, and to be the beginning of that which *ends* in death, which ends in impenitence, ends in quenching those gracious influences, by which alone we are able to do any good. And this is a very serious thought to all who sin wilfully ; that though their sin be slight, they are beginning a course, which, if let run

<hr>

[1] James i. 15.   [2] Heb. xii. 13.

on freely, ends in apostasy and reprobation. Hence the force of the following passage, which describes the ultimate result of a course of wilful sin, or what every wilful sin tends to become : " It is impossible for those who were once enlightened, and have tasted of the heavenly gift, and were made partakers of the Holy Ghost, and have tasted of the good word of God, and the powers of the world to come, *if they shall fall away,*" so as utterly to quench the grace given them, " to renew them again to repentance." [1]

On the whole, then, this may be considered a Christian's state, ever about to fall, yet by God's mercy never falling ; ever dying, yet always alive ; full of infirmities, yet free from transgressions : and, as time goes on, more and more free from infirmities also, as tending to that perfect righteousness which is the fulfilling of the Law ;—on the other hand, should he fall, recoverable, but not without much pain, with fear and trembling.

I conclude with advising you, my brethren, one thing, which is obviously suggested by what I have said. Never suffer sin to remain upon you ; let it not grow old in you ; wipe it off while it is fresh, else it will stain ; let it not get ingrained ; let it not eat its way in, and rust in you. It is of a consuming nature ; it is like a canker ; it will eat your flesh. I say, beware, my brethren, of suffering sin in yourselves, and this for a great many reasons. First, if for no other than this, you will forget you have committed it, and never repent of it at all. Repent of it while you know it ; let it not be

[1] Heb. vi. 6.

wiped from your memory without being first wiped away from your soul. What may be the state of our souls from the accumulating arrears of the past! Alas! what difficulties we have involved ourselves in, without knowing it. Many a man doubtless in this way lives in a languid state, has a veil intercepting God from him, derives little or no benefit from the ordinances of grace, and cannot get a clear sight of the truth. Why? His past sins weigh upon him like a load, and he knows it not. And then again, sin neglected not only stains and infects the soul, but it becomes habitual. It perverts and deforms the soul; it permanently enfeebles, cripples, or mutilates us. Let us then rid ourselves of it at once day by day, as of dust on our hands and faces. We wash our hands continually. Ah! is not this like the Pharisees, unless we wash our soiled souls also? Let not then this odious state continue in you; in the words of the prophet, "Wash you, make you clean, put away the evil of your doings" from before the eyes of your Lord and Saviour. Make a clean breast of it. You sin day by day; let not the sun go down upon your guilt. You sin continually, at least so far as to make you most miserable, most offensive, most unfit for the Angels who are your companions. Come then continually to the Fount of cleansing for cleansing. St. John says that the Blood of Jesus Christ cleanseth from all sin. Use the means appointed,—confession, prayer, fasting, making amends, good resolves, and the ordinances of grace. Do not stop to ask the degree of your guilt,— whether you have actually drawn back from God or not. Let your ordinary repentance be as though you had

You cannot repent too much. Come to God day by day, intreating Him for all the sins of your whole life up to the very hour present. This is the way to keep your baptismal robe bright. Let it be washed as your garments of this world are, again and again ; washed in the most holy, most precious, most awfully salutary of all streams, His Blood, who is without blemish and without spot. It is thus that the Church of God, it is thus that each individual member of it, becomes all glorious within, and filled with grace.

Thus it is that we return in spirit to the state of Adam on his creation, when as yet the grace and glory of God were to him for a robe, and rendered earthly garments needless. Thus we prepare ourselves for that new world yet to come, for the new heavens and the new earth, and all the hosts of them, in the day when they shall be created ;—when the marriage of the Lamb shall come, and His wife shall make herself ready, and to her shall be granted to be arrayed in fine linen clean and white; for the fine linen is the righteousness of Saints.

SERMON XV.

SINS OF INFIRMITY.

*" The flesh lusteth against the Spirit, and the Spirit against the flesh ;
and these are contrary the one to the other, so that ye cannot do the things
that ye would."*

IT is not uncommonly said of the Church Catholic,
and we may humbly and thankfully receive it, that
though there is error, variance, and sin in an extreme
degree in its separate members, yet what they do all in
common, what they do in combination, what they do
gathered together in one, or what they universally
receive or allow, is divine and holy; that the sins of
individuals are overruled, and their wanderings guided
and brought round, so that they end in truth, in spite,
or even in one sense, by means of error. Not as if
error had any power of arriving at truth, or were a
necessary previous condition of it, but that it pleases
Almighty God to work out His great purposes in and
through human infirmity and sin. Thus Balaam had a
word put in his mouth in the midst of his enchantments,
and Caiaphas prophesied in the act of persuading our
Lord's death.

v]   P

What is true of the Church as a body, is true also of each member of it who fulfils his calling: the continual results, as I may call them, of his faith, are righteous and holy, but the process through which they are obtained is one of imperfection; so that could we see his soul as Angels see it, he would, when seen at a distance, appear youthful in countenance, and bright in apparel; but approach him, and his face has lines of care upon it, and his dress is tattered. His righteousness then seems, I do not mean superficial, this would be to give a very wrong idea of it, but though reaching deep within him, yet not whole and entire in the depth of it; but, as it were, wrought out of sin, the result of a continual struggle,—not spontaneous nature, but habitual self-command.

True faith is not shown here below in peace, but rather in conflict; and it is no proof that a man is not in a state of grace that he continually sins, provided such sins do not remain on him as what I may call ultimate results, but are ever passing on into something beyond and unlike themselves, into truth and righteousness. As we gain happiness through suffering, so do we arrive at holiness through infirmity, because man's very condition is a fallen one, and in passing out of the country of sin, he necessarily passes through it. And hence it is that holy men are kept from regarding themselves with satisfaction, or resting in any thing short of our Lord's death, as their ground of confidence; for, though that death has already in a measure wrought life in them, and effected the purpose for which it took place, yet to themselves they seem but sinners, their renewal being hidden from them by the circumstances attending it. The utmost they can say of themselves is, that they are not in the commission of any such sins as would plainly exclude them from grace; but how little of firm hope can be placed on such negative evidence is plain from St. Paul's own words on the subject, who, speaking of the censures passed upon him by the Corinthians, says, "I know nothing by myself," that is, I am conscious of nothing, "yet am I not hereby justified; but He that judgeth me is the Lord." As men in a battle cannot see how it is going, so Christians have no certain signs of God's presence in their hearts, and can but look up towards their Lord and Saviour, and timidly hope. Hence they will readily adopt the well-known words, not as expressing a matter of doctrine, but as their own experience about themselves. "The little fruit which we have in holiness, it is, God knoweth, corrupt and unsound; we put no confidence at all in it; ... our continual suit to Him is, and must be, to bear with our infirmities and pardon our offences."[1]

Let us then now enumerate some of the infirmities which I speak of; infirmities which, while they certainly beset those who are outcasts from God's grace, and that with grievous additions and fatal aggravations, yet are also possible in a state of acceptance, and do not in themselves imply the absence of true and lively faith. The review will serve to humble all of us, and perhaps may encourage those who are depressed by a sense of their high calling, by reminding them that they are not reprobate, though they be not all they should be.

[1] Hooker on Justification, § 9.

1. Now of the sins which stain us, though without such a consent of the will as to forfeit grace, I must .mention first original sin.　How it is that we are born under a curse which we did not bring upon us, we do not know; it is a mystery; but when we become Christians, that curse is removed.　We are no longer under God's wrath; our guilt is forgiven us, but still the infection of it remains.　I mean, we still have an evil principle within us, dishonouring our best services. How far, by God's grace, we are able in time to chastise, restrain, and destroy this infection, is another question; but still it is not removed at once by Baptism, and if not, surely it is a most grievous humiliation to those who are striving to "walk worthy of the Lord unto all pleasing."[1]　It is involuntary, and therefore does not cast us out of grace; yet in itself it is very miserable and very humbling: and every one will discover it in himself, if he watches himself narrowly.　I mean, what is called the old Adam, pride, profaneness, deceit, unbelief, selfishness, greediness, the inheritance of the Tree of the knowledge of good and evil; sins which the words of the serpent sowed in the hearts of our first parents, which sprang up and bore fruit, some thirty-fold, some sixty, some an hundred, and which have been by carnal descent transmitted to us.

2. Another class of involuntary sins, which often are not such as to throw us out of grace, any more than the infection of nature, but are still more humbling and distressing, consists of those which arise from our ·former habits of sin, though now long abandoned.　We

[1] Col. i. 10.

cannot rid ourselves of sin when we would; though we repent, though God forgives us, yet it remains in its power over our souls, in our habits, and in our memories. It has given a colour to our thoughts, words, and works; and though, with many efforts, we would wash it out from us, yet this is not possible except gradually. Men have been slothful, or self-conceited, or self-willed, or impure, or worldly-minded in their youth, and afterwards they turn to God, and would fain be other than they have been, but their former self clings to them, as a poisoned garment, and eats into them. They cannot do the things that they would, and from time to time they seem almost reduced back again to that heathen state, which the Apostle describes, when he cries out, "O wretched man that I am! who shall deliver me from the body of this death?"[1]

3. Another class of involuntary sins are such as arise from want of self-command; that is, from the mind being possessed of more light than strength, the conscience being informed, but the governing principle weak. The soul of man is intended to be a well-ordered polity, in which there are many powers and faculties, and each has its due place; and for these to exceed their limits is sin; yet they cannot be kept within those limits except by being governed, and we are unequal to this task of governing ourselves except after long habit. While we are learning to govern ourselves, we are constantly exposed to the risk, or rather to the occurrence, of numberless failures. We have failures by the way, though we triumph in the end; and thus, as I just now

<hr>

[1] Rom. vii. 24.

implied, the process of learning to obey God is, in one sense, a process of sinning, from the nature of the case. We have much to be forgiven; nay, we have the more to be forgiven the more we attempt. The higher our aims, the greater our risks. They who venture much with their talents, gain much, and in the end they hear the words, "Well done, good and faithful servant;" but they have so many losses in trading by the way, that to themselves they seem to do nothing but fail. They cannot believe that they are making any progress; and though they do, yet surely they have much to be forgiven in all their services. They are like David, men of blood; they fight the good fight of faith, but they are polluted with the contest.

I am not speaking of cases of extraordinary devotion, but of what every one must know in his own case, how difficult it is to command himself, and do that he wishes to do;—how weak the governing principle of his mind is, and how poorly and imperfectly he comes up to his own notions of right and truth; how difficult it is to command his feelings, grief, anger, impatience, joy, fear; how difficult to govern his tongue, to say just what he would; how difficult to rouse himself to do what he would, at this time or that; how difficult to rise in the morning; how difficult to go about his duties and not be idle; how difficult to eat and drink just what he should, how difficult to fix his mind on his prayers; how difficult to regulate his thoughts through the day; how difficult to keep out of his mind what should be kept out of it.

We are feeble-minded, excitable, effeminate, wayward, irritable, changeable, miserable. We have no lord over us, because we are but partially subject to the dominion of the true King of Saints. Let us try to do right as much as we will, let us pray as earnestly, yet we do not, in a time of trial, come up even to our own notions of perfection, or rather we fall quite short of them, and do perhaps just the reverse of what we had hoped to do. While there is no external temptation present, our passions sleep, and we think all is well. Then we think, and reflect, and resolve what we will do; and we anticipate no difficulty in doing it. But when the temptation is come, where are we then? We are like Daniel in the lions' den; and our passions are the lions; except that we have not Daniel's grace to prevail with God for the shutting of the lions' mouths lest they devour us. Then our reason is but like the miserable keeper of wild beasts, who in ordinary seasons is equal to them, but not when they are excited. Alas! Whatever the affection of mind may be, how miserable it is! It may be a dull, heavy sloth, or cowardice, which throws its huge limbs around us, binds us close, oppresses our breath, and makes us despise ourselves, while we are impotent to resist it; or it may be anger, or other baser passion, which, for the moment, escapes from our control after its prey, to our horror and our disgrace; but anyhow, what a miserable den of brute creatures does the soul then become, and we at the moment (I say) literally unable to help it! I am not, of course, speaking of *deeds* of evil, the fruits of wilfulness,—malice, or revenge, or uncleanness, or intemperance, or violence, or robbery, or fraud;—alas! the sinful heart often goes on to commit sins which hide from it at once the light of God's countenance; but I am supposing what was Eve's case, when she looked at the tree and saw that the fruit was good, but before she plucked it, when lust had conceived and was bringing forth sin, but ere sin was finished and had brought forth death.   I am supposing that we do not exceed so far as to estrange God from us; that He mercifully chains the lions at our cry, before they do more than frighten us by their moanings or their roar,—before they fall on us to destroy us: yet, at best, what misery, what pollution, what sacrilege, what a chaos is there then in that consecrated spot, which is the temple of the Holy Ghost!   How is it that the lamp of God does not go out in it at once, when the whole soul seems tending to hell, and hope is almost gone?   Wonderful mercy indeed it is, which bears so much! Incomprehensible patience in the Holy One, so to dwell, in such a wilderness, with the wild beasts! Exceeding and divine virtue in the grace given us, that it is not stifled! Yet such is the promise, not to those who sin contentedly after they have received grace; there is no hope while they so sin; but where sin is not part of a course, though it is still sin, whether sin of our birth, or of habits formed long ago, or of want of self-command which we are trying to gain, God mercifully allows and pardons it, and "the blood of Jesus Christ cleanseth us from" it all.

4. Further, I might dwell upon sins which we fall into from being taken unawares,—when the temptation

is sudden,—as St. Peter, when he first denied Christ; though whether it became of a different character, when he denied twice and thrice, is a further question.

5. And again, those sins which rise from the devil's temptations, inflaming the wounds and scars of past sins healed, or nearly so; exciting the memory, and hurrying us away; and thus making use of our former selves against our present selves contrary to our will.

6. And again, I might speak of those which rise from a deficiency of practical experience, or from ignorance how to perform duties which we set about. Men attempt to be munificent, and their acts are prodigal; they wish to be firm and zealous, and their acts are cruel; they wish to be benevolent, and they are indulgent and weak; they do harm when they mean to do good; they engage in undertakings, or they promote designs, or they put forth opinions, or they set a pattern, of which evil comes; they countenance evil; they mistake falsehood for truth; they are zealous for false doctrines; they oppose the cause of God. One can hardly say all this is without sin, and yet in them it may be involuntary sin and pardonable on the prayer of faith.

7. Or I might speak of those unworthy motives, low views, mistakes in principle, false maxims, which abound on all sides of us, and which we catch (as it were) from each other;—that spirit of the world which we breathe, and which defiles all we do, yet which can hardly be said to be a wilful pollution; but rather it is such sin as is consistent with the presence of the

grace of God in us, which that grace will blot out and put away.

8. And, lastly, much might be said on the subject of what the Litany calls "negligences and ignorances," on forgetfulnesses, heedlessnesses, want of seriousness, frivolities, and a variety of weaknesses, which we may be conscious of in ourselves, or see in others.

Such are some of the classes of sins which may be found, if it so happen, where the will is right, and faith lively; and which in such cases are not inconsistent with the state of grace, or may be called infirmities. Of course it must be ever recollected, that infirmities are not always to be regarded *as* infirmities; they attach also to those who live in the commission of wilful sins, and who have no warrant whatever for considering themselves in a saving state. Men do not cease to be under the influence of original sin, or sins of past years, they do not gain self-command, or un-learn negligences and ignorances, by adding to these offences others of a more grievous character. Those who are out of grace, have infirmities and much more. And there will always be a tendency in such persons to explain away their wilful sins into infirmities. This is ever to be borne in mind. I am not attempting to draw the line between infirmities and transgressions; I only say, that to whomsoever besides such infirmities do attach, they may happen to attach to those who are free from transgressions, and who need not despond, or be miserable on account of failings which in them are not destructive of faith or incompatible with grace. Who these are He only knows for certain, who " tries the reins and the heart," who "knoweth the mind of the Spirit," and "discerns between the righteous and the wicked." He is able, amid the maze of contending motives and principles within us, to trace out the perfect work of righteousness steadily going on there, and the rudiments of a new world rising from out the chaos. He can discriminate between what is habitual and what is accidental; what is on the growth and what is in decay; what is a result and what is indeterminate; what is of us and what is in us. He estimates the difference between a will that is honestly devoted to Him, and one that is insincere. And where there is a willing mind, He accepts it "according to that a man hath, and not according to that he hath not."[1] In those whose wills are holy, He is present for sanctification and acceptance; and, like the sun's beams in some cave of the earth, His grace sheds light on every side, and consumes all mists and vapours as they rise.

We indeed have not knowledge such as His; were we ever so high in God's favour, a certainty of our justification would not belong to us. Yet, even to know only thus much, that infirmities are no necessary mark of reprobation, that God's elect have infirmities, and that our own sins may possibly be no more than infirmities, this surely, by itself, is a consolation. And to reflect that at least God continues us visibly in His Church; that He does not withdraw from us the ordinances of grace; that He gives us means of instruction,

---

[1] 2 Cor. viii. 12.

patterns of holiness, religious guidance, good books; that He allows us to frequent His house, and to present ourselves before Him in prayer and Holy Communion; that He gives us opportunities of private prayer; that He has given us a care for our souls; an anxiety to secure our salvation; a desire to be more strict and conscientious, more simple in faith, more full of love than we are; all this will tend to soothe and encourage us, when the sense of our infirmities makes us afraid. And if further, God seems to be making us His instruments for any purpose of His, for teaching, warning, guiding, or comforting others, resisting error, spreading the knowledge of the truth, or edifying His Church, this too will create in us the belief, not that God is certainly pleased with us, for knowledge of mysteries may be separated from love, but that He has not utterly forsaken us in spite of our sins, that He still remembers us, and knows us by name, and desires our salvation. And further, if, for all our infirmities, we can point to some occasions on which we have sacrificed anything for God's service, or to any habit of sin or evil tendency of nature which we have more or less overcome, or to any habitual self-denial which we practise, or to any work which we have accomplished to God's honour and glory; this perchance may fill us with the humble hope that God is working in us, and therefore is at peace with us. And, lastly, if we have, through God's mercy, an inward sense of our own sincerity and integrity, if we feel that we can appeal to God with St. Peter, that we love Him only, and desire to please Him in all things,—in proportion as we feel this, or at such times as we feel it, we have an assurance shed abroad on our hearts, that we are at present in His favour, and are in training for the inheritance of His eternal kingdom.

SERMON XVI.

SINCERITY AND HYPOCRISY.

2 Cor. viii. 12.

" If there be first a willing mind, it is accepted according to that a man hath, and not according to that he hath not."

MEN may be divided into two great classes, those who profess religious obedience, and those who do not; and of those who do profess to be religious, there are again those who perform as well as profess, and those who do not. And thus on the whole there are three classes of men in the world, open sinners, consistent Christians, and between the two, (as speaking with the one, and more or less acting with the other,) professing Christians, or, as they are sometimes called, nominal Christians. Now the distinction between open sinners and consistent Christians is so clear, that there is no mistaking it; for they agree in nothing; they neither profess the same things nor practise the same. But the difference between professing Christians and true Christians is not so clear, for this reason, that true Christians, however consistent they are, yet do sin, as being not yet perfect; and so far as they sin, are inconsistent, and this is all that professing Christians are. What then, it may be asked, is the real difference between true and professing Christians, since both the one and the other profess more than they practise? Again, if you put the question to one of the latter class, however inconsistent his life may be, yet he will be sure to say that he wishes he was better; that he is sorry for his sins; that the flesh is weak; that he cannot overcome it; that God alone can overcome it; that he trusts God will, and that he prays to Him to enable him to do it. There is no form of words conceivable which a mere professing Christian cannot use,—nay, more, there appears to be no sentiment which he cannot feel,—as well as the true Christian, and at first sight apparently with the same justice. He *seems* just in the very position of the true Christian, only perhaps behind him; not *so* consistent, not advanced so much; still, on the same line. Both confess to a struggle within them; both sin, both are sorry; what then is the difference between them?

There are many differences; but, before going on to mention that one to which I shall confine my attention, I would have you observe that I am speaking of differences in God's sight. Of course, we men may after all be unable altogether, and often are unable, to see differences between those who, nevertheless, are on different sides of the line of life. Nor may we judge anything absolutely before the time, whereas God "searcheth the hearts." He alone, "who searcheth the

hearts," "knoweth what is the mind of the Spirit."
We do not even know ourselves absolutely. "Yea, I
judge not mine own self," says St. Paul, "but He that
judgeth me is the Lord." God alone can unerringly
discern between sincerity and insincerity, between the
hypocrite and the man of perfect heart. I do not, of
course, mean that we can form no judgment at all
upon ourselves, or that it is not useful to do so; but
here I will chiefly insist upon the point of *doctrine*,
viz., how does the true Christian differ in God's sight
from the insincere and double-minded?—leaving any
practical application which it admits, to be incidentally
brought out in the course of my remarks.

Now the real difference between the true and the
professing Christian seems to be given us in the text,—
"If there be a willing mind, it is accepted." St. Paul
is speaking of almsgiving; but what he says seems to
apply generally. He is laying down a principle, which
applies of course in many distinct cases, though he uses
it with reference to one in particular. An honest, unaf-
fected *desire* of doing right is the test of God's true
servants. On the other hand, a double mind, a pursuing
other ends besides the truth, and in consequence an
inconsistency in conduct, and a half-consciousness (to
say the least) of inconsistency, and a feeling of the
necessity of defending oneself to oneself, and to God,
and to the world; in a word, hypocrisy; these are the
signs of the merely professed Christian. Now I am
going to give some instances of this distinction, in
Scripture and in fact.

For instance. The two great Christian graces are

faith and love. Now, how are these characterised in Scripture?—By their being honest or single-minded. Thus St. Paul, in one place, speaks of "the end of the commandment being love;" what love?—"love *out of a pure heart*," he proceeds, "and of a *good conscience;*" and still further, "and of faith,"—what kind of faith?— "faith *unfeigned;*" or, as it may be more literally translated, "unhypocritical faith;" for so the word means in Greek. Again, elsewhere he speaks of his "calling to remembrance the *unfeigned* faith" which dwelt in Timothy, and in his mother and grandmother before him; that is, literally, "unhypocritical faith." Again, he speaks of the Apostles approving themselves as the ministers of God, "by kindness, by the Holy Ghost, by love *unfeigned*," or, more literally, "unhypocritical love." Again, as to love towards man. "Let love be *without dissimulation*," or, more literally, as in the other cases, "let love be unhypocritical." In like manner, St. Peter speaks of Christians "having purified their souls in obeying the truth through the Spirit unto unhypocritical love of the brethren." And in like manner, St. James speaks of "the wisdom that is from above, being first *pure* . . ." and, presently, "without partiality, and *without hypocrisy.*"[1] Surely it is very remarkable that three Apostles, writing on different subjects and occasions, should each of them thus speak about whether faith or love as without hypocrisy.

A true Christian, then, may almost be defined as one who has a ruling sense of God's presence within him. As none but justified persons have that privilege, so

____
[1] 2 Cor. vi. 6. Rom. xii. 9. 1 Pet. i. 22. James iii. 17.

none but the justified have that practical perception of it.   A true Christian, or one who is in a state of acceptance with God, is he, who, in such sense, has faith in Him, as to live in the thought that He is present with him,—present not externally, not in nature merely, or in providence, but in his innermost heart, or in his *conscience.*   A man is justified whose conscience is illuminated by God, so that he habitually realizes that all his thoughts, all the first springs of his moral life, all his motives and his wishes, are open to Almighty God. Not as if he was not aware that there is very much in him impure and corrupt, but he wishes that all that is in him should be bare to God.   He believes that it is so, and he even joys to think that it is so, in spite of his fear and shame at its being so.   He alone admits Christ into the shrine of his heart; whereas others wish in some way or other, to be by themselves, to have a home, a chamber, a tribunal, a throne, a self where God is not,— a home within them which is not a temple, a chamber which is not a confessional, a tribunal without a judge, a throne without a king;—that self may be king and judge; and that the Creator may rather be dealt with and approached as though a second party, instead of His being that true and better self, of which self itself should be but an instrument and minister.

Scripture tells us that God the Word, who died for us and rose again, and now lives for us, and saves us, is "quick and powerful, and sharper than any two-edged sword, piercing even to the dividing asunder of soul and spirit, and of the joints and marrow, and a discerner of the thoughts and intents of the heart.   Neither is there any creature that is not manifest in His sight; but all things are naked and opened unto the eyes of Him with whom we have to do."[1] Now the true Christian realizes this; and what is the consequence ?—Why, that he enthrones the Son of God in his conscience, refers to Him as a sovereign authority, and uses no reasoning with Him. He does not reason, but he says, "Thou, God, seest me." He feels that God is too near him to allow of argument, self-defence, excuse, or objection. He appeals in matters of duty, not to his own reason, but to God Himself, whom with the eyes of faith he sees, and whom he makes the Judge; not to any fancied fitness, or any preconceived notion, or any abstract principle, or any tangible experience.

The Book of Psalms continually instances this temper of profound, simple, open-hearted confidence in God. "O Lord, Thou hast searched me out and known me. Thou knowest my downsitting and mine uprising. Thou understandest my thoughts long before . . . There is not a word in my tongue but Thou knowest it altogether." "My soul hangeth upon Thee. Thy right hand hath upholden me." "When I wake up, I am present with Thee." "Into Thy hands I commend my spirit, for Thou hast redeemed me, O Lord, Thou God of Truth." "Commit thy way unto the Lord, and put thy trust in Him, and He shall bring it to pass. He shall make thy righteousness as clear as the light, and thy just dealing as the noonday." "Against Thee only have I sinned, and done this evil in Thy sight." "Hear the right, O Lord, consider my complaint, and hearken

[1] Heb. iv. 12, 13.

unto my prayer that goeth not out of feigned lips. Let my sentence come forth from Thy presence, and let Thine eyes look upon the thing that is equal. Thou hast proved and visited mine heart in the night season. Thou hast tried me, and shalt find no wickedness in me; for I am utterly purposed that my mouth shall not offend." Once more, "Thou shalt guide me with Thy counsel, and after that receive me with glory. Whom have I in heaven but Thee? and there is none upon earth that I desire in comparison of Thee. My flesh and my heart faileth, but God is the strength of mine heart and my portion for ever." [1]

Or, again, consider the following passage in St. John's First Epistle. "If our heart condemn us, God is greater than our heart and knoweth all things. Beloved, if our heart condemn us not, then have we confidence towards God." And in connexion with this, the following from the same Epistle: "God is Light, and in Him is no darkness at all. If we say that we have fellowship with Him, and walk in darkness, we lie, and do not the truth. . . . If we confess our sins, He is faithful and just to forgive us our sins, and to cleanse us from al' unrighteousness." Again, "the darkness is past, and the true light now shineth." Again, "Hereby we know that He abideth in us, by the Spirit which He hath given us." And again, "He that believeth on the Son of God, hath the witness in himself." And, in the same connexion, consider St. Paul's statement, that "the

---

[1] Ps. cxxxix. 1, 2, 4; lxiii. 8; xxxi. 5; xxxvii. 5, 6; li. 4; xvii. 1—3; lxxiii. 24—26.

Spirit itself beareth witness with our spirit, that we are the children of God." [1]

And, now, on the other hand, let us contrast such a temper of mind, which loves to walk in the light, with that of the merely professing Christian, or, in Scripture language, of the *hypocrite*. Such are they who have two ends which they pursue, religion *and* the world; and hence St. James calls them "double-minded." Hence, too, our Lord, speaking of the Pharisees who were hypocrites, says, "Ye cannot serve God *and* mammon." [2] A double-minded man, then, as having two ends in view, dare not come to God, lest he should be discovered; for "all things that are reproved are made manifest by the light." [3] Thus, whereas the Prodigal Son "rose and came to his father," on the contrary, Adam hid himself among the trees of the garden. It was not simple dread of God, but dread joined to an unwillingness to be restored to God. He had a secret in his heart which he kept from God. He felt towards God,—as it would seem, or at least his descendants so feel,—as one man often feels towards another in the intercourse of life. You sometimes say of a man, "he is friendly, or courteous, or respectful, or considerate, or communicative; but, after all, there is something, perhaps without his knowing it, in the background. He professes to be agreed with me; he almost displays his agreement; he says he pursues the same objects as I; but still I do not know him, I do not make progress with him, I have no confidence in him, I

1 1 John iii. 20, 21; i. 5—9; ii. 8; iii. 24; v. 10. Rom. viii. 16.
2 Luke xvi. 13.　　　　　　　　3 Ephes. v. 13.

do not know him better than the first time I saw him." Such is the way in which the double-minded approach the Most High,—they have a something private, a hidden self at bottom. They look on themselves, as it were, as independent parties, treating with Almighty God as one of their fellows. Hence, so far from seeking God, they hardly like to be sought by Him. They would rather keep their position and stand where they are,—on earth, and so make terms with God in heaven; whereas, "he that doeth truth, cometh to the light, that his deeds may be made manifest that they are wrought in God."[1]

This being the case, there being in the estimation of the double-minded man two parties, God and self, it follows (as I have said), that reasoning and argument is the mode in which he approaches his Saviour and Judge; and that for two reasons,—first, because he will not *give* himself up to God, but stands upon his rights and appeals to his notions of fitness : and next, because he has some secret misgiving after all that he is dishonest, or some consciousness that he may appear so to others; and therefore, he goes about to fortify his position, to explain his conduct, or to excuse himself.

Some such argument or excuse had the unprofitable servant, when called before his Lord. The other servants said, "Lord, Thy pound hath gained ten," or "five pounds." They said no more; nothing more was necessary; the case spoke for itself. But the unprofitable servant did not dare leave his conduct to tell its own tale at God's judgment-seat; he said not merely, "Lord, I have kept Thy pound laid up in a napkin :" he

[1] John iii. 21.

appealed, as it were, to the reasonableness of his conduct against his Maker: he felt he must make out a case, and he went on to attempt it. He trusted not his interests to the Eternal and All-perfect Reason of God, before whom he stood, but entrenched himself in his own.

Again :—When our Lord said to the scribe, who had answered Him that eternal life was to be gained by loving God and his neighbour, "Thou hast answered right," this ought to have been enough. But his object was not to please God, but to exalt himself. And, therefore, he went on to make an objection. "But he, willing to *justify himself*, said unto Jesus, And who is my neighbour?" whereas they only are justified in God's judgment, who give up the notion of justifying themselves by word or deed, who start with the confession that they are unjust, and who come to God, not upon their own merits, but for His mercy.

Again : we have the same arguing and insincere spirit exposed in the conduct of the Pharisees, when they asked Christ for the authority on which He acted. They said, "By what authority doest thou these things?" This might be the question of sincere inquirers or mere objectors, of faith or of hypocrisy. Observe how our Lord detects it. He asked them about St. John's baptism; meaning to say, that if they acknowledged St. John, they must acknowledge Himself, of whom St. John spake. They, unwilling to submit to Christ as a teacher and Lord, preferred to deny John to going on to acknowledge Him. Yet, on the other hand, they dare not openly deny the Baptist, because of the people; so, between hatred of our Lord and dread of the people, they would give no answer at all. "They *reasoned* among themselves," we are told. In consequence, our Lord left them to their reasonings; He refused to tell them what, had they reasoned sincerely, they might learn for themselves.

What is seen in the Gospels, had taken place from the beginning. Our first parents were as ready with excuses, as their posterity when Christ came. First, Adam says, "I hid myself, for I was afraid;" though fear and shame were not the sole or chief reasons why he fled, but an incipient hatred, if it may be said, of his Maker. Again, he says, "The woman, whom Thou gavest me . . . . she gave me of the tree." And the woman says, "The serpent beguiled me." They did not honestly surrender themselves to their offended God, but had something to say in their behalf. Again, Cain says, when asked where his brother was, whom he had murdered, "Am I my brother's keeper?"

Balaam, again, is a most conspicuous instance of a double mind, or of hypocrisy. He has a plausible reason for whatever he does; he can so skilfully defend himself, that to this day he looks like a good man, and his conduct and fortunes are a perplexity to many minds. But it is one thing to have good excuses, another to have good motives. He had not the love of the truth, the love of God, in his heart; he was covetous of worldly goods; and, therefore, all his excuses only avail to mark him as double-minded.

Again :—Saul is another very remarkable instance of a man acting for his own ends, and yet having plausible *reasons* for what he did. He offered sacrifice on one occasion, not having a commission ; this was a sin ; yet what was his excuse ?—a very fair one. Samuel had promised to come to offer the sacrifice, and did not. Saul waited some days, the people grew discouraged, his army fell off, and the enemy was at hand,—so, as he says, he "*forced* himself."[1]

Such is the conduct of insincere men in difficulty. Perhaps their difficulty may be a real one ; but in this they differ from the sincere :—the latter seek God *in* their difficulty, feeling that He only who imposes it can remove it ; but insincere men do not like to go to God ; and to them the difficulty is only so much gain, for it gives them an apparent reason, a sort of excuse, for not going by God's rule, but for deciding in their own way. Thus Saul took his own course ; thus Jeroboam, when in a difficulty, put up calves of gold and instituted a new worship without Divine command. Whereas, when Hezekiah was in trouble, he took the letter of Senna-cherib, " and went up into the house of the Lord, and spread it before the Lord."[2] And when St. Peter was sinking in the water, he cried out to Christ, " Lord, save me."[3] And in like manner holy David, after he had sinned in numbering the people, and was told to choose between three punishments offered him, showed the same honest and simple-hearted devotion in choos-ing that of the three which might be the most exactly called falling into the Lord's hands. If he must suffer, let the Lord chastise him.—" I am in a great strait," he says ; " let us fall now into the hands of the Lord ; for

1 1 Sam. xiii. 12.   2 Isa. xxxvii. 14.
3 Matt. xiv. 30.

His mercies are great; and let me not fall into the hand
of man."[1]

Great, then, is the difference between sincere and
insincere Christians, however like their words may be
to each other; and it is needless to say, that what I
have shown in a few examples, might be instanced
again and again from every part of Scripture, particularly from the history of the Jews, as contained in the
Prophets.   All men, even after the gift of God's grace,
sin : God's true servants profess and sin,—sin, and are
sorry; and hypocrites profess and sin,—sin and are
sorry.   Thus the two parties look like each other.   But
the word of God discriminates one from the other by
this test,—that Christ dwells in the conscience of one,
not of the other; that the one opens his heart to God, the
other does not; the one views Almighty God only as an
accidental guest, the other as Lord and owner of all that
he is; the one admits Him as if for a night, or some stated
season, the other gives himself over to God, and considers
himself God's servant and instrument now and for ever.
Not more different is the intimacy of friends from mere
acquaintance; not more different is it to know a person
in society, to be courteous and obliging to him, to inter-
change civilities, from opening one's heart to another,
admitting him into it, seeing into his, loving him, and
living in him ;—than the external worship of the hypocrite, from the inward devotion of true faith; approaching God with the lips, from believing on Him with
the heart; so opening to the Spirit that He opens to us,
from so living to self as to exclude the light of heaven.

[1] 2 Sam. xxiv. 14.

Now, as to applying what I have been showing from Scripture to ourselves, this shall here be left, my brethren, to the consciences of each of us, and a few words will suffice to do this. Do you, then, habitually thus unlock your hearts and subject your thoughts to Almighty God? Are you living in this conviction of His Presence, and have you this special witness that that Presence is really set up within you unto your salvation, viz. that you live in the sense of it? Do you believe, and act on the belief, that His light penetrates and shines through your heart, as the sun's beams through a room? You know how things look when the sun's beams are on it,—the very air then appears full of impurities, which, before it came out, were not seen. So is it with our souls. We are full of stains and corruptions, we see them not, they are like the air before the sun shines; but though we see them not, God sees them: He pervades us as the sunbeam. Our souls, in His view, are full of things which offend, things which must be repented of, forgiven, and put away. He, in the words of the Psalmist, "has set our misdeeds before Him, our secret sins in the light of His countenance."[1] This is most true, though it be not at all welcome doctrine to many. We cannot hide ourselves from Him; and our wisdom, as our duty, lies in embracing this truth, acquiescing in it, and acting upon it. Let us then beg Him to teach us the Mystery of His Presence in us, that, by acknowledging it, we may thereby possess it fruitfully. Let us confess it in faith, that we may possess it unto justification. Let us so

[1] Ps. xc. 8.

own it, as to set Him before us in everything. "I have set God always before me," says the Psalmist, "for He is on my right hand, therefore I shall not fail."[1] Let us, in all circumstances, thus regard Him. Whether we have sinned, let us not dare keep from Him, but with the prodigal son, rise and go to Him. Or, if we are conscious of nothing, still let us not boast in ourselves or justify ourselves, but feel that "He who judgeth us is the Lord." In all circumstances, of joy or sorrow, hope or fear, let us aim at having Him in our inmost heart; let us have no secret apart from Him. Let us acknowledge Him as enthroned within us at the very springs of thought and affection. Let us submit ourselves to His guidance and sovereign direction; let us come to Him that He may forgive us, cleanse us, change us, guide us, and save us.

This is the true life of saints. This is to have the Spirit witnessing with our spirits that we are sons of God. Such a faith alone will sustain the terrors of the Last Day; such a faith alone will be proof against those fierce flames which are to surround the Judge, when He comes with His holy Angels to separate between "those who serve God, and those who serve Him not."[2]

---

[1] Ps. xvi. 8.   [2] Mal. iii. 18.

SERMON XVII.

THE TESTIMONY OF CONSCIENCE.

2 Cor. i. 12.

*" Our rejoicing is this, the testimony of our conscience, that in sim-
plicity and godly sincerity, not with fleshly wisdom, but by the grace of
God, we have had our conversation in the world, and more abundantly
to you-ward."*

IN these words the great Apostle appeals to his
conscience that he had lived in simplicity and sincerity, with a single aim and an innocent heart, as one
who was illuminated and guided by God's grace. The
like appeal he makes on other occasions; when brought
before the Jewish council he says, " Men and brethren,
I have lived in all good conscience before God until this
day."[1] And in his Second Epistle to Timothy he speaks
of having served God from his forefathers "with pure
conscience."[2]

And in the text he expressly says, what he implies,
of course, whenever he appeals to his conscience at all,
that he is able to rejoice in this appeal. He was given
to know his own sincerity in such measure, that he

[1] Acts xxiii. 1.   [2] 2 Tim. i. 2, 3.

could humbly take pleasure in it, and be comforted by it. "Our *rejoicing* is this," he says, "the testimony of our conscience." In like manner he says to the Galatians, "Let every man prove his own work, and then shall he have *rejoicing* in himself alone, and not in another."[1] And so also speaks St. John: "If our heart condemn us not, then have we *confidence* towards God."[2] Such was the confidence, such the rejoicing of St. Paul and St. John; not that they could do anything acceptable to God by their unaided powers, but that by His grace they could so live as to enjoy a cheerful hope of His favour, both now and evermore.

The same feeling is frequently expressed in the Psalms: a consciousness of innocence and integrity, a satisfaction in it, an appeal to God concerning it, and a confidence of God's favour in consequence. For instance, "Be thou my judge, O Lord," says David; he appeals to the heart-searching God, "for I have walked innocently; my trust hath been also in the Lord, therefore shall I not fall." He proceeds to beg of God to aid him in this self-knowledge: "Examine me, O Lord, and prove me; try out my reins and my heart," that is, lest he should be deceived in thinking himself what he was not. He next enumerates the special points in which God had enabled him to obey: "I have not dwelt with vain persons; neither will I have fellowship with the deceitful; I have hated the congregation of the wicked, and will not sit among the ungodly. . . . As for me, I have walked innocently; O deliver me, and be merciful unto me. My foot standeth

---

[1] Gal. vi. 4.　　　　[2] 1 John iii. 21.

right; I will praise the Lord in the congregations."[1] In this and other passages of the Psalms two points are brought before us : that it is possible to be innocent, and to have that sense of our innocence which makes us happy in the thought of God's eye being upon us. Let us then dwell on a truth, of which Apostles and Prophets unite in assuring us.

What the text means by "simplicity and sincerity," I consider for all practical purposes to be the same as what Scripture elsewhere· calls "a perfect heart;" at least this latter phrase will give us some insight into the meaning of the former. You know that it is a frequent account of the kings of Judah in the Sacred history, that they walked or did not walk with God, *with a perfect heart.* In contrast with this phrase, consider what our Saviour says of the attempt made by the Pharisees to serve God *and* mammon, and St. James's account of a *double-minded* man. A man serves with a perfect heart, who serves God in all parts of his duty ; and, not here and there, but here and there and everywhere ; not perfectly indeed as regards the quality of his obedience, but perfectly as regards its extent; not completely, but consistently. So that he may appeal to God with the Psalmist, and say, "Examine me, O Lord, and prove me : and seek the ground of my heart," with the humble trust that there is no department of his duty on which Almighty God can put His hand, and say, "Here thou art not with Me:" no part in which he does not set God before him, and desire to please Him, and to be governed by Him. And something like

[1] Ps. xxvi. 1, 2, &c.

this seems to be St. James's meaning, when he says, on the other hand, that " Whosoever shall keep the whole law, and yet offend in one point, he is guilty of all;"[1] for such a one is of imperfect heart, or double-minded.

Again, such seems to be our Saviour's meaning when He uses the word *hypocrite.* A hypocrite is one who professes to be serving God faithfully, while he serves Him in only some one part of his duty, not in all parts. The word is now commonly taken to mean one who uses a profession of religion as a mere instrument of gaining his worldly ends, or who wishes to deceive men into thinking that he is what he is not. This is not exactly its Scripture sense, which seems rather to denote a person who would (if I may use the words) deceive God; one who, though his heart would tell him, were he honest with it, that he is *not* serving God perfectly, yet will not *ask* his heart, will not listen to it, trifles with his conscience, is *determined* to believe that he *is* religious, and (as if to strengthen himself in his own false persuasion, and from a variety of mixed motives difficult to analyse) protests his sincerity and innocence before God, appeals to God, and thus claims as his own the reward of innocence.

Now then to attempt to describe that state of heart, which Scripture calls simple and sincere, or perfect, or innocent; and which is such, that a man may know he has it, and humbly rejoice in it.

We are by nature what we are; very sinful and corrupt, we know; however, we like to be what we are, and for many reasons it is very unpleasant to us to

[1] James ii. 10.

change. We cannot change ourselves; this too we know full well, or, at least, a very little experience will teach us. God alone can change us; God alone can give us the desires, affections, principles, views, and tastes which a change implies: this too we know; for I am all along speaking of men who have a sense of religion. What then is it that we who profess religion lack? I repeat it, this: a willingness to *be* changed, a willingness to suffer (if I may use such a word), to suffer Almighty God to change us. We do not like to let go our old selves; and in whole or part, though all is offered to us freely, we cling hold to our old selves. Though we were promised no trouble at all in the change, though there were no self-denial, no exertion in changing, the case would not be altered. We do not like to be new-made; we are afraid of it; it is throwing us out of all our natural ways, of all that is familiar to us. We feel as if we should not *be* ourselves any longer, if we do not keep some portion of what we have been hitherto; and much as we profess in general terms to wish to be changed, when it comes to the point, when particular instances of change are presented to us, we shrink from them, and are content to remain unchanged.

It is this principle of self-seeking, so to express myself, this influence of self upon us, which is our ruin. I repeat, I am speaking of those who make a *profession* of religion. Others, of course, avowedly follow self altogether; they indulge the flesh, or pursue the world. But when a man comes to God to be saved, then, I say, the essence of true conversion is a *surrender* of himself, an unreserved, unconditional surrender; and this is a saying which most men who come to God cannot receive. They wish to be saved, but in their own way; they wish (as it were) to capitulate upon terms, to carry off their goods with them ; whereas the true spirit of faith leads a man to look off from self to God, to think nothing of his own wishes, his present habits, his importance or dignity, his rights, his opinions, but to say, " I put myself into Thy hands, O Lord ; make Thou me what Thou wilt ; I forget myself ; I divorce myself from myself ; I am dead to myself ; I will follow Thee." Samuel, Isaiah, and St. Paul, three Saints in very different circumstances, all instance this. The child Samuel, under Eli's instruction, says, " Speak, Lord ; for Thy servant heareth."[1] The prophet Isaiah says, " Here am I : send me."[2] And still more exactly to the point are St. Paul's words, when arrested by the miraculous vision, " Lord, what wilt Thou have me to do?"[3] Here is the very voice of self-surrender, " What wilt thou have me to do ? Take Thy own way with me ; whatever it be, pleasant or painful, I will do it." These are words worthy of one who was to be to after-ages the pattern of simplicity, sincerity, and a pure conscience : and as he spake, so he acted ; for in his own narrative of what happened, he goes on to say, " I was not disobedient unto the heavenly vision."

Now to give some instances in illustration.

1. One very common case, though it is not one in which men have any pretensions to be considered as sincere, is when they determine to repent more fully by and by, or to be more strict in their mode of living

<hr>

[1] 1 Sam. iii. 9.   [2] Isa. vi. 8.   [3] Acts ix. 6.

by and by. However, it will serve to explain what I would say. Alas! so common is it, that I should not wonder if some persons here present, were they but honest, would confess it of themselves, that they dare not put themselves into God's hands, lest He should make them what they love not. Here then is the absence of a perfect heart, a shrinking from the absolute surrender and sacrifice of self to God.

2. Again, in a number of cases want of perfectness is shown in their keeping away, as they obstinately do, from the Lord's Supper. I am not speaking of the case of open sinners. Of course, it is well that they should feel reluctant; it would be dreadful indeed if they did not. Nor do I mean to say that many are not kept away by fears, which they ought not to have, which are mistaken. But still there are a great number, who have good words in their mouth, who profess all reverence, all service towards God, acknowledge His power and love, believe in what Christ has done for them, and say they desire to be ruled by Him, and to die the death of the righteous, who yet are quite unmovable on this particular point. Why is this? I fear, for this reason. They dare not profess in God's sight that they will serve Him. They dare not promise; they dare not pray to Him. They dare not beg Him to make them wholly His. They dare not ask Him to disclose to them their secret faults. They dare not come to an Ordinance, in which God meets them face to face. As many a man will tell an untruth who dare not swear it, so there are many men who make random professions of obedience, who dare not put themselves in circumstances when perhaps

they may be taken at their word. And as cowards disguise from themselves their own cowardice, till brought into danger, so do these their hypocrisy, till obliged to take a side. They profess vaguely; but they dare not definitely and solemnly say, "And here we offer and present unto Thee, O Lord, our souls and bodies, to be a reasonable, holy, and lively sacrifice unto Thee."

3. Another instance of insincerity is set before us in the conduct of the young man in the Gospel, who came running to Christ, and saying, "Good Master." He did not justly know himself, and he flattered himself that he was perfect in heart when he had a reserve in his obedience. You will observe he was even forward and rude in his manner; and here we seem to gain a lesson. When young persons address themselves to religious subjects without due reverence and godly fear, when they rush towards them impetuously, engage in them hotly, talk about them vehemently, and profess them conspicuously, they should be very suspicious of themselves, lest there be something or other wrong about them. Men who are quite honest, who really wish to surrender themselves to Christ, have counted the cost. They feel it is no slight sacrifice which they are making; they feel its difficulty and its pain; and therefore they cannot make an impetuous offer of their services. They cannot say, "Lord, I will follow Thee whithersoever Thou goest;" it is too great a profession. They dare not say, "All these have I kept from my youth up;" lest, after all, they discover something in themselves lacking. They have no heart to say, "Good Master," in a familiar, light manner, before him who stands to

them instead of God, and whose words involve duties. The young ruler came running, not waiting till Christ should look on him or call—not fearing, but intruding himself. Christ exposed what was in his heart, and he who ran to accost Him, stole away sorrowing.

4. And here perhaps we shall understand something of the contrast between St. Peter's first and second profession of service to Christ. He made the first of his own accord. Christ had said, "Whither I go, thou canst not follow Me now."[1] He answered, "Lord, why cannot I follow Thee now? I will lay down my life for Thy sake." Now, we may indeed say that his fall was merely an instance of weakness;—so it may have been;—yet it does seem likely too, that, at the time he said it, he had not that perfect devotion to Christ which he had afterwards. Let it not be imagined that on that former occasion, when "he forsook all and followed" Christ, or again, when he went to meet Him on the sea, the holy Apostle did not act out of the fulness of a perfect heart; but may we not reverently suppose that till Pentecost his state of mind was variable, and sometimes had more of heaven in it than at other times? We may surmise that he, who first said, "Thou art the Christ," and next, "Be it far from Thee, Lord," earning blessing and rebuke almost in one breath, on this occasion came short of the sincerity which he showed before and afterwards. We may surmise that his fault was not merely self-deception, but, in a measure, a reserved devotion; that there was one corner (as it were) of his heart, which at that moment was not

---

[1] John xiii. 33.

Christ's; for the more that is the case, the louder men commonly talk, in order to beat down the risings of conscience. When a man half suspects his own honesty, he makes loud professions of it. Contrast, with this, St. Peter's words after our Lord's resurrection. First, he waits for Christ to say, " Follow Me ;" next, observe his answer to Christ, " Lord, Thou knowest all things ; Thou knowest that I love Thee."[1] Then he felt that he dare appeal to his heart-searching Judge, in witness that he was making an unreserved surrender of himself. He did not thus speak before.

5. Another illustration may be drawn from the state of mind which not unfrequently is found in a person who has been injured or insulted, and is bound in duty to forgive the offenders. I am supposing a well-meaning and religious man ; and he often lies under the temptation to forgive them up to a certain point, but at the same time to make a reserve in favour of his own dignity, or to satisfy his sense of justice, and thus to take the matter in part into his own hands. He cannot get himself honestly to surrender every portion of resentment, and to leave his cause simply to God, as remembering the words, " Vengeance is Mine ; I will repay."[2] This reluctance is sometimes seen very clearly under other circumstances, in the instance of children, who, whether they be out of temper, or obstinate, or otherwise what they should not be, cannot bring themselves to do that very thing which they ought to do, which is enough, which comes up to the mark. They are quite conscious that they are wrong, and they wish

[1] John xxi. 15.   [2] Rom. xii. 19.

to be right; and they will do a number of good things short of what is required of them; they will show their wish to be at one again with the parties who are displeased with them; they will go round about their duty,—but from pride, or other wrong feeling, they shrink from going close to it, and, as it were, embracing it. And so again, if they have been in fault, they will make excuses, or half confess; they will do much, but they cannot bring themselves to do a whole deed, and make a clean breast of it.

6. Lastly may be mentioned, the case of persons seeking the truth. How often are they afraid or loth to throw themselves on God's guidance, and beg Him to teach them! how loth to promise in His sight that they will follow the truth wherever it leads them! but whether from fear of what the world will say, fear of displeasure of friends, or of ridicule of strangers, or of triumph of enemies, or from entertaining some fancy or conceit of their own, which they are loth to give up, they hang back, and think to gain the truth, not by rising and coming for it, but, as it were, by a mere careless extension and grasp of the hand, while they sit at ease, or proceed with other work that employs them. Much might be said on what is a very fertile part of the subject.

In all these ways, then, to which many more might be added, men serve God, but do not serve Him with a *perfect* heart, or "in simplicity and sincerity." And in explaining what I consider Scripture to mean by perfectness of purpose, I have explained also in a measure how it is that a person must know if he has it. For it is a state of mind which will not commonly lie hid from those who are blest with it. Not more different is ice from the flowing stream, than a half purpose from a whole one. "He bloweth with His wind, and the waters flow." So is it when God prevails on a heart to open itself to Him, and admit Him wholly. There is a perceptible difference of feeling in a man, compared with what he was, which, in common circumstances, he cannot mistake. He may have made resolves before, he may have argued himself into a belief of his own sincerity, he may have (as it were) convinced himself that nothing can be required of him more than he has done, he may have asked himself what more *is* there to do, and yet have felt a something in him still which *needed* quieting, which was ever rising up and troubling him, and had to be put down again. But when he really gives himself up to God, when he gets himself honestly to say, "I sacrifice to Thee this cherished wish, this lust, this weakness, this scheme, this opinion: make me what *Thou* wouldest have me; I bargain for nothing; I make no terms; I seek for no previous information whither Thou art taking me; I will be what Thou wilt make me, and all that Thou wilt make me. I say not, I will follow Thee whithersoever Thou goest, for I am weak; but I give myself to Thee, to lead me anywhither. I will follow Thee in the dark, only begging Thee to give me strength according to my day. Try me, O Lord, and seek the ground of my heart; prove me, and examine my thoughts; look well if there be any way of wickedness in me;" search each dark recess with Thy own bright light, "and lead me in the way everlasting,"—what a difference is this! what a plain perceptible change, which cannot be mistaken! what a feeling of satisfaction is poured over the mind! what a sense that at length we are doing what we should do, and approving ourselves to God our Saviour! Such is the blessedness and reward of confession. " I said I will confess my sins unto the Lord, and so Thou forgavest the wickedness of my sin." It matters little whether it is a resolve for the future or a confession of the past; the same temper is involved in both. If a person does not confess with a desire of amendment, it is not a real confession; but he who comes to God to tell before Him sorrowfully all that he knows wrong in himself, is thereby desiring and beginning what is right and holy; and he who comes to beg Him to work in him all that is right and holy, does thereby implicitly condemn and repent of all that is wrong in him. And thus he is altogether innocent; for all his life is made up either of honest endeavour or of honest confession, exactness in doing or sorrow for not doing, of simplicity and sincerity, repentance being on the one side of it, and obedience on the other. Such is the power divinely vouchsafed in the Gospel to an honest purpose. It either *does*, or blots out what is *not* done; or rather by one act, and in itself which is one, it both performs part, and blots out the rest.

And here it is obvious to point out the bearing of what has been said on the subject of Justification. We know that faith justifies us; but what is the test of true faith? Works are its evidence; but they are so on the whole, after a sufficient period of time, to others, and at the judgment of the last day. They scarcely can be considered an evidence definite and available for a man's own comfort at any moment when he seeks for one. He does some things well, some ill; and he is more clear-sighted and more sensitive in the instance of his failings than of his successful endeavours. If what he does well be an evidence of faith, what he does ill will be to him a more convincing proof that he has not faith; and thus he cannot conclusively appeal to his works. Now, I suppose, absolute certainty about our state cannot be attained at all in this life; but the nearest approach to such certainty which is possible, would seem to be afforded by this consciousness of openness and singleness of mind, this good understanding (if I may use such an expression) between the soul and its conscience, to which St. Paul so often alludes. "Our rejoicing is this," he says, "the testimony of our conscience, that in simplicity and godly sincerity we have had our conversation in the world." He did not rejoice in his faith, but he was justified by faith, because he could rejoice in his sincerity. Perfectness of heart, simple desire to please God, "a spirit without guile," a true and loyal will, where these are present, faith is justifying; and whereas those who have this integrity will more or less be conscious of it, therefore, after all exceptions duly made on the score of depression of spirits, perplexity of mind, horror at past sins, and the like, still, on the whole, really religious persons will commonly enjoy a subdued but comfortable hope and trust that they are in a state of justification. They may have this hope more or less; they may deserve to have it more or less; at times they may even be unconscious of it, and yet it may secretly support them; they may fancy themselves in perfect darkness, yet it may be a light cheering them forward; they may vary in their feelings about their state from day to day, and yet, whether or not they can collect evidence to satisfy their reason, still if they be really perfect in heart, there will be this secret sense of their sincerity, with their reason or against reason, to whisper to them peace. And on the other hand, it never will rise above a sober trust, even in the most calm, peaceful, and holy minds. They to the end will still but say, " Lord, I believe; help Thou mine unbelief." They still will say, in St. Paul's words, " I am conscious to myself of nothing, yet am I not hereby justified, but he that judgeth me is the Lord." " Judge me, O Lord; examine me; search the ground of my heart; judge *Thou* me, who art the sole Judge; I judge not myself. I do but say, *Thou* knowest me; I say not, I know." It was but the Pharisee that said, " Lord, I thank Thee I am not as other men are." We can but "gird up the loins of our minds, be sober, and hope to the end, and pass the time of our sojourning here in fear,"[1] though "the day has dawned, and the day star has arisen in our hearts."[2]

One more remark must be made. It may be objected, that, if the feeling of a good conscience be the evidence

---

[1] 1 Pet. i. 13—17.　　　　[2] 2 Pet. i. 19.

to us of our justification, then are persons in a justified state who are external to the Church, provided they have this feeling. I reply briefly,—for to say much here would be out of place,—that every one will be judged according to his light and his privileges; and any man who has really the testimony of a good conscience is acting up to his light, whatever that is. This does not, however, show that he has always so acted; nor determine what his light is; nor what degree of favour he is in; nor whether he might have been in greater, had his past actions been other than they have been. It but shows that he is accepted *in* that state in which he is, be it one of greater favour or less, heathenism,[1] schism, superstition, or heresy; and that, because his faults and errors *at present* are not wilful. And in like manner, in the case of members of the Church, a good conscience evidences God's acceptance, according to that measure of acceptance which He gives in His Church,—that is, it evidences their justification; whereas what privileges attach to bodies or creeds external to the Church we do not know. No inward feeling can do more than what is here assigned to it, unless an inward feeling can be the evidence of an external revelation.

But here I am speaking to members of the Church; to those who, if they serve God with a perfect heart, are justified. Let us then, since this is our privilege, attempt to share in St. Paul's sincerity, that we may share in his rejoicing. Let us endeavour to become friends of God and fellow-citizens with the saints; not

<hr>

[1] Acts x. 35

by sinless purity, for we have it not; not in our deeds of price, for we have none to show; not in our privileges, for they are God's acts, not ours; not in our Baptism, for it is outward; but in that which is the fruit of Baptism within us, not a word but a power, not a name but a reality, which, though it can claim nothing, can beg everything;—an honest purpose, an unreserved, entire submission of ourselves to our Maker, Redeemer, and Judge. Let us beg Him to aid us in our endeavour, and, as He has begun a good work in us, to perform it until the day of the Lord Jesus.

SERMON XVIII.

MANY CALLED, FEW CHOSEN.

(SEPTUAGESIMA.)

1 Cor. ix. 24.

" Know ye not that they which run in a race run all, but one receiveth
the prize ?   So run, that ye may obtain."

NOTHING is more clearly brought out in Scripture, or more remarkable in itself than this, that in every age, out of the whole number of persons blessed with the means of grace, few only have duly availed them of this great benefit. So certain, so uniform is the fact, that it is almost stated as a doctrine. " Many are called, few are chosen." Again, " Strive to enter in at the strait gate ; for many, I say unto you, shall seek to enter in, and shall not be able." And again, " Wide is the gate, and broad is the way, that leadeth to destruction, and many there be which go in thereat. . . . Strait is the gate, and narrow is the way that leadeth unto life, and few there be that find it." And St. Paul seems expressly to turn the historical fact into a doctrine, when he says, by way of remark upon his own day, as compared with former ages of the Church,

"Even so then, at this present time also," that is, as formerly, "there is a *remnant*, according to the election of grace." [1]

The word "remnant" is frequent with the prophets, from whom St. Paul takes it. Isaiah, for instance, says, "Though the number of the children of Israel be as the sand of the sea, a *remnant* shall be saved." Jeremiah speaks of "the *remnant* of Judah," and the "small number," to which a return was promised. Ezekiel, too, declares that God "will leave a *remnant*," "that ye may have some," continues the divine oracle, "that shall escape the sword among the nations, when ye shall be scattered through the countries. And they that escape of you shall remember Me among the nations, whither they shall be carried captives." And so well understood was this, that the hope of good men never reached beyond it. Neither the promise, on the one hand, nor the hope, on the other, ever goes beyond the prospect of a remnant being saved. Thus the consolation given to the Church in the Book of Jeremiah is, that God "will not make a *full* end;" and Ezra, confessing the sins of his people, expresses his dread lest there should be "*no* remnant." [2] Thus Christ, His Apostles, and His Prophets, all teach the same doctrine, that the chosen are few, though many are called: that one gains the prize, though many run the race.

This rule in God's dispensations is most abundantly and awfully illustrated in their history. At the time of

<hr>

[1] Matt. xx. 16.   Luke xiii. 24.   Matt. vii. 13, 14.   Rom. xi. 5.
[2] Rom. ix. 27.   Jer. xliv. 28.   Ezek. vi. 8, 9.   Jer. xlvi. 28. Ezra ix. 14.

the Flood, out of a whole world, in spite of Adam's punishment, in spite of Enoch's preaching, in spite of Noah's setting about the ark, eight only found acceptance with God, and even one of these afterwards incurred a curse. When the Israelites were brought out of Egypt by miracle, two only of the whole generation entered the land of promise. Two tribes alone out of twelve remained faithful at the time of the great schism, and continued in possession of God's covenanted mercies. And when Christ came, the bulk of His own people rejected Him, and His Church came but of the scanty remnant, "as a root out of a dry ground."

Moreover, it is observable that Almighty God seems as if to rejoice, and deigns to delight Himself in this small company who adhere to Him, as if their fewness had in it something of excellence and preciousness. "Fear not," he says, "little flock, for it is your Father's good pleasure to give you the kingdom." "Behold, I send you forth as sheep in the midst of wolves." "I pray not for the world, but for those whom Thou hast given Me." In a like spirit, St. Paul says, "Whom He did foreknow, He also did predestinate." And in the time of Elijah, "I have reserved to Myself seven thousand men, who have not bowed the knee to the image of Baal." And in the time of Moses, "The Lord did not set His love upon you, nor choose you, because ye were more in number than any people, for ye were the fewest of all people."[1]

And it need scarcely be added, that the same

[1] Luke xii. 32. Matt. x. 16. John xvii. 9. Rom. viii. 29 ; xi. 4. Deut. vii. 7.

bountifulness on God's part, the same ingratitude on the part of man, the same scarcity of faith, sanctity, truth, and conscientiousness, have marked the course of the Christian Dispensation, as well as of those former ones of which the inspired volume is the record.

So clear is this, that persons who, from unwillingness to take the narrow way, or from other like cause, have disputed it, have scarcely anything left them to urge but certain false views or consequences, which have been, or may be, entertained concerning the doctrine. And as these misconceptions tend at once to prejudice the mind against it, and to pervert its reception of it, I shall now examine one or two of the objections to which it is exposed.

1. Now, first, it has often happened that, because the elect are few, serious men have considered that this took place in consequence of some fixed decree of God. They have thought that they were few, because it was God's will that they should not be many. Now it is doubtless a great mystery, why this man receives the truth and practises it, and that man does not. We do not know how it comes to pass; but surely we do not tend to solve it, by saying God has so decreed it. If you say that God does absolutely choose the one and reject the other, then *that* becomes the mystery. You do but throw it back a step. It is as difficult to explain this absolute willing or not willing, on the part of Almighty God, as to account for the existence of free will in man. It is as inexplicable why God should act differently towards this man and that, as it is why this man or that should act differently towards God. On the other hand, we

are solemnly assured in Scripture that God "hath no pleasure in the death of the wicked;" that He is "not willing that any should perish, but that all should come to repentance."[1]

The doctrine, then, which is implied in the text, does not lead us to any hard notions of God. He is a most loving Father still, though few are chosen. His mercy is over all His works, and to no one does the word of life come but with the intent that he may live. If the many remain in unbelief, they "are not straitened" in God's love, but they "are straitened in their own bowels." Man will not be what by God's renewing and co-operating grace he might be. It is man's doing, not God's will, that, while the visible Church is large, the Church invisible is small.

2. But it may be said that this doctrine lies open to another objection: that to believe that few only find the gate of life, necessarily makes a man self-confident and uncharitable towards others, whether he considers himself predestined to life or not. Every one, it is said, will place himself on the safe side of the line, and, of course, will place his friends with him; and all others he will give over, as if they were to be classed among the many. Now the text, and the verses which follow it, supply the readiest answer to this objection. St. Paul speaks as if the Christian course were a race, in which one only out of many could succeed. And what is the conclusion he arrives at? "I keep under my body, and bring it into subjection, lest that by any means when I have

<hr>

[1] Ezek. xxxiii. 11. 2 Pet. iii. 9.

preached to others, I myself should be a castaway." You see how far the holy Apostle was from security and self-satisfaction, though he, if any one, would have had a right to feel easy about his state. And the exhortation he gives his brethren is, "So run, that ye may obtain." Are candidates for a prize confident, because only one can gain it? What is the meaning then of asserting that "they which run in a race" take it for granted that they are on the winning side?

And yet it is quite true that there are men who, in consequence of holding the doctrine that the chosen are few, instead of exerting themselves, become proud and careless. But then, let it be observed, these persons hold another doctrine besides, which is the real cause of their carnal security. They not merely think that Christ's flock is small, but that every man can tell whether or no he belongs to it, and that they do know that they themselves belong to it. Now, if a man thinks he knows for certain that he shall be saved, of course he will be much tempted to indulge in a carnal security, and to look down upon others, and that, whether the true flock of Christ is large or small. It is not the knowledge that the chosen are *few* which occasions these bad feelings, but a man's private assurance that *he* is chosen.

St. Paul tells us, that whom God "did foreknow He also did predestinate," and "whom he did predestinate, them He also called; and whom He called them He also justified; and whom He justified, them He also glorified;" but he does not say that God discloses this to the persons who are subjects of it.

He has deep and eternal counsels, but they are secret ones; He has a decree, founded on righteousness and truth, but it is not revealed. We know not, we cannot know, whom God has chosen for salvation; and while we understand this, and keep it before us, we shall not be puffed up about ourselves, nor harsh and censorious towards others, though we bear in mind ever so much that the gate of heaven is narrow, and few there be that find it.

This, I think, is very plain; yet it may be useful to enlarge upon it. Let us take an illustration, not exact, but sufficient for the purpose. Supposing we had to cast lots for some worldly benefit, a sum of money, or some desirable post, or the like, and only three or four out of a great number could succeed, how should we be affected beforehand? Should we be at all led to speculate or judge who were to be successful, who unsuccessful? And why not? Because it would be idle to employ our thoughts about an event which nothing we saw before us, nothing we could see, tended to discover to us; idle to attempt to decide in a case where there were no means of deciding. For what any of us could know, one man had as good a prospect as another. We should feel as much as this, that a certain prize was destined for some out of all of us; we should feel anxious and expectant, and that would be the end of the matter. Now, as regards our heavenly prospects, the decision indeed is not a matter of chance; God forbid!—but yet it is as much hid from us as if it were. Nothing that we see, or think we see, can enable us to decide about the future. We do not know but those who are the greatest sinners now, may repent, reform, and in severity and austereness of life surpass ourselves; the last oftentimes become the first. Nor do we know about ourselves, however fair we seem, but we may fall away. We cannot compare ourselves with others at all. All we know is, and a most awful thought it is, that out of the whole number of those who have received the Christian calling, out of ourselves and our friends, and all whom we see and hear of in the intercourse of life, but a few are chosen; but a few act up to their privileges. Now, considering the inscrutable darkness in which the event lies, hid almost like the time of judgment in the prescience of Almighty God, is this a thought to fill us with confidence and pride, or is it not rather an exceedingly solemn and dreadful thought? Should a prophet declare that out of a given number of persons but a few would be alive this time next year, that the greater part would die, should we, under any circumstances, feel altogether easy, were our health ever so good in appearance, or were there ever so many older persons than ourselves in the number addressed ? Should we not be made very anxious at every little indisposition, or at every symptom of illness, or at every chance of accident from without? Should we have much heart for speculating about others?

And this surely is the real state of the case. Our means of judging ourselves or others are so very insufficient, that they are practically nothing; and it is our wisdom to let the attempt alone. We may know about ourselves, that at present we are sincere and earnest, and so far in God's favour; we may be able to say that such and such words or deeds are right or wrong in another; but how different is this from having the capacity to decide absolutely about our or his eternal doom! How different this from being able to take in the whole compass of our lives, the whole range and complication of our thoughts, words, deeds, habits, principles, and motives! How different from being able to argue from what we see to what God knows, or from discerning whether the divine seed has taken root in particular minds! St. Paul himself, though conscious of nothing, says to the Corinthians, "Yet am I not hereby justified, but He that judgeth me is the Lord; therefore judge nothing before the time, until the Lord come, who both will bring to light the hidden things of darkness, and will make manifest the counsels of the hearts."[1] We cannot estimate the real value of anything which we or others do; or how it stands in making up their or our final account in God's sight. What is a sign of faith in one man, is not in another; what is a great deed in one man, is not in another. The differences of disposition, education, and guidance are so great, and make the problem so intricate, that it would seem to be the height of madness (were it not sometimes attempted by persons not mad) to attempt to solve it. St. Paul says in one place that he has not "attained." On the contrary, at the end of his life, after fighting a good fight, then he says that "henceforth there *was* laid up for him a crown of righteousness."[2] Thus there was a point at which, and not before, his

---

[1] 1 Cor. iv. 5.   [2] Phil. iii. 12.   2 Tim. iv. 8.

salvation was, practically speaking, secured. What happened in his case, may, for what we know to the contrary, happen in ours also; and the point at which victory is certain may vary in the case of every one of us.

Or, again, let us recur to the Apostle's words in the text: "Know ye not," he says, "that they which run in a race run all, but one receiveth the prize? So run, that ye may obtain." When a number of persons are contending for a prize, since one alone can obtain it, it is plain that no one, from what he knows about himself, can conclude anything concerning his own success; because, even be he ever so likely in himself, yet another may be more likely. The event is utterly and totally hid from him, unless he be very well acquainted with his rivals. Now here, again, the illustration used is not altogether parallel. In the prize which we run for, praised be God, there is no such rivalry of one against another; there is no restriction; and if all did their duty, all would succeed. Yet the effect is the same as regards our knowledge, as if only one could succeed; I mean, we do not know the *standard* by which God will judge us. Nothing that we are can assure us that we shall answer to what He expects of us; for we do not know what that is; what we are can but cheer us and give us hopes and good spirits. In contending for the prize, it is of no use to be second best. He who comes second, as little gains it as he who comes last. And so in striving to enter in at the strait gate, unless we rise to that which God requires of us, unless we attain, no matter how near we once were to attaining;—after all, it has come to this, that we have not attained. This thought will surely ever keep us from dwelling on our own proficiency, whatever it is; rather it will lead us, with the great Apostle, to "follow after, if that we may apprehend that for which we are apprehended of Christ Jesus." It is not till life is over, when we have lived in the fear of God consistently, when death has put its seal upon us, and cut us off from the chance of falling, that others, surveying us, and observing our consistency and perseverance in well-doing, will humbly trust that we are in St. Paul's case, to whom, after "finishing his course," it was revealed that "a crown of righteousness was laid up for him."

The doctrine, then, that few are chosen though many be called, properly understood, has no tendency whatever to make us fancy ourselves secure and others reprobate. We cannot see the heart, we can but judge from externals, from words and deeds, professions and habits. But these will not save us, unless we persevere in them to the end; and they are no evidence that we shall be saved, except so far as they suggest hope that we shall persevere. They are but a beginning; they tell for nothing till they are completed. Till we have done all, we have done nothing; we have but a prospect, not possession. If we ultimately do attain, every good thing we shall have done will have tended to that attainment, as a race tends to a goal; but, unless we attain, it will not have so tended; and, therefore, from no good thing which we do can we argue that we are sure to attain.

3. One other misconception of this doctrine shall be mentioned, and then I will conclude. It may be said, then, that the belief that true Christians are few leads men to isolate themselves in their own opinions, to withdraw from the multitude, to adopt new and extravagant views, and to be singular in their conduct, as if what the many held and did could not be right. This may sometimes be the case; but I would have it remarked, that if true Christians are few, they must in a certain sense be singular. Singularity indeed is no proof that we are right in our opinions, or are Christ's chosen, because there are a great many ways of being singular, and all cannot be right. And persons are often, as is objected, singular, from love of being so, from conceit, or desire to excite remark; and therefore it does not follow that even those who profess the views of Christ's true servants, are themselves in their number. But, on the other hand, neither does it follow, because men are singular in their opinions, that they are wrong, nor, because other opinions are generally received in their day, that therefore these are right. If the multitude of men are ever in the broad way "that leadeth to destruction," there is no ground for maintaining that, in order to be right in our religious views, we must agree with the many; rather, if such as persons are, their opinions are also, it would seem to be certain that those opinions which are popular will ever be mistaken and dangerous as being popular opinions. Those who serve God faithfully must ever look to be accounted, in their generation, singular, intemperate, and extreme. They are not so; they must guard against becoming so; if they are so,

they are equally wrong as the many, however they may
in other respects, differ from them; but still it is no proof
that they are so, because the many call them so. It is
no proof that they are so, because others take it for
granted that they are, pass their doctrines over, put
their arguments aside without a word,—treat them
gravely, or are vexed about them, or impatient with
them, or ridicule them, or fiercely oppose them. No;
there are numberless clouds which flit over the sky,
there are numberless gusts which agitate the air to and
fro : as many, as violent, as far-spreading, as fleeting, as
uncertain, as changing, are the clouds and the gales of
human opinion; as suddenly, as impetuously, as fruit-
lessly, do they assail those whose mind is stayed on
God. They come and they go; they have no life in
them, nor abidance. They agree together in nothing
but in this, in threatening like clouds, and sweeping
like gusts of wind. They are the voice of the many;
they have the strength of the world, and they are
directed against the few. Their argument, the sole
argument in their behalf, is their prevalence at the
moment; not that they existed yesterday, not that they
will exist to-morrow; not that they base themselves on
reason, or ancient belief, but that they are merely what
every one now takes for granted, or, perhaps, supposes
to be in Scripture, and therefore not to be disputed :—
not that they have most voices through long periods,
but that they happen to be most numerously professed
in the passing hour. On the other hand, divine truth
is ever one and the same; it changes not, any more
than its Author: it stands to reason, then, that those

who uphold it must ever be exposed to the charge of singularity, either for this or for that portion of it, in a world which is ever varying.

What a most awful view does human society present to those who would survey it religiously! Go where you will, you find persons with their own standards of right and wrong, yet each different from each. Thus everywhere you find both a witness that there is a standard, and yet an evidence everywhere that that standard is lost. Go where you will, you find in each separate circle certain persons held in esteem as patterns of what men should be; each sect and party has its Doctors, its Confessors, and its Saints. And in all parties you will find so many men possessed of good points of character, if not exemplary in their lives, that to judge by appearances, you do not know why the chosen should not be many instead of few. Your very perplexity in reconciling the surface of things with our Lord's announcements, the very temptation you lie under to explain away the plain words of Scripture, shows you that your standard of good and evil, and the standard of all around you, must be very different from God's standard. It shows you, that if the chosen are few, there must be some particular belief necessary, or some particular line of conduct, or something else different from what the world supposes, in order to account for this solemn declaration. It suggests to you that perchance there must be a certain perfection, completeness, consistency, entireness of obedience, for a man to be chosen, which most men miss in one point or another. It suggests to you that there is a great difference between

being a hearer of the word and a doer; a well-wisher of
the truth, or an approver of good men or good actions,
and a faithful servant of the truth. It suggests to you
that it is one thing to be in earnest, another and higher
to be "rooted and grounded in love." It suggests to
you the exceeding dangerousness of single sins, or particular bad habits. It suggests to you the peril of
riches, cares of this life, station, and credit.

Of course we must not press the words of Scripture;
we do not know the exact meaning of the word
" chosen;" we do not know what is meant by being
saved " so as by fire;" we do not know what is meant
by " few." But still the few can never mean the many;
and to be called without being chosen cannot but be a
misery. We know that the man, in the parable, who
came to the feast without a wedding garment, was "cast
into outer darkness." [1] Let us then set at nought the
judgment of the many, whether about truth and falsehood, or about ourselves, and let us go by the judgment
of that line of Saints, from the Apostles' times down-
wards, who were ever spoken against in their generation,
tion, ever honoured afterwards,—singular in each point
of time as it came, but continuous and the same in the
line of their history,—ever protesting against the many,
ever agreeing with each other. And, in proportion as we
attain to their judgment of things, let us pray God to
make it live in us; so that at the Last Day, when all
veils are removed, we may be found among those who
are inwardly what they seem outwardly,—who with
Enoch, and Noah, and Abraham, and Moses, and Joshua,

[1] Matt. xxii. 13.

and Caleb, and Phineas, and Samuel, and Elijah, and
Jeremiah, and Ezekiel, and the Baptist, and St. Paul,
have " borne and had patience, and for His Name-sake
laboured and not fainted," watched in all things, done
the work of an Evangelist, fought a good fight, finished
their course, kept the faith.

SERMON XIX.

PRESENT BLESSINGS.

(SEPTUAGESIMA.)

PHIL. iv. 18.

" I have all, and abound : I am full."

SUCH is St. Paul's confession concerning his temporal condition, even in the midst of his trials. Those trials brought with them spiritual benefits ; but, even as regarded this world, he felt he had cause for joy and thankfulness, in spite of sorrows, pains, labours, and self-denials. He did not look on this life with bitterness, complain of it morosely, or refuse to enjoy it ; he was not soured, as the children of men often are, by his trials ; but he felt, that if he had troubles in this world, he had blessings also ; and he did not reject these, but made much of them. "I have all, and abound: I am full," he says. And, elsewhere, he tells us, that "every creature of God is good," and that "godliness is profitable unto all things, having the promise of the life that now is, and of that which is to come."[1]

[1] 1 Tim. iv. 4, 8.

Gloom is no Christian temper; that repentance is not real, which has not love in it; that self-chastisement is not acceptable, which is not sweetened by faith and cheerfulness. We must live in sunshine, even when we sorrow; we must live in God's presence, we must not shut ourselves up in our own hearts, even when we are reckoning up our past sins.

These thoughts are suitable on this day, when we first catch a sight, as it were, of the Forty Days of Lent. If God then gives us grace to repent, it is well; if He enables us to chasten heart and body, to Him be praise; and for that very reason, while we do so, we must not cease rejoicing in Him. All through Lent we must rejoice, while we afflict ourselves. Though "many be called, but few chosen;" though all run in the race, but "one receiveth the prize;" though we must "so run that we may obtain;" though we must be "temperate in all things," and "keep under our body and bring it into subjection, lest we be castaways;" yet through God alone we can do this; and while He is with us, we cannot but be joyful; for His absence only is a cause for sorrow. The Three Holy Children are said to have stood up in the midst of the fire, and to have called on all the works of God to rejoice with them; on sun and moon, stars of heaven, nights and days, showers and dew, frost and cold, lightnings and clouds, mountains and hills, green things upon the earth, seas and floods, fowls of the air, beasts and cattle, and children of men,— to praise and bless the Lord, and magnify Him for ever. We have no such trial as theirs; we have no such awful suspense as theirs, when they entered the burning fiery furnace; we attempt for the most part what we know; we begin what we think we can go through. We can neither instance their faith nor equal their rejoicing; yet we can imitate them so far, as to look abroad into this fair world, which God made " very good," while we mourn over the evil which Adam brought into it; to hold communion with what we see there, while we seek Him who is invisible; to admire it, while we abstain from it; to acknowledge God's love, while we deprecate His wrath; to confess that, many as are our sins, His grace is greater. Our sins are more in number than the hairs of our head; yet even the hairs of our head are all numbered by Him. He counts our sins, and, as He counts, so can He forgive; for that reckoning, great though it be, comes to an end; but His mercies fail not, and His Son's merits are infinite.

Let us, then, on this day, dwell upon a thought, which it will be a duty to carry with us through Lent, the thought of the blessings and mercies of which our present life is made up. St. Paul said that he had all, and abounded, and was full; and this, in a day of persecution. Surely, if we have but religious hearts and eyes, we too must confess that our daily and hourly blessings in this life are not less than his. Let us recount some of them.

1. First, then, we ought to bless and praise God that we have the gift of life. By this I mean, not merely that we live, but for those blessings which are included in the notion of our living. He has made life in its very nature to imply the existence of certain blessings which are themselves a happiness, and which bring it

to pass that, in spite of all evils, life in itself, except in rare cases, cannot be otherwise than desirable. We cannot live without the means of life; without the means of life we should die; and the means of life are means of pleasure. It might have so been ordered that life could not have been sustained without the use of such means as were indifferent, neither pleasurable nor painful,—or of means which were even painful; as in the case of illness or disease, when we actually find that we cannot preserve it without painful remedies. Now, supposing the ordinary ways of preserving it had been what are now but extraordinary : supposing food were medicine; supposing wounds or blows imparted health and strength. But it is not so. On the contrary, life consists in things pleasant; it is sustained by blessings. And, moreover, the Gospel, by a solemn grant, guarantees these things to us. After the Flood, God Almighty condescended to promise that there never should be such a flood again; that seed-time and harvest should not fail. He ratified the stability of nature by His own Word, and by that Word it is upheld. And in like manner He has, in a special way, guaranteed to us in the Gospel that law of nature whereby good and pleasant gifts are included in our idea of life, and life becomes a blessing. Did He so will, He might sustain us Christians, not by bread only, but by every word that proceedeth out of His mouth. But He has not done so. He has pledged to us those ordinary means of sustenance which we naturally like : " bread shall be given us ; our water shall be sure ; " " all these things shall be added unto us." He has not indeed promised us what the world calls its great prizes; He has not promised us those goods, so called, of which the goodness depends on the imagination; He has not promised us large estates, magnificent domains, houses like palaces, sumptuous furniture, retainers and servants, chariots and horses, rank, name, credit, popularity, power, the deference of others, the indulgence of our wills, luxuries, sensual enjoyments. These, on the contrary, He denies us; and, withal, He declares, that, specious and inviting as they are, really they are evil. But still He has promised that this shall be His rule,—that thus shall it be fulfilled to us as His ordinary providence, viz.—that life shall not be a burden to us, but a blessing, and shall contain more to comfort than to afflict. And giving us as much as this, He bids us be satisfied with it; He bids us confess that we "have all" when we have so much: that we "abound" when we have enough; He promises us food, raiment, and lodging; and He bids us, "having food and raiment, therewith to be content."[1] He bids us be content with those gifts, and withal unsolicitous about them; tranquil, secure, and confident, because He has promised them; He bids us be sure that we shall have so much, and not be disappointed that it is no more. Such is His merciful consideration of us; He does not separate us from this world, though He calls us out of it; He does not reject our old nature when He gives us a new one; He does but redeem it from the curse, and purify it from the infection which came through Adam, and is none of His. He especially blesses the creation to our use, though we be regenerate.

---

[1] 1 Tim. vi. 8.

'Every creature of God," says the Apostle, "is good, and nothing to be refused, if it be received with thanksgiving, for it is sanctified by the word of God and prayer."[1] He does not bid us renounce the creation, but associates us with the most beautiful portions of it. He likens us to the flowers with which He has ornamented the earth, and to the birds that live solitary under heaven, and makes them the type of a Christian. He denies us Solomon's regal magnificence, to unite us to the lilies of the field and the fowls of the air. "Take no thought for your life, what ye shall eat or what ye shall drink ; nor yet for your body, what ye shall put on. Is not the life more than meat, and the body than raiment ? Behold the fowls of the air, for they sow not, neither do they reap, nor gather into barns ; yet your heavenly Father feedeth them. Are ye not much better than they ? .... And why take ye thought for raiment ? Consider the lilies of the field, how they grow ; they toil not, neither do they spin ; and yet I say unto you, that even Solomon in all his glory was not arrayed like one of these."[2]

Here then, surely, is a matter for joy and thankfulness at all seasons, and not the least at times when, with a religious forbearance, and according to the will of the Giver, not from thanklessness but from prudence, we, for a while, more or less withhold from ourselves His good gifts. Then, of all times, when we think it right to suspend our use of the means of life, so far as may not hurt that life, His gift, and to prove how pleasant is the using them by the pain of abstaining from them,—

<hr>

[1] 1 Tim. iv. 4, 5.   [2] Matt. vi. 25—29.

now especially, my brethren, in the weeks in prospect, when we shall be called on to try ourselves, as far as may be, by hunger, or cold, or watching, or seclusion, that we may be brought nearer to God,—let us now thank God that He has not put us into an evil world, or subjected us to a cruel master, but has given us a continual record of His own perfections in all that lies around us. Alas! it will be otherwise hereafter with those whom God puts out of His sight for ever. Their world will be evil; their life will be death; their rulers will be the devil and his angels; flames of fire and the lake of brimstone will be their meat and drink; the heaven above them will be brass; their earth will be dust and ashes; the blood in their veins will be as molten lead. Fearful thought! which it is not right to do more than glance at. Let us utter it, and pass by. Rather it is for us to rejoice that we are still in the light of His countenance, on His good earth, and under His warm sun. Let us thank Him that He gives us the fruits of the earth in their season; that He gives us " food out of the earth, and wine that maketh glad the heart of man, and oil to make him a cheerful countenance, and bread to strengthen man's heart." [1] Thus was it with our fathers of old time; thus is it with us now. After Abraham had fought with the kings, Melchizedek brought forth bread and wine to refresh him The Angels who visited him made themselves men, and ate of the calf which he dressed for them. Isaac blessed Jacob after the savoury meat. Joseph's brethren ate and drank, and were merry with him. The seventy

[1] Ps. civ. 14, 15.

elders went up Mount Sinai with Moses, Aaron, Nadab, and Abihu, and they saw God, and moreover "did eat and drink." David, after his repentance, had "bread set before him, and he did eat." When Elijah went for his life, and requested that he might die, "an Angel touched him, and said unto him, Arise and eat;" and he did eat and drink, once and twice, and lay down to sleep between his meals; and when he arose, he "went in the strength of that meat forty days and forty nights unto Horeb the mount of God." St. Paul also, after his conversion and baptism, "received meat and was strengthened."[1]

2. Again, what a great blessing is that gift, of which I have just spoken in Elijah's case, the gift of sleep! Almighty God does not suffer us to be miserable for a long while together, even when He afflicts us; but He breaks our trial into portions; takes us out of this world ever and anon, and gives us a holy-day time, like children at school, in an unknown and mysterious country.

All this then must be borne in mind, in reflecting on those solemn and sobering truths concerning the Christian's calling, which it is necessary often to insist upon. It is often said, and truly, that the Christian is born to trouble,—that sorrow is the rule with him, and pleasure the exception. But when this is said, it is with reference to seasons, circumstances, events, such things as are adventitious and additional to the gift of life itself. The Christian's *lot* is one of sorrow, but, as

---

[1] Gen. xiv. 18; xviii. 8; xxvii. 25; xliii. 34. Exod. xxiv. 11. 2 Sam. xii. 20. 1 Kings xix. 5—8. Acts ix. 19.

the regenerate *life* with him is happiness, so is the gift of natural life also. We live, therefore we are happy; *upon* this life of ours come joys and sorrows; and in proportion as we are favourites of God, it is sorrow that comes, not joy. Still after all considered in ourselves, that we live; that God breathes in us; that we exist in Him; that we think and act; that we have the means of life; that we have food, and sleep, and raiment, and lodging; and that we are not lonely, but in God's Church, and are sure of brethren by the very token of our having a Father which is in heaven; so far, rejoicing is the very condition of our being, and all pain is little more than external, not reaching to our inmost heart. So far all men almost are on a level, seasons of sickness excepted. Even delicate health and feebleness of life does not preclude these pleasures. And as to seasons of sickness, or even long and habitual pain or disease, the good Lord can compensate for them in His own way by extraordinary supplies of grace, as in early times He made even the torments of Christians in persecution literally pleasant to them. He who so ordered it, that even the red-hot iron did feel pleasant to the Martyrs after a while, cannot fail of means to support His servants when life becomes a burden. But, generally speaking, it is a happiness, and that to all ranks. High and low, rich and poor, have the same refreshment in their pilgrimage. Hunger is as pleasantly appeased by the low as by the high, on coarse fare as on delicate. Sleep is equally the comfort and recruiting of rich and poor. We eat, drink, and sleep, whether we are in sorrow or in joy, in anxiety or in hope. Our natural life is the type of our spiritual life, and thus, in a literal as well as higher sense, we may bless Him "who saveth our life from destruction, and crowneth us with mercy and loving-kindness; who satisfieth our mouth with good things, making us young and lusty as an eagle."[1]

3. Now, again, consider the blessings which we have in Christian brotherhood. In the beginning, woman was made, that man might not be alone, but might have a help meet for him; and our Lord promised that all who gave up this world and this world's kindred for Him, should "receive manifold more in this present time, houses, and brethren, and sisters, and mothers, and children, and lands, with persecutions."[2] You see He mentions the troubles of Christians, which were their lot *as* Christians; but still these did not interfere with the prior law of their very nature, that they should not be friendless. As food and raiment are necessary conditions of life, society is an inseparable adjunct of it. God does not take away food and raiment when He gives grace, nor does He take away brotherhood. He removes from the world to put into the Church. Religion without a Church is as unnatural as life without food and raiment. He began our life anew, but He built it up upon the same foundations; and as He did not strip us of our body, when He made us Christians, neither did He of social ties. Christ finds us in the double tabernacle, of a house of flesh and a house of brethren, and He sanctifies both, not pulls them down. Our first life is in ourselves; our second in our friends.

[1] Ps. ciii. 4, 5.   [2] Mark x. 30.

They whom God forces to part with their near of kin, for His sake, find brethren in the spirit at their side. They who remain solitary, for His sake, have children in the spirit raised up to them. How should we thank God for this great benefit! Now especially, when we are soon to retire, more or less, into ourselves, and to refrain from our ordinary intercourse with one another. let us acknowledge the blessing, whether of the holy marriage bond, or of family affection, or of the love of friends, which He so bounteously bestows. He gives, He takes away; blessed be His Name. But He takes away to give again, and He withdraws one blessing, to restore fourfold. Abraham offered his only son, and received Him back again at the Angel's voice. Isaac "took Rebekah, and she became his wife, and he loved her; and Isaac was comforted after his mother's death." Jacob lost Joseph, and found him governor of Egypt. Job lost all his children, yet his end was more blessed than his beginning. We too, through God's mercy, whether we be young or old, whether we have many friends or few, if we be Christ's, shall all along our pilgrimage find those in whom we may live, who will love us and whom we may love, who will aid us and help us forward, and comfort us, and close our eyes. For His love is a secret gift, which, unseen by the world, binds together those in whom it lives, and makes them live and sympathise in one another.

4. Again, let us bless and praise God for the present peace of the Church, and the freedom of speech and action which He has vouchsafed to us. There have been times when, to be a Christian, was to be an out-

cast and a criminal, when to profess the faith of the Saints would have subjected us to bonds and imprisonment. Let us thank God that at present we have nothing to fear, but may serve Him zealously, "no man forbidding" us. No thanks indeed to the world, which has given us this peace, not from any love to the Church or the Truth, but from selfish and ungodly principles of its own; but great thanks to God, who has made use of the world, and has overruled its course of opinion to our benefit. We have large and noble Churches to worship in; we may go freely to worship when we will; we may enjoy the advice of those who know better than ourselves; we may speak our mind one to another; we may move about freely; we may hold intercourse with whom we will; we may write what we will, explaining, defending, recommending, spreading the truth, without suffering or inconvenience. This is the blessing which we pray for in our Collects; and wonderfully has God granted it for very many years past. We pray daily that God would " give peace in our time." We pray three times a week that " those evils, which the craft and subtilty of the devil or man worketh against us, be brought to nought;" and " that, being hurt by no persecutions, we may evermore give thanks unto God in His Holy Church." We pray yearly that " the course of this world may be so peaceably ordered by His governance, that His Church may joyfully serve Him in all godly quietness;" and that He may " keep His household. the Church, in continual godliness, that through His protection it may be free from all adversities, and devoutly given to serve Him, in good works, to the glory of His Name." Now all this is most wonderfully fulfilled to us at this day,—praised be His great mercy! You will ask, perhaps, whether too much prosperity is not undesirable for the Church? —It is so; but I am speaking, not of the Church, but of ourselves as individuals: what is dangerous to the body, may be a blessing to the separate members. As to ourselves, one by one, God has His own secret chastisements for us, which, if He loves us, He will apply when we need them; but, if we know how to use the blessing duly, it is, I say, a great gift, that we are allowed to serve God with such freedom and in such peace as are now vouchsafed us. Great mercy indeed, which we forget because we are used to it; which many prophets and righteous men in the first ages of the Gospel had not, yet which we have had from our youth up. We from our youth up have lived in peace; with no persecution, no terror, no hindrance in serving God. The utmost we have had to endure, is what is almost too trifling for a Christian to mention,—cold looks, or contempt, or ridicule, from those who have not the heart themselves to attempt the narrow way.

5. Lastly, and very briefly, my brethren, let us remind ourselves of our own privileges here in this place. How great is our privilege, my brethren!—every one of us enjoys the great privilege of daily Worship and weekly Communion. This great privilege God has given to me and to you,—let us enjoy it while we have it. Not any one of us knows how long it may be his own. Perhaps there is no one among us all who can reckon upon it for a continuance. Perhaps, or rather probably, it is

a bright spot in our lives. Perhaps we shall look upon these days or years, time hence ; and then reflect, when all is over, how pleasant they were ; how pleasant to come, day after day, quietly and calmly, to kneel before our Maker,—week after week, to meet our Lord and Saviour. How soothing will then be the remembrauce of His past gifts ! we shall remember how we got up . early in the morning, and how all things, light or darkness, sun or air, cold or freshness, breathed of Him,—of Him, the Lord of glory, who stood over us, and came down upon us, and gave Himself to us, and poured forth milk and honey for our sustenance, though we saw Him not. Surely we have all, and abound : we are full.

SERMON XX.

ENDURANCE, THE CHRISTIAN'S PORTION.

(SEXAGESIMA.)

GEN. xlii. 36.

" All these things are against me."

SO spoke the Patriarch Jacob, when Joseph had been made away with, Simeon was detained in Egypt, Benjamin threatened, and his remaining sons suspected by him and distrusted; when out of doors, nay, at his door, was a grievous famine, enemies or strangers round about, evil in prospect, and in the past a number of sad remembrances to pain, not to cheer him,—the dreadful misconduct of his own family and its consequences, and, further back, the wrath of Esau, his separation from his father's house, his wanderings, and his ill-usage by Laban. From his youth upwards he had been full of sorrows, and he bore them with a troubled mind. His first words are, "If God will be with me . . . then shall the Lord be my God." His next, "Deliver me, I pray Thee." His next, "Ye have troubled me." His next, "I will go down into the grave unto my son mourning." His next, "All these things are against me." And his next, "Few and evil have the days of the years of my life been."[1] Blow after blow, stroke after stroke, trouble came like hail. That one hailstone falls is a proof, not that no more will come, but that others are coming surely; when we feel the first, we say, " It *begins* to hail,"—we do not argue that it is over, but that it is to come. Thus was it with Jacob: the storm muttered around him, and heavy drops fell while he was in his father's house; it drove him abroad. It did not therefore cease because he was out in it: it did not end because it had begun. Rather, it continued, because it had begun; its beginning marked its presence; it began upon a law, which was extended over him in manhood also and old age, as in early youth. It was his calling to be in the storm : it was his very life to be a pilgrimage; it was the very thread of the days of his years to be few and evil.

And what Jacob was all his life, that was his son Joseph at least in the early part of it; for thirteen years, from seventeen to thirty, he was in trouble far greater than Jacob's;—in captivity, in slavery, in prison, in bonds so tight that the iron is said to have entered into his soul. And what Joseph was in the beginning of life, such was Abraham, his forefather, in the latter half of it. For seventy-five years he lived in his "father's house;" but henceforward he was a wanderer. Thus did Almighty God, by the instance of the patriarchs of His ancient people, remind that

---

[1] Gen. xxviii. 20, 21 ; xxxii. 11 ; xxxiv. 30 ; xxxvii. 35 ; xlii. 36 ; xlvii. 9.

people themselves that this world was not their rest; thus did He foreshadow that condition of life, which is not only a lesson, but a pattern to us of our very state of life, "if we live godly in Christ Jesus."[1] He Himself, the Lord Incarnate, chose only to sojourn on earth; He had not where to lay His head. "Let us go forth, therefore, unto Him without the camp, bearing His reproach, for here we have no continuing city, but we seek one to come."[2] In Jacob is prefigured the Christian. He said, "All these things are against me;" and what he said in a sort of dejection of mind that must the Christian say, not in dejection, not sorrowfully, or passionately, or in complaint, or in impatience, but calmly, as if confessing a doctrine. "All these things are against me;" but it is my portion; they are against me, that I may fight against them and overcome them. If there were no enemy, there could be no conflict; were there no trouble, there could be no faith; were there no trial, there could be no love; were there no fear, there could be no hope. Hope, faith, and love are weapons, and weapons imply foes and encounters; and, relying on my weapons, I will glory in my suffering, being "persuaded that neither death, nor life, nor Angels, nor principalities, nor powers, nor things present, nor things to come, nor height, nor depth, nor any other creature, shall be able to separate us from the love of God which is in Christ Jesus our Lord."[3]

That trouble and sorrow are in some especial sense

---

[1] 2 Tim. iii. 12.　　　　　[2] Heb. xiii. 13, 14.
[3] Rom. viii. 38, 39.

the lot of the Christian, is plain from such passages
of Scripture as the following:—For instance, St. Paul
and St. Barnabas remind the disciples "that we must
through much tribulation enter into the kingdom of
God." Again, St. Paul says, "If so be that we suffer
with Him, that we may be also glorified together."
Again, "If we suffer, we shall also reign with Him."
Again, "Yea, and all that will live godly in Christ
Jesus, shall suffer persecution." Again, St. Peter, "If,
when ye do well, and suffer for it, ye take it patiently,
this is acceptable with God; for even hereunto were
ye called." And our Saviour declares, that those who
have given up the relations of this world "for His sake
and the Gospel's" shall receive "an hundred-fold"
now, "with persecutions." And St. Paul speaks in
his own case of his "perils," by sea and land, from
friend and foe, without and within him, of the body
and of the soul. Yet he adds, "I will glory of the
things which concern mine infirmities."[1]

To passages, however, like these, it is natural to
object that they do not apply to the present time; that
they apply to a time of persecution, which is past and
over; and that men enter the kingdom now, without
the afflictions which it once involved. What we see, it
may be said, is a disproof of so sad and severe a doctrine.
In this age, and in this country, the Church surely
is in peace; rights are secured to it, and privileges
added. Christians now, to say the very least, have
liberty of person and property; they live without dis-

[1] Acts xiv. 22. Rom. viii. 17. 2 Tim. ii. 12; iii. 12. 1 Pet. ii. 20.
Matt. xix. 29. Mark x. 30. 2 Cor. xi. 30.

quietude, and they die happily. Nay, they have much more than mere toleration, they have possession of the whole country; there are none but Christians in it; and if they suffer persecution, it must be (as it were) self-inflicted from the hands of each other. Christianity is the law of the land; its ministry is a profession, its offices are honours, its name a recommendation. So far from Christians being in trial because they are Christians, those who are not Christians, infidels and profligates, it is they who are under persecution. Under disabilities indeed these are, and justly; but it would be as true to say that Christians are justly in trouble, as to say that they are in trouble at all. What confessorship is there in a man's putting himself in the front of the Christian fight, when that front is a benefice or a dignity? Rulers of the Church were aforetime marks for the persecutor; now they are but forced into temporal rank and power. Aforetime, the cross was in the inventory of holy treasures, handed down from Bishop to Bishop; but now what self-denial is there in the Apostolate, what bitterness in Christ's cup, what marks of the Lord Jesus in the touch of His Hand, what searching keenness in His sacred Breath? Of old time, indeed, as the Spirit forthwith drave Him into the wilderness to be tempted of the devil, so they, also, who received the Almighty Comforter, in any of His high gifts, were at once among the wild beasts of Ephesus, or amid the surges of the sea; but there are no such visible proofs now of the triumphs of God's grace, humbling the individual, while using him for heavenly purposes.

This is what objectors may say; and, in corroboration, they may tell us to look at the feelings of the world towards the Church and its sacred offices, and to judge for ourselves whether they have not the common sense of mankind with them. For is not the ministry of the Church what is called an easy profession? Do we not see it undertaken by those who love quiet, or who are unfit for business; by those who are less keen, less active-minded, less venturous than others? Does it not lead rather to a land of Canaan, as of old time, than to the narrow rugged way and the thorny couch of the Gospel? Has it not fair pastures, and pleasant resting-places, and calm refreshing streams, and milk and honey flowing, according to the promise of the Old Covenant, rather than that baptism and that draught which is the glory of the New? Facts then, it will be said, refute such notions of the suffering character of the Christian Church. It suffered at first,—suffering was the price of its triumphing; and since that, it has ceased to suffer. It is as truly in peace now, as it was truly in suffering then;— one might as well deny that it did suffer, as that it is in peace; and to apply texts which speak of what it was then to what it is now, is unreal, offends some hearers, and excites ridicule in others. This is what may be said.

Yet is it so indeed? Let us look into the Bible again. Are we to go by faith or by sight?—for surely, whatever conclusions follow from what we see, these cannot undo what is written. What is written remains; and if sight is against it, we must suppose that there is some way of solving the difficulty, though we may not see how; and we will try, as well as we can, to solve it in the case before us.

Let us, I say, consider the words of Scripture again. Surely, if endurance be not in some sense or other the portion of Christians, the whole New Testament itself has but a temporary meaning; for it is all built upon this doctrine as a groundwork. If "the present distress,"[1] of which St. Paul speaks, does not denote the ordinary state of the Christian Church, the New Testament is scarcely written for us, but must be re-modelled before it can be made apply. There are men of the world in this day who are attempting to supersede the precepts of Christ about almsgiving and the maintenance of the poor. We are accustomed to object, that they contravene Scripture. Again, we hear of men drawing up a Church government for themselves, or omitting Sacraments, or modifying doctrines. We say they do not read Scripture rightly. They answer, perhaps, that Scripture commands or countenances many things which are not binding on us eighteen hundred years after. They consider that the management of the poor, the form of the Church, the power of the State over it, the nature of its faith, or the choice of its ordinances, are not points on which we need rigidly keep to Scripture; that times have changed. This is what they say; and can we find fault with them if we ourselves allow that the New Testament is a dead letter in another most essential part of it? Is it strange that they should think that the world may now tyrannize over the Church, when we allow that the Church

[1] 1 Cor. vii. 26.

may now indulge in the world? Surely they do but make a fair bargain with us; both they and we put aside Scripture, and then agree together, we to live in ease, and they to rule. We have taken the world's pay, and must not grudge its yoke. Independence surely is not the Church's privilege, unless hardship is her portion.

Well, and perhaps affliction, hardship, distress, ill-usage, evil report, are her portion, both promised and bestowed, though at first sight they may seem not to be. What proof is there that temporal happiness was the gift of the Law, which will not avail for temporal adversity being that of the Gospel? You say the Jews had the promise of this world. True. But look at their history. Is that promise fulfilled on its surface? Had they not long periods of captivity, war, famine, pestilence, weakness, internal division? Look at their history as a whole. Is it not very like other histories? Had not their power a beginning, a progress, and an end? Did they not pass through those successive stages which other states pass through? What prosperity had they, to go by appearances, which other states had not? What trouble had other states which they were spared? If, then, the face of things be taken to prove that the Christian Church is not born to trouble, would it not also prove that the Jewish Church was not allotted prosperity? And if, in spite of appearances, we yet say that the Israelites had special temporal blessings, why may we not, in spite of the appearance, say that Christians have special temporal trials?

You will say, perhaps, that the Jewish promise was

suspended on a condition, the condition of obedience, and that the Jews forfeited the reward, because they did not merit it. True; let it be so. And what hinders, in like manner, if Christians are in prosperity, not in adversity, that it is because they too have forfeited the promise and privilege of affliction by disobedience? And what hinders that, as in spite of the sins of the people, the Jewish Church still in some sufficient sense did obtain the temporal promise; so, in like manner, in spite of the sins of the multitude of Christians, the Christian Church as a whole, and her true children in particular, may partake in the promise of distress?

It is very difficult then to argue from what we see, and there are many ways in which what is written may be fulfilled in spite, or by means, of it. All that clearly can be pointed out is the word of promise. It was said of Israel, "He loved the people; all His saints are in Thy hand; and they sat down at Thy feet; every one shall receive of Thy words. . . . Let Reuben live and not die; and let not his men be few. . . . Hear, Lord, the voice of Judah, and bring him unto his people. Let his hands be sufficient for him, and be Thou an help to him from his enemies." And of Levi; "Let Thy Thummim and Thy Urim be upon Thy Holy One. . . . Bless, Lord, his substance, and accept the work of his hands: smite through the loins of them that rise against him, and of them that hate him, that they rise not again." And of Benjamin: "The Beloved of the Lord shall dwell in safety by Him." And of Joseph: "Blessed of the Lord be his land, for the precious things of heaven, for the dew, and for the deep that coucheth beneath, and for the precious things brought forth by the sun, and for the precious things brought forth by the moon, and for the chief things of the ancient mountains, and for the precious things of the lasting hills, and for the precious things of the earth, and the fulness thereof." And of Zebulun: "Rejoice, Zebulun; in thy going out; and, Issachar, in thy tents . . . . they shall suck of the abundance of the seas, and of treasures hid in the sand." And, "Blessed be he that enlargeth Gad; he dwelleth as a lion, and teareth the arm with the crown of the head." And, "O Naphtali, satisfied with favour, and full of the blessing of the Lord, possess thou the west and the south." And, "Let Asher be blessed with children; thy shoes shall be iron and brass; and as thy days, so shall thy strength be." And of all of them together it was said, "Israel shall dwell in safety alone; the fountain of Jacob shall be upon a land of corn and wine; and his heavens shall drop down dew."[1] These were the bright and pleasant things promised to the first people of God, in the plains of Moab, on their entering into the land. And now in turn, what did the second and greater Prophet of the Church declare, when He was set upon the mount, with the people around Him, and published His covenant of grace. "He opened His mouth and said, Blessed are the poor in spirit, for theirs is the kingdom of heaven. Blessed are they that mourn, for they shall be comforted. Blessed are the meek. . . . Blessed are they which do hunger and thirst after righteousness. . . . Blessed are the merciful. . . . Blessed are the pure in heart. . . . Blessed are the peacemakers."

[1] Deut. xxxiii.

And lastly, " Blessed are ye when men shall revile you and persecute you, and shall say all manner of evil against you falsely for my sake. Rejoice, and be exceeding glad ; for great is your reward in heaven; for so persecuted they the Prophets which were before you." And by contrast, He added, " But woe unto you that are rich, for ye have received your consolation. Woe unto you that are full, for ye shall hunger. Woe unto you that laugh now, for ye shall mourn and weep. Woe unto you when all men shall speak well of you, for so did their fathers unto the false prophets."

At another time He spoke thus : " Sell that ye have, and give alms." " If thou wilt be perfect, go and sell that thou hast, and give to the poor." " It is easier for a camel to go through the eye of a needle, than for a rich man to enter into the kingdom of God." " Whosoever will be chief among you, let him be your servant." " If any man will come after Me, let him deny himself, and take up his cross, and follow Me." And, in a word, the doctrine of the Gospel, and the principle of it, is thus briefly stated by the Apostle, in the words of the Wise Man. " Whom the Lord loveth He chasteneth, and scourgeth every son whom He receiveth. If ye endure chastening, God dealeth with you as with sons. . . . If ye be without chastisement, *whereof all are partakers,* then are ye bastards, and not sons." [2] Can words speak it plainer, that, as certainly as temporal prosperity is the gift of the Law, so also are hardship and distress the gift of the Gospel ?

[1] Matt. v. 2—12. Luke vi. 24—26.
[2] Luke xii. 33. Matt. xix. 21, 24; xx. 27; xvi. 24. Heb. xii. 6—8.

Take up thy portion, then, Christian soul, and weigh it well, and learn to love it. Thou wilt find, if thou art Christ's, in spite of what the world fancies, that after all, even at this day, endurance, in a special sense, *is* the lot of those who offer themselves to be servants of the King of sorrows. There is an inward world, which none see but those who belong to it; and though the outside robe be many-coloured, like Joseph's coat, inside it is lined with camel's hair, or sackcloth, fitting those who desire to be one with Him who fared hardly in the wilderness, in the mountain, and on the sea. There is an inward world into which they enter who come near to Christ, though to men in general they seem the same as before. They hold the same place as before in the world's society; their employments are the same, their ways, their comings in and goings out. If they were high in rank, they are still high; if they were in active life, they are still active; if they were wealthy, they still have wealth. They have still great friends, powerful connexions, ample resources, fair name in the world's eye; but, if they have drunk of Christ's cup, and tasted the bread of His Table in sincerity, it is not with them as in time past. A change has come over them, unknown indeed to themselves, except in its effects, but they have a portion in destinies to which other men are strangers, and, as having destinies, they have conflicts also. They drank what looked like a draught of this world, but it associated them in hopes and fears, trials and purposes, above this world. They came as for a blessing, and they have found a work. They are soldiers in Christ's army; they fight against "things that are

seen," and they have "all these things against them."
To their surprise, as time goes on, they find that their
lot is changed. They find that in one shape or other
adversity happens to them. If they refuse to afflict
themselves, God afflicts them. One blow falls, they
are startled; it passes over, it is well; they expect
nothing more. Another comes; they wonder; "Why
is this?" they ask; they think that the first should be
their security against the second; they bear it, however;
and it passes too. Then a third comes; they almost
murmur; they have not yet mastered the great doctrine
that endurance is their portion. O simple soul, is it
not the law of thy being to endure since thou camest to
Christ? Why camest thou but to endure? Why didst
thou taste His heavenly feast, but that it might work in
thee? Why didst thou kneel beneath His hand, but
that He might leave on thee the print of His wounds?
Why wonder then that one sorrow does not buy off the
next? Does one drop of rain absorb the second? Does
the storm cease because it has begun? Understand thy
place in God's kingdom, and rejoice, not complain, that
in thy day thou hast thy lot with Prophets and Apostles.
Envy not the gay and thriving world. Religious persons ask, "Why are we so marked out for crosses?
Others get on in the world; others are prosperous;
their schemes turn out well, and their families settle
happily; there is no anxiety, no bereavement among
them, while the world fights against us." This is what
they sometimes say, though with some exaggeration
certainly, for almost all men, sooner or later, have their
troubles, and Christians, as well as others, have their

continual comforts. But what then, be it ever so true? If so, it is but what was foretold long ago, and even under the Law fulfilled in its degree. "They have children at their desire, and leave the rest of their substance for their babes." "They are in no peril of death, but are lusty and strong. They come in no misfortune like other folk, neither are they plagued like other men. . . . Their eyes swell with fatness, they do even what they lust. . . . Lo, these are the ungodly, these prosper in the world, and these have riches in possession." Such is the portion, such the punishment of those who forsake their God. "Verily, I say unto you, They have their reward."[1]

When, then, my brethren, it is objected that times are changed since the Gospel was first preached, and that what Scripture says of the lot of Christians does not apply to us, make answer, that the Church of Christ doubtless is in high estate everywhere, and so must be, for it is written, "I will give Thee the heathen for Thine inheritance, and the uttermost parts of the earth for Thy possession." Yet that while she maintains her ground, she ever suffers *in* maintaining it; she has to fight the good fight, in order to maintain it : she fights and she suffers, in proportion as she plays her part well; and if she is without suffering, it is because she is slumbering. Her doctrines and precepts never can be palatable to the world; and if the world does not persecute, it is because she does not preach. And so of her individual members : they in their own way suffer; not after her manner, perhaps, nor for the same reason,

---

[1] Ps. xvii. 15; lxxiii. 4—12. Matt. vi. 5.

nor in the same degree, but more or less, as being under the law of suffering which Christ began. Judge not then by outward appearance; think not that His servants are in ease and security because things look smooth, else you will be startled, perhaps, and offended, when suffering falls upon you. Temporal blessings, indeed, He gives to you and to all men in abundance; " He maketh His sun to rise upon the just and unjust;" but in your case it will be " houses and brethren and lands, with persecutions." Judge not by appearance, but be sure that, even when things seem to brighten and smile upon God's true servants, there is much within to try them, though you see it not. Of old time they wore clothing of hair and sackcloth under rich robes. Men do not observe this custom now-a-days; but be quite sure still, that there are as many sharp distresses underneath the visible garb of things, as if they did. Many a secret ailment or scarcely-observed infirmity exercises him who has it, better than thorns or knotted cord. Many a silent grief, lying like lead within the breast, or like cold ice upon the heart. Many a sad secret, which a man dare not tell lest he should find no sympathy. Many a laden conscience, laden because the owner of it has turned to Christ, and which he would not have felt, had he kept from Him. Many an apprehension for the future, which cannot be spoken; many a bereavement which has robbed the world's gifts of their pleasant savour, and leads the heart but to sigh at the sight of them. No; never while the Church lasts, will the words of old Jacob be reversed,—all things here are against us but God; but if God be for us, who can really be against us ? If He is in the midst of us, how shall we be moved ? If Christ has died and risen again, what death can come upon us, though we be made to die daily ? what sorrow, pain, humiliation, trial, but must end as His has ended, in a continual resurrection into His new world, and in a nearer and nearer approach to Him ? He pronounced a blessing over His Apostles, and they have scattered it far and wide all over the earth unto this day. It runs as follows : " Peace I leave with you, My peace. I give unto you; not as the world giveth, give I unto you." " These things I have spoken unto you, that in Me ye might have peace. In the world ye shall have tribulation; but be of good cheer, I have overcome the world." [1]

[1] John xiv. 27 ; xvi. 33.

SERMON XXI.

AFFLICTION, A SCHOOL OF COMFORT.

(SEXAGESIMA).

2 Cor. i. 4.

" Who comforteth us in all our tribulation, that we may be able to comfort them which are in any trouble, by the comfort wherewith we ourselves are comforted of God."

IF there is one point of character more than another which belonged to St. Paul, and discovers itself in all he said and did, it was his power of sympathising with his brethren, nay, with all classes of men. He went through trials of every kind, and this was their issue, to let him into the feelings, and thereby to introduce him to the hearts, of high and low, Jew and Gentile. He knew how to persuade, for he knew where lay the perplexity; he knew how to console, for he knew the sorrow. His spirit within him was as some delicate instrument, which, as the weather changed about him, as the atmosphere was moist or dry, hot or cold, accurately marked all its variations, and guided him what to do. " To the Jews he became as a Jew, that he might gain the Jews; to them that were under the Law, as under the Law, that he might gain them that were under the Law: to them that were without Law, as without Law, that he might gain them that were without Law." "To the weak," he says, "became I as weak, that I might gain the weak. I am made all things to all men, that I might by all means save some." And so again, in another place, after having recounted his various trials by sea and land, in the bleak wilderness and the stifling prison, from friends and strangers, he adds, "Who is weak, and I am not weak? who is offended, and I burn not? If I must needs glory, I will glory of the things which concern mine infirmities." Hence, in the Acts of the Apostles, when he saw his brethren weeping, though they could not divert him from his purpose, which came from God, yet he could not keep from crying out, " What mean ye to weep, and to break my heart? for I am ready, not to be bound only, but also to die at Jerusalem, for the Name of the Lord Jesus." And even of his own countrymen who persecuted him, he speaks in the most tender and affec- tionate terms, as understanding well where they stood, and what their view of the Gospel was. " I have great heaviness and continual sorrow in my heart; for I could wish that myself were accursed from Christ for my brethren, my kinsmen according to the flesh." And again, " Brethren, my heart's desire and prayer to God for Israel is, that they might be saved. For I *bear them record* that they have a zeal of God, but not according to knowledge." And hence so powerful was he in speech with them, wherever they were not repro- bate, that even King Agrippa, after hearing a few words of St. Paul's own history, exclaimed, "Almost thou persuadest me to be a Christian!"[1]   And what he was in persuasion, such he was in consolation.   He himself gives this reason for his trials in the text, speaking of Almighty God's comforting him in all his tribulation, in order that he might be able to comfort them which were in any trouble, by the comfort wherewith he himself was comforted of God.

Such was the great Apostle St. Paul, the Apostle of grace, whom we hold in especial honour in the early part of the year.   At this season we commemorate his conversion; and at this season we give attention, more than ordinary, to his Epistles.   And on Sexagesima Sunday we almost keep another Festival in his memory, the Epistle for the day being expressly on the subject of his trials.   He was beaten, he was scourged, he was chased to and fro, he was imprisoned, he was ship-wrecked, he was in this life of all men most miserable, that he might understand how poor a thing mortal life is, and might learn to contemplate and describe fitly the glories of the life immortal.

" Experience," he tells us elsewhere, " worketh hope," —that grace which of all others most tends to comfort and assuage sorrow.   In somewhat a similar way our Lord says to St. Peter, " Simon, Simon, behold, Satan hath desired to have you, that he may sift you as wheat : but I have prayed for thee, that thy faith fail not; and when thou art converted, strengthen thy brethren."[2]   Nay, the same law was fulfilled, not only

[1] 1 Cor. ix. 20—22.   2 Cor. xi. 29, 30.   Acts xxi. 13.   Rom. ix. 3; x. 1, 2.   Acts xxvi. 28.
[2] Luke xxii. 31, 32.

in the case of Christ's servants, but even He Himself, "who knoweth the hearts," condescended, by an ineffable mystery, to learn to strengthen man, by the experiencing of man's infirmities. "In all things it behoved Him to be made like unto His brethren, that He might be a merciful and faithful High Priest in things pertaining to God, to make reconciliation for the sins of the people; for in that He Himself suffered being tempted, He is able to succour them that are tempted." "We have not a High Priest who cannot be touched with the feeling of our infirmities, but was in all points tempted like as we are, yet without sin."[1]

Such is one chief benefit of painful trial, of whatever kind, which it may not be unsuitable to enlarge on. Man is born to trouble, "as the sparks fly upward." More or less, we all have our severe trials of pain and sorrow. If we go on for some years in the world's sunshine, it is only that troubles, when they come, should fall heavier. Such at least is the general rule. Sooner or later we fare as other men; happier than they only if we learn to bear our portion more religiously; and more favoured if we fall in with those who themselves have suffered, and can aid us with their sympathy and their experience. And then, while we profit from what they can give us, we may learn from them freely to give what we have freely received, comforting in turn others with the comfort which our brethren have given us from God.

Now, in speaking of the benefits of trial and suffering, we should of course never forget that these things by

<hr>

[1] Heb. ii. 17; iv. 15.

themselves have no power to make us holier or more heavenly. They make many men morose, selfish, and envious. The only sympathy they create in many minds, is the wish that others should suffer with them, not they with others. Affliction, when love is away, leads a man to wish others to be as he is; it leads to repining, malevolence, hatred, rejoicing in evil. "Art thou also become weak as we? art thou become like unto us?" said the princes of the nations to the fallen king of Babylon. The devils are not incited by their own torments to any endeavour but that of making others devils also. Such is the effect of pain and sorrow, when unsanctified by God's saving grace. And this is instanced very widely and in a variety of cases. All afflictions of the flesh, such as the Gospel enjoins, and St. Paul practised, watchings and fastings, and subjecting of the body, have no tendency whatever·in themselves to make men better; they often have made men worse; they often (to appearance) have left them just as they were before. They are no sure test of holiness and true faith, taken by themselves. A man may be most austere in his life, and, by that very austerity, learn to be cruel to others, not tender. And, on the other hand (what seems strange), he may be austere in his personal habits, and yet be a waverer and a coward in his conduct. Such things have been,—I do not say they are likely in this state of society,—but I mean, it should ever be borne in mind, that the severest and most mortified life is as little a passport to heaven, or a criterion of saintliness, as benevolence is, or usefulness, or amiableness. Self-discipline is a necessary condition, but not a sure sign of holiness. It may leave a man worldly, or it may make him a tyrant. It is only in the hands of God that it is God's instrument. It only ministers to God's purposes when God uses it. It is only when grace is in the heart, when power from above dwells in a man, that anything outward or inward turns to his salvation. Whether persecution, or famine, or the sword, they as little bring the soul to Christ, as they separate it from Him. He alone can work, and He can work through all things. He can make the stones bread. He can feed us with " every word which proceedeth from His mouth." He could, did He so will, make us calm, resigned, tender-hearted, and sympathising, without trial; but it is His will ordinarily to do so by means of trial. Even He Himself, when He came on earth, condescended to gain knowledge by experience; and what He did Himself, that He makes His brethren do.

And while affliction does not necessarily make us gentle and kind, nay, it may be, even makes us stern and cruel, the want of affliction does not mend matters. Sometimes we look with pleasure upon those who never have been afflicted. We look with a smile of interest upon the smooth brow and open countenance, and our hearts thrill within us at the ready laugh or the piercing glance. There is a buoyancy and freshness of mind in those who have never suffered, which, beautiful as it is, is perhaps scarcely suitable and safe in sinful man. It befits an Angel; it befits very young persons and children, who have never been delivered over to their three great enemies. I will not dare to deny that there are those whom white garments and unfading chaplets show that they have a right thus to rejoice always, even till God takes them. But this is not the case of the many, whom earth soils, and who lose their right to be merry-hearted. In them lightness of spirits degenerates into rudeness, want of feeling, and wantonness; such is the change, as time goes on, and their hearts become less pure and child-like. Pain and sorrow are the almost necessary medi-cines of the impetuosity of nature. Without these, men, though men, are like spoilt children; they act as if they considered everything must give way to their own wishes and conveniences. They rejoice in their youth. They become selfish; and it is difficult to say which selfishness is the more distressing and disagreeable, self in high spirits, or self in low spirits; self in joy, or self in sorrow; in the rude health of nature, or in the languor and fretfulness of trial. It is difficult to say which will comfort the worse, hearts hard from suffering, or hard from having never suffered; cruel despair, which rejoices in misery, or cruel pride, which is impatient at the sight of it. The cruelty, indeed, of the despairing is the more hateful, for it is more after Satan's pattern, who feels the less for others, the more he suffers himself; yet the cruelty of the prosperous and wanton is like the excesses of the elements, or of brute animals, not designed, more at random, yet perhaps even more keen and trying to those who incur it.

Such is worldly happiness and worldly trial; but

Almighty God, while He chose the latter as the portion of His Saints, sanctified it by His heavenly grace, to be their great benefit. He rescues them from the selfishness of worldly comfort without surrendering them to the selfishness of worldly pain. He brings them into pain, that they may be like what Christ was, and may be led to think of Him, not of themselves. He brings them into trouble, that they may be near Him. When they mourn, they are more intimately in His presence than they are at any other time. Bodily pain, anxiety, bereavement, distress, are to them His forerunners. It is a solemn thing, while it is a privilege, to look upon those whom He thus visits. Why is it that men would look with fear and silence at the sight of the spirit of some friend departed, coming to them from the grave? Why would they abase themselves and listen awfully to any message he brought them? Because he would seem to come from the very presence of God. And in like manner, when a man, in whom dwells His grace, is lying on the bed of suffering, or when he has been stripped of his friends and is solitary, he has, in a peculiar way, tasted of the powers of the world to come, and exhorts and consoles with authority. He who has been long under the rod of God, becomes God's possession. He bears in his body marks, and is sprinkled with drops, which nature could not provide for him. He comes "from Edom, with dyed garments from Bozrah," and it is easy to see with whom he has been conversing. He seems to say to us in the words of the Prophet, "I am the man that hath seen affliction by the rod of His wrath. He hath led me and brought me into darkness, but not into light . . . . He hath bent His bow, and set me as a mark for the arrow."[1]   And they who see him, gather around like Job's acquaintance, speaking no word to him, yet more reverently than if they did; looking at him with fear, yet with confidence, with fellow-feeling, yet with resignation, as one who is under God's teaching and training for the work of consolation towards his brethren.   Him they will seek when trouble comes on themselves; turning from all such as delighted them in their prosperity, the great or the wealthy, or the man of mirth and song, or of wit, or of resource, or of dexterity, or of knowledge; by a natural instinct turning to those for consolation whom the Lord has heretofore tried by similar troubles.   Surely this is a great blessing and cause of glorying, to be thus consecrated by affliction as a minister of God's mercies to the afflicted.

Some such thoughts as these may be humbly entertained by every one of us, when brought even into any ordinary pain or trouble.   Doubtless if we are properly minded, we shall be very loth to take to ourselves titles of honour.   We shall be slow to believe that we are specially beloved by Christ.   But at least we may have the blessed certainty that we are made instruments for the consolation of others.   Without impatiently settling anything absolutely about our own real state in God's sight, and how it will fare with us at the last day, at least we may allow

[1] Lam. iii. 1, 2, 12.

ourselves to believe that we are at present evidently blessed by being made subservient to His purposes of mercy to others; as washing the disciples' feet, and pouring into their wounds oil and wine. So we shall say to ourselves, Thus far, merciful Saviour, we have attained; not to be assured of our salvation, but of our usefulness. So far we know, and enough surely for sinful man, that we are allowed to promote His glory who died for us. Taught by our own pain, our own sorrow, nay, by our own sin, we shall have hearts and minds exercised for every service of love towards those who need it. We shall in our measure be comforters after the image of the Almighty Paraclete, and that in all senses of the word,—advocates, assistants, soothing aids. Our words and advice, our very manner, voice, and look, will be gentle and tranquillizing, as of those who have borne their cross after Christ. We shall not pass by His little ones rudely, as the world does. The voice of the widow and the orphan, the poor and destitute, will at once reach our ears, however low they speak. Our hearts will open towards them; our word and deed befriend them. The ruder passions of man's nature, pride and anger, envy and strife, which so disorder the Church, these will be quelled and brought under in others by the earnestness and kindness of our admonitions.

Thus, instead of being the selfish creatures which we were by nature, grace, acting through suffering, tends to make us ready teachers and witnesses of Truth to all men. Time was when, even at the most necessary times, we found it difficult to speak of heaven to another; our mouth seemed closed, even when our heart was full; but now our affection is eloquent, and "out of the abundance of the heart our mouth speaketh." Blessed portion indeed, thus to be tutored in the sweetest, softest strains of Gospel truth, and to range over the face of the earth pilgrims and sojourners, with winning voices, singing, as far as in the flesh it is possible to sing, the song of Moses the servant of God, and the song of the Lamb;[1] severed from ties of earth by the trials we have endured, without father, without mother, without abiding place, as that patriarch whom St. Paul speaks of, and, like him, allowed to bring forth bread and wine to refresh the weary soldiers of the most High God. Such too was our Lord's fore-runner, the holy Baptist, an austere man, cut off from among his brethren, living in the wilderness, feeding on harsh fare, yet so far removed from sternness towards those who sincerely sought the Lord, that his preaching was almost described in prophecy as the very language of consolation, " Comfort ye, comfort ye My people ... speak ye comfortably to Jerusalem."

Such was the high temper of mind instanced in our Lord and His Apostles, and thereby impressed upon the Church of Christ. And for this we may thank God, that much as the Church has erred in various ways since her setting up, this great truth she never has forgotten, that we must all "take up our cross daily," and " through much tribulation enter into the kingdom of God." She has never forgotten that she was set apart for a comforter of the afflicted, and that to comfort

[1] Rev. xv. 3.

well we must first be afflicted ourselves. St. Paul was consecrated by suffering to be an Apostle of Christ; by fastings, by chastisements, by self-denials for his brethren's sake, by his forlorn, solitary life, thus did he fill up day by day those intervals of respite which the fury of his persecutors permitted. And so the Church Catholic after him has never forgotten that ease was a sin, favoured as she might be with peace from external enemies. Even when riches and honours flowed in upon her, still has she always proclaimed that affliction was her proper portion. She has felt she could not perform the office of a comforter, if she enjoyed this world; and, though doubtless her separate branches have at times forgotten this truth, yet it remains, and is transmitted from age to age; and though she has had many false sons, yet even they have often been obliged to profess what they did not practise. This indeed is strange news to men of the world, who are bent on gratifying themselves, and who think they have gained a point, and have just cause for congratulation, when they have found out a way of saving themselves trouble, and of adding to their luxuries and conveniences. But those who are set on their own ease, most certainly are bad comforters of others; thus the rich man, who fared sumptuously every day, let Lazarus lie at his gate, and left him to be " comforted " after this life by Angels. As to comfort the poor and afflicted is the way to heaven, so to have affliction ourselves is the way to comfort them.

And, lastly, let us ever anxiously remember that affliction is sent for our own personal good also. Let us fear, lest, after we have ministered to others, we ourselves should be castaways; lest our gentleness, consideration, and patience, which are so soothing to them, yet should be separated from that inward faith and strict conscientiousness which alone unites us to Christ; —lest, in spite of all the good we do to others, yet we should have some secret sin, some unresisted evil within us, which separates us from Him. Let us pray Him who sends us trial, to send us a pure heart and honesty of mind wherewith to bear it.

SERMON XXII.

THE THOUGHT OF GOD, THE STAY OF THE SOUL.

(QUINQUAGESIMA.)

ROM. viii. 15.

" Ye have not received the spirit of bondage again to fear, but ye have received the Spirit of adoption, whereby we cry, Abba, Father."

WHEN Adam fell, his soul lost its true strength ; he forfeited the inward light of God's presence, and became the wayward, fretful, excitable, and miserable being which his history has shown him to be ever since ; with alternate strength and feebleness, nobleness and meanness, energy in the beginning and failure in the end. Such was the state of his soul in itself, not to speak of the Divine wrath upon it, which followed, or was involved in the Divine withdrawal. It lost its spiritual life and health, which was necessary to complete its nature, and to enable it to fulfil the ends for which it was created,—which was necessary both for its moral integrity and its happiness ; and as if faint, hungry, or sick, it could no longer stand upright, but sank on the ground. Such is the state in which every one of us lies as born into the world ; and Christ has come to reverse this state, and restore us the great gift which Adam lost in the beginning. Adam fell from his Creator's favour to be a bond-servant; and Christ has come to set us free again, to impart to us the Spirit of adoption, whereby we become God's children, and again approach Him as our Father.

I say, by birth we are in a state of defect and want; we have not all that is necessary for the perfection of our nature. As the body is not complete in itself, but requires the soul to give it a meaning, so again the soul till God is present with it and manifested in it, has faculties and affections without a ruling principle, object, or purpose. Such it is by birth, and this Scripture signifies to us by many figures; sometimes calling human nature blind, sometimes hungry, sometimes un-clothed, and calling the gift of the Spirit light, health, food, warmth, and raiment; all by way of teaching us what our first state is, and what our gratitude should be to Him who has brought us into a new state. For instance, "Because thou sayest, I am rich, and increased in goods, and have need of nothing; and knowest not that thou art wretched, and miserable, and poor, and blind, and naked: I counsel thee to buy of Me gold tried in the fire, that thou mayest be rich; and white raiment, that thou mayest be clothed, . . . and anoint thine eyes with eye-salve, that thou mayest see." Again, "God, who commanded the light to shine out of darkness, hath shined in our hearts, to give the light of the knowledge of the glory of God, in the face of Jesus Christ." Again, "Awake, thou that sleepest, and arise from the dead, and Christ shall give thee light." Again,

" Whosoever drinketh of the water that I shall give him, shall never thirst; but the water that I shall give him shall be in him a well of water springing up into everlasting life." And in the Book of Psalms, "They shall be satisfied with the plenteousness of Thy house; and Thou shalt give them drink of Thy pleasures as out of the river. For with Thee is the well of life, and in Thy Light shall we see light." And in another Psalm, "My soul shall be satisfied, even as it were with marrow and fatness, when my mouth praiseth Thee with joyful lips." And so again, in the Prophet Jeremiah, "I will satiate the souls of the priests with fatness; and My people shall be satisfied with My goodness. . . . I have satiated the weary soul, and I have replenished every sorrowful soul." [1]

Now the doctrine which these passages contain is often truly expressed thus: that the soul of man is made for the contemplation of its Maker; and that nothing short of that high contemplation is its happiness; that, whatever it may possess besides, it is unsatisfied till it is vouchsafed God's presence, and lives in the light of it. There are many aspects in which the same solemn truth may be viewed; there are many ways in which it may be signified. I will now dwell upon it as I have been stating it.

I say, then, that the happiness of the soul consists in the exercise of the affections; not in sensual pleasures, not in activity, not in excitement, not in self-esteem, not in the consciousness of power, not in

[1] Rev. iii. 17, 18.　2 Cor. iv. 6.　Ephes. v. 14.　John iv. 14.
Ps. xxxvi. 8, 9; lxiii. 5. Jer. xxxi. 14, 25.

knowledge; in none of these things lies our happiness, but in our affections being elicited, employed, supplied. As hunger and thirst, as taste, sound, and smell, are the channels through which this bodily frame receives pleasure, so the affections are the instruments by which the soul has pleasure. When they are exercised duly, it is happy; when they are undeveloped, restrained, or thwarted, it is not happy. This is our real and true bliss, not to know, or to affect, or to pursue; but to love, to hope, to joy, to admire, to revere, to adore. Our real and true bliss lies in the possession of those objects on which our hearts may rest and be satisfied.

Now, if this be so, here is at once a reason for saying that the thought of God, and nothing short of it, is the happiness of man; for though there is much besides to serve as subject of knowledge, or motive for action, or means of excitement, yet the affections require a something more vast and more enduring than anything created. What is novel and sudden excites, but does not influence; what is pleasurable or useful raises no awe; self moves no reverence, and mere knowledge kindles no love. He alone is sufficient for the heart who made it. I do not say, of course, that nothing short of the Almighty Creator can awaken and answer to our love, reverence, and trust; man can do this for man. Man doubtless is an object to rouse his brother's love, and repays it in his measure. Nay, it is a great duty, one of the two chief duties of religion, thus to be minded towards our neighbour. But I am not speaking here of what we can do, or ought to do, but what it is our happiness to do; and surely it may be said that though the love of the brethren, the love of all men, be one half of our obedience, yet exercised by itself, were that possible, which it is not, it would be no part of our reward. And for this reason, if for no other, that our hearts require something more permanent and uniform than man can be. We gain much for a time from fellowship with each other. It is a relief to us, as fresh air to the fainting, or meat and drink to the hungry, or a flood of tears to the heavy in mind. It is a soothing comfort to have those whom we may make our confidants; a comfort to have those to whom we may confess our faults; a comfort to have those to whom we may look for sympathy. Love of home and family in these and other ways is sufficient to make this life tolerable to the multitude of men, which otherwise it would not be; but still, after all, our affections exceed such exercise of them, and demand what is more stable. Do not all men die? are they not taken from us? are they not as uncertain as the grass of the field? We do not give our hearts to things irrational, because these have no permanence in them. We do not place our affections in sun, moon, and stars, or this rich and fair earth, because all things material come to nought, and vanish like day and night. Man, too, though he has an intelligence within him, yet in his best estate he is altogether vanity. If our happiness consists in our affections being employed and recompensed, "man that is born of a woman" cannot be our happiness; for how can he stay another, who "continueth not in one stay" himself?

But there is another reason why God alone is the

happiness of our souls, to which I wish rather to direct attention:—the contemplation of Him, and nothing but it, is able fully to open and relieve the mind, to unlock, occupy, and fix our affections. We may indeed love things created with great intenseness, but such affection, when disjoined from the love of the Creator, is like a stream running in a narrow channel, impetuous, vehement, turbid. The heart runs out, as it were, only at one door; it is not an expanding of the whole man. Created natures cannot open us, or elicit the ten thousand mental senses which belong to us, and through which we really live. None but the presence of our Maker can enter us; for to none besides can the whole heart in all its thoughts and feelings be unlocked and subjected. "Behold," He says, "I stand at the door and knock; if any man hear My voice and open the door, I will come in to him, and will sup with him, and he with Me." "My Father will love him, and We will come unto him, and make Our abode with him." "God hath sent forth the Spirit of His Son into your hearts." "God is greater than our heart, and knoweth all things."[1] It is this feeling of simple and absolute confidence and communion, which soothes and satisfies those to whom it is vouchsafed. We know that even our nearest friends enter into us but partially, and hold intercourse with us only at times; whereas the consciousness of a perfect and enduring Presence, and it alone, keeps the heart open. Withdraw the Object on which it rests, and it will relapse again into its state of confinement and constraint; and in proportion as it is limited, either to certain seasons or to certain

1 Rev. iii. 20. John xiv. 23. Gal. iv. 6. 1 John iii. 20.

affections, the heart is straitened and distressed. If it be not over bold to say it, He who is infinite can alone be its measure; He alone can answer to the mysterious assemblage of feelings and thoughts which it has within it. "There is no creature that is not manifest in His sight, but all things are naked and opened unto the eyes of Him with whom we have to do."[1]

This is what is meant by the peace of a good conscience; it is the habitual consciousness that our hearts are open to God, with a desire that they should be open. It is a confidence in God, from a feeling that there is nothing in us which we need be ashamed or afraid of. You will say that no man on earth is in such a state; for we are all sinners, and that daily. It is so; certainly we are quite unfitted to endure God's all-searching Eye, to come into direct contact (if I may so speak) with His glorious Presence, without any medium of intercourse between Him and us. But, first, there may be degrees of this confidence in different men, though the perfection of it be in none. And again, God in His great mercy, as we all well know, has revealed to us that there is a Mediator between the sinful soul and Himself. And as His merits most wonderfully intervene between our sins and God's judgment, so the thought of those merits, when present with the Christian, enables him, in spite of his sins, to lift up his heart to God; and believing, as he does, that he is (to use Scripture language) in Christ, or, in other words, that he addresses Almighty God, not simply face to face, but in and through Christ, he can bear to submit and open his heart

[1] Heb. iv. 13.

to God, and to wish it open.   For while he is very conscious both of original and actual sin, yet still a feeling
of his own sincerity and earnestness is possible; and in
proportion as he gains as much as this, he will be able
to walk unreservedly with Christ his God and Saviour,
and desire His continual presence with him, though he
be a sinner, and will wish to be allowed to make Him
the one Object of his heart.   Perhaps, under somewhat
of this feeling, Hagar said, "Thou, God, seest me."   It
is under this feeling that holy David may be supposed
to say, "Examine me, O Lord, and prove me; try out
my reins and my heart." "Try me, O God, and seek
the ground of my heart; prove me, and examine my
thoughts.   Look well, if there be any way of wickedness in me; and lead me in the way everlasting."[1]
And especially is it instanced in St. Paul, who seems to
delight in the continual laying open of his heart to God,
and submitting it to His scrutiny, and waiting for His
Presence upon it; or, in other words, in the joy of a
good conscience.   For instance, "I have lived in all
good conscience before God until this day."   "Herein
do I exercise myself, to have always a conscience void
of offence toward God, and toward men."   "I say the
truth in Christ, I lie not; my conscience also bearing
me witness in the Holy Ghost."   "Our rejoicing is
this, the testimony of our conscience, that in simplicity
and godly sincerity, not with fleshly wisdom, but by the
grace of God, we have had our conversation in the
world, and more abundantly to you-ward."[2]   It is, I say,

[1] Ps. xxvi. 2; cxxxix. 23, 24.
[2] Acts xxiii. 1; xxiv. 16.   Rom. ix. 1.   2 Cor. i. 12.

the characteristic of St. Paul, as manifested to us in his Epistles, to live in the sight of Him who " searcheth the reins and the heart," to love to place himself before Him, and, while contemplating God, to dwell on the thought of God's contemplating him.

And, it may be, this is something of the Apostle's meaning, when he speaks of-the witness of the Spirit. Perhaps he is speaking of that satisfaction and rest which the soul experiences in proportion as it is able to surrender itself wholly to God, and to have no desire, no aim, but to please Him. When we are awake, we are conscious we are awake, in a sense in which we cannot fancy we are, when we are asleep. When we have discovered the solution of some difficult problem in science, we have a conviction about it which is distinct from that which accompanies fancied discoveries or guesses. When we realize a truth we have a feeling which they have not, who take words for things. And so, in like manner, if we are allowed to find that real and most sacred Object on which our heart may fix itself, a fulness of peace will follow, which nothing but it can give. In proportion as we have given up the love of the world, and are dead to the creature, and, on the other hand, are born of the Spirit unto love of our Maker and Lord, this love carries with it its own evidence whence it comes. Hence the Apostle says, " The Spirit itself beareth witness with our spirit, that we are the children of God." Again, he speaks of Him " who hath sealed us, and given the earnest of the Spirit in our hearts." [1]

1 Rom. viii. 16.   2 Cor. i. 22.

I have been saying that our happiness consists in the contemplation of God;—(such a contemplation is alone capable of accompanying the mind always and everywhere, for God alone can be always and everywhere present;)—and that what is commonly said about the happiness of a good conscience, confirms this; for what is it to have a good conscience, when we examine the force of our words, but to be ever reminded of God by our own hearts, to have our hearts in such a state as to be led thereby to look up to Him, and to desire His eye to be upon us through the day? It is in the case of holy men the feeling attendant on the contemplation of Almighty God.

But, again, this sense of God's presence is not only the ground of the peace of a good conscience, but of the peace of repentance also. At first sight it might seem strange how repentance can have in it anything of comfort and peace. The Gospel, indeed, promises to turn all sorrow into joy. It makes us take pleasure in desolateness, weakness, and contempt. " We glory in tribulations also," says the Apostle, " because the love of God is shed abroad in our hearts by the Holy Ghost which is given unto us." It destroys anxiety : " Take no thought for the morrow, for the morrow shall take thought for the things of itself." It bids us take comfort under bereavement : " I would not have you ignorant, brethren, concerning them which are asleep, that ye sorrow not, even as others which have no hope."[1] But if there be one sorrow, which might seem to be unmixed misery, if there be one misery left under the

<hr>

[1] Rom. v. 3, 5. Matt. vi. 34. 1 Thess. iv. 13.

Gospel, the awakened sense of having abused the Gospel might have been considered that one. And, again, if there be a time when the presence of the Most High would at first sight seem to be intolerable, it would be then, when first the consciousness vividly bursts upon us that we have ungratefully rebelled against Him. Yet so it is that true repentance cannot be without the thought of God; it has the thought of God, for it seeks Him; and it seeks Him, because it is quickened with love; and even sorrow must have a sweetness, if love be in it. For what is to repent but to surrender ourselves to God for pardon or punishment; as loving His presence for its own sake, and accounting chastisement from Him better than rest and peace from the world? While the prodigal son remained among the swine, he had sorrow enough, but no repentance; remorse only; but repentance led him to rise and go to his Father, and to confess his sins. Thus he relieved his heart of its misery, which before was like some hard and fretful tumour weighing upon it. Or, again, consider St. Paul's account of the repentance of the Corinthians; there is sorrow in abundance, nay, anguish, but no gloom, no dryness of spirit, no sternness. The penitents afflict themselves, but it is from the fulness of their hearts, from love, gratitude, devotion, horror of the past, desire to escape from their present selves into some state holier and more heavenly. St. Paul speaks of their "earnest desire, their mourning, their fervent mind towards him." He rejoices, "not that they were made sorry, but that they sorrowed to repentance." "For ye were made sorry," he proceeds, "after a godly manner, that ye might receive damage by us in nothing." And he describes this "sorrowing after a godly sort," to consist in "carefulness, which it wrought in them," "clearing of themselves,"—"indignation,"—"fear,"—"vehement desire,"—"zeal,"—"revenge,"[1]—feelings, all of them, which open the heart, yet, without relaxing it, in that they terminate in acts or works.

On the other hand, remorse, or what the Apostle calls "the sorrow of the world," worketh death. Instead of coming to the Fount of Life, to the God of all consolation, remorseful men feed on their own thoughts, without any confidant of their sorrow. They disburden themselves to no one : to God they will not, to the world they cannot confess. The world will not attend to their confession ; it is a good associate, but it cannot be an intimate. It cannot approach us or stand by us in trouble; it is no Paraclete; it leaves all our feelings buried within us, either tumultuous, or, at best, dead: it leaves us gloomy or obdurate. Such is our state, while we live to the world, whether we be in sorrow or in joy. We are pent up within ourselves, and are therefore miserable. Perhaps we may not be able to analyse our misery, or even to realize it, as persons oftentimes who are in bodily sicknesses. We do not know, perhaps, what or where our pain is ; we are so used to it that we do not call it pain. Still so it is ; we need a relief to our hearts, that they may be dark and sullen no longer, or that they may not go on feeding upon themselves; we need to escape from ourselves to something beyond; and

1 2 Cor. vii. 7, 9, 11.

much as we may wish it otherwise, and may try to make idols to ourselves, nothing short of God's presence is our true refuge; everything else is either a mockery, or but an expedient useful for its season or in its measure.

How miserable then is he, who does not practically know this great truth! Year after year he will be a more unhappy man, or, at least, he will emerge into a maturity of misery at once, when he passes out of this world of shadows into that kingdom where all is real. He is at present attempting to satisfy his soul with that which is not bread; or he thinks the soul can thrive without nourishment. He fancies he can live without an object. He fancies that he is sufficient for himself; or he supposes that knowledge is sufficient for his happiness; or that exertion, or that the good opinion of others, or (what is called) fame, or that the comforts and luxuries of wealth, are sufficient for him. What a truly wretched state is that coldness and dryness of soul, in which so many live and die, high and low, learned and unlearned. Many a great man, many a peasant, many a busy man, lives and dies with closed heart, with affections undeveloped, unexercised. You see the poor man, passing day after day, Sunday after Sunday, year after year, without a thought in his mind, to appearance almost like a stone. You see the educated man, full of thought, full of intelligence, full of action, but still with a stone heart, as cold and dead as regards his affections, as if he were the poor ignorant countryman. You see others, with warm affections, perhaps, for their families, with benevolent feelings towards their fellow-men, yet stopping there; centring their hearts on what is sure to fail them, as being perishable. Life passes, riches fly away, popularity is fickle, the senses decay, the world changes, friends die. One alone is constant; One alone is true to us; One alone can be true; One alone can be all things to us; One alone can supply our needs; One alone can train us up to our full perfection; One alone can give a meaning to our complex and intricate nature; One alone can give us tune and harmony; One alone can form and possess us. Are we allowed to put ourselves under His guidance? this surely is the only question. Has He really made us His children, and taken possession of us by His Holy Spirit? Are we still in His kingdom of grace, in spite of our sins? The question is not whether we should go, but whether He will receive. And we trust, that, in spite of our sins, He will receive us still, every one of us, if we seek His face in love unfeigned, and holy fear. Let us then do our part, as He has done His, and much more. Let us say with the Psalmist, "Whom have I in heaven but Thee? and there is none upon earth I desire in comparison of Thee. My flesh and my heart faileth; but God is the strength of my heart, and my portion for ever."[1]

[1] Ps. lxxiii. 25, 26.

SERMON XXIII.

LOVE, THE ONE THING NEEDFUL.

(QUINQUAGESIMA.)

1 Cor. xiii. 1.

*" Though I speak with the tongues of men and of angels, and have not
charity, I am become as sounding brass, or a tinkling cymbal."*

I SUPPOSE the greater number of persons who try to
live Christian lives, and who observe themselves with
any care, are dissatisfied with their own state on this
point, viz. that, whatever their religious attainments may
be, yet they feel that their motive is not the highest ;—
that the love of God, and of man for His sake, is not
their ruling principle. They may do much, nay, if it
so happen, they may suffer much ; but they have little
reason to think that they love much, that they do and
suffer for love's sake. I do not mean that they thus
express themselves exactly, but that they are dissatisfied with themselves, and that when this dissatisfaction
is examined into, it will be found ultimately to come to
this, though they will give different accounts of it.
They may call themselves cold, or hard-hearted, or
fickle, or double-minded, or doubting, or dim-sighted, or

weak in resolve, but they mean pretty much the same thing, that their affections do not rest on Almighty God as their great Object.   And this will be found to be the complaint of religious men among ourselves, not less than others; their reason and their heart not going together; their reason tending heavenwards, and their heart earthwards.

I will now make some remarks on the defect I have described, as thinking that the careful consideration of it may serve as one step towards its removal.

Love, and love only, is the fulfilling of the Law, and they only are in God's favour in whom the righteousness of the Law is fulfilled.   This we know full well; yet, alas! at the same time, we cannot deny that whatever good thing we have to show, whether activity, or patience, or faith, or fruitfulness in good works, love to God and man is not ours, or, at least, in very scanty measure; not at all proportionately to our apparent attainments.   Now, to enlarge upon this.

In the first place, love clearly does not consist merely in great sacrifices.   We can take no comfort to ourselves that we are God's own, merely on the ground of great deeds or great sufferings.   The greatest sacrifices without love would be nothing worth, and that they are great does not necessarily prove they are done with love.   St. Paul emphatically assures us that his acceptance with God did not stand in any of those high endowments, which strike us in him at first sight, and which, did we actually see him, doubtless would so much draw us to him.   One of his highest gifts, for instance, was his spiritual knowledge.   He shared, and felt the sinfulness and infirmities of human nature; he had a deep insight into the glories of God's grace, such as no natural man can have. He had an awful sense of the realities of heaven, and of the mysteries revealed. He could have answered ten thousand questions on theological subjects, on all those points about which the Church has disputed since his time, and which we now long to ask him. He was a man whom one could not come near, without going away from him wiser than one came; a fount of knowledge and wisdom ever full, ever approachable, ever flowing, from which all who came in faith, gained a measure of the gifts which God had lodged in him. His presence inspired resolution, confidence, and zeal, as one who was the keeper of secrets, and the revealer of the whole counsel of God; and who, by look, and word, and deed encompassed, as it were, his brethren with God's mercies and judgments, spread abroad and reared aloft the divine system of doctrine and precept, and seated himself and them securely in the midst of it. Such was this great servant of Christ and Teacher of the Gentiles; yet he says, "Though I speak with the tongues of men and of Angels, though I have the gift of prophecy, and understand all mysteries, and all knowledge, and have not charity, I am become as sounding brass, or a tinkling cymbal. . . . I am nothing." Spiritual discernment, an insight into the Gospel covenant, is no evidence of love.

Another distinguishing mark of his character, as viewed in Scripture, is his faith, a prompt, decisive, simple assent to God's word, a deadness to motives of earth, a firm hold of the truths of the unseen world, and keenness in following them out; yet he says of his faith also, "Though I have all faith, so that I could remove mountains, and have not charity, I am nothing." Faith is no necessary evidence of love.

A tender consideration of the temporal wants of his brethren is another striking feature of his character, as it is a special characteristic of every true Christian; yet he says, "Though I bestow all my goods to feed the poor, and have not charity, it profiteth me nothing." Self-denying alms-giving is no necessary evidence of love.

Once more. He, if any man, had the spirit of a martyr; yet he implies that even martyrdom, viewed in itself, is no passport into the heavenly kingdom. "Though I give my body to be burned, and have not charity, it profiteth me nothing." Martyrdom is no necessary evidence of love.

I do not say that at this day we have many specimens or much opportunity of such high deeds and attainments; but in our degree we certainly may follow St. Paul in them,—in spiritual discernment, in faith, in works of mercy, and in confessorship. We may, we ought to follow him. Yet though we do, still, it may be, we are not possessed of the one thing needful, of the spirit of love, or in a very poor measure; and this is what serious men feel in their own case.

Let us leave these sublimer matters, and proceed to the humbler and continual duties of daily life; and let us see whether these too may not be performed with considerable exactness, yet with deficient love. Surely they may; and serious men complain of themselves here, even more than when they are exercised on greater subjects. Our Lord says, "If ye love Me, keep My commandments;" but they feel that though they are, to a certain point, keeping God's commandments, yet love is not proportionate, does not keep pace, with their obedience; that obedience springs from some source short of love. This they perceive; they feel themselves to be hollow; a fair outside, without a spirit within it.

I mean as follows :—It is possible to obey, not from love towards God and man, but from a sort of conscientiousness short of love; from some notion of acting up to a *law;* that is, more from the fear of God than from love of Him. Surely this is what, in one shape or other, we see daily on all sides of us; the case of men, living to the world, yet not without a certain sense of religion, which acts as a restraint on them. They pursue ends of this world, but not to the full; they are checked, and go a certain way only, because they dare not go further. This external restraint acts with various degrees of strength on various persons. They all live to this world, and act from the love of it; they all allow their love of the world a certain range; but, at some particular point, which is often quite arbitrary this man stops, and that man stops. Each stops at a different point in the course of the world, and thinks every one else profane who goes further, and superstitious who does not go so far,—laughs at the latter, is shocked at the former. And hence those few who are miserable enough to have rid themselves of all scruples, look with great contempt on such of their companions as have any, be those scruples more or less, as being inconsistent and absurd. They scoff at the principle of mere fear, as a capricious and fanciful principle; proceeding on no rule, and having no evidence of its authority, no claim on our respect; as a weakness in our nature, rather than an essential portion of that nature, viewed in its perfection and entireness. And this being all the notion which their experience gives them of religion, as not knowing really religious men, they think of religion, only as a principle which interferes with our enjoyments unintelligibly and irrationally. Man is made to love. So far is plain. They see that clearly and truly; but religion, as far as they conceive of it, is a system destitute of objects of love; a system of fear. It repels and forbids, and thus seems to destroy the proper function of man, or, in other words, to be un-natural. And it is true that this sort of fear of God, or rather slavish dread, as it may more truly be called, *is* unnatural; but then it is not religion, which really con-sists, not in the mere fear of God, but in His love; or if it be religion, it is but the religion of devils, who believe and tremble; or of idolaters, whom devils have seduced, and whose worship is superstition,—the attempt to appease beings whom they love not; and, in a word, the religion of the children of this world, who would, if possible, serve God and Mammon, and, whereas religion consists of love *and* fear, give to God their fear, and to Mammon their love.

And what takes place so generally in the world at large, this, I say, serious men will feel as happening, in its degree, in their own case. They will understand that even strict obedience is no evidence of fervent love, and they will lament to perceive that they obey God far more than they love Him. They will recollect the instance of Balaam, who was even exemplary in his obedience, yet had not love; and the thought will come over them as a perplexity, what proof they have that they are not, after all, deceiving themselves, and thinking themselves religious when they are not. They will indeed be conscious to themselves of the sacrifice they make of their own wishes and pursuits to the will of God; but they are conscious also that they sacrifice them because they know they *ought* to do so, not simply from love of God. And they ask, almost in a kind of despair, How are we to learn, not merely to obey, but to love?

They say, How are we to fulfil St. Paul's words, "The life which I now live in the flesh I live by the faith of the Son of God, who loved me, and gave Himself for me"? And this would seem an especial difficulty in the case of those who live among men, whose duties lie amid the engagements of this world's business, whose thoughts, affections, exertions, are directed towards things which they see, things present and temporal. In their case it seems to be a great thing, even if their *rule* of life is a heavenly one, if they *act* according to God's will; but how can they hope that heavenly Objects should fill their heart, when there is no room left for them? how shall things absent displace things present, things unseen the things that are visible? Thus they seem to be reduced, as if by a sort of necessity, to that state, which I just now described as the state of men of the world, that of having their hearts set on the world, and being only restrained outwardly by religious rules.

To proceed. Generally speaking, men will be able to bring against themselves positive charges of want of love, more unsatisfactory still. I suppose most men, or at least a great number of men, have to lament over their hardness of heart, which, when analysed, will be found to be nothing else but the absence of love. I mean that hardness which, for instance, makes us unable to repent as we wish. No repentance is truly such without love; it is love which gives it its efficacy in God's sight. Without love there may be remorse, regret, self-reproach, self-condemnation, but there is not saving penitence. There may be conviction of the reason, but not conversion of the heart. Now, I say, a great many men lament in themselves this want of love in repenting; they are hard-hearted; they are deeply conscious of their sins; they abhor them; and yet they can take as lively interest in what goes on around them, as if they had no such consciousness; or they mourn this minute, and the next are quite impenetrable. Or, though, as they think and believe, they fear God's anger, and are full of confusion at themselves, yet they find (to their surprise, I may say) that they cannot abstain from any indulgence ever so trivial, which would be (as their reason tells them) a natural way of showing sorrow. They eat and drink with as good a heart, as if they had no distress upon their minds; they find no difficulty in entering into any of the recreations or secular employments which come in their way.

They sleep as soundly; and, in spite of their grief, perhaps find it most difficult to persuade themselves to rise early to pray for pardon. These are signs of want of love.

Or, again, without reference to the case of penitence, they have a general indisposition towards prayer and other exercises of devotion. They find it most difficult to get themselves to pray; most difficult, too, to rouse their minds to attend to their prayers. At very best they do but feel satisfaction in devotion *while* they are engaged in it. Then perhaps they find a real pleasure in it, and wonder they can ever find it irksome; yet if any chance throws them out of their habitual exercises, they find it most difficult to return to them. They do not like them well enough to seek them *from* liking them. They are kept in them by habit, by regularity in observing them; not by love. When the regular course is broken, there is no inward principle to act at once in repairing the mischief. In wounds of the body, nature works towards a recovery, and, left to itself, would recover; but we have no spiritual principle strong and healthy enough to set religious matters right in us when they have got disordered, and to supply for us the absence of rule and custom. Here, again, is obedience, more or less mechanical, or without love.

Again :—a like absence of love is shown in our proneness to be taken up and engrossed with trifles. Why is it that we are so open to the power of excitement? why is it that we are looking out for novelties? why is it that we complain of want of variety in a religious life? why that we cannot bear to go on in an ordinary round of duties year after year? why is it that lowly duties, such as condescending to men of low estate, are distasteful and irksome? why is it that we need powerful preaching, or interesting and touching books, in order to keep our thoughts and feelings on God? why is it that our faith is so dispirited and weakened by hearing casual objections urged against the doctrine of Christ? why is it that we are so impatient that objections should be answered? why are we so afraid of worldly events, or the opinions of men? why do we so dread their censure or ridicule?—Clearly because we are deficient in love. He who loves, cares little for any thing else. The world may go as it will; he sees and hears it not, for his thoughts are drawn another way; he is solicitous mainly to walk with God, and to be found with God; and is in perfect peace because he is stayed in Him.

And here we have an additional proof how weak our love is; viz. when we consider how little adequate our professed principles are found to be, to support us in affliction. I suppose it often happens to men to feel this, when some reverse or unexpected distress comes upon them. They indeed most especially will feel it, of course, who have let their words, nay their thoughts, much outrun their hearts; but numbers will feel it too, who have tried to make their reason and affections keep pace with each other. We are told of the righteous man, that " he will not be afraid of any evil tidings, for his heart standeth fast, and believeth in the Lord. His heart is established, and will not shrink."[1]

<hr>

[1] Ps. cxii. 7, 8.

Such must be the case of every one who realizes his own words, when he talks of the shortness of life, the wearisomeness of the world, and the security of heaven. Yet how cold and dreary do all such topics prove, when a man comes into trouble? and why, except that he has been after all set upon things visible, not on God. while he has been speaking of things invisible? There has been much profession and little love.

These are some of the proofs which are continually brought home to us, if we attend to ourselves, of our want of love to God; and they will readily suggest others to us. If I must, before concluding, remark upon the mode of overcoming the evil, I must say plainly this, that, fanciful though it may appear at first sight to say so, the comforts of life are the main cause of it ; and, much as we may lament and struggle against it, till we learn to dispense with them in good measure, we shall not overcome it. Till we, in a certain sense, detach ourselves from our bodies, our minds will not be in a state to receive divine impressions, and to exert heavenly aspirations. A smooth and easy life, an uninterrupted enjoyment of the goods of Providence, full meals, soft raiment, well-furnished homes, the pleasures of sense, the feeling of security, the consciousness of wealth,—these, and the like, if we are not careful, choke up all the avenues of the soul, through which the light and breath of heaven might come to us. A hard life is, alas! no certain method of becoming spiritually minded, but it is one out of the means by which Almighty God makes us so. We must, at least at seasons, defraud ourselves of nature, if we would not be defrauded of grace. If we attempt to force our minds into a loving and devotional temper, without this preparation, it is too plain what will follow,—the grossness and coarseness, the affectation, the effeminacy, the unreality, the presumption, the hollowness, (suffer me, my brethren, while I say plainly, but seriously, what I mean,) in a word, what Scripture calls the Hypocrisy, which we see around us; that state of mind in which the reason, seeing what we should be, and the conscience enjoining it, and the heart being unequal to it, some or other pretence is set up, by way of compromise, that men may say, " Peace, peace, when there is no peace."

And next, after enjoining this habitual preparation of heart, let me bid you cherish, what otherwise it were shocking to attempt, a constant sense of the love of your Lord and Saviour in dying on the cross for you. "The love of Christ," says the Apostle, "constraineth us;" not that gratitude leads to love, where there is no sympathy, (for, as all know, we often reproach ourselves with not loving persons who yet have loved us,) but where hearts are in their degree renewed after Christ's image, there, under His grace, gratitude to Him will increase our love of Him, and we shall rejoice in that goodness which has been so good to us. Here, again, self-discipline will be necessary. It makes the heart tender as well as reverent. Christ showed His love in deed, not in word, and you will be touched by the thought of His cross far more by bearing it after Him, than by glowing accounts of it. All the modes by which you bring it before you must be simple and severe; "excellency of speech," or "enticing words," to

use St. Paul's language, is the worst way of any. Think
of the Cross when you rise and when you lie down,
when you go out and when you come in, when you eat
and when you walk and when you converse, when you
buy and when you sell, when you labour and when you
rest, consecrating and sealing all your doings with this
one mental action, the thought of the Crucified. Do
not talk of it to others; be silent, like the penitent
woman, who showed her love in deep subdued acts.
She "stood at His feet behind Him weeping, and began
to wash His feet with tears, and did wipe them with the
hairs of her head, and kissed His feet, and anointed
them with the ointment." And Christ said of her,
"Her sins, which are many, are forgiven her, for she
loved much; but to whom little is forgiven, the same
loveth little."[1]

And, further, let us dwell often upon those His manifold mercies to us and to our brethren, which are the
consequence of His coming upon earth; His adorable
counsels, as manifested in our personal election,—how
it is that we are called and others not; the wonders of
His grace towards us, from our infancy until now; the
gifts He has given us; the aid He has vouchsafed; the
answers He has accorded to our prayers. And, further,
let us, as far as we have the opportunity, meditate upon
His dealings with His Church from age to age; on His
faithfulness to His promises, and the mysterious mode
of their fulfilment; how He has ever led His people
forward safely and prosperously on the whole amid so
many enemies; what unexpected events have worked

[1] Luke vii. 38, 47.

His purposes; how evil has been changed into good; how His sacred truth has ever been preserved unimpaired; how Saints have been brought on to their perfection in the darkest times. And, further, let us muse over the deep gifts and powers lodged in the Church: what thoughts do His ordinances raise in the believing mind!—what wonder, what awe, what transport, when duly dwelt upon!

It is by such deeds and such thoughts that our services, our repentings, our prayers, our intercourse with men, will become instinct with the spirit of love. Then we do everything thankfully and joyfully, when we are temples of Christ, with His Image set up in us. Then it is that we mix with the world without loving it, for our affections are given to another. We can bear to look on the world's beauty, for we have no heart for it. We are not disturbed at its frowns, for we live not in its smiles. We rejoice in the House of Prayer, because He is there "whom our soul loveth." We can condescend to the poor and lowly, for they are the presence of Him who is Invisible. We are patient in bereavement, adversity, or pain, for they are Christ's tokens.

Thus let us enter the Forty Days of Lent now approaching. For Forty Days we seek after love by means of fasting. May we find it more and more, the older we grow, till death comes and gives us the sight of Him who is at once its Object and its Author.

SERMON XXIV.

THE POWER OF THE WILL.

(QUINQUAGESIMA.)

EPHES. vi. 10.

" Finally, my brethren, be strong in the Lord, and in the power of His might."

WE know that there are great multitudes of professed
Christians, who, alas! have actually turned from
God with a deliberate will and purpose, and, in consequence, are at present strangers to the grace of God;
though they do not know, or do not care about this.
But a vast number of Christians, half of the whole
number at least, are in other circumstances. They
have not thrown themselves out of a state of grace, nor
have they to repent and turn to God, in the sense in
which those must, who have allowed themselves in wilful
transgression, after the knowledge of the truth has been
imparted to them. Numbers there are in all ranks of
life, who, having good parents and advisers, or safe
homes, or religious pursuits, or being without strong
feelings and passions, or for whatever reason, cannot
be supposed to have put off from them the garment of

divine grace, and deserted to the ranks of the enemy.
Yet are they not safe, nevertheless. It is plain,—for
surely it is not enough to avoid evil in order to attain
to heaven,—we must follow after good. What, then, is
their danger?—That of the unprofitable servant who hid
his lord's money. As far removed as that slothful servant
was from those who traded with their talents, in his
state and in his destiny, so far separate from one
another are two classes of Christians who live together
here as brethren,—the one class is using grace, the other
neglecting it ; one is making progress, the other sitting
still ; one is working for a reward, the other is idle and
worthless.

This view of things should ever be borne in mind
when we speak of the state of grace. There are different
degrees in which we may stand in God's favour; we
may be rising or sinking in His favour; we may not
have forfeited it, yet we may not be securing it; we
may be safe for the present, but have a dangerous prospect before us. We may be more or less " hypocrites,"
" slothful," "unprofitable," and yet our day of grace not
be passed. We may still have the remains of our new
nature lingering on us, the influences of grace present
with us, and the power of amendment and conversion
within us. We may still have talents which we may
put to account, and gifts which we may stir up. We
may not be cast out of our state of justification, and yet
may be destitute of that love of God, love of God's
truth, love of holiness, love of active and generous
obedience, that honest surrender of self, which alone
will secure to us hereafter the blessed words, "·Well

done, good and faithful servant; enter thou into the joy of thy Lord."[1]

The only qualification which will avail us for heaven is the love of God. We may keep from gross sinning, and yet not have this divine gift, "without which we are dead" in God's sight. This changes our whole being; this makes us live; this makes us grow in grace and abound in good works; this makes us fit for God's presence hereafter.

Now, here I have said a number of things, each of which will bear drawing out by itself, and insisting on.

No one can doubt that we are again and again exhorted in Scripture to be holy and perfect, to be holy and blameless in the sight of God, to be holy as He is holy, to keep the commandments, to fulfil the Law, to be filled with the fruit of righteousness. Why do we not obey as we ought? Many people will answer that we have a fallen nature, which hinders us; that we cannot help it, though we ought to be very sorry for it; that this is the reason of our shortcomings. Not so: we can help it; we are not hindered; what we want is the will; and it is our own fault that we have it not. We have all things granted to us; God has abounded in His mercies to us; we have a depth of power and strength lodged in us; but we have not the heart, we have not the will, we have not the love to use it. We lack this one thing, a desire to be new made; and I think any one who examines himself carefully, will own that he does, and that this is the reason why he cannot and does not obey or make progress in holiness.

<hr>

[1] Matt. xxv. 21.

That we have this great gift within us, or are in a state of grace, for the two statements mean nearly the same thing, is very plain of course from Scripture. We all know what Scripture says on the subject, and yet even here it may be as well to dwell on one or two passages by way of reminding and impressing ourselves.

Consider then our Saviour's words: "The water that I shall give him, shall be in him a *well of water* springing up into everlasting life."[1] Exhaust the sea, it will not fill the infinite spaces of the heavens, but the gift within us may be drawn out till it fills eternity.

Again, consider St. Paul's most wonderful words in the Epistle from which the text is taken, when he gives glory to "Him who is able to do exceeding abundantly above all that we ask or think, according to the power that worketh in us."[2] You observe here, that there is a power given to us Christians, which "worketh in us," a special hidden mysterious power, which makes us its instruments. Even that we have souls, is strange and mysterious. We do not see our souls; but we see in others and we are conscious in ourselves of a principle which rules our bodies, and makes them what the brutes are not. We have that in us which informs our bodies, and changes them from mere animal bodies into human. Brutes cannot talk; brutes have little expression of countenance; they cannot form into societies; they cannot progress. Why? Because they have not that hidden gift which we have?—reason. Well, in like manner St. Paul speaks of Christians too as having a special power within

[1] John iv. 14.　　　　　　　[2] Ephes. iii. 20.

them, which they gain because they are, and when they become Christians ; and he calls it, in the text to which I am referring, " the power that worketh in us." In a former chapter of the Epistle, he speaks of " the exceeding greatness of His power to us-ward who believe, according to the working of His mighty power;"[1] and he says that our eyes must be enlightened in order to recognise it ; and he compares it to that divine power in Christ our Saviour, by which, working in due season, He was raised from the dead, so that the bonds of death had no dominion over Him. As seeds have life in them, which seem lifeless, so the Body of Christ had life in itself, when it was dead ; and so also, though not in a similar way, we too, sinners as we are, have a spiritual principle in us, if we did but exert it, so great, so wondrous, that all the powers in the visible world, all the conceivable forces and appetites of matter, all the physical miracles which are at this day in process of discovery, almost superseding time and space, dispensing with numbers, and rivalling mind, all these powers of nature are nothing to this gift within us. Why do I say this? because the Apostle tells us that God is able thereby "to do *exceeding abundantly above all* that we ask or think." You see he labours for words to express the exuberant, overflowing fulness, the vast and unfathomable depth, or what he has just called " the breadth, and length, and depth, and height" of the gift given us. And hence he elsewhere says, " I can do *all things* through Christ, which *strengtheneth* me;"[2] where he uses the same word which occurs also

<hr>

[1] Ephes. i. 19.   [2] Phil. iv. 13.

in the text,—" My brethren, be *strong* in the Lord, and in the power of His might." See, what an accumulation of words! First, be *strong*, or be ye made strong. Strong in what? strong in power. In the power of what? in the power of His might, the might of God. Three words are used one on another, to express the manifold gift which God has given us. He to might has added power, and power He has made grow into strength. We have the power of His might; nor only so, but the strength of the power of His might who is Almighty.

And this is the very account which St. Luke gives us of St. Paul's own state in the Acts, after his conversion. The Jews wondered, but " Saul increased the more in *strength*, and confounded the Jews who dwelt at Damascus."[1] He became more and more strong. And, at the end of his course, when brought before the Romans, "The Lord," as he says, " stood with him, and *strengthened* him ;" and in turn he too exhorts Timothy, " Thou, therefore, my son, be *strong* in the grace that is in Christ Jesus ; and the things that thou hast heard of me among many witnesses, the same commit thou to faithful men, who shall be able to teach others also. Thou therefore endure hardness, as a good soldier of Jesus Christ."[2]

I said just now that we did not need Scripture to tell us of our divinely imparted power ; that our own consciousness was sufficient. I do not mean to say that our consciousness will enable us to rise to the fulness of the Apostle's expressions ; for trial, of course, cannot

---

[1] Acts ix. 22.   [2] 2 Tim. ii. 1—3 ; iv. 17.

ascertain an inexhaustible gift. All we can know of it by experience is, that it goes beyond *us*, that *we* have never fathomed it, that we have drawn from it, and never emptied it; that we have evidence that there is *a* power with us, how great we know not, which does for us what we cannot do for ourselves, and is always equal to all our needs. And of as much as this, I think, we have abundant evidence.

Let us ask ourselves, why is it that we so often wish to do right and cannot? why is it that we are so frail, feeble, languid, wayward, dim-sighted, fluctuating, perverse? why is it that we cannot "do the things that we would?" why is it that, day after day, we remain irresolute, that we serve God so poorly, that we govern ourselves so weakly and so variably, that we cannot command our thoughts, that we are so slothful, so cowardly, so discontented, so sensual, so ignorant? Why is it that we, who trust that we are not by wilful sin thrown out of grace (for of such I am all along speaking), why is it that we, who are ruled by no evil masters and bent upon no earthly ends, who are not covetous, or profligate livers, or worldly-minded, or ambitious, or envious, or proud, or unforgiving, or desirous of name, —why is it that we, in the very kingdom of grace, surrounded by Angels, and preceded by Saints, nevertheless can do so little, and instead of mounting with wings like eagles, grovel in the dust, and do but sin, and confess sin, alternately? Is it that the *power* of God is not within us? Is it literally that we are *not able* to perform God's commandments? God forbid! We are able. We have that given us which makes us

able. We are not in a state of nature. We have had
the gift of grace implanted in us. We have a power
within us to do what we are commanded to do. What
is it we lack? The power? No; the will. What we
lack is the real, simple, earnest, sincere inclination and
aim to use what God has given us, and what we have in
us. I say, our experience tells us this. It is no matter
of mere doctrine, much less a matter of words, but of
things; a very practical plain matter.

To take an instance of the simple kind. Is not the
power to use our limbs our own, nay, even by nature?
What then is sloth but a want of will? When we are
not set on an object so greatly as to overcome the inconvenience of an effort, we remain as we are;—when
we ought to exert ourselves we are slothful. But is the
effort any effort at all, when we desire that which needs
the effort?

In like manner, to take a greater thing. Are not the
feelings as distinct as well can be, between remorse and
repentance? In both a man is very sorry and ashamed
of what he has done; in both he has a painful fore-
boding that he may perchance sin again in spite of his
present grief. You will hear a man perhaps lament
that he is so weak, so that he quite dreads what is to
come another time, after all his good resolutions. There
are cases, doubtless, in which a man *is* thus weak in
power, though earnest in will; and, of course, it continually happens that he has ungovernable feelings and
passions in spite of his better nature. But in a very
great multitude of cases this pretence of want of power
is really but a want of will. When a man complains

that he is under the dominion of any bad habit, let him seriously ask himself whether he has ever *willed* to get rid of it. Can he, with a simple mind, say in God's sight, " I wish it removed ?"

A man, for instance, cannot attend to his prayers; his mind wanders; other thoughts intrude; time after time passes, and it is the same. Shall we say, this arises from want of power? Of course it may be so ; but before he says so, let him consider whether he has ever roused himself, shaken himself, awakened himself, got himself to will, if I may so say, attention. We know the feeling in unpleasant dreams, when we say to ourselves, "This is a dream," and yet cannot exert ourselves to will to be free from it; and how at length by an effort we will to move, and the spell at once is broken; we wake. So it is with sloth and indolence ; the Evil One lies heavy on us, but he has no power over us except in our unwillingness to get rid of him. He cannot battle with us; he flies; he can do no more, as soon as we propose to fight with him.

There is a famous instance of a holy man of old time, who, before his conversion, felt indeed the excellence of purity, but could not get himself to say more in prayer than " Give me chastity, but not yet." I will not be inconsiderate enough to make light of the power of temptation of any kind, nor will I presume to say that Almighty God will certainly shield a man from temptation for his wishing it ; but whenever men complain, as they often do, of the arduousness of a high virtue, at least it were well that they should first ask themselves the question, whether they desire to have it. We hear

much in this day of the impossibility of heavenly
purity;—far be it from me to say that every one has
not his proper gift from God, one after this manner,
another after that;—but, O ye men of the world, when
ye talk, as ye do, so much of the impossibility of this
or that supernatural grace, when you disbelieve in the
existence of severe self-rule, when you scoff at holy
resolutions, and affix a slur on those who make them,
are you sure that the impossibility which you insist
upon does not lie, not in nature, but in the will? Let
us but will, and our nature is changed, "according to
the power that worketh in us." Say not, in excuse for
others or for yourselves, that you cannot be other than
Adam made you; you have never brought yourselves to
will it,—you cannot bear to will it. You cannot bear
to be other than you are. Life would seem a blank
to you, were you other; yet what you are from not
desiring a gift, this you make an excuse for not
possessing it.

Let us take what trial we please,—the world's ridicule
or censure, loss of prospects, loss of admirers or friends,
loss of ease, endurance of bodily pain,—and recollect
how easy our course has been, directly we had once
made up our mind to submit to it; how simple all
that remained became, how wonderfully difficulties
were removed from without, and how the soul was
strengthened inwardly to do what was to be done.
But it is seldom we have heart to throw ourselves, if
I may so speak, on the Divine Arm; we dare not trust
ourselves on the waters, though Christ bids us. We
have not St. Peter's love to ask leave to come to Him

upon the sea. When we once are filled with that heavenly charity, we can do all things, because we attempt all things,—for to attempt is to do.

I would have every one carefully consider whether he has ever found God fail him in trial, when his own heart had not failed him; and whether he has not found strength greater and greater given him according to his day; whether he has not gained clear proof on trial that he *has* a divine power lodged within him, and a certain conviction withal that he has not made the extreme trial of it, or reached its limits. Grace ever outstrips prayer. Abraham ceased interceding ere God stayed from granting. Joash smote upon the ground but thrice, when he might have gained five victories or six. All have the gift, many do not use it at all, none expend it. One wraps it in a napkin, another gains five pounds, another ten. It will bear thirty-fold, or sixty, or a hundred. We know not what we are, or might be. As the seed has a tree within it, so men have within them Angels.

Hence the great stress laid in Scripture on growing in grace. Seeds are intended to grow into trees. We are regenerated in order that we may be renewed daily after the Image of Him who has regenerated us. In the text and verses following, we have our calling set forth, in order to " stir up our pure minds, by way of remembrance,"[1] to the pursuit of it. " Be strong in the Lord," says the Apostle, " and in the power of His might. Put on the whole armour of God," with your loins girt about with truth, the breastplate of righteousness, your

---

[1] 2 Pet. iii. 1.

feet shod with the preparation of the gospel of peace, the shield of faith, the helmet of salvation, the sword of the Spirit. One grace and then another is to be perfected in us. Each day is to bring forth its own treasure, till we stand, like blessed spirits, able and waiting to do the will of God.

Still more apposite are St. Peter's words, which go through the whole doctrine which I have been insisting on, point by point. First, he tells us that "divine power hath given unto us all things that pertain unto life and godliness;"[1] that is, we have the *gift*. Then he speaks of the *object* which the gift is to effect,— "exceeding great and precious promises are given unto us, that by these we may be *partakers of the divine nature;*" that we who, by birth, are children of wrath, should become inwardly and really sons of God ; putting off our former selves, or, as he says, "having escaped the corruption that is in the world through lust;" that is, cleansing ourselves from all that remains in us of original sin, the infection of concupiscence. With which closely agree St. Paul's words to the Corinthians, "Having these promises," he says, "dearly beloved, let us cleanse ourselves from all defilement of the flesh and spirit, perfecting holiness in the fear of God."[2] But to continue with St. Peter,—" Giving all diligence," he says, "add to your faith virtue, and to virtue knowledge, and to knowledge temperance, and to temperance patience, and to patience godliness, and to godliness brotherly kindness, and to brotherly kindness charity." Next he speaks of those who, though they cannot be

----

[1] 2 Pet. i. 3.   [2] 2 Cor. vii. 1.

said to have forfeited God's grace, yet by a sluggish will and a lukewarm love have become but unprofitable, and "cumber the ground" in the Lord's vineyard. "He that lacketh these things is blind, and cannot see afar off, and hath forgotten that he was purged from his old sins,"—has forgotten that cleansing which he once received, when he was brought into the kingdom of grace. "Wherefore the rather, brethren, give diligence to make your calling and election sure; for if ye do these things, ye shall never fall; for so an entrance shall be ministered unto you abundantly, into the everlasting kingdom of our Lord and Saviour Jesus Christ." Day by day shall ye enter deeper and deeper into the fulness of the riches of that kingdom, of which ye are made members.

Or, lastly, consider St. Paul's account of the same growth, and of the course of it, in his Epistle to the Romans. "Tribulation worketh patience, and patience experience, and experience hope, and hope maketh not ashamed." Such is the series of gifts, patience, experience, hope, a soul without shame,—and whence all this? He continues, "because the *love* of God is shed abroad in our hearts, by the Holy Ghost which is given unto us."[1]

Love can do all things; "charity never faileth;" he that has the will, has the power. You will say, "But is not the will itself from God? and, therefore, is it not after all *His* doing, not ours, if we have *not* the will?" Doubtless, by nature, our will is in bondage; we cannot will good; but by the grace of God our

[1] Rom. v. 3—5.

will has been set free; we obtain again, to a certain extent, the gift of free-will; henceforth, we can will, or not will.　If we will, it is doubtless from God's grace, who gave us the power to will, and to Him be the praise; but it is from ourselves too, because we have used that power which God gave.　God enables us to will and to do; by nature we cannot will, but by grace we can; and now if we do not will, we are the cause of the defect.　What can Almighty Mercy do for us which He hath not done?　"He has given *all* things which pertain to life and godliness;" and we, in consequence, can "make our calling and election sure," as the holy men of God did of old time.　Ah, how do those ancient Saints put us to shame! how were they "out of weakness made strong," how "waxed" they "valiant in fight," and became as Angels upon earth instead of men!　And why?—because they had a heart to contemplate, to design, to *will* great things. Doubtless, in many respects, we all are but men to the end; we hunger, we thirst, we need sustenance, we need sleep, we need society, we need instruction, we need encouragement, we need example; yet who can say the heights to which in time men can proceed in all things, who beginning by little and little, yet in the distance shadow forth great things?　"Enlarge the place of thy tent, and let them stretch forth the curtains of thine habitations; spare not, lengthen thy cords, and strengthen thy stakes; for thou shalt break forth on the right hand and on the left. . . . Fear not; for thou shalt not be ashamed; neither shalt thou be confounded, for thou shalt not be put to shame. . . .

In righteousness shalt thou be established; thou shalt be far from oppression, for thou shalt not fear; and from terror, for it shall not come near thee. . . . This is the heritage of the servants of the Lord, and their righteousness is of Me, saith the Lord."[1]

High words like these relate in the first place to the Church, but doubtless they are also fulfilled in their measure in each of her true children. But we sit coldly and sluggishly at home; we fold our hands and cry "a little more slumber;" we shut our eyes, we cannot see things afar off, we cannot "see the land which is very far off;" we do not understand that Christ calls us after Him; we do not hear the voice of His heralds in the wilderness; we have not the heart to go forth to Him who multiplies the loaves, and feeds us by every word of His mouth. Other children of Adam have before now done in His strength what we put aside. We fear to be too holy. Others put us to shame; all around us, others are doing what we will not. Others are entering deeper into the kingdom of heaven than we. Others are fighting against their enemies more truly and bravely. The unlettered, the ungifted, the young, the weak and simple, with sling and stones from the brook, are encountering Goliath, as having on divine armour. The Church is rising up around us day by day towards heaven, and we do nothing but object, or explain away, or criticise, or make excuses, or wonder. We fear to cast in our lot with the Saints, lest we become a party; we fear to seek the strait gate, lest we be of the few not the

[1] Isa. liv. 2—4, 14, 17.

many. Oh may we be loyal and affectionate before our race is run! Before our sun goes down in the grave, oh may we learn somewhat more of what the Apostle calls the love of Christ which passeth knowledge, and catch some of the rays of love which come from Him! Especially at the season of the year now approaching, when Christ calls us into the wilderness, let us gird up our loins and fearlessly obey the summons. Let us take up our cross and follow Him. Let us take to us " the whole armour of God, that we may be able to stand against the wiles of the devil; for we wrestle not against flesh and blood, but against principalities, against powers, against the rulers of the darkness of this world, against spiritual wickedness in high places; wherefore, take unto you the whole armour of God, that ye may be able to withstand in the evil day, and, having done all, to stand."

END OF VOL. V.

9 783337 319939